Love Stories
for Wilkes Ferry

Love Stories
for Wilkes Ferry

Christina Jacqueline Johns

Library of Congress Control Number:		2010911630
ISBN:	Hardcover	978-1-4535-2497-8
	Softcover	978-1-4535-2496-1

This book was printed in the United States of America.

To order additional copies of this book, contact:
Xlibris Corporation
1-888-795-4274
www.Xlibris.com
Orders@Xlibris.com
51054

Contents

For my father

The Biggest Liar

This is a memoir of a sort. But it's the kind of memoir Southerners write. In other words, it's full of truths, half-truths, shadings of the truth, and outright lies. It's tall tales and what wasn't the truth but should have been.

It is, I think, the art of the storyteller to conjure into being what should have been. Sometimes that altered version, almost unrecognizable as the truth, is more the truth than truth.

My mother hated talking about the past, hated telling or listening to stories about the past. Most of the time, when I would ask her to tell me which doctor did what or whose coffin it was that showed up at the railroad station, she would refuse. "He was the husband of my dearest friend," she might say and then conclude, as she always did, "*I* have to live in this town even though *you* don't."

I tried to reason with her. "Mama, if you don't tell me, I'll just make it up, and you know the version I make up will be trashier than the truth." But getting a story out of Mama was like pulling teeth out of a mule's mouth. She was a stubborn woman and only became more so the older she got. And as I was to learn very late in life, she was a woman with things to hide. She was not above creating her own stories about the past, stories that suited her, some of them outrageous.

I inherited every bit of Mama's stubbornness but very little of her shame. A friend was recently telling me about the book written by Joyce Maynard, J. D. Salinger's one-time lover. The book was about their affair.

"I think it's a betrayal," my friend said.

"Do you?" I replied.

My friend turned to me. "Wouldn't you consider it a betrayal if your friend Carla wrote a book about her experiences with you forty years ago?"

I considered this unlikely possibility. "I don't think so," I said. "If anybody thought the time they spent with me was interesting enough to write about, I'd take it as a compliment. Besides," I added, "there's not much anybody could tell about me that I haven't already told myself."

I am, for better or worse, a talker, a writer, and a spinner of tales. In other words, I am a fabricator. If you try to figure out who the people are in this book, or even where Wilkes Ferry is, you're bound to be frustrated. There are characters in these stories who existed but are depicted in situations I have invented. There are characters who never existed put in situations I remember vividly. Names are changed, and some characters are made up of two or more real people. In some cases, I have taken small characteristics of real people and magnified them so that they become major character flaws.

Southerners are just naturally drawn to embroidery. My father was the storyteller of our family. He told, edited, revised, and retold the same stories for years. I used to find fascinating the twists and turns of different versions of the same story as he improved on it. I think it's where I got my love of storytelling.

I remember once sitting at the dining room table in my parents' house on Christmas or Thanksgiving. Daddy was feeling expansive and tried out a particularly inventive version of a story. The embroidery was not what got him in trouble. What got him in trouble was trying to enlist my grandmother in attesting to his veracity. Somebody at the table expressed doubt about the details of Daddy's story. Daddy, knowing exactly where to go for reliable back up, turned to his mother.

"Isn't that right, DeeMama?" he asked, already smiling in anticipation of the answer.

My tiny Scottish grandmother, almost overwhelmed by the size of a standard dining room chair, sat silently, looking down into her lap.

Two beers beyond taking the hint, my father repeated his question. "Isn't that right, DeeMama?"

My grandmother swallowed and, never lifting her eyes, softly drawled, "Honey, I don't want to dispute your word but . . ."

That's as far as she got. The entire table howled with laughter, including my father. I love this genteel Southern way of saying "You're lying."

My grandmother would have eaten her left arm off before admitting that my father was less than perfect, but on this occasion, her stiff-necked, rigid Southern Baptist background might tolerate silence before a lie but not active participation in it.

There will be a lot of people who will choose to "dispute my word" about these stories if not call me an outright liar. And I will not object. But everyone must remember that these are only stories, stories out of one person's memory, from one participant's imagination, from one listener who made up the bits she didn't know or which she thought worked better than the strict truth.

Even though most of the characters in this book are imaginary, I can talk about them and their histories in detail because over the years, they have become real to me, as real as those who actually existed. There are times when I actually have to stop and try to remember whether Wilkie Dunn or Pickering Head were people.

In the final instance, what everybody has to remember is that memory is the biggest liar of all.

Closing Over My Head

For years, I told people that after Daddy died, celebrating Christmas just didn't seem worth it anymore. Then I realized that after Daddy died, nothing seemed worth it anymore. All the joy in my life slowly drained out over the next ten years until I was left with nothing. No joy, no interest, no gladness, no pleasure, no reason to get up in the morning.

But I did get up. Like millions of other people I thought I'd never become. I dressed (most of the time). I cooked. I cleaned. I washed clothes. I took the cat for a walk. But I became a ghost. Even though I could feel it happening, I could not seem to stop my withdrawal.

Most of the time, I kept something on—the radio, the television, my iPod (trusty friend of the insomniac). But there were times when I had none of these, and my mind would start reaching back, wherever I was, to Daddy and Mama, to Drew and Margaret Ann, to Joe Ed and Miss Mary Francis, Elizabeth Ann and Mattie Mae, to Wilkes Ferry.

I remember once, when I was around thirteen, sitting on the front steps of my house on a summer night with one of the boys in my class.

"I hadn't thought about it before," he said, "but you'll never find anywhere else home."

He was referring to my parents' house in Wilkes Ferry. At the time, I thought it was foolishness, just another bit of evidence of how little he understood me. For years, I thought the best thing I'd ever seen was Wilkes Ferry in the rearview mirror.

But now, almost fifty years later, there is nothing so real as the memory of wet Georgia clay between my toes, the sound of long-leaf pines whispering in the summer breeze, or the cool feel of the deep rust red water of the Catawba River closing over my head. My mind runs over the memories like a green lizard skittering across the porch.

A Blanket Over His Feet

One of the last things my daddy ever did was to go fishing on an August afternoon. Standing on the bank of his beloved Catawba River, he had a heart attack and never regained consciousness. But even so, he waited for me before he left that last time. He waited for me to drive two hundred miles with a husband and six cats.

I kissed his cheek and put a blanket over his feet, which were always so cold. As I did so, I remembered a black-and-white photograph of him taken in Scotland during the war. He was wearing his army uniform, lying on his left side on a bench, sleeping. His hands had sought warmth between his thighs. His feet were covered with layers of newspaper. That photograph was taken in 1944 by one of his army buddies. He was twenty-three years old.

Looking at him there in the hospital, it never once entered my mind that he was dying.

"Lydia."

That was my mother's voice. She was standing silhouetted in the doorway, the stark garish lights of the hospital hallway behind her. She was holding out a small lovely hand. I followed her down the hall and into the room where she had arranged for us to spend the night.

I was walking in familiar territory. I had been born in Cobb Memorial Hospital. I started working there at the age of fourteen as a candy striper and at sixteen as a nurses' aide, not because we needed the money, but because I wanted the independence. I knew every hallway of that hospital, every storage closet, every shortcut from one end of the building to the other. Very little had changed in thirty-five years.

In the room, I sat down on one of the beds. But before Mother and I even had time to brush our teeth, the nurse came back.

"Y'all better come on if you wanna see Mr. Will Lee."

Dazed, I stood at the foot of Daddy's bed again, holding his feet in my hands, as if by that one action I could hold him to life.

Mama bent down and put her cheek near Daddy's. Her face never touched his.

"Lee," she said, "we've been through so much together. Don't you think we could go on a little longer?"

We've been through so much together. Don't you think we could go on a little longer? Those two sentences went round and round in my head for years. Every time I looked into my mother's face, they came back to me. They were, most probably, the last thing Daddy heard before silence closed around him.

Years later, I was driving a boat with heavy sheets of construction plywood stacked in the bow. One of the construction workers, John Wesley Lemon, was sitting on top of the plywood. For some reason, John Wesley stood up, and the wind slipped its strong dangerous fingers underneath two of the massive pieces of lumber and hurled them backward. The first one hit me squarely on the forehead.

I heard the crack, and then there was silence. I felt myself beginning to slide to the bottom of the boat.

Is this how death comes? I asked myself. Then everything within me rebelled. *No, I have too much left to do.*

It was as if my whole body along with my mind screamed rejection of what was happening to me although I hadn't made a sound.

"Miss Lydia?"

That was John Wesley. I could hear again. I reached out and closed my fingers around the turned-up cuff of his wet jeans. I felt the smooth skin of his hand as it passed through my hair and across my forehead.

After that day, I often wondered if at some crucial point, when the body receives a life-threatening assault like a blow to the head or a heart attack, the mind or the will or the spirit somehow makes a decision. At one pivotal instant, something decides to fight or to give up. Had I made the decision to give up or simply been too tired or too discouraged to fight, would my body and spirit have just let go as clearly and as irrevocably as my fingers eventually let go of the cuff of John Wesley's jeans.

So many times, especially at night when I couldn't sleep, I have wondered if that was what happened to Daddy. All he heard was Mother's voice, a voice he had heard since he was thirteen years old, a voice he knew as well as his own breath. "*Lee. We've been through so much together. Don't you think we could go on a little longer?*" And the wispy fingers of his soul just opened and let go.

"She'd be happier if I died," he had said to me several times during the last few years of his life. I never replied when he said this, partly because I didn't know what to say and partly because I was almost certain he was right.

It took me years to admit it to myself. And it is still hard for me to say, but she wanted him to die.

Settling a Score

A few years after Daddy's funeral, I moved back to Wilkes Ferry, back beside the Catawba River, to the Valley where Daddy raised me and where he himself had been raised. I thought I moved back to the little cotton-mill town to take care of my mother. But I really moved back to settle a score.

I didn't go back there, saying to myself, *I'm going to settle a score.*

Hell, if I had known that was what I was doing, I could have settled the score without going through all the trouble of moving back to town.

But you see, the score was so old I didn't even know it was there anymore. And I was so confused in my mind that even though it had been driving my life for well over half a century, I couldn't have told you about it at the time had you asked me.

That's what's so fascinating about the human heart and the human mind. They can jump up and down, dance, do the tango, do cartwheels. They can scatter magic, like glitter, in your face or blow on dry ice and create a fog so dense you can't even see yourself. And they do all this just so you can survive.

The human heart and the human mind can take you into a house of mirrors like they used to have at the county fair and hold up one that distorts you so you see yourself as completely different from what you are. The heart and the mind can change the distorting mirrors over time, or they can just jump in front of you no matter which way you look with the same mirror. And they do this just so you can survive.

But the human mind and the human heart are unpredictable. They can cavort and dance and distract your attention for decades, and then one day, they can sit straight up and reach out for your hand and say, "Come on, baby. We can do better than this."

When I think of what my mind and heart did to me when I moved back to Wilkes Ferry, it reminds me of those men who used to work at filling stations.

These were the men who always came right out to your car before you even got it into "Park," filled your tank up with gas, changed your oil, and washed your windows. And they didn't even mind doing it. This was, of course, before it became necessary to get completely filthy, crawling out of your own car to pump gas.

Well, life did me just like one of those men. Life tapped on my window to get my attention and said, "You won' back 'at up here darlin' an' lemme see dem tires?"

I just went along for the ride.

The Fall Line

The Catawba River starts out high in the Blue Ridge mountains as a mere trickle, on land properly belonging to Cherokee and Creek. As it flows west, it slowly grows into a wide powerful river, red with mud. Just north of the small town of Wilkes Ferry, the Catawba turns abruptly south and descends some three hundred feet in a few dozen miles. After that, the river relaxes and stretches itself out to the sea.

It is this drop in elevation that determined the initial founding of Wilkes Ferry, and the fate of the town and the people in it for more than a hundred years. For the drop in elevation forms the fall line, the point at which mountain gives way to sea, the point at which the crystalline rock of the north encounters the sedimentary rock of the south. It is called the fall line because the encounter between mountain and sea creates waterfalls. North of the fall line, the soil tends to be clay. South of it, sandy. North of the fall line, there are narrow stream valleys. South of the fall line, wide flood plains developed.

How quickly, in other words, in what distance the elevation of the land descends, determines the character and direction of development of the surrounding community. The location of Wilkes Ferry was initially determined by the relatively calm water just above the fall line. The site of the old ferry was the southernmost point at which a ferry could easily be pulled from one side of the river to the other year-round. In fact, before the town came to be known as Wilkes Ferry, it was commonly referred to as South Point, an approximation of the Indian words for "lower paw."

For the Indians in and around Lower Paw, this particular spot in the river was a grand place to fish. A small island just north of where the ferry was established provided an excellent camping site where potential enemies could be spotted as they paused on the riverbank, preparing to cross. This delay by the riverside became especially important when what must have seemed like hordes of determined white settlers came to South Paw to cross the Catawba on their way west.

As soon as the ferry was established, the Catawba along the fall line changed. It ceased to be primarily a mode of transportation and object of beauty and became a work horse. Technology closed its grip around the current of the river and to this day, the rush of the Catawba, the wild, free Catawba, is subservient to the desires of man.

There's Nothing I Can Do

I didn't cry when Daddy died—not at the hospital, not at home, not at the funeral. I didn't cry early on that morning when I phoned my brother Drew from the nurses' station as my mother had instructed me to do. But even though I didn't cry, I somehow could not make myself say the word "dead." I started the sentence repeatedly but could not bring myself to finish it.

"Daddy is . . . Daddy has . . . Daddy . . ." The charge nurse took the phone away from me, told Drew that Daddy had died, and handed the receiver back.

After that, there was nothing to cry about, nothing even to say.

Drew was annoyed. If you listened to him, you would have thought Daddy had chosen to die right then just to be difficult. To Drew, it was all just a great big whopping inconvenience.

"Well," Drew huffed, exasperated, "I can't imagine how I'm going to get four members of a family all to Wilkes Ferry at the same time in the middle of August. They're all over the country."

I didn't say a word.

Once a younger sibling, always a younger sibling. I have seen it in cats and in human beings. It was nowhere within my behavioral repertoire to confront Drew over his behavior, actually to confront Drew over anything. I didn't confront my mother over her tinny deathbed plea, and I didn't confront Drew over his self-obsessed response to Daddy's death. For you see, Drew had not only married Mother, he was also very much like her. Had I told him he was being an ass, he would have, with devastating speed, implemented a verbal-scorched earth policy that would have left me emotional and intellectual toast. I knew. I had grown up on it. Mother and Drew and Drew's dreadful wife all knew how to make disagreement, much less confrontation, way too costly to be worth it.

I could, at the time, count on one hand the number of times Drew had seen Daddy in the past forty years, and those times were when Mama made Daddy go to New York to visit. Daddy hated going anywhere. I think this was partly because he didn't like the fuss of traveling, but the primary reason was that he didn't want to suffer through trying to travel with my mother who was, most of the time, utterly impossible. He especially didn't want to travel to New York and have to put up with both mother and Drew's dreadful wife in close quarters for two weeks. I'm also sure Drew hated having Daddy there.

But Drew and his tribe swept down onto Wilkes Ferry like a visiting theatrical troop. Once the engagement had been made, the show had to go on, and once into the swing of the performance, it all became what appeared to be a downright pleasure.

In fact, the funeral, far from being an inconvenience, was just the sort of thing Drew seemed to thrive on. He was making phone calls, cancelling engagements, constructing and elaborating on the narrative, managing his family, mobilizing his tribe, making sure he was the center of attention. After all, *his* father had died.

For me, it was like sleep walking. I didn't cry or think or even remember. I made small talk, I ate, I smiled at people who seemed to be everywhere around us, but none of it seemed real. Sometimes I wonder if anything has been real since. Now, as I look back on it, it feels as if I became a spectator in my own life the minute Daddy left my world.

It seems, sitting here now, trying to write it all down, as if a klieg light went out when Daddy died. There are other lights besides the enormous warming klieg light of my father. But without him, there is just something wrong. I can't leave the stage, and I can't do a thing about it, but I keep walking into dark spots.

During the two weeks my husband, Lee Ray Macon, and I stayed in Wilkes Ferry after Daddy died, Mother slept in the bedroom she had occupied for decades. Lee Ray and I slept in Daddy's room. I could still smell my daddy's scent if I opened his wardrobe door. It makes me cry, even now, every time I think about it. My bedroom in their house no longer existed. It had been turned into Mother's study years before.

At some point, in the days after the funeral, I woke up during the night with the moon shining into the window of Daddy's bedroom. I remembered that Mother had still been sleeping in that bedroom with Daddy the night of the telephone call with Drew. I heard the conversation, or at least Daddy's end of it, because there was only one telephone in the house then, in the downstairs hallway. Daddy was talking loud, arguing with Drew who was in Boston. Daddy wanted Drew to come home for the summer as he had done every year before when we was in college, but Drew was refusing.

Daddy was mad, and he was frustrated. I had never heard him sound quite so angry, and there was an edge to his tone that was unfamiliar to me even though I had heard him yell on numerous occasions. I opened the door to my bedroom and crept into the hallway.

Daddy was wearing his light blue summer pajamas with the dark blue cord. He was standing barefoot with the phone in his hand. Every muscle in his body seemed to be straining.

"Don't you understand?" he was yelling. "You have to come home. You can work in the mill for the summer and make good money. I know it's not what you want to do, but it's the best money you'll get. Dammit, can't you understand?"

But Drew didn't understand. I don't remember what else Daddy said to Drew; I just remember that shortly afterward, the phone slammed down. I darted back inside my bedroom and closed the door except for a crack. Daddy careened unsteadily back up the stairs and into my parents' bedroom. Then I could hear crying—Daddy crying. I had never heard my daddy cry before. It terrified me, and I realized later, it broke my heart.

I had no idea what to do. I just stood there inside the door. Then suddenly, Daddy walked out of the bedroom and went into Drew's bedroom and slammed the door. I could hear him sobbing.

I walked to the door of my parents' bedroom and looked in. My mother was sitting, propped up on some pillows against the headboard, her arms folded over her chest. There was no light on, and I couldn't see her eyes.

"Do something," I pleaded.

There was a pause, and I felt cold air coming up from the stairway, surrounding me. "There's nothing I can do," she said with finality.

I didn't have to see her eyes then. I knew what they would look like.

I don't think Drew ever voluntarily came back to the house after that, and sometime around then, Mother started sleeping in Drew's bedroom.

The Divided Town

The Catawba River forms the boundary line between two deep South states. It also divides the small cotton-mill town of Wilkes Ferry. On the west side of the river, the town side, there is one main intersection and a few cross streets—five traffic lights in all. On the east side of the river, most of the houses, the churches, and the schools are located.

When I was growing up in Wilkes Ferry during the fifties and early sixties, the town side was the center of excitement, interest, and activity.

Wyatt's Drug Store, Byron's Market with Lambe's Butcher Shop, Salzburg's Jewelers, Anderson Brothers Shoe Store, Lyle's Café, George's Record Store, the Last Chance Pool Room, Patterson's Boarding House, and the incomparable Woolworths were all packed together on those few dusty streets. They offered what seemed to me, at the time, to be an endless variety of diversion.

We ordered groceries over the telephone from Byron's Market. When my mother would let me, I would sit at the mahogany telephone desk in the hallway off our dining room and read the grocery list to whoever answered the phone at Byron's. Sometimes, I even read out the list to Mr. Lambe, the dark-eyed, long-lashed, black-haired butcher whose large, soft, tender hands handled meat in a way that impressed me even as a child.

I can still see Mr. Lambe in my mind's eye, standing behind the butcher's counter, leaning over at the waist, writing with one stub of a pencil while another rested behind his ear. His apron was always smudged, but as a child, I never realized the smudges were blood. From time to time, he ran the blunt fingers of his free hand through his thick, glossy black hair.

Sometimes Mama and I picked up the groceries. She would drive us to town and stop the car in front of Byron's. I would run up the steps to tell them we were there. Every store in Wilkes Ferry was built up from the level of the street. There were six cement steps running the length of every downtown block. The Catawba River flooded regularly every year, and after the 1920 flood wiped out all the downtown stores, the city built an elevated slab on which the store owners rebuilt. So all through downtown, there was the street, six cement steps, the sidewalk, and the stores.

Inside Byron's, there would always be a black man bagging groceries or just sitting on the wooden Coca-Cola crates stacked at the front of the store, waiting for some little girl like me to run inside and announce a pick up. The man would then collect the boxes of groceries marked "McPherson" and carry them out to the car. That's what happened if Mama was in a hurry.

When Mama wasn't in a hurry, Byron's would deliver the groceries to our house. A black man in a dull green truck with wooden panels on the side would come up our driveway. He would knock on the back door, wait for someone to come, and then bring the boxes in.

I have photographs in my mind from those years, photographs of Wilkes Ferry and things that happened there. Some of the photographs are of me, others are of things I saw, and still others are of events I wasn't even present to observe but only heard about later on.

In one of those photographs, I am standing in the back room of our house, the large utility room between the back door and the kitchen. I am facing the colored man from Byron's, who is holding a heavy box of canned goods. I am talking to him. But he is not looking at me. He is studying the floor. I am little more than a child. It is the first time a grown man has ever said "Yes, ma'am" to me.

I don't have any idea how long we stood there, the colored man and I, before I figured out I was blocking his way to the kitchen. I stepped aside but kept on blabbing away, trying to make up for whatever I had done wrong, whatever I had done to make him not want to look at me. It never occurred to me that he was afraid. But there he was, every time he made a delivery, inside a white person's house. This was not a good place to be if you were a black man in the 1950s. In this case, the man from Byron's was inside a seemingly empty house with a little white girl. He wasn't about to look me in the eye or talk to me if he could help it.

I never heard, when I was growing up, of an instance when a black man was accused of being too friendly (if not more) with a white girl, but it certainly could have happened. It's the sort of thing my mother would have never told me. But Wilkes Ferry was and is still a small town. There's not much that goes on that everybody in town doesn't know about sooner or later.

There were certainly lots of people around town who hated colored people. My step-granddaddy, for example, bragged about being a Night Rider for the Ku Klux Klan. Of course, he did this bragging from the comfortable position of a rocking chair. But even so, I remember how mad it made my father. Daddy got furious because Mr. Younger would bring these Night Rider stories up in front of us on Sunday's when we went to my grandmother's house for dinner. So Mama and Daddy did shield us from hearing absolutely everything, or at least they tried.

I knew there were violent racial incidents, and there was an almost ubiquitous use of the word "nigger" everywhere outside our house. And there was the systematic racism of excluding colored people from any of the jobs in the mills. But there was also a strange kind of respect between some colored people and some whites. A kind of comradeship was still possible.

In the fifties, white people who treated colored people with decency and respect were highly regarded by members of the black community. Black people appreciated white people with character, and they weren't afraid to show it.

As a child, I noticed this when I was with Mama downtown. In the South, especially in small towns, people speak to, or at least acknowledge, everyone they pass on the street. It is considered the height of bad manners not to exchange some kind of greeting with every person you encounter.

Now it's not like there were a lot of black people strolling the streets of Wilkes Ferry. They were usually there doing business for whites or tending to young children. But I noticed how these black people nodded at Mama. Usually, black people would give a perfunctory tight smile and a quick dipping of the head. Men would bow their heads slightly and take the rim of their hats between their thumb and first finger. But when they passed Mama, there was a lingering eye contact and a genuine softness to the expression on their faces. They were acknowledging something about Mama's decency. They were giving her respect.

I recently read an article by a black author who said that in the fifties and sixties, black people saw their problem as racism. Now they see their problem as white people.

My Daddy's Passing

Two days after Daddy died, I found Mother and Drew arranged in a conspiratorial tableau in Mother's immaculate mauve living room. Mother was sitting center stage on the right end of the newly upholstered Duncan Phyfe sofa. Drew had drawn up one of the solid mauve end chairs so close to her that their knees were almost touching. There was a large Bible on the end table beside Mother and music scattered all over the sofa, table, and floor.

I pulled up an end chair and sat down, exhausted. Mother and Drew barely acknowledged my presence. I laid my head back to rest my neck, just like Daddy used to do, and listened to Mama and Drew discuss the merits of various pieces of music. Every once in a while, one or the other reached for the Bible and paged through, looking for a particular scripture. Gradually, I realized they were planning the funeral—Daddy's funeral. But nobody was talking about Daddy. Nobody was saying, "Oh, Daddy would have liked this scripture, or Will Lee would have loved that piece of music."

Don't get me wrong, my father was a good man, but he had never been to church in his life unless Mother or his mother, DeeMama, had badgered him into it. Daddy's church was the cottage he had built us with his own hands on the Catawba River. He liked nothing better than being at the "backwater"—boating, fishing, or just sitting, looking out over the water.

To my knowledge, he never, on his own volition, listened to a piece of classical music unless it was played by Drew in some recital or performance. Even then, although he was enormously proud, he fidgeted and stretched his neck and prayed for at least an intermission, if not the end of the program. Now that I think about it, that may have been the only time he ever prayed in his life unless, which is likely, he prayed in France during the war.

The longer I sat there in my mother's living room, the more clear it became to me that this funeral was going to be a performance, an opportunity to display that the McPherson family had high-church taste. It was going to be an opportunity for Drew to show off his prodigious musical and verbal talents in front of the small town he and Mother felt had rejected him years before. Drew, it seemed, was also delivering the eulogy.

"When you get through with the music and Drew's eulogy, I'm going to do a eulogy and a piece of music of my own," I announced flatly. They both looked up at me like my hair had suddenly caught fire.

I got up and went back to bed. I have no idea what they said after I left or what they thought about it. I also had no idea what I was going to say or play at Daddy's funeral.

The morning of the funeral, I sat down and wrote my eulogy. I delivered it at Daddy's funeral.

Norman Rockwell did a series of oil paintings he called the four freedoms. The *Freedom of Speech, Freedom from Want, Freedom to Worship*, and *Freedom from Fear*.

In the painting he called *Freedom of Speech*, a young man stands in a room full of seated people, at what might be a town meeting.

He is a young man, not as well dressed as some of the rest of the people in the room. He has thick hands, and he just might have a little dirt underneath his fingernails. They are hands that just might have worked in a cotton mill when he was thirteen years old.

The other people in the room are looking up at the young man, some with admiration and some with a touch of fear. But the young man is oblivious to all of them. He is speaking. And he is proud and strong and confident. You can see in his face that he considers himself no better but certainly no worse than anyone else in the room. You know from his face and his eyes that he is standing up, speaking up for something right and just.

That's my daddy.

The first time I ever saw that painting, I said to myself, *That's my daddy.*

My daddy came from a background that would have destroyed a lot of people or twisted them and made them greedy and climbing, willing to step over anybody just to get something in the world.

But my daddy?

For my daddy, that background forged a fine, independent young man who knew how to fight and who understood the importance of fighting. That background made of my daddy a man whose integrity was not and would never be for sale to the highest bidder. For my daddy, that background helped fashion a man who was never ashamed of where he came from and never forgot who he was.

Out of that background, he made his own epic, his own story, and as he grew older, we all listened as he worked on that epic, telling it over and over again, rewriting some parts of it until he got it right. I think he was happy with the epic he wrote, with the story of his life, before he died. And he was what most people never manage to become—proud and content.

He was proud of himself and his family, and he was content that he had done what he was supposed to do, lived the way he was supposed to live.

He made a good life for his wife, his son, and his daughter, and he stood beside and cared for his sister, his nieces and nephews, his grandchildren, his son-in-law, and his mother.

As far as I'm concerned, and I know as far as he was concerned, he and my mother were about the best thing that ever happened to each other. For over six decades, they struggled and they worked and they laughed and they loved and they shared that love not only with their family, but also with anyone who was wise enough to come close and accept it.

They engendered in my brother and I, a core of fierce integrity and independence of thought. This has not always made my life easy nor made me the best daughter, but I would not trade it for anything in the world. It is what I consider my most treasured legacy.

At the end of Harper Lee's novel *To Kill a Mockingbird*, Atticus, the father, has put his heart and his soul and his intellect into fighting an unpopular battle, not for himself, but for a black man falsely accused of raping a white woman. In that battle, Atticus demonstrated his character as did my daddy in his life. The important thing about Atticus was not that he won. He didn't. But that he stood up, stood tall for what was right and just.

So did my daddy.

In the last scene of the novel, Atticus's daughter, Scout, is sitting in the balcony of the courthouse watching her father pack up his things.

As Atticus closes his briefcase and walks from the courtroom, everyone in the balcony stands. An elderly black man leans down and says to Scout, "Stan' up, chile', you daddy's passing."

I'm glad that when this ceremony is over, we'll all be standing because my daddy's passing.

Off the Road to Hamilton

Daddy's funeral was held in the First Baptist Church, a place I knew even better than Cobb Memorial Hospital. I had been dragged to and around inside that church every week and sometimes twice a week since I was old enough to walk. Mama, unfortunately, was big on church. Daddy and I went because she made us. Daddy would have been happier at the "backwaters," an immense lake and river system backed up from the Catawba River. I would have been happier reading a book or listening to records or watching television. I would have been happier getting a root canal.

Mama and Daddy moved to Wilkes Ferry when I was two years old, so I never saw the inside of another church unless it was on the few occasions I went to the Episcopal Church with my schoolmate Lauren Wainwright or the Methodist Church with Gaynell Woodham. But the Episcopal and the Methodist and the First Baptist churches were "town churches," where the parishioners were expected to stay seated after the service began and where the preacher was not expected to raise his voice above the level of polite conversation. There was no hell fire and perdition here; it was all very civilized.

I had only one occasion to see the inside of what we called a "country church." It was a "country church" even though it wasn't a quarter mile outside the Wilkes Ferry city limits.

I think I was in the eighth grade when, for some reason beyond my comprehension even now, the gorgeous, long-haired, guitar-playing Larry Davis asked me for a date. I was over the moon with excitement. Larry Davis was the closest thing to a living, breathing teen idol Wilkes Ferry had to offer. He was a member of the most popular and best-paid teenaged band in two states. The

Bushmen played all over Georgia and Alabama, and Larry Davis, rhythm-guitar player and lead singer of The Bushmen, asked me out on a date.

Larry was several years older than I was, probably four years older. I think the only reason my parents allowed me to go out with him was because he had asked me to go to a service at his parents' church. I guess they thought I couldn't possibly get into any trouble at a church. They were, of course, wrong.

Larry Davis could have easily asked out any girl in town. His celebrity status elevated him out of his working-class background, at least for a date if not as a marriage partner. Most of the kids Larry's age, four years older than we were, thought seriously about marriage. Some of them got married right out of high school (one of them even married the assistant coach). But there was a big difference between the class of '65 and the class of '69. For most of the kids in the class of '69, college was a foregone conclusion. Not many of them even thought about getting married right out of high school. Kids in the class of '65 listened to Elvis Presley. They were still in the 1950s, with crew cuts and bobby socks. The class of '69 was obsessed with The Beatles.

The difference between kids that listened to Elvis and those who listened to The Beatles was not just a difference in musical preference, it was a difference in culture. In Larry's class, kids bought designer bags and labeled clothes. They had never even heard of drugs. By the time I was in high school, we shopped at Goodwill for Midi skirts, wore jeans, and had at least heard of people smoking marijuana.

Larry Davis and his crowd were almost out of high school by the time The Beatles and rock bands appeared. Instead of getting married or trying to find jobs, they grew their hair and started a band. They were only one among a number of bands, but they were the best.

When I look back at it, I wonder if Larry Davis asked me out because he had noticed me mooning around the bandstand over him at dances, but all the girls did that. Maybe somebody told him I had a crush on him. Maybe he just couldn't get another date on a Sunday night, or he couldn't get another date on a Sunday night who would agree to go to church with him, or he couldn't get another date on a Sunday night who would agree to go to his parents' church. If so, the others were way smarter than I was.

As it turned out, I had never even seen this church his parents went to. It was hiding out in a not very nice subdivision near where the colored theater used to be. The church was actually just a house, a regular house they had changed into a church. There wasn't even a sign out in front of it.

Now Larry Davis, like all the members of The Bushmen, had a reputation as being fast, smooth, and very successful with girls. I was disappointed when he never even made a pass at me. He picked me up and drove me to this makeshift church and he drove me home. He could have probably driven me to hell that night, and I wouldn't have raised the slightest objection. But he didn't. Even forty years later, I wish that the night had turned out better.

I don't remember the denomination of the church. It may have been a Primitive Baptist or Holiness Church or Christian Scientist, something like that, although I have never been able to remember the difference between the Christian Scientists and the Jehovah's Witnesses.

The church sat back on a little street off the road to Hamilton. If you turned up onto that street and continued going down it, you ran into a dead end. Larry Davis and his family lived just at the end of that dead-end street. I knew exactly where Larry Davis lived because Margaret Ann Patterson, my best friend, and I used to joke about driving down that road to see if The Bushmen were in town. This was our amusement on an otherwise boring day. Tells you just about how exciting Wilkes Ferry was.

But that summer evening, I was being escorted to church with Larry Davis's hand cupping my elbow. It took my breath away. It made it almost worth sitting through a sermon. I was so excited I even remember what I wore. It was a high-waisted, pale pink, checked cotton dress. Those Empire-waisted dresses had a shorter hemline, but they were a version of the Empire-style dresses worn in the day of the Bronte sisters. My dress had smocking just below the breasts and a strip of white cotton lace attached to the smocking. There was a pink ribbon threaded through the lace. I loved that dress.

When Larry and I walked into his parents' church, Larry guided me into the first pew we came to. It was the pew at the very back of the church. I must admit that it crossed my mind that this might mean we were going to leave early. If so, I couldn't think of anything better than to get off alone with Larry Davis. I can still remember the sleeve of his starched short-sleeved shirt brushing up against my arm, the clean male smell of him, maleness and *Canoe*.

As soon as the service started, I bowed my head. While giving the outward appearance of reverent concentration, this was really a way of blotting out everything except the feel and the smell of Larry Davis. I wasn't paying the least bit of attention to anything going on except some teenaged version of a romance novel I was writing in my head.

With my head bowed, my long hair covered the sides of my face. This blocked out a view of anything to the side of me. Long red bangs blocked out anything in front of me. So there I sat, blissful, in a world of my own creation. I am sure I was rehearsing in my head some melodrama like the building catching fire and Larry Davis sweeping me up in his arms and carrying me to safety. Snuggling in each other's arms, we would watch as the church burned to the ground. Or more realistically, I might have been fantasizing about being taken parking at Flat Shoal's Creek. In this fantasy, I am sure we did little more than talk. Larry might tell me he had been secretly in love with me for years and had only dated other girls while biding his time, waiting for me to reach an age when he could decently ask for my hand. This is the sort of nonsense that was going around in my head at the time. I was only fourteen, after all.

At some point in this idiotic adolescent reverie, I got the uncomfortable feeling that something had changed in the room. I looked up and was shocked to see that there was nobody else still sitting in the pews but Larry and I. Everybody in the congregation, including both Larry's parents, had gone to the front of the church, and as I was trying to figure this out, some of these adults fell to the floor and began to writhe and talk in tongues.

Now you might ask how I knew they were talking in tongues. But believe me, I knew. I watched Oral Roberts on television every Sunday morning when I had to go to church. This was not from religious zeal but because it was one of the standard ploys my brother and I used when we were trying to talk Mama into letting us stay at home. We would dutifully promise Mama that if she allowed us to stay home from church, we would sit and watch Oral Roberts for an hour nearly breaking people's necks with his hands as he yelled, "Heaaaaaaaaaaaaaaaaaaaal."

I don't remember that this ploy ever worked, but I do remember going through it over and over, complete with a pantomime of the "healing" bit. My brother and I would exchange roles, sometimes being the healer and sometimes being the healed. I think my father appreciated the humor of this little drama more than Mama ever did. Anyway, I was well acquainted with talking in tongues.

That evening in Larry's church, there were people on the floor talking and yelling and other people standing around watching the ones writhing on the floor. The preacher was moving from one writhing group to the other, holding a Bible in his left hand. With his right hand, he was making the sign of the cross over them. For some silly reason, now, this seemed oddly out of kilter. The gesture is more like something the Pope would do than an evangelical preacher. Maybe this "cross with the hand" gesture is a reconstructed memory since I'm not even sure I knew there was a Pope at that time.

I had certainly never seen anything like what was going on in the front of that church. I was mesmerized. Especially engaging was the activity around a vastly overweight woman who was talking in tongues and writhing on the floor while two other women tried to keep her dress down below her waist. These were grown people. To this day, I have never seen anything like it outside of the movies.

Needless to say, I forgot completely that rock star Larry Davis was sitting next to me. I was just riveted by the scene playing itself out at the front of the church. I guess I would have felt more uncomfortable had any of them paid the slightest bit of attention to Larry and I, the only heathen holdouts hiding in the back of the church. But they were oblivious.

What I became afraid of though, was that any minute one of them might get the call and be prompted to come to the back of the church and drag us up there with them. I quickly looked behind me and sized up the fact that I would have to dive up and over the back of our pew to get out the door.

Amid all this, the magnificent Larry Davis sat perfectly still beside me, relaxed, as if this was something that happened on a regular basis in his living room. It probably was, now that I think about it.

Now something you have to understand about the South is that poisonous snakes are just a part of life. You spend your entire childhood listening to one adult or the other yelling warnings about what to do or what not to do so you won't get bitten by a snake. Every minute you're outside in the South, snakes are in the back of your mind, along with giant black grasshoppers with pink and yellow wings which are unpleasant, to say the least, first crunching and then squishing between the toes. But, even though snakes were ubiquitous, I never got even remotely comfortable with them.

As I was watching these folks, grown-up people, in the front of the little church flailing about on the floor or bending over backward calling out praises to "Jeaaaaaaaaaaaaaaaazus," somebody (I have no idea who) threw a thick coiled-up length of rope toward the preacher.

As I watched, hypnotized, the preacher simply extended the thumb of the hand he was using to bless people, and the rope fell right into his grip. He didn't look at his hand or follow the progress of the rope through the air. And it was only when he caught the rope that I realized it was not a rope. It was . . .

"A snake!"

Both my elbows hit the back of the pew so hard that even the imperturbable Larry Davis jumped in his seat. I looked over at him, desperate. *Get me out of here.* But Larry Davis was calmly looking straight ahead just like the people in the room weren't stark raving mad. In fact, the only response I saw from Larry Davis was that he flicked his head and threw back the long straight brown hair out of his eyes. I was in a dead panic, and he looked like he was watching football on a Saturday night.

By this time, the preacher had the snake, a cottonmouth moccasin, I knew that much, around his neck.

"We will drive out demons," he intoned. "Demons. We will speak in tongues. We will pick up snakes with our hands . . ."

Fuck, I thought. *What was this "we" business.* I wasn't about to pick up any snakes with my hand or any other part of my body.

"When we drink poison and it will not hurt. It will not hurt."

Then all of them, except those who were still busy babbling something they thought was a facsimile of a language, started to chant. "It will not hurt. It will not hurt."

By this time, the snake had recovered from his trip through the air. His head was up and his neck crooked. That was snake body language I recognized almost by instinct. The sight of it was something I felt down to my toes. That snake was taking in the movement all around him with his beady little snake eyes, and I knew it was only a matter of seconds before the reptilian brain chose a victim. I couldn't move. Besides, any move I made (unless I did dive up and over the back of the pew) would put me closer to the snake (even if by inches) before I could run or crawl on my hands and knees, whatever was necessary to get out of that room. Fourteen years of admonitions hadn't totally fallen on deaf ears. I had it embedded in my DNA that what you did if you saw a snake was to freeze.

So I sat frozen. The preacher put his hand around the snake's neck and unbelievably tried to get the snake to look him in the eye. *Are you completely crazy?* I thought. But the snake wouldn't look at him. Every time the preacher turned the snake so that the snake would be looking into his face, the snake turned away.

Well, this really sent people in the front of the church into a frenzy, and they started to chant louder. "It will not hurt. It will not hurt."

It might well not hurt, I thought, *but as Rhett Butler said, this seemed "a minor point at such a moment."*

I just knew this situation was going to end in tears and ambulances, and I wanted to make damn sure they weren't my tears flowing inside an ambulance headed toward Cobb Memorial Hospital with some part of my body swelling up. My mother would kill me.

Then suddenly, all at once, it was like the preacher and the congregation (if not the snake) had worn themselves out. The activity died down as did the sound. I took the opportunity to make a move. I started to get up, but Larry Davis grabbed my wrist and pulled me back down.

"Just wait," he said out of the side of his mouth.

Foolishly, I sat down, and then everybody in the church seemed to be coming toward us. Larry stood up and pulled me up with him. There were smiles everywhere and hands reaching out to shake mine. Women tried to hug me over the back of the pew in front of us. All I could do was look frantically from one body to the next, one hand to the next, like a Secret Service agent in a crowd looking for a gun. I, however, was looking for that damn snake.

Larry guided me out into the aisle and backward toward the door.

When we reached the foyer, I had had enough. I turned and bolted. I'll be damned if I didn't run right smack-dab into a wooden box that was being carried by an old man from the congregation. Suddenly, I found myself face-to-face not with one, but with a box full of cottonmouth moccasins.

I could feel the bile rising in my throat and my knees weakening. I was sure I was going to throw up. Either throw up or faint or both.

But then, something stopped me. I was so shocked I couldn't even think, much less throw up. The snakes had clothes on. Let me repeat that, the snakes had clothes on. The people around me were starting to laugh, even Larry. In this box were three cottonmouth moccasins. One of them had a bonnet tied onto its head. Another had a cowboy hat on, and the third had a tiny saddle strapped on his back and a halter affair on his head with the reins coming back onto his neck.

The laughter got louder. I felt like I was losing my mind. I looked up into the face of the man who was carrying the box, and he howled with amusement. Finally, Larry, smooth ladies man, Larry Davis took my arm and started pulling me through the foyer and out toward his car. He opened the door and I got in.

Larry Davis drove me home. He didn't say a word, and I couldn't say a word. I was afraid if I opened my mouth, I would hurt his feelings. When we got to my house, he parked the car and went around to open the car door for me. He walked me to our front door. Then, Larry Davis got back into his car and drove away. He never asked me out again.

I saw him at a class reunion years later, when we were all in our late fifties. I'll be damned if he didn't look as good at sixty as he did at nineteen. How do men do that?

At one point in the reunion, I found myself next to Larry Davis, and I worked up the courage to tell him I would like to dance with him later on. He smiled and agreed. But when the dancing came around, Larry Davis was nowhere to be found. Elizabeth Ann, Tamyra, and I found out where he was though. We met him coming back inside the Country Club when we were leaving. Lula Hill was striding up the sidewalk looking exhilarated. She had in tow a subdued and exhausted-looking Larry Davis. It was obvious he had gotten a better offer than dancing.

I never got to ask him about the snakes.

Drowned in the Blood

Aside from the one rather eventful church service with Larry Davis and the few odd visits to neighborhood churches with my girlfriends, I spent seventeen years, at least an hour a week, looking at the inside of the First Baptist Church of Wilkes Ferry. That works out to be almost nine hundred hours of intense examination.

There was not much you could do besides examine the inside of the church when you were there. There was absolutely no possibility of talking to pass the time. Not in a church that small. Not even in the back. You couldn't even talk in the balcony, where the teenagers usually fled to avoid sitting with their parents.

Even though in the balcony we were above and behind everyone in the church, Mrs. Hester, the organist, could still see us in the mirror she used to watch the music director. We could see her every Sunday just after the morning hymns were over, adjusting that mirror to tilt upward so she could supervise the balcony. She must have been over sixty at the time, as I am startled to remember I am now, but Mrs. Hester must have had much better long distance vision than I do. She had eyes like diamond lasers, and she would not hesitate to tell your parents if you leaned over to share a joke with a friend. As we would have phrased it then, she would tell on you for "talking." This, of course, meant talking when you weren't supposed to be talking. The subject of "talking" seemed to follow me throughout my school years. *This* happened because I was "talking." *That* happened because I was "talking." Finally, I got expelled from school for "talking" a little bit too long and a little bit too publically about the obese and totally humorless football coach. Mama had to come and pick me up. All the way home, she berated me for "talking." Then she accused me of deliberately getting myself expelled from school just to embarrass her. The thing you have to remember about my Mama is that everything, everything was about her.

It's funny, but Daddy apologized to me years later for them getting so upset about the incident. He told me that they should have congratulated me instead of castigating me for pointing out to the football coach that my profanity was nothing compared to the profanity he regularly doled out on the football field. It's the story of my life, never being able to keep myself from talking.

And I guess I'm still talking. My mother would be mortified if she knew I was telling all of this. She's probably having a hissy-fit right now, looking down at me, or up at me, as the case may be. And if there are doors wherever she is, you can bet money she's slamming them.

But, back in the First Baptist Church, the only way to survive Sunday services was to look around the sanctuary and try to entertain yourself. I think even today, fifty years later, I could draw from memory every detail of the inside of that church—the large wooden chairs with red velvet cushions, one on either side of the preacher's podium, the choir loft with the polished dark-wood flat rail that enclosed it, and the stained glass window on the wall behind the choir loft. I think I could make that window from memory.

At the center of the stained glass window was an enormous long-haired Jesus, who stood full frontal, wearing a white robe, his arms extended, his hands held palms out to receive. He stood in the center of the window and also in the middle of a pond, on top of the water, of course. The water from the pond flowed around his feet and then appeared to flow over the lip of the bottom of the window and into the choir loft.

Actually, there was a rectangular brass receptacle in front of the stained glass window. This is where people were baptized, but you couldn't see that from the congregation. So Sunday after Sunday, I contemplated that water flowing into the choir loft, creeping up the legs of Mrs. Hester and Miss Mary Francis, floating Mrs. Hester's glasses off her face.

I know exactly what the brass receptacle looked like because I had to walk into it when I was baptized. I was very young, and I had, for some reason that I can now not fathom, "answered the call" of Kirk Steadman one Sunday morning and walked down the aisle (I was still sitting with my parents at that time), indicating by this action that I wanted to be "saved." My mother was thrilled. That's probably, now that I think about it, why I did it. I wanted to please Mama. God, that should be put on my fucking tombstone—She wanted to please Mama. Don't get me wrong, I never did please Mama, but I wanted to, desperately and for most of my life.

After the walk down the aisle came weeks of visits by Kirk Steadman, visits that I found more than a little bit embarrassing. I would be left alone with Kirk Steadman for little lecture and question sessions in my own house. I didn't like it. I didn't like it one bit. It made me feel creepy and uncomfortable. But that discomfort was nothing compared to what was in store for me—the ritual of baptism in front of the whole church one Sunday morning.

The victim, in this case me, was dressed like a sacrificial princess in a white dress, new white panties, a white petticoat, and white socks. I descended the three steps into the thing which I think is called a baptismal font. Now on the face of it, this doesn't sound so bad, but you have to remember that I was slowly immersing myself in lukewarm water inside a tinny basin. I was wet but fully clothed and with a grown man. It gave me the same strange forbidden sensation I used to have when I wet my pants. And like wetting my pants, it was more than distasteful. For some reason probably understood by people with more church experience than I have, there was a sheen of something like motor oil floating on the top of the water. Maybe this was some kind of holy oil or something, but I don't remember Baptists as going in for that kind of thing.

Anyway, after I had reluctantly walked down into the basin, Kirk Steadman put one hand behind my head and the other on my chest and pushed my entire body backward under the water. After I was ducked, he pulled me up with enormous force. Somehow, and this was not supposed to happen, I got water up my nose. And when I came up from being dunked, or baptized, I was choking and sputtering like a drowned puppy. Since I felt like I was suffocating, I reached out to clutch at whatever was nearest and that was Kirk Steadman.

I wrapped my arms around his head and all but smothered him in the process of trying to get myself out of the water. It was a most undignified performance. The baptism was suppose to make me feel like I was being hoisted into the future, a new person, reborn.

But I didn't feel reborn. I felt like I was being murdered, and I am sure Kirk Steadman felt like he had been humiliated. He unceremoniously pushed me away from him, and I sputtered and splashed toward the steps.

The memory of that water, even now, leaves a metallic taste in my mouth, sort of like the way George Orwell described Victory Gin in the book *1984*. And the feel of dragging myself out the other side of the receptacle, soaking wet with a dress and petticoat sticking to me, was just horrible. I knew, when I took one look at Kirk Steadman in a robe, standing in that greasy water, that this was going to end in tears. And before I had even taken one step into that receptacle thing, I was sorry I had ever gotten myself into it. I felt like a horse who wanted to bolt in the starting gate. But I had promised my mother, and the whole congregation was watching, and it was too late.

Let me tell you, that experience didn't leave me feeling blessed or clean as the driven snow or any of the other things that I was supposed to feel. It left me feeling wet and cold, embarrassed, uncomfortable, and more than slightly exposed since my white dress, when I finally dragged myself out of the water, was stuck to my body and all but transparent. This was another of those occasions when I rode home with Mother, silent, waiting for her to start in on me.

I can't remember anybody else's baptism, only mine. I am sure that the other people were better behaved and didn't act like they were being killed in front of the congregation of the First Baptist Church. But either I was never permitted to see another baptism, or I just repressed the whole thing. Kirk Steadman gave me a wide berth after that.

But you know, it was the strangest experience in the world for me at that age to have a grown man, a stranger, in that much control of my body. I had given myself as I was supposed to do, and he had half-drowned me. There's a reason why baptism is so often portrayed in the movies as a sexual experience.

But aside from the stained glass window and the font (if that's what it's called), the thing that there was more of than anything else in that church was walls, chalk green walls. Now green is a color I like, but the green of the First Baptist Church was not a light airy green or even a deep comforting green. It was just green, drab gray-green like the walls of a funeral home. It was, I noted, the same shade of green thirty-five years later. Where did they get that paint? The Southern Baptist Convention must distribute it in buckets full.

I must have examined those walls hundreds of times. I certainly don't remember listening to any of the interminable sermons that went on while I was sitting there. Church for me was something to get through, something to grit your teeth and endure, like torture.

Religion was just something I could never get into. Whether it was Bobby White, the football captain, talking about Jesus being a quarterback calling the plays in life, or Kirk Steadman, handsome as he was, droning away in the main church about Paul the Baptist. I just never could bring myself to believe in it. I tried, as I said, with that pathetic little attempt when I was baptized, but I wasn't very old before I decided that it was most probably a load of hokum. I kept my mouth shut about it, or at least I think I did, but after I left home, I never went back inside another church unless it was for a wedding or a funeral. Even then, I always felt uncomfortable and found myself struggling with the desire to do something outrageous.

As I remember it, the real parting of the way between me and religion came on the day that Mrs. Hawkins, Drew's home room teacher when he was in the seventh grade and I was in the third, towered over me, looked down at me with her icy cold blue eyes, and told me that animals were most certainly not allowed to go to heaven.

I was shocked. I can remember looking up into her big-boned, wide face. I must have stood there staring up at her for a long time. Finally, she raised her eyebrows and made a face at me, turned, and walked off across the elementary school playground.

After that day, when I learned that cats and dogs and horses couldn't go to heaven, I decided that heaven was not a place I was ever going to set foot in, especially not for fucking eternity.

After that, what went on in church had nothing to do with me.

Sometimes, when I was a teenager and sitting in the balcony, I watched Mrs. Heard and her chubby little husband.

Stout is a word that was invented for Mrs. Heard. Her flesh didn't even move when she walked. She looked like a barrel with legs or a stuffed pork sausage, and she was about twice as big as her husband. To make matters worse, she always sat in church beside her husband with her right arm over the back of the pew and her hand draped over his shoulder.

It seems now a small thing, but in the 1950s South, this was an extraordinarily unladylike thing to do. I don't remember one single other woman in the whole church doing anything even remotely similar

It fascinated me, that one bit of body language. I spent a considerable amount of time thinking about Mrs. Heard and her husband and what this arm over the shoulder might mean and why it was so exceptional. But aside from that one little bit of behavior, Mrs. Heard and her husband were completely uninteresting. The only other thing I can remember about them is that they had a son who was a big football player. He went bald at an early age, and Mrs. Heard firmly believed that he had lost his hair from too many locker room showers.

Sometimes, I watched the McGregors and the McKeans, wealthy and big givers to the church, always looking around and smiling as if they were welcoming everybody to their own house. Mr. Ben McKean was Mr. McGregor's son-in-law. Ben McKean married one of old Mr. McGregor's two daughters, who Mr. McGregor, and therefore everybody else in town, called "Sweet" and "Honey." Mr. McKean and old Mr. McGregor (I have no idea why he was called "old" Mr. McGregor. There was no young Mr. McGregor.) were deacons, and the two families were considered to be the financial and social backbone of the church.

I also sometimes watched Mr. Riley, Daddy's good friend, when he bothered to show up for church. Mr. Riley stood out in my mind because he looked exactly like the actor William Bendix. And like William Bendix, Mr. Riley was always making jokes and kidding around. For this reason, it was just fascinating to watch him.

I remember once when he was sitting in the back of the church, one of the ushers tried to give him a visitor's ribbon. Mr. Riley kept pushing the usher's hand away, and the usher kept offering the ribbon back. There were not many funny things that happened during that long hour in the First Baptist Church every Sunday, but this was one of the funniest things I ever saw, with the exception of Miss Sudie, Margaret Ann's grandmother, trying to get past the other people in the pew and run up the aisle holding a hymnal in one hand and her skirt, which had fallen down around her knees in the other. Margaret Ann and I got tickled every time one of us remembered that scene.

Mr. Riley, Mrs. Hawkins, Mrs. Herd, Kirk Steadman, Miss Sudie, Margaret Ann, the baptism, the long boring hours, all of it went round and round in my head as I walked into that same church for Daddy's funeral.

Reasons to Love My Father

My brother, Drew, did his monologue at the funeral. It was a good piece of theater, well written and performed. Throughout, Drew was wearing that little smile of his. The smile says, "I'm a good person, a kind and tolerant person, but I'm a tiny bit above it all. And more importantly, I'm a tiny bit above you." It is a look of benign detachment, similar to the expression one might wear talking with a child one dislikes but to whom one has to be gracious.

Drew's monologue was entitled "Reasons to Love My Father." I don't now remember all the reasons Drew gave for loving Daddy, partly because I was stuck thinking about the title. "Reasons to Love My Father." There were, evidently (since Drew went on for quite a while), numerous reasons to love my daddy, but Drew never said once that *he* loved Daddy. So as far as I was concerned, Drew might as well have gotten up in front of everybody who ever knew Daddy and said, "There are a number of reasons to love my father, but I didn't."

One of the other things Drew said that struck me later on was that water was always my father's friend. Now Daddy loved the water, it was true. But Drew said the water lovingly held my father up after he had a heart attack. Lovingly held him up? It fucking drowned him. Where do people get this shit

The content of Drew's eulogy was bad enough, but the tone was worse. It was flat around the edges in a way that I was sure nobody else noticed. It was very much like Mother's tone when she made the "Will Lee, can't we go on a little longer" plea.

The funeral was a performance for Drew, and I was beginning to wonder if Drew's entire life was a performance, something I hadn't really thought about before. I guess I should have felt sorry for him and for mother, both of them damaged beyond repair. I didn't want to even think what that said about me.

Drew and his family seemed to have a great good time during their brief stay in Wilkes Ferry. At the viewing, they set up a little shrine for Daddy. They kept coming into Snipes's Funeral Home with items to add to the shrine. Here came a photograph of Daddy in his football uniform, spread legged, holding the ball in his left hand and the knuckles of his right hand on the ground, looking straight into the camera. That photograph sat on Daddy's chest of drawers for as long as I can remember. He must have loved looking at it. Then came Daddy's pocket watch. Then his alcoholic father's pocket watch. Then came a golf club and, finally, a remote control from the television.

I thought it was sweet at first, but I also thought they were having way too much fun. And somewhere, beneath it all, there was a hollow tone of mockery in it. It was the same when Drew drove Daddy's pickup truck to the grave site. Drew was smiling, pleased with what he thought was a clever joke. It set my teeth on edge.

I never, ever thought I'd hear myself say this, but Daddy looked good in his coffin. He made a nice corpse. He looked young, like he did in photographs of him in the army during WWII, full faced and healthy with ruddy cheeks. It was the way he looked when he came back to me those two times after he died.

But at the "viewing," after I slipped a piece of paper with a poem I had written into his shirt pocket, I felt sick. I felt as if I might just collapse on the floor. We stood in a line—Mother, Drew, his dreadful wife, his tribe, Mattie Mae, and I—to receive the guests. After a few minutes, Mattie Mae leaned over to me and said she couldn't stand up anymore.

I took her arm, and we walked over to a large upholstered chair in the corner. She sat down and I sat down beside her. I leaned my head up against her as if I were a child again, seeking comfort in her arms.

We sat there together, not speaking for most of the viewing. People came over and shook hands, and I smiled and nodded my head. That was about all I could do.

As I remember the events of that two weeks after Daddy's death, they seem to have no particular order. Scenes float in and out of my memory without context.

At some point, when I was sitting in the living room, I became aware that Drew and his dreadful wife and daughters were piling Daddy's clothes on the dining room table. I watched with very little understanding of what they were doing. The wife or a daughter would come down the stairs with an arm full of clothes which they deposited on the table. Then another would come down with even more clothes. They cleared out Daddy's closets and his drawers and God knows what else the day after the funeral. They gave some of Daddy's things to Looney, the yard man, and took the rest to Goodwill. They offered some of it to Mattie Mae, but she waved them off with tears in her eyes. "I couldn't take none of Mr. Will Lee's things," she said simply.

When I thought about it later, I wondered if they were all mad.

Who in the hell did they think they were to dispose of Daddy's belongings the day after his funeral? I was only surprised they didn't fumigate the damn house.

None of them had loved Daddy. The wife and daughters hadn't even set eyes on him more than a half dozen times in their lives. Daddy remarked once that when he was with them in New York, they treated him like he was a sexual predator. It was demented. They swept into town, took over the funeral, disposed of Daddy's body and his belongings, and were carried to the airport laughing and talking. Lee Ray, who drove them to the airport, said it made him feel really bad for Daddy. It was, he said, like they were on holiday instead of at a funeral. The psychotic nature of my brother and his tribe's behavior was so evident and deep, it rivaled only that of my mother. Mother, by the way, didn't make a peep of objection to the disposal of Daddy's things. She wouldn't. Nobody even asked me.

Drew and his family were there, and they were gone, and it occurred to me that in over fifty years of living, Drew had phoned me once—once, just to talk. That once, he phoned me because he had gotten a new cell phone and was calling everybody he knew to try it out.

The River, the Rails, and King Cotton

For over a hundred years, life in the Catawba River Valley centered around three things—the river, the railroad, and king cotton. They all met in Wilkes Ferry. Before the railroad and the cotton, was the river. For Native Americans, the river was a means of transportation. They cut trees from its banks, hollowed them out, and delivered goods too heavy to carry downstream. But even more importantly, the river system was a map. There were paths along both sides of the river, like the one still on our back land when Lee Ray and I lived in Wilkes Ferry, that Native Americans followed down river to the coast or upriver to the headwaters of the Catawba. When they got to the headwaters, it was a short walk to the headwaters of other river systems. These were well-worn trails from one river system to the other, and using them, the Natives could travel as far as the Mississippi River Valley.

Native Americans fished in the Catawba for trout and catfish. They bathed in the river, drank its waters, and played in it. Food, transportation, recreation, an unfailing travel guide, the river was essential. The Creek Indians were called Creek by white settlers because they always found the Indians near the water.

Native Americans farmed the land around Wilkes Ferry for centuries before the settlers came. Native trade routes met there. The Creek met up with the odd explorer like de Soto. But when settlers started coming in waves from the east, it was the beginning of disaster.

The Creek Indians made a settlement on an island just off the western bank of the Catawba River, a little north of what is now Wilkes Ferry. They chose that spot because when settlers arrived from the east with their wagons and horses and children and guns, they would have to stand on the eastern bank for at least as long as it took to organize the river crossing. This gave the Creek time to suss out the settlers' intentions. There is something quaint and more than a little tragic about the Creek thinking all they needed was a few minutes of advanced warning to protect themselves from the settlers. They should have strangled all of them.

There's a saying in Mexico that everything the Spanish ever touched turned to shit. Similarly, every time European settlement started, it bulldozed everything in its path and, to this day, has left behind it nothing but devastation.

The Creek, the Cherokee, Choctaws, and the Chickasaw were all eventually either killed or driven out of the region. By the 1830s, the Choctaws and the Chickasaw were driven out. Planters had to get rid of them to consolidate their land holdings. When gold was found in 1838 on land belonging to Cherokee and later in 1842 on land belonging to the Seminole, that sealed their fates. There were trashy squatters all over what had been Creek land. Criminals and exploiters were drawn to the Creek because they were such easy marks. In 1832, an agreement was signed that essentially dissolved the Creek nation, ceding all Creek land east of the Mississippi. The land was divided up into individual plots. Lots were drawn for free homesteads on their land. But the poor whites who took over plots after the lottery were mostly not able to keep the holdings away from land speculators who bought them up.

Sometime in the 1840s, the river crossing moved south of the Creek village, about two miles, and a ferry was started near where the river bridge in Wilkes Ferry is now. When the river is low, you can still see the large metal hooks sunk into rocks that were used to pull the ferry across the river. When we were living in Wilkes Ferry and boated on the river, we often picnicked on those rocks. Cotton went down river on barges, and groceries and supplies came upriver on pole boats. The river was essential as a way out of subsistence farming.

Cotton was originally grown only for domestic use. There was too much work involved in handpicking the debris out of the cotton and separating it from the seed. Then there was pulling and twisting and spinning. The cotton gin changed all that. The cotton gin made growing cotton commercially possible. But cotton needed water, so the large plantations located all up and down the river, with widespread clearing of the land to make room for the increased capacity of cotton processing. Erosion started washing iron-rich soil into the Catawba, turning it from the crystal-clear water the natives swam and fished in to the muddy red of today.

By 1835, two dozen steam-powered river boats plied the Catawba. By the 1840s and 1850s, there were as many as two hundred going up the Catawba, at least as far as Wilkes Ferry. Steamboat captains often paid Indians for cords of wood they would cut and stack at landings along the river. The once-proud natives, without land, were reduced to canoeing up and down the Catawba begging for food.

Steam engines pushing a paddle were perfect for the shallow water of the Catawba. The paddle went only one to two feet under the water. Most of the paddle wheelers had two paddles, one on either side, so they could go backward and maneuver quite capably.

One of these steamboats sank while tied to the wharf on the town side of the river and still remains there covered with mud. I know this because the state paid divers an outrageous sum of money to explore the river at Wilkes Ferry, and there was a proposal to devise underwater tours of the river bottom. This idea will probably be about as successful as was the idea to flood over half the county to build a dam in the mid-seventies.

After the flooding, a lake was advertised. The county was filled with tourists. After that, the water became so polluted the dead fish floating down the river had blisters on them. The tourists stopped coming and never came back. And even with the dam and all the promises that this meant never having a flood again, the Catawba flooded the year we moved back to town. This flood was a disaster since most people near the river hadn't bothered to hold onto their flood insurance after the dam was built.

The old docks where the steamboat sank were located on a bluff high above the river. At other points, the land running beside the river is not so steep. Just downstream from the river bridge on bottomland next to the river, deer can easily walk down to the river for a drink as can black-gloved foxes and coyotes and racoons.

The Wilkes Ferry docks were located where the bank was high for the same reason they were located at similar spots in Columbus and Montgomery. Bales of cotton and other cargo could be easily pushed down the steep incline and onto waiting boats. Wooden scutes were built, and the bales pushed down those wooden scutes and onto the boats. There were even men who specialized in pushing the bales, brave men. This was dangerous work. A man could lose a hand or break an arm if he got caught up in a bale of cotton plummeting down one of the scutes. He could also get killed. The men who specialized in this work were called "Pushadors." The men whose job was less dangerous, those who got the bales onto the boat at the bottom of the scutes, were called "Stevedores."

The river was the preferred form of transportation for people and cargo until the railroad took over. The roads were so bad some people said the only maintenance work that was done on them was the pressure of the wheels of the conveyances that were unlucky enough to travel down them.

Even so, transport on the river was not problem-free. A trip from Wilkes Ferry to the coast took five days. Of course, that was if the boat didn't encountered stumps, roots, strong currents, low water, or flooding. Boats loaded with cotton regularly ran aground on sandbars. For this reason, many of the riverboats had extremely shallow drafts for navigating in the dry season. It was said that the riverboat Ben Franklin could navigate the Catawba if the river bottom was moist.

Even so, boats and barges ran aground or hit rocks and sank. Some even caught fire. The river changed with such rapidity that boats could be grounded in the mud before their crews had a chance to move them. It might take months to dig them out. When the Catawba flooded, it was impossible for boats to get underneath bridges. One time, the flooding was so extensive, a riverboat was able to solve the problem by going around the river bridge instead of under it.

The unpredictability and shallowness of the muddy river made it one of the most expensive rivers in the country on which to move cotton, or any other cargo for that matter. It was said to have cost three times more to insure a boatload of cotton from Wilkes Ferry to the sea as it was to ship it from the coast to any port in Europe. But traffic up and down the river continued.

In fact, the river and the cotton crop provided the rhythm of life in the river valley. In the summer, when the river was low and sometimes even dry, commerce virtually came to a stop. This was also when the cotton was most vulnerable to drought. The river rose in the autumn, when the cotton was being ginned and baled. The harvest was complete by October. By Christmas, when the cotton was being chopped, the river was at its highest.

The bridge over the Catawba at Wilkes Ferry was built in the early 1800s. The first bridge was designed by a slave named Cicero, who had been taught to design and build bridges by his master. Cicero and his master traveled around constructing bridges all over the region. When the master got older, he was afraid he would die suddenly, and Cicero would be considered as just another part of his estate. So he freed Cicero.

After Cicero was freed, he continued to work with his former master as a partner. After the master's death, Cicero and his sons designed bridges all over the Southeast. Cicero didn't design the bridge that crossed the Catawba at Wilkes Ferry in the '50s when I was growing up. I don't know who did, but he must have been a very disturbed man because the bridge was nothing less than fiendish.

I Believed She Could

When I was a child, Mattie Mae Hollis, our maid, would regularly take my brother and I downtown. We loved *being* downtown. It was *going* downtown that was the problem, most particularly one part of the journey—the river bridge.

Downtown Wilkes Ferry was about two miles from our house. At that time, Wilkes Ferry was a collection of lovely, well-tended houses with trimmed lawns and shady gardens. There were a few large plantation-style houses, where very rich people lived, and then the more modest frame-and-brick houses of the middle class. All of them contained people who were proud of what they had and who were also afraid of what the neighbors might say if they didn't keep what they had neat. None of them would have considered letting their grass grow up or leaving their children's toys all over the yard.

It was a delightful walk from our house to the river. Usually, Mattie Mae and my brother and I would take the streets down by the river where the trees made a canopy over the road, and it was cool even on the hottest day.

But as pleasurable as it was to walk down that canopied street, the end of that street brought on a vision of unutterable terror—the bridge.

This was no ordinary bridge. This was a bridge designed by a maniac who detested animals and children. I am absolutely sure the only thing that prevented him from committing the most heinous crimes was the construction of bridges like this all over the South and the knowledge that it made little girls squeal in hysterical terror.

You might ask what made the bridge so frightening. In the center of the bridge, where the cars and the occasional mule-drawn wagon passed, everything was normal. But then, there were two pedestrian walkways, one on either side of the bridge. They were not normal. I have had nightmares about those walkways for most of my life.

The pedestrian walkways should have been smooth concrete like the roadway. They were not. They were instead made up of thirty or forty large cement blocks set side by side into a metal frame. At the center of each of these large blocks was a smaller cement square which fit down into the larger block. These squares moved when you stepped on them. Some of them were cracked. A few were even broken.

To make matters worse, there was a hole in the center of each of the smaller blocks. Through this hole you could see down, down, down what seemed like a thousand feet to the muddy red Catawba River passing below.

Because the hole was small and the river far away, the water seemed to be rushing by so furiously that if you fell into it, you would be consumed in a second and never appear again.

The whole thing terrified me. I knew it was only a matter of time before I would step on one of those blocks, the block would crack and drop me into the dark red water of the Catawba River like a condemned man dropping through the trap door at a hanging. I also feared that the entire bridge might fall down and the river would suck the three of us, Mattie May, my brother, and I, away without a trace.

I don't think anybody but Mattie Mae Hollis could have dragged me across that bridge without gagging me and putting me in a straight jacket. But every time, when we got to the beginning of the bridge, Mattie Mae would bend down, sweep me up into her powerful arms, and say the same thing: "Hush you cryin' now, chile'. Dat bridge fall down, I'll jump in the riber myself and hol' it up till you gets across."

I think Mattie Mae loved me so much she would have held that bridge up for me. I loved her so much I believed she could.

The War Zone

When I was a teenager, our dinner table was like a war zone. Every night we sat down with dinner and the nightly news. In the early sixties, that nightly news was usually from Selma or Montgomery, Little Rock or Birmingham.

Sometimes my father would slam his fist on the dinner table and walk out. One night, my mother provoked just such an event by setting the plates on the table and then sitting down and saying, "If I was colored, I'd burn down everything in sight."

Mother didn't move when Daddy hit the table. In fact, her response was to sit up a little straighter. When Daddy slammed the back door, she closed her eyes for a moment and said calmly, "Colored people fix our food and virtually raise our children. I can't imagine anybody objecting to sitting at a lunch counter with them."

Wyatt's Pharmacy

There were fifteen children in the photograph of Mrs. Tigner's 1957 kindergarten class. Lined up facing the camera were Margaret Ann Patterson, Elizabeth Ann Wyatt, Tamyra Tanner, Danny McKean, Robbie Hopewell, Gaynell Woodham, Marie Scroggs, and David Sumerland. I was the one dressed like a clown.

I started kindergarten with those children, and I graduated from high school with them. By the time we graduated, we knew each other so well, the boys were more brothers than possible boyfriends.

From the time I was around eight until we started to drive at sixteen, the little girls in that photograph, along with a few others, went downtown every Saturday morning. We would either walk there along with one of the family maids—Pearl or Mary or Mattie Mae or Mildred—across the dreaded river bridge, or one of our mothers would drive us there and let us out for a few hours.

We would walk from the stoplight in the center of town one block to Wyatt's Pharmacy. Once there, we ordered cherry sodas and strawberry floats and rocky-road malts at the old-fashioned soda fountain. The soda fountain was glossy black, and the milk-shake makers and other equipment was gleaming silver. We took our drinks from the soda counter to the black lacquered booths at the back of the store. We then spent a couple of hours talking and giggling and heaven knows what else.

When we were a little older, we would arrange during the week to meet the boys from our class. I danced my very first dance with a boy (outside of dancing class) in that pharmacy between the lacquered booths. It's hard now to imagine we had enough room to dance back there where the jukebox was, but dance we did. I danced then and numerous times afterward with Billy Cooper, a tall lanky boy whose father had died when we were little. Billy was a great friend, a talented artist and always up for any kind of crazy, wacky fun.

I remember vividly sitting in one of those booths with Margaret Ann, holding a Pez dispenser shaped like Donald Duck or Mickey Mouse. She had one and I had the other, but I can't remember who had which. You pushed back Donald's or Mickey's head, and a white or green or pink tablet would slide out ready for small fingertips to grasp. The thought of those chalky tablets now gives me indigestion. I am sure that just one of them would rot the lining out of an iron stomach.

Sometimes when we were at Wyatt's, Elizabeth Ann would show us how to shoplift lipsticks and perfumes. This seemed like a terribly daring thing to do, and it made me nervous as a squirrel just watching her. But it was, after all, her father's store. All Elizabeth Ann was really risking was that her father, Mr. Jim William, or more likely her mother, Miss Fern, would yell at her if what she shoplifted was too expensive.

Miss Fern, before she became a wife and mother, was a school teacher and she had very little tolerance for nonsense. She was proper, upright, and most importantly, severe. I know I have seen her laugh, but I can't remember when. She also had a peculiar way of speaking. She would say "Elizabeth Ann-uh" or "Come-uh back here-uh." No other person in Wilkes Ferry that I can remember talked like that, and it was enough to freeze me in my tracks. The possibility of Miss Fern being mad would have been enough to deter me from any behavior but not Elizabeth Ann.

Elizabeth Ann was one of those people who, as they say, marched to her own drummer. And her drummer had little, if any, feel for the rhythm of the drummer's keeping time in the rest of our heads. Elizabeth Ann's drummer, in fact, couldn't keep time at all. Margaret Ann and I often talked her into trying to do dance steps while clapping her hands to the music. The result was highly entertaining not only for us but also for Elizabeth Ann, who seemed hilariously baffled at her own inability to do something everyone else found so natural.

Elizabeth Ann was by no means stupid. She was probably one of those children who had severe learning disabilities before anyone knew what a learning disability was, so when she failed the seventh grade, everyone was shocked. Failing was simply unheard of in Wilkes Ferry. The only children who failed were the one or two really poor children who sometimes showed up in the middle of a school year. Children in our little group of families did not fail. It just wasn't done.

Wilkes Ferry, you see, was the white-collar town in the Catawba River Valley, or just "the Valley" as the collection of mill towns running up and down the Catawba River was referred to. Everybody and everything was defined by its connection to the Cobb Cotton Manufacturing Company. The offices of the Company (pronounced *Cumpny*), were located in Wilkes Ferry, so the population was largely made up of middle-class families with children headed for college. The other towns "down the Valley" (including the one my mother and father came from) had grown up around cotton mills, and the population was overwhelmingly working class. Children in those schools, most of them, would take their places in the mills when they graduated from high school. In the Valley, people owned the white wooden houses which had been part of the mill villages built and owned by the Cobb Manufacturing Company years before. In Wilkes Ferry, most of the houses were brick or stone.

For a child to fail in Wilkes Ferry was an oddity. You can imagine how upset Miss Fern was when Elizabeth Ann failed. But Elizabeth Ann was just, or seemed to be, oblivious to the shame and embarrassment of her mother. She was quietly transferred over the summer to the closest mill-town school to repeat the seventh grade. Elizabeth Ann didn't skip a beat. She just barreled on through life, enjoying herself, doing as she damn well pleased, like a bull in a china shop. I liked and still do like Elizabeth Ann very much. She is cynical, irreverent, and absolutely fearless.

Needless to say, when we were growing up, an afternoon with Elizabeth Ann was an adventure.

The Wyatts lived in a large solid brick house on a hill right next to the First Baptist Church. Almost forty years after we graduated from high school and Elizabeth Ann had moved back in with Miss Fern, we had a conversation about neighborhoods. Elizabeth Ann remarked in an offhand way that she had deeply resented the fact that she was looked down on because her family didn't live in Indian Hills, where the big plantation houses were located along with more expensive houses like the Oriental Tea Garden house built by Mr. Morgan, one of the big managers of "the Company."

The hurt and anger with which Elizabeth Ann made the comment brought me up short. I never felt looked down on because my family didn't live in Indian

Hills. It was like telling someone they had been poor as a child when they had never noticed. It reminded me of a statement my friend Carol made to me once about what she called her "dysfunctional family."

"Oh," I said, "I didn't know you had a dysfunctional family."

"Neither did I," she responded, "until I read this book a few years ago."

Don't get me wrong, I was not above envy. The Morgan's Tea Garden house, for example, was a spectacular house with an open courtyard in the center. Nobody had even seen a house like it outside of the movies. When it was first completed in the 1960s, people from all over town and even down the Valley would drive by just to look at it. Oh, I envied Sister and Lara Jane Morgan but not for their house. I envied them their horses—two giant Thoroughbred jumpers.

And not everybody who lived in Indian Hills was rich. There were some small houses. The Tates, for example, lived in a little brick box of a house, new but tiny, not half a mile from the Fallon Mansion and the Oriental Tea Garden house.

Joe Ed Montgomery's House was also in Indian Hills. It was larger than the Tate's house, but it was hardly a mansion. It was 1950s modern though, with sliding glass doors going out to a brick patio in the back. In the 1950s, this was very sophisticated stuff. It was TV stuff. I don't remember seeing sliding glass doors in anybody else's house until the Pattersons, Margaret Ann's family, added a downstairs kitchen and living room to their then tiny house over on the town side of Wilkes Ferry.

But even with modern sliding glass doors, neither the Montgomerys nor the Pattersons had any living room furniture. The Pattersons didn't even have carpeting. They had linoleum tile. Now that I think about it, that living room never had any furniture in it until Margaret Ann's grandmother, Miss Sudie, died and that was after Margaret Ann and I left for college.

In fact, I remember just after Miss Corinne's funeral, Margaret Ann saying, "I'm so glad Mama got her living room before she died."

No, I don't remember pining away for a house in Indian Hills or feeling in any way resentful or envious of those who lived there. I am sure part of this was due to my parents, who were adamant (for reasons I didn't then understand) that we were as good as anybody in town and that we were no better than anybody in town. But like so many things my mother espoused, what was said and deeply held were different things.

I was fifty years old before I realized how much Mama resented people wealthier than she was and how scarred she had been by poverty and public shame. When I was fifty and had moved back to Wilkes Ferry, she was becoming unable to maintain the facade she had cultivated for so many years. The walls were starting to crack, and meanness and insecurity started appearing in the breech.

I am grateful that my parents believed (or in mother's case tried to believe) that people were equals. I am grateful they inculcated that sentiment in me. It is that populist base that has been a central part of my makeup for sixty years. Daddy believed it to his core. But, Mother was the kind of person who dredged up a little too much anger and pain when asserting her equality. She said "I am (or you are) just as good as anybody in this town" a little too often, with a little too much vehemence. But I didn't pick up that up at the time. So I was never aware, or at least I can't remember ever being aware, of a social distinction between myself and the other children living in Indian Hills. No, I didn't envy the Morgans and their house or their location in Indian Hills.

What I wanted was one of the oldest houses in Wilkes Ferry—Crawford House, a classic antebellum, white-columned *Gone with the Wind* mansion. It had a balcony on the second floor accessed by old wavy-glass French doors and was built at the highest point in Wilkes Ferry, higher even than Fort Butler across the river where the last battle of the Civil War was fought. Crawford House was, and still is, the best house in Wilkes Ferry. It was, if anything, at the periphery of Indian Hills, only a few blocks from our house.

When I walked to Gaynell's house or Joe Ed's house as a child, I would pass by the Crawford House, and the rest of the way, I would spin dreams. I could see Southern belles jostling each other on the balcony to get a glimpse of some beau who had ridden up on a shiny leather-bridled, silky black horse. I could feel the necklaces and ribbons they wore and a turquoise-colored fan partially hiding my face as I looked down into the drive with them. I could hear the swish of silk petticoats and feel them brushing against my legs. Crawford House was all romance.

There was not much romance to Elizabeth Ann's house. It was very much like Miss Fern—formal and rigid. It was a solid, respectable house and way too close to the Baptist Church for me to invent any imaginative stories about it.

What I do remember is that the Wyatt's house was cool and dark like a cave. And the lights were always off when I was there in the afternoon, perhaps to save electricity. It gave the house an eerie green look that, now that I think about it, was very much like the inside of the Baptist Church. Maybe the Wyatts used the leftover paint from the Baptist Church, although I could not imagine Miss Fern ever doing such a thing.

Curiously, I don't remember Miss Fern or Mildred ever being there in the house with us. It seems that when I was there, we were unsupervised. It seems odd though that Mildred wasn't somewhere in the house. That's what Pearl and Mattie Mae and Mary and Mildred did—worked and kept an eye on us while our mothers went to bridge club or golf dates or cocktail parties. But either Mildred kept a low profile, and I'm not sure I wouldn't have done the same thing if I had to supervise Elizabeth Ann and her brother Charlie, or we were very often alone in the house.

Elizabeth Ann's brother Charlie also marched very much to his own distinct drummer. The family had relegated him, or he had relegated himself to a room in the basement, where he spent every waking minute (at least every waking minute I knew of) talking to people all over the world on his CB radio. He was like a troll there in the basement, always a presence but hardly ever seen.

I'm not sure if it was Charlie who created the ominous, heavy feeling in the Wyatt house or the White brothers, the only friends Charlie seemed to have. But the door to the basement where Charlie stayed, was always kept closed. But, even when I didn't see Charlie, I was keenly aware of his presence. There's a photograph in my mind of that closed door to the basement in the hallway smothered in green light.

Once, when I was walking from the kitchen back to Elizabeth Ann's bedroom, Danny White came unexpectedly out of that door. I think Charlie was behind him, but in the photograph in my memory, Danny alone is there within my vision. He is standing much too close to me, blocking my way down the hall to Elizabeth Ann's room.

He is standing so close I can feel the heat of his breath on my face. He is smiling but not the way Joe Ed or Morgan or Michael would smile at me. There is something menacing in the smile, menacing and ridiculing at the same time. It made me feel as if he knew some secret about me.

Danny and his older brother Steve were star high school football players. They were considered attractive, but they had canines, top and bottom, that were a little bit too large. This made their smiles disturbing at the best of times, and this wasn't the best of times. Both brothers had bodies that were tight, compact, and coordinated. They were born competitors—fast, athletic, and aggressive.

The hallway in Elizabeth Ann's house was narrow, and I began to perspire even in that cool green house. I was stuck, and I knew that no matter which way I tried to move, Danny could block me. If I panicked, he could outmaneuver me sure as the world. Then I would not only be trapped, I would be humiliated. If I made the mistake of turning this into a test of physical prowess, he would no doubt be the winner. Perhaps this was the secret he knew about me.

I don't remember how the moment resolved itself. I don't remember how a lot of moments like that resolved themselves. Perhaps Elizabeth Ann came along, perhaps Mildred. Perhaps Danny backed off, content to leave me swallowing the realization that he had spared me from something. I don't know, but I do know the moment was significant enough to remain in my brain for forty years.

Another less ominous photograph I have in my mind is Elizabeth Ann kneeling on her bed showing me how to create farts. She is bending down until her forehead touches the bedspread and then straightening up.

Somehow she was sucking air into her anus and producing fart after reliable fart. I don't know whether the attempts to teach me how to perform this extraordinary feat would have been successful. I was too embarrassed to try. I don't think I ever said the word fart until I was in my thirties and living in Scotland, where the word was more commonly used. Fart was definitely a word that was unacceptable in our house. In fact, no word even remotely related to bodily functions was permitted in our house. Well-bred ladies didn't talk about bodily functions to anyone, even if they were dying. So even though I admired Elizabeth Ann's liberation from the normal constraints of conventional manners, I could not bring myself to join her. What she was doing embarrassed me even though her single-minded pursuit amused me. Finally, that afternoon, Elizabeth Ann despaired of getting me to participate in the farting contest. I am sure she thought I was a party pooper. We must have been very bored since the next activity Elizabeth Ann thought up was to explore the drawers in her mother's bathroom.

There was a bathroom between Elizabeth Ann's bedroom and that of her parents. This very fact should spell trouble to any adult. I know that I would certainly never want a child sharing a bathroom with me. To illustrate why, that afternoon Elizabeth Ann started exploring in depth her mother's bathroom drawers. She was again on her knees, but this time she was littering the floors with items that were largely of no interest.

Then Elizabeth Ann took an object out of one of the drawers and held it up for me to see. It was a rubber circular thing wider in diameter than the length of an adult's finger. In the center was a layer of thin rubber. Around the edges the rubber was, or appeared to be, tightly rolled up. We sat, two little girls in the middle of the bathroom floor on the black-and-white tiles looking at the curious object.

"What is it?" I asked Elizabeth Ann as she compressed the circle and then allowed it to pop out and regain shape.

"Oh, you dummy," she responded. "Don't you know anything? It's a rubber."

I stared at the circular object. I reached out and Elizabeth Ann dropped it in my hand. I examined it, turning it around and around. "Are you sure?"

"Of course, I'm sure," she responded. "What else could it be?"

I shrugged my shoulders. I then positioned the rubber thing between my legs which were outstretched on the floor. I looked up at Elizabeth Ann whose eyes met mine. Both sets of eyes widened with realization.

Suddenly, Elizabeth Ann threw herself backwards on to the tile and let out a moan. "Agggggggggggggggggggggg." She started grasping her skull. "Shut up. Shut up," Elizabeth Ann wailed.

"Shut up?" I said. "I didn't say anything."

"You didn't have to," she replied, still holding her head and groping around with her fingers through her hair.

"You were the one who started all this."

I tossed the rubber thing to her and, at that moment, saw a drop of blood hit Elizabeth Ann's shoulder.

"Oh," I said. "You're bleeding."

We scrambled up from the floor and examined Elizabeth Ann's head in the mirror. Elizabeth Ann had a great deal of glossy black hair, and we had a hard time finding the cut.

When we did, Elizabeth Ann strained to get close enough to the mirror to see. "It's nothing," she said, dropping her hair.

I stared at her. "But what if you need stitches?"

Elizabeth Ann cocked her head. "Don't be a ninny. It's just a cut."

"But what are we going to tell Miss Fern?" I could feel myself getting hysterical.

Elizabeth Ann gazed unseeingly into my eyes. She was thinking.

"Oh, hell. Anything," she finally said. "Help me clean this stuff up."

Elizabeth Ann then threw everything back into Miss Fern's drawers. I stood wondering how she thought Miss Fern was going to miss the fact that somebody had been rummaging around in her drawers with all the mess Elizabeth Ann was leaving. When I got up enough nerve to even open one of my mother's drawers, I memorized the exact position of the contents before moving anything. But Miss Fern would probably come home and give Elizabeth Ann a lecture about playing in her drawers. Elizabeth Ann would pretend to listen but ignore her, and life would go on.

I often wished I could manage to be that blasé about my mother's anger. I couldn't even manage to be that impervious when I was fifty, much less when I was a child. I had antennae that were so fine-tuned I would start to get nervous if my mother even adopted body language indicating she was mad. I could even tell from another car if my mother was *getting* mad.

Oh, after finding what we thought was the rubber in Miss Fern's bathroom (and later realized was a diaphram), I never looked at Mr. Jim William quite the same way.

Margaret Ann Patterson

When I was growing up, I spent time playing with all of the little girls in Mrs. Tigner's kindergarten—Elizabeth Ann Wyatt, Gaynell Woodham, Marie Scroggs, Tamyra Tanner, Susan Turner. Magaret Ann Patterson wasn't one of those little girls who started out at Mrs. Tigner's, I can't remember why, but for most of my childhood and adolescence, Margaret Ann and I were inseparable. We spent so much time together we might as well have been sisters. Even though we now no longer speak, she was my closest childhood friend.

Margaret Ann says we became best friends in Mrs. Ayers's fifth grade homeroom when I was moved to a desk right in front of hers. I don't remember this at all, but photographs were taken every year of each class. When I looked through Mama's things, I found the fifth-grade photo, and there we are, Margaret Ann and I. I am in the first desk of the row next to the door. Margaret Ann is right behind me. Margaret Ann has an amazing memory for the details of those years. She maintains I was moved for "talking," which lends further credibility to her version of events. It has been one of the great misfortunes of my life, that I seem to be constitutionally incapable of keeping my mouth shut.

One of my theories about why I almost compulsively write (which is a form of talking) is that I have been trying for over fifty years to tell a story, one story. It's just that I still haven't figured out yet what that story is.

In the photograph of Mrs. Ayers's fifth grade class, we are all seated at our wooden lift-top desks, four rows of children, four children per row. Margaret Ann and I both have long hair, pulled straight back into ponytails. I can still remember sitting on the bench of my mother's dresser and watching her brush my hair in the large circular mirror. When she was ready to put the rubber band on, she pulled my hair so tight I felt like my eyes were going to start to slant.

To prevent the shorter ends of hair from falling down in our faces, both Margaret Ann and I wore what we called "bandos." They are now called hair bands. The bandos matched our dresses as closely as possible. I used to take that bando off my head and use it to comb back the hair off my face so often it became like a behavioral tic, much like some people repeatedly push glasses up on their noses.

I have always loved fabric and color, dresses and petticoats. I remember vividly the dress I am wearing in that photograph. It was a sleeveless print dress with an olive green background and little beige flowers that resembled the blooms of African violets. The dress had a solid green collar so deep it capped the tops of my bare shoulders. Around the edge of the collar were three rows of piping, handmade by rolling the olive green print fabric, seaming it, and then attaching it onto the collar. The dress had a gathered skirt with a deep hem since Teresa Linley was even taller than I was. The dress was a hand-me-down made by Teresa's mother, Carolee Linley. Miss Carolee was a tall raven-haired beauty with eyebrows that only went up and not back down and glamourously slanted eyes (that were natural and not caused by a tight ponytail).

I wore Teresa Linley's hand-me-downs for years. Margaret Ann wore hand-me-downs from her sister, Frankie. Frankie wore hand-me-downs from her cousin Betty. Even though the families of the girls I grew up with were solidly middle class, in the fifties, none of them could afford to turn down perfectly good clothes for growing children. I don't remember anybody being self conscious about it or ashamed of it.

The only reason I knew Margaret Ann got Frankie's hand-me-downs was that it was part of the continuing internecine war that went on between Margaret Ann and Frankie for at least as long as we were in school. I have no idea why they were always at each other's throats except that they were very different. Frankie was devilish, cunning, always on the make. Margaret Ann was quiet, moody, and lived in her own world. Margaret Ann wanted little more than to be left alone, but I cannot now remember one single kind word either of them had for the other during the years we were growing up.

I was always on Margaret Ann's side, of course, whatever the issue in the fight, but I was not very good back-up. I had no experience with the particular brand of female bickering Margaret Ann and Frankie engaged in. The few times I tried to intervene on Margaret Ann's behalf were laughable, and my reward was that both Margaret Ann and Frankie laughed at me. Frankie was three years older than we were, and therefore always better at fighting, and she was really just plain mean. She was mean when she was a child, and she was mean as an adult.

In the photograph I have in my mind of Frankie, she is sitting in her bedroom at the dresser, filing her fingernails. For some crazy reason, Frankie carefully filed each of her fingernails so that it came to a very sharp point. It looked crazy and I never had courage to think about what she intended to do with those nails. I sure wouldn't have wanted to get in a cat fight with her.

You know, now that I think about it, I probably also loved that green dress because it was unlike anything my mother would have ever made for me or bought for me. It was a creation of Miss Carolee Linley and therefore it was, like her, a little bit eccentric. Mother was far from anything that could be called eccentric, at least on the outside.

In the class photograph, Margaret Ann had on a pale blue shirtwaist dress much like mine except that it was store-bought, had a small round collar, four creamy white decorative buttons down the front of the bodice, and a cloth belt made out of the same pale blue material.

We both had on white tennis shoes and white socks, folded down once. Margaret Ann had sandy blonde hair. Mine was red. But we both, even in the fifth grade, shared the same half-cynical expression. We had lost the sweet look of childhood, even then. It is amazing how very quickly we all start to be what we will eventually become.

Since I never had children, I have no experience with them, but I have seen it in cats over and over. They are what they are going to be almost as soon as they are born. Very few of them change significantly in basic character unless something deeply traumatic happens to them.

We were an odd mix, Margaret Ann and I. We were as different as we could be but also like two peas in a pod. Margaret Ann was quiet and shy. I was loud and talkative. Margaret Ann hated boys and I loved them. I think the thing that held us together was the fact that we both had the same jaundiced view of the world and the same cynical sense of humor. We made fun of everything and everybody, including each other.

Also, our mothers encouraged us to spend time together. Mama and Miss Corinne had known each other when they were in high school and got along as well as my mother could ever get along with anybody. I remember Mama telling me that Margaret Ann was a good playmate for me because her family and mine were from similar circumstances. Mama had also warned me of another little girl who, Mama said, "could have anything she wanted."

It was only later in life that it occurred to me that Margaret Ann was also suitable as a friend because she was somebody my mother could easily control. In the end, Mother managed, before she died, to cause a rift between Margaret Ann and I that has continued for almost a decade. Even from the grave, Mama managed to have enormous power over my life. That would please her. Nothing could make her happy, but that would please her.

The Happiness of Joe Ed Montgomery

It was on the street right in front of Wyatt's Pharmacy that I had, at the age of ten, my second romantic rendezvous. Joe Ed Montgomery asked me to meet him there on the night of the 1961 centennial parade to celebrate the beginning of the Civil War. Even at the age of ten, it hardly seemed like the beginning of the Civil War was something the whole town would turn out to celebrate. But turn out they did. I guess they figured they had to celebrate the beginning of the war since they certainly couldn't celebrate the end.

I remember that dress too, the one I wore to the Civil War parade. It was a gray-blue twill dress, a shirtwaist that reached down to my ankles. The dress had long sleeves and a scooped out neckline. It was a plain dress, no frills, no ribbons, no turquoise and gold fan like the one I fantasized about holding when I imagined myself on the upstairs porch of the Crawford house. Only the teenaged girls on floats wore the elaborate hoop-skirted Southern-belle costumes.

Mama explained to me that most people in the South had not been wealthy nor had they owned slaves at the time of the Civil War. She told me my dress was far more historically accurate than were the fancy plantation dresses donned by the teenaged girls on the floats. This story must have appeased me because I remember loving the dress and being very proud of it. Besides, nothing could have spoiled the excitement of being asked to meet Joe Ed Montgomery.

When the telephone call came, I answered it in the back room where the black delivery man from Byron's had refused to look at me. I remember it well since it's another of those photographs that have stayed with me over the years. The event was significant enough for me to remember my surroundings in detail. I held the phone and listened as Joe Ed Montgomery asked me whether I would

agree to watch the parade with him. Afterward, his mother, Miss Belle, would
bring us home.

I was breathless with anticipation.

If the truth is told, I would have to say that I have loved Joe Ed Montgomery
my entire life. I used to pray, when I still did pray as a child, for his happiness,
whether that happiness came with me or with somebody else.

"Really?" Kitty Kelly said once looking over at me with astonishment from
the top bunk of the next bed. We were at summer camp, and she had overheard
me praying for Joe Ed's happiness.

She rolled onto her stomach and studied me. "You don't care if he marries
somebody else?"

"I care," I responded. "But what I want most is for him to be happy." This
lofty and self-sacrificing little line was something I had heard at one of the revivals
Mama was constantly dragging the family to.

The sermon was "Youth." There was at least one "Youth Night" sermon in
every week-long revival. Proud mothers and bored fathers sat in the sweltering
heat under a tent on an otherwise perfectly pleasant summer evening, trying
to cool themselves with cardboard fans distributed by Pickering Head's Funeral
Home on which was printed a dreadful portrait of Jesus.

"You-ah should be praying-ah for your future husbands and wives-ah." That
summer's evangelist said, looking down at all of us sitting chastely on the front
row as demanded by our watchful mothers. "Even though-ah you don't know
who they are-ah right now. Pray-ah for their happiness and pray-ah that God
leads them to you. Pray-ah for their happiness even if they don't become your
future husbands and wives-ah."

Now I never understood quite how the objects of our prayers could qualify as
our "future husbands and wives" even if they weren't going to become our future
husbands and wives, but I was always getting into trouble for saying things like
this, so I tried not to mention the inherent contradiction in logic. Once, when I
was coming out of a revival tent sweaty and bored, with my mother, I asked if she
felt "revived." She didn't speak to me for a week.

Revivals were serious business in the South, especially for Mama, and I
quickly learned that they were not appropriate subjects of childish critique, well

reasoned or otherwise. There was no reward in anything that even resembled logical consistency when the subject was church. I learned that quickly.

But I prayed fervently for the happiness of Joe Ed Montgomery.

My prayers for Joe Ed went the same way as most of the other prayers I dutifully and trustingly sent up to heaven during those years. What I didn't realize was that Joe Ed Montgomery was simply never destined to be happy, and no amount of prayer was going to change that.

Sweet, Happy, and the Same

For most of my childhood, there was only one small bathroom in our house. Right outside that bathroom was, and still is, a large painting. The painting takes up almost the entire wall in the hallway right outside the small green bathroom. In the painting, a woman with long auburn hair sits in a meadow. She is wearing a long yellow dress that spreads out around her. She has a ribbon in her hair. Sitting next to her is a little girl. The little girl is an exact replica of the mother, just smaller. She has the same hairstyle, the same yellow dress, and the same yellow ribbon in her hair at exactly the same place as that of her mother. The mother and daughter are romanticized figures in a romanticized setting. They are sweet and happy and the same. The two of them form a complete little world.

Grandiose Dreams

Joe Ed Montgomery certainly never ended up where any of us, including him, thought he would. He didn't even end up better off than we or he thought he would. He ended up worse.

There was, of course, no Wal-Mart then. The only chain stores around were Woolworths and Pennys and the ubiquitous Sears. But it would have been inconceivable to us that the little boy who would become captain of the football team, Mr. Wilkes Ferry High School, Mr. Popularity, and Most Likely to Succeed, would end up as the manager of a Sears or a Pennys, much less the housewares manager in a Wal-Mart.

It was inconceivable because we were blinded by our own somewhat grandiose dreams for the future, fueled by postwar parents who had succeeded beyond anything they had ever imagined and believed their children would do the same.

Any fool with eyes though should have been able to see that Joe Ed Montgomery, Mr. Popularity, Mr. Wilkes Ferry High School, football, baseball, and basketball hero, was a really good-looking big fish in a very small pond.

You know, people never seem to learn that being a high school football hero is the kiss of death. Every high school football hero I have ever known or heard about has had a dismal life after the age of eighteen. It's like being a child star. Well hell, it *is* being a child star in the South. Everything from then on out is guaranteed to go downhill.

Plus, anybody should have known that the son of bigger-than-life Ed Montgomery and the grandson of Big D. Duncan didn't have anywhere to go but down.

But we weren't looking at the past then, at family history, at blood, at destiny. In the 1960s, the world was a place where you could leave your family history behind and carve out your own fate. At least that's what we thought.

Now fifty years later, I have come to understand that blood and history always will out, not sometimes, always. Under the circumstances, Joe Ed Montgomery was lucky to have a job thirty years later. Hell, he was lucky to be alive.

In the graduating kindergarten class of 1957, there were fifteen children. Joe Ed Montgomery and I were the tallest boy and girl among them. Because of this, we were paired as a couple and chosen to walk down the auditorium aisle first, like a bride and groom. We ascended the steps to the stage and assumed our central position waiting to be flanked by the other children as they came after us.

Joe Ed wore a white linen suit, a white shirt starched by Lena, their maid, who was there (wouldn't have missed it), and a red bow tie. I wore a long full white satin dress with yards and yards of lace netting in layers from the waist. I had a row of lace netting at my neck, and I wore three petticoats. To this day, I love a petticoat and would wear one around the house if they weren't such a pain in the ass, always getting in the way.

That afternoon, in the Wilkes Ferry Elementary School auditorium, I carried a small bouquet of pink rosebuds surrounded by baby's breath and more lace. Two pink silk ribbon streamers, almost long enough to reach the floor, were attached to the bouquet and rested lightly on the front of my dress as I walked down the aisle on the arm of Joe Ed Montgomery.

I never got over the romance of that afternoon. From that day on, I believed Joe Ed Montgomery and I were destined, no matter what happened in between, to walk together, stand together like that at our wedding, flanked by those same children, grown-up and dressed as bridesmaids and whatever you call the men in a wedding. As far as I was concerned, it was written in the stars. So when I prayed for Joe Ed Montgomery to be happy no matter whom he married, it wasn't as self-sacrificing as it seemed. I never for a second believed he would marry anybody but me.

As things turned out though, I only ever had three dates with Joe Ed Montgomery. One date was in an Atlanta bar when we were grown. One was for the Civil War parade, and the third was when we were around six years old.

The six-year-old date was by far the most romantic. When Joe Ed phoned, I don't remember where I was, but I remember hearing his mother, Belle, in the background prompting him in her musical Southern accent. He asked me quite formally if I would honor him by allowing him to escort me to dinner at the General Butler Hotel. The glamorous, elegant General Butler Hotel was owned by Big D. Duncan, Joe Ed's grandfather.

In the not-much-better-than-rural South in the 1950s, middle-class children like us were still raised to live in a courtly agrarian culture that died before our parents were born. Southerners hadn't been able to hold onto their land or their fortunes or their way of life or the way of life they imagined they had had or had thought they would have, but at least they could hold onto some of the gentility, the manners, and courtly customs of a former age.

Joe Ed Montgomery, under his mother's tutelage, was being socialized into the world of a Southern gentleman, where ladies, even six-year-old ladies, were escorted to hotel restaurants by young men wearing white suits and bow ties. A gentleman knew how to treat a lady, how to hold out a chair, how to escort a lady, and how to manage waiters in starched white jackets and food courses. Joe Ed was simply being schooled to assume his position in society. That the society he was being schooled into was dead was irrelevant. Faulkner once wrote that for Southerners the past is not dead. It isn't even past. He was right.

Sitting there in the General Butler Hotel, my little white gloves with the pearl button on the wrist carefully folded on the table in a dining room with chandeliers and mirrors, I felt like a princess. Black waiters hovered around us, catered to our every whim, bowed, and smiled. Miss Belle looked on benevolently.

To Miss Belle, these dinners were a training school, guaranteeing that Joe Ed would have the social skills and the attitudes to assume his position as heir to the Duncan and Montgomery fortunes. That these fortunes, like so many others, later proved to be nonexistent was also irrelevant.

I have no idea exactly why Joe Ed liked me so much when we were children nor why his mother thought for an instant I would be a suitable partner for him. But when we were children, I was Joe Ed's favorite, and he chose me. I cannot tell you how much that meant to me. Joe Ed Montgomery picked me to be the head cheerleader of his first little league football team, inventively named the Blue Team. The cheerleaders wore white blouses underneath navy blue short-skirted pinafore affairs. We twirled and leaped and clapped and cheered on the Little League football heroes of which Joe Ed was the greatest, even then. In high school, Joe Ed was the quarterback and the captain of the team and the central talent in an otherwise mediocre group of athletes.

During those years in high school, I watched Joe Ed Montgomery play every football, basketball, and baseball game he ever played. I was sitting in the bleachers one spring afternoon when he was hit with a baseball.

He was beautiful up there at bat, wearing a clean white uniform with red piping and a Creek Warrior emblem embroidered on the chest. His skin was smooth and tanned and creamy, and the muscles in his arms were visible from the stands. If I think of him, standing there at bat, long enough, I can feel his creamy skin on my lips.

That afternoon, the tip of Joe Ed's bat circled above his head as he positioned his feet in anticipation of the pitch. I was floating in a dream of admiration and pride as I watched him.

Then the pitch, a hard fastball, hit Joe Ed squarely in the head. The crowd sucked in a collective breath; Joe Ed landed on his side right on top of home plate. But he was up almost as soon as he hit the ground. He hopped, dancing on one foot. He then threw the bat to the side and started out for first base.

Then just as everyone had begun to relax, he crumpled to the ground. He was holding himself up, his chest at least, with one arm, but his legs were frozen, useless. Joe Ed Montgomery was paralyzed.

Everyone in the bleachers stood. Big Ed Montgomery, Joe Ed's father, wasn't there that day. I remember because had Big Ed been there, he would have pitched a fit. Screaming at the umpire or referee or the coach of the other team or even at the players was not uncommon for Big Ed. Nor was it uncommon for him to scream obscenities at his own son.

Although she never gave any indication that it bothered her, I think even Miss Belle was embarrassed by Big Ed. She was just too much of a lady, or too tipsy, to let on. I know Joe Ed was embarrassed on many occasions. Big Ed found fault with his own son more than all the others combined.

Had Big Ed been there, I would have remembered. But that afternoon, there were no scenes, there was no cursing or screaming at the offending pitcher, just hushed silence as the coaches gathered around Joe Ed, and the rest of us strained to see what was happening.

It was perhaps five or ten minutes before Joe Ed Montgomery, hero that he was, pulled himself up, hopped a little on one leg again, and trotted off to first base.

The crowd roared, even the fans for the opposing team. There was very little you could do to resist this charming, beautiful young man whose behavior so uniformly matched his legend.

It was said later that the pitch was intentional, meant to take our pitcher, Joe Ed, out of the game. The Creek Warriors, of course, never engaged in such dishonorable and unsportsmanlike tactics. Other teams however, were frequently guilty of such dastardly Yankee-like acts.

At another game, a football game this time, I sat in my cheerleader's uniform until 3:00 AM in a hospital emergency waiting room while doctors put Joe Ed's eyeball back into the socket after it had been knocked out onto his cheek. Fifteen years later, Joe Ed told me that when he had cried on the way to the hospital that night, Big Ed had told him to stop acting like a sissy. Joe Ed also told me that he never played another game of football without standing over a toilet and throwing up.

The other boys on the high school football team must have known about this, must have seen and heard Joe Ed retching in the locker room. But those boys kept the secret. They knew how damaging the story would be if it got out, especially to the scouts. I never heard a word about it until, as an adult, I listened to Joe Ed Montgomery talk for hours over a small table in a darkened Atlanta bar.

The General Butler Hotel

The General Butler Hotel had been located on South Main Street since before the Civil War. It was even used as a hospital during the last years of the war. It was burned down in the battle for control of the railroad, the river bridge, and what later became known as Fort Butler.

Soon after the war, the Duncans rebuilt and named the hotel after the one-legged general who fought that last battle for the town. The General Butler Hotel was right there beside the railroad tracks and only a half a block from the train station itself. The new General Butler was more elaborate and lovely than ever. The General Butler Hotel, like many buildings after the war, was an act of defiance. It therefore held a special place in the hearts of the people in the community.

It was a monument to defiance and romance and I suppose also a monument to the repression of reality that necessarily accompanies romance and lost causes. I felt as if it had been built for me.

When I was a child, Big D. Duncan and his wife lived in the hotel. Joe Ed and I played in their apartment. I couldn't imagine anything more elegant except perhaps living in Miss Mary Francis's house. The apartment was different from all the obsessively neat houses of the 1950s middle class, the houses of my schoolmates. There were what I now know to be oriental carpets on the high polish hardwood floors, enormous majesty palms in elaborate pots, and books everywhere. There were books on built-in shelves, not tidily arranged as in our house, but stacked and leaning and even left open, book on top of book. When you were there, it always looked like someone had been going through the books just before you walked into the room. Even in an empty room, it felt like something was going on there. The atmosphere invited you to pick up a book, open a book, and leave it there waiting just in case you came back to it. Joe Ed and I spent long afternoons doing just that. He loved the *National Geographic* magazines, and I loved the books of paintings and drawings and anything about animals.

There were even books in the bathroom piled on the floor in stacks and haphazardly arranged on a white wrought-iron stand made to look like it had vines and leaves on it. The bathroom was a private jungle or a rain forest haven, wild with tropical plants, books, magazines, layers of fabric, and even a parrot in a cage.

Miss Gay, Joe Ed's grandmother, glided through the rooms like a ghost, most often wearing a dressing gown. She never scolded or even directed our activities there. She most often came into the room without our even knowing it, ran a gentle hand over the top of Joe Ed's head, absently looked through the reading material, satisfied herself, and disappeared into her bedroom.

I fantasized about living in the General Butler Hotel with Joe Ed Montgomery just like Miss Gay, cocooned in a chaotic but all-consuming world of rooms.

Miss Mary Francis's Tony

"And a one, and a two, and a three, and a four . . . and a one, and a two, and a three, and a four . . . Tony. Tonyeeeeeeeeeeeeeeeeeeeeeeeeeeee. Stop that barking this instant. You know very well you can't come out of that kitchen until the little gurls are gone . . . and a three and a four."

During the 150 years I took piano lessons as a child from Miss Mary Francis Cobb, I must have heard that refrain a thousand times.

I don't suppose Miss Mary Francis was much more than forty when we were suffering through *Tiny Toe Dancer*, *Waltz of the Gypsies*, and *Hoe Cake Shuffle*, but she already had the whitest hair, and we thought of her as being very old indeed. This was also a time when people still whispered the exceptionally cruel phrase "old maid."

But as far as I was concerned, if Miss Mary Francis was an old maid, it couldn't be that bad a thing to be. She had inherited all her daddy's money and a beautiful white colonial mansion with columns.

She was tall and thin and elegant, with skin like alabaster and patrician pale blue eyes. And she carried herself like a queen, pacing and counting time up and down that enormous piano room of hers, complete with two gleaming black baby grand pianos and furnished in beige silk and white lace.

Most of the time, she wore pencil-straight skirts, rounded-collar white linen blouses, and one simple strand of pearls. She wore no makeup, and I am sure she would have considered doing so whorish, although she would have never allowed such a word to cross her lips. Instead, she would have probably said something like, "Makeup is for showgurls."

Hundreds of little boys and girls must have sat in that piano room over the years, mutilating Miss Mary Francis's most cherished pieces of music. Although how anyone could appreciate or even sit through the *Brownie's Carnival* is beyond me.

But Miss Mary Francis was determined that even pieces like *Elves in the Moonlight* were practiced to perfection. From time to time, she would scare the living hell out of you by walking up suddenly behind you and forcing an errant finger onto the right key rather more violently than necessary.

But nothing, nothing could strike horror in our hearts like hearing Miss Mary Francis's lilting voice calling out from the kitchen, "Now Tony, you come back here . . ."

Like lightning, we would snatch our hands off the piano keyboard, fold our little legs underneath us, and scramble to stand up on the piano benches, even though we were strictly forbidden to do so. With practice, this could be accomplished just in time to keep the horrid tan miniature Chihuahua with his razor-sharp gnashing little teeth from tearing our ankles apart.

But even after years of canine terrorism, Miss Mary Francis never ever yelled at Tony or even scolded him. She would instead stand in the doorway, her hands on her hips, and look at us all as if she were deeply disappointed.

"Now Tony, don't you snap at those little gurls. They think you're gonna bite them."

Think? We knew he was going to bite us if he got half a chance. Then she would turn her narrowed eyes on us. "Ladies, do not stand on piano benches."

We would slowly climb down, and Tony would trot off behind Miss Mary Francis toward the kitchen, giving us a spiteful backward glance for which we would wait so we could stick out our tongues.

Only a mother could have loved this psychotic creature. But love him she did. The most extraordinary thing of all was seeing Miss Mary Francis Cobb, linen and pearls, the soul of propriety, chewing up chocolate and spitting it out in her hand for Tony to eat.

There is no accounting for taste—in animals, music, people, or anything else as far as I can see.

Sittin' There Waitin' for Him

Just like Big Ed wanted him to, Joe Ed Montgomery went off to college on a football scholarship. He had been a big fish in a small pond in Wilkes Ferry. He wasn't such a big fish in a university though, where every player had been selected because he too was the best of his own small pond.

Joe Ed wasn't the best player on the team anymore, and it was the sixties. Cool kids were out protesting the war in Vietnam, questioning authority, doing psychedelic drugs, and dressing in beads and long hair. The world was changing radically around us, and Joe Ed Montgomery was running laps.

Joe Ed and I were sitting in a deserted Atlanta bar as he was telling me all this. We were talking as grown-ups for the first time.

"Marry me," he said abruptly in the middle of his story.

I must tell you, there are no two words in the English language for which I am a bigger sucker. I'm not a three, not a four, but a five-time repeat offender, a serial monogamist. And, in that Atlanta bar, I was more than tempted, staring into Joe Ed's familiar blue eyes.

"I can at least keep a roof over your head," he added.

I blinked, the waltz suddenly coming to an end. *A roof over my head? I can very well keep a roof over my own damn head.* I heard this sentence as if it were hanging in the air waiting for me and my red-wine-addled brain. In fact, I had a perfectly adequate roof over my head a few hours from London at the time.

I looked down and tried to hide what I was thinking. I knew he hadn't meant to insult me, but I felt insulted. I felt like a racehorse suddenly yanking its head up, rearing, and refusing the gate.

"You're meeting who?" my friend Carol had asked me as I was dressing to meet Joe Ed Montgomery at the bar.

"Joe Ed Montgomery."

"*The* Joe Ed Montgomery?" she said, her eyes widened. "The one from the reunion?"

"The same."

"What went wrong at the reunion? I can't remember."

"I looked great," I sighed. "I felt great. I was in a long, ankle-length Indian print dress. I had picked out a pair of bone-colored sandals with just the tiniest of heels. The leather straps of the sandals made a knot at the toe. The dress swayed and flowed around my legs, and I wore no bra and no panties."

"And . . ."

"And I walked into the Country Club and looked across the room and there he was at the bar. I couldn't believe I had been so lucky. If I hadn't known better, I'd have thought it was fate. And then, I walked across the dance floor and, like magic, the person on the stool to Joe Ed's left slid off and vacated the seat. I sat down on the empty stool and ordered a drink. When Joe Ed turned to his left, we exchanged smiles and then a warm hug. Then the imbecile on the stool to my left said something, and I had to turn to answer. When I looked back for Joe Ed . . . he was gone. Everyone was looking at the floor, and when I looked down, there was Joe Ed, sprawled on the floor in a less than flattering manner, his mouth open, passed out.

"He stayed passed out all night. Michael and Morgan and Mike and Jamie each took an appendage and threw him into the backseat of somebody's car when we left the Country Club and went to Gus's house. They carried him in and deposited him on the living room sofa, and everybody just drank and partied around him like he was a dead man at his own wake.

"The last I saw of him, he was being deposited in somebody else's backseat when the night was over. I have no idea what happened after that."

I continued to brush my cheeks with blush.

"And tonight . . . ," Carol said, mimicking Mammy in *Gone with the Wind.* "You gonna be sittin' there waiting for him jes' like a spider."

I couldn't help but laugh.

Lottie's Babies

Mattie Mae Hollis was a part of our family for over fifty years. During those years, Mama and Mattie Mae helped each other a great many times. I, of course, remember only the most dramatic occasions, and most particularly, I remember the time Pickering Head had those two dead babies at Snipes's funeral home.

Mattie Mae was the one who phoned Mama for help that crisp autumn day, but the help wasn't for her this time. It was for Lottie, Mattie Mae's best friend.

Mattie Mae was phoning from Mr. George Reed's gas station, about a block from Snipes's Funeral Home. To my consternation, Mama hadn't seen fit to pass on the information that Lottie's house had burned down that past weekend and that her twin babies were killed in the fire.

This was the kind of thing Mama never told me. She always thought I had a morbid turn of mind, and I suppose she saw herself as not feeding what she and my grandmother deemed my unhealthy and definitely unladylike obsession with all things secret.

Of course, the minute I heard the words "dead" and "babies" and then "funeral home" in the same few sentences, my ears cranked around like those of a cat hearing footsteps in the leaves.

Now there are a lot of peculiar things about this story. One of them is that Lottie's two babies were even taken to Snipes's Funeral Home. You see, Snipes was a white funeral home, and if there was any life function in the 1950s South that was more segregated than religion, it was death.

The only thing I can figure out is that the babies had somehow wound up there because it was an accident, a fire, and somebody got put through to the wrong funeral home. But even so, it seemed like somebody would have realized the mistake and phoned a black mortician. It doesn't make a lot of sense.

Mama was never any help with this story. She refused to talk about the incident, and when I pressed her, she denied it even happened. "Lydia, this is just something you've made up. You were always such a strange child."

She always did this to me. It took me over fifty years to work out that my mama, Frances Sarah Ward McPherson, had a lot of secrets. She didn't like talking about the past, and whenever anything "uncomfortable" came up, her way of dealing with it was to just deny it ever happened.

But I remember as clearly as I remember the color of the Catawba River that Lottie's two precious babies were left in the cold waxy hands of Pickering Head.

The problem Mattie Mae was phoning about on that crisp autumn day was that Pickering wouldn't let Lottie look at the bodies. I stood just inside the white swinging door to the breakfast room, my ear pressed to the crack, and listened to Mama talk.

Seems Pickering said he'd already closed the coffins, that the bodies were too badly burned, and that Lottie didn't need to see them. Pickering, of course, being white, thought he knew better than Lottie what she needed. He also probably thought that once this poor black woman was told with some authority by a white man that she didn't need to see her own dead children, she would go away and let it be.

But Pickering Head didn't figure on the combination of Mama and Mattie Mae Hollis.

Lottie was brokenhearted when she found out she couldn't see her babies. She walked all the way home to grieve and wait for the funeral, but Mattie Mae was at her house to hear the story.

Now Mattie Mae Hollis didn't have much to say on a day-to-day basis, but she was about as determined, when she got her mind set about something, as anybody I've ever seen, except my mama.

Mattie Mae and Lottie walked the five miles back to Snipes's Funeral Home and knocked on the screen door to the side porch. They wouldn't have even thought about knocking on the front door. Pickering Head, the director of the funeral home, opened the glass door to the porch and walked out.

"What y'all want?" he asked as he reached the screen door.

"We wants to see the chillin'," Mattie Mae told him.

Pickering Head opened the door with his left hand and pointed to Lottie with his right. "I already tol' Lottie, those children are beyond recognizing. Now she's got no business bothering us and upsetting herself more than she's already upset by pawing all over them. I got better things to do."

"She they mama," Mattie Mae said, standing firm on her two enormous flat feet.

"Now y'all go on away from here before I call the law," Pickering said. "I already explained it to you. Now, git."

Mattie Mae told Mama later that he said "git" like he was talking to a pack of dogs.

Mattie Mae Hollis stood on the side steps of Snipes's Funeral Home, staring at Pickering Head. She did not move one inch.

"When you gon' send the babies to the church?" she asked.

Pickering gave an exasperated sigh. "Mattie Mae, I'm gonna' send the babies to the church when I get the money for doing 'em and not before."

Pickering Head closed the screen door to the porch, and when he went inside the house, he locked the glass door behind him. He left Mattie Mae and Lottie standing on the steps. Lottie was crying.

Mattie Mae put her arm around Lottie.

"You stay right here," she said. "I be back. Me and Miss Sarah Ward straighten this out." Mattie Mae strode across the street toward Reed's gas station. "Me and Miss Sarah Ward gon' jerk a knot in Mr. Pickering Head's tail," she muttered to herself.

When the phone call from Mattie Mae came, I could see my mama reddening in outrage. "Why, that's ridiculous," she said, "absolutely ridiculous. He has no choice but to let Lottie see them if she wants to."

Mama cast a worried glance in my direction and then said into the telephone. "There's nobody here to stay with Lydia."

"I'll go, Mama," I said, perhaps a bit too eagerly under the circumstances. "I don't mind."

She shook her head. "I don't want you at a funeral home. I don't even like funeral homes, and this thing might be ugly business."

My eyes widened. Ugly business was just my cup of tea at that age. "Please, Mama," I begged.

"Oh, all right," Mama said exasperated by my eagerness. "I'm coming, Mattie Mae. Y'all just wait right there." She put the telephone down.

"Come on, Lydia, if you're coming," she called.

I raced to find my tennis shoes and then got to the back door, so Mama wouldn't have to wait.

Mama stood there, tying a scarf around her head, looking down at me. "You are the strangest child," she said, but she was always saying that. I didn't take it personally. I couldn't even tell you how many times Mama or my grandmother, DeeMama, said that to me from the time I was about four to the time I left home at nineteen.

By the time Mama drove up to Snipes's Funeral Home in our car, I was sitting forward in the seat with my face almost on the window. I was craning my neck to see what was happening.

"Lydia, sit back in the seat. You could at least try to act like a lady in public instead of a gaping monkey."

Lottie and Mattie Mae were standing on the wooden steps outside the screened porch of the enormous old house that used to belong to one of the Cobbs before it was turned into a funeral home.

"You stay in the car," Mama ordered as she got her pocketbook and gloves and started to get out.

"Mama," I whined.

Mama stopped moving. She raised her eyebrows, and her eyes became big as saucers. I knew that look. It could have frozen me in hell. What it meant was stop whatever you were doing instantly. In this case, it was whining. "Stay," she said.

I knew there was no point in arguing. So I watched Mama walk across the front lawn, her light navy blue coat trailing behind her, her beige gloves clutched in her tiny hand, to talk with Mattie Mae and poor Lottie, who was still crying.

They were obviously not paying a bit of attention to me, so I rolled down the window to see if I could hear. But all I could hear was the exchange of women's voices. Mama's little frame got straighter and straighter; Mattie Mae and Lottie were gesturing with their hands, and every few minutes, Lottie would cover her face with both hands and drag them down her cheeks, sobbing.

All of a sudden, Mama turned and walked up the steps to the door of the screened-in porch. She rapped so hard on the door with her little fist, I could see the wood frame moving from across the street.

She waited like a soldier ready for battle. Nothing. She rapped again. Then I started to see what Daddy called "the Irish" rising in her, and I knew what was going to happen. Mama was about to lose her temper.

"Pickering Head," she shouted out right there in the front yard of Snipes's Funeral Home. "You come out here. I know you're in there. You answer the door this minute."

The glass door to the house opened, and out came Pickering Head even more ashen and unctuous than usual.

"Why, Miss Sarah Ward," he said, feigning surprise. "I didn't know you were out here. You could have just come right on in the front door. It's always open."

"The point is not where I could have come in, Pickering. The point is where they could have come in." Mama's left arm flew out, pointing behind her at Mattie Mae and Lottie, without taking her eyes off the pitiable Pickering Head. Mattie Mae and Lottie both stood up straighter.

"And the point is that you have to let this woman see her children. And the point is that you don't slam the door in a woman's face and tell her to "git" like she was a dog. And the last point, Pickering Head, is that I've known you for a long time, a very long time. I knew you when you still had cotton lint in your hair and were sneaking up behind women in the mill and pinching fannies. You have never had and never deserved the least little bit of power or authority or respect. And so you're just the sort of man to lord your imaginary authority over two women who you think can't do anything to you. You are not going to call the law on these women. I am going to call the law on you if you don't open those coffins and let Lottie see her children right this minute while I'm standing here."

All the time Mama had been delivering this breathtaking soliloquy, Pickering Head had been bending and bowing and holding his hands up in front of him and putting the fingertips of both hands on his cheeks in an attempt to somehow appease Mama.

Oh, Mama knew Pickering Head all right, but Pickering Head sure didn't know my mama. If he had, he would have known that after what he had done, trying to appease Mama would have been just about as easy as appeasing Hitler.

Pickering Head grew paler and paler as he realized he was dead meat. He moved backward and held the screened door while Mattie Mae and Lottie and then Mama filed inside. They all went into the house, and the glass door closed behind them.

I couldn't believe all this was going on, and I was sitting in the car.

I sat there trying to weigh the trouble I would be in for disobeying Mama against the chance that she would be so distracted when she came out, she wouldn't even notice if I were in the car.

Mama, Lottie, and Mattie Mae stayed inside Snipes's for what seemed like hours. I slumped down in the seat, keeping my eyeballs just high enough to see out the window. The sun was getting hotter and hotter, and what had been an autumn day was fast turning into summer. I lifted my thighs off the seat, trying to keep them from sticking to the upholstery. I knew Mama wasn't ever going to tell me what was happening inside. I let my hand stray over onto the door handle and then pushed it down. The sound it made seemed very loud. I wasn't really going to get out, just open the door for some air. I scanned the front of the funeral home for activity. None. I scanned the street in front of the car and then turned around and scanned the area toward Reed's filling station. Nobody.

I twisted in the seat and pushed open the door, putting my two tennis-shoed feet on the asphalt. Just getting some air. Then I darted across the enormous lawn and into the azaleas next to the house.

The windows of the old Cobb house were that wavy, old-timey glass. Fortunately for my purposes, the windows on the front porch went from floor to ceiling, and the ceilings were at least sixteen or eighteen feet high. I jumped sideways onto the staircase and ran across the porch, flattening myself against the house. God help me if Mama came out the front door.

I peered into one of the windows, trying to do so without being seen. But it didn't matter. There was nobody there. Turning, I ran toward the end of the porch and jumped off again into the azaleas. It was then that I saw the back of the old Cobb house, where they had evidently built an addition. It went straight back from the old house, a long, low monstrosity of a structure built with cinder blocks and aluminum windows.

I could hear voices now, women's voices, my mother's voice. And I could hear crying, wailing like I'd never heard before, even at a funeral. I turned and headed for the car as fast as my crooked polio legs would carry me. I almost dove into the window of the car I was so afraid. But, I was able to jerk the door open and sit down before I heard the front door of Snipes's slam with a force that might well have shattered all the panes.

I sat up straight to see Mama storming down the stairs and across the lawn. I had never seen her look quite so furious. Mattie Mae and Lottie were trailing behind her, looking very much like they had seen a ghost. Lottie was wailing as she walked, and Mattie Mae was staring straight in front of her with an expression that, to this day, I would not even try to describe.

Then I saw the front door of the house open, and an ashen Pickering Head emerged cautiously onto the porch. He held his arms out with his palms open and shrugged his shoulders. "Miss Sarah Ward," he called, "I'm sure we can work this out. It's just a mistake. Somebody in the back just made a little mistake."

Mama stopped dead in her tracks. Her hand was holding her gloves so tightly I could see her knuckles whiten. She stood there for a minute, and then she turned around. She marched back up the walkway, circling around Mattie Mae and Lottie. She climbed up the stairs, and Pickering Head walked toward her in relief. Just before Mama got to Pickering, she transferred the beige gloves from one hand to the other. I guess Pickering was suffering under the delusion that she was going to shake hands. But what she did was to rear back and slap Pickering Head across the face.

He put one hand on his cheek and stood there with a red splotch spreading down his neck.

I couldn't have been more shocked if Mama had taken all her clothes off and set her hair on fire.

While Pickering Head stood there with his hand on his cheek, Mama bent down and picked up the beige gloves she had dropped. Finished, she turned and descended the steps.

When Mama and Mattie Mae and Lottie and I got to our house, I was banished (under protest) to the yard while telephone calls were made and voices were raised and Lottie wailed. Finally, I was allowed to ride along while Mama took everybody home. Nobody said a word, and I knew that my continued existence on the earth depended on my keeping my own mouth shut.

Mama took Lottie home first and then Mattie Mae. When Mattie Mae got out of the car, Mama held up her hand before I could even open my mouth.

"Not one question Lydia, not one. I know you don't believe this, but there are some things you don't need to know about."

I couldn't believe it, and I sunk back into the seat in frustration and disappointment. What on earth could there be that you didn't need to know about? Weren't she and Daddy always telling me to learn everything? "Look it up in the dictionary, go look in the encyclopedia." Wasn't that the constant refrain of our house? But, now there were things I didn't need to know.

Of course, to be fair, my mother knew that if she told me, I'd tell everybody else in the known universe that would listen; and in a small town like Wilkes Ferry, even if people commit murder, you still had to live with them and get along. In a town like Wilkes Ferry, you couldn't afford to have too many enemies, and Mama had just slapped a grown man in the street.

When I couldn't find something out any other way, there was always spying, and the best time to spy was at night, after everybody else had gone to bed, everybody except me. I would wait, pretending I was asleep, until all the lights were out and Daddy went around locking the doors. Then there was a time when Mama and Daddy talked to each other. That was the time I waited for, the time I had to stay awake if I wanted to learn anything important.

What I heard was that when Mama and Mattie Mae and Lottie had gone into the funeral home, Pickering Head had tried his best to talk them out of having him open the coffins, but Mama and Mattie Mae had insisted. Mama even had to threaten to phone the sheriff.

Faced with three determined women and the threat of the sheriff, Pickering relented. When he took them to the back though, he didn't have to open two coffins, only one. Both babies were together in the first little white coffin, laying on top of each other like they'd been thrown in by a garbage collector.

The real kicker, though, was that they hadn't even been embalmed. Pickering Head (even though he denied it) was going to charge Lottie a fortune on time for the burial of two embalmed babies in two coffins, when in fact, he had done nothing to the bodies except throw them in together.

"I've never seen anything quite so heartbreaking in my whole life as those two babies all crumpled in together in each other's arms," Mama said to Daddy in their bedroom while I leaned with my back up against their bedroom door. Mama was crying, something she never ever did. "And Will Lee, I'll never forget that smell if I live to be a hundred. Poor Lottie, poor, poor Lottie."

I stayed up a long time that night, imagining the two babies together in that coffin, playing back in my mind the scene when Mama slapped Pickering Head. I was wondering what on earth Lottie must be feeling and knowing in my heart of hearts that nothing, absolutely nothing, would happen to Pickering Head or Snipes's Funeral Home. Pickering Head was probably asleep.

I wondered, for the first time in my life, if it had bothered Mattie Mae to have to phone Mama to get Pickering Head's face slapped. Mattie Mae did things for Mama all the time, favors. They were friends. But somehow this was different. Mattie Mae was a big woman. She had hands that could wrench a chicken's head off without hardly noticing it. I unfortunately knew this from personal experience. Mattie Mae was so strong she could probably have pinched Pickering's head off herself. Now Mama could scare the living hell out of me and even Daddy, but she wasn't five feet tall with her heels on. I wondered that night if Mattie Mae resented the fact that she had had to get Mama involved for anything to be done.

I knew Mama wasn't going to talk about it, and I knew what Daddy would say if I asked him: "That's just the way things are, Liddy."

I sat and stared out my bedroom window. Everybody in Wilkes Ferry, Georgia, all five hundred souls, seemed to be peacefully asleep. Everybody except me and Lottie. Poor Lottie.

The Hot Potato

"All they cared about was my body," Joe Ed said later that night when we were propped up, talking, in his bed.

"I was a thing to them. They owned me—everything I did, everything I said, everything I ate. The only thing they didn't control was what I thought, and they tried hard to control that."

"You were a commodity," I said.

He looked over at me. "You know what it's like to travel for hours in a bus full of football jocks and assistant coaches screaming and chanting and butting heads and working themselves up into a frenzy?"

"I can imagine," I answered.

"You can't," he said. "That's the thing. It's like some weird movie you can't believe you're in. The assistant coaches, old enough to act like adults, old enough to know how insane it all was, up there at the front, getting a bunch of young guys charged up. They were talking about fucking, fucking the shit out of Tennessee, chanting, 'Kill, kill, kill the cunts.'"

There was a silence.

"No, you're right," I finally said. "I can't imagine."

"The minute I didn't perform, the minute I got hurt, the minute I stopped being a maniac just like them, they'd drop me like a hot potato." He paused. "And Big Ed would never speak to me again."

This threat of Big Ed never speaking to him again was no exaggeration. Big Ed had done just that once before when Joe Ed was in high school.

The enormous, sloppy head coach who made it a practice to regularly rearrange his hemorrhoids and balls in public did something that the team got upset over.

I can't imagine what this could have been since Coach Dwyer regularly abused all the players both verbally and physically and used language that was more crude and foul than anything a person of good breeding could possibly imagine. But he did something so bad that Joe Ed and Brennan Quinn walked out of practice.

By that afternoon, the entire town had heard about it, and Big Ed Montgomery and Mr. Brennan Quinn Sr. had stopped talking to their sons. The pleading and reasoning of mothers did no good. The fathers were resolute. It was devastating for Joe Ed and Brennan. Even though they had known full well how football crazy their fathers were, they thought their fathers would support them on a matter of principle.

But, neither father supported them. They weren't supported and they weren't even talked to. They no longer enjoyed the confidences or praise or even the disapproval of their fathers. Joe Ed and Brennan, although they tried to act as if they weren't bothered, walked around like stunned, condemned men for weeks.

I can't remember now how this was finally resolved. Somehow, it seems like I can't remember how a lot of things were resolved. But things did get back to normal. Fathers talked to sons who were back on the practice field after apologizing to the coach. But the important thing was that these two men had taken sides against their own sons. It was a betrayal that I think had a lasting effect on both Brennan and Joe Ed.

Joe Ed, for his part, lasted about two years in college before he drank and partied himself not only off the football team, but also out of the university. Joe Ed never said so, but I think it was the only way he could escape from the pressure, the expectations. It was a way to escape without directly taking the action of escaping. It was like what Teddy Kennedy accomplished with Chappaquiddick. He eliminated himself from the running without himself taking the action of bowing out. Kennedy could always tell himself that something external eliminated his candidacy.

Joe Ed spent the next ten years working different jobs, trying to make up for lost time by drinking and doing drugs. He worked for a short time for a professional football team, not as a player, but as a manager of some sort—a kind of athletic Stepin Fetchit. Again, who would ever have thunk (least of all him) that Joe Ed Montgomery would be a hanger-on rather than the most valuable player of the team? It must have stuck in his craw like a fried catfish fin battered in cornmeal.

Joe Ed married one of the blonde bombshell football groupies who hung around the team. Not the wisest of decisions, but hey, who am I to talk? She promptly left him for one of the professional football players when she got the chance and took everything Joe Ed owned, which, even he admitted, wasn't much.

Then there was a photography shop backed by Big D. Duncan in a last-ditch attempt to drag Joe Ed up out of self-destruction. Joe Ed drank the proceeds, failed to open the shop for weeks when he was on a toot, totaled several cars, and finally lost the photo shop entirely.

But every few years, when Joe Ed Montgomery came back to the high school reunions in Wilkes Ferry, he was once again the captain of the football team, Mr. Wilkes Ferry High School, Most Likely to Succeed. The other guys idolized him. Even at the age of forty-five, they treated him like he was a celebrity. While I could hardly remember the names of the men I had been married to, those guys would sit for hours and go over every play of God knows how many football games. Joe Ed was always the hero.

Over the years, they created a lore together by telling and retelling the stories, elaborating on them. Joe Ed became even more central and even more of a hero. Any failure to come through with the promise of his early years was blamed on various coaches who were said to have used and abused him to feed their own career goals. Joe Ed was thus said to have been ruined for college and the pros. His drinking and drug taking were attributed to his various injuries. Coach Dwyer let him throw his arm out in the game against Manchester. Coach Sandford made him play to the end of the game against Lee County with an ice pack on his knee.

In short, no reality was allowed to tarnish the image. It was as if all those boys, and then men, had a vested interest in maintaining the overblown fiction of Joe Ed Montgomery, the tragic hero. Joe Ed's talents and stunning accomplishments meant that they themselves were part of something great, something astounding. They didn't need their own legends, they had Joe Ed. And Joe Ed loved every minute of it. I sometimes wondered if he thought about these reunions for years, lived off them.

He may well have, but somewhere inside him, he felt that it was mostly exaggeration, mostly lie, mostly lore, because he hated himself. Deep down where it always counts, he loathed Joe Ed Montgomery.

So Joe Ed Montgomery didn't turn out at all the way we thought he would, the way he thought he would, but then again, who did? There's something very sad about high school being the best time in your life. But at this age, not many of us are heroes or ever have been. And I suppose to be a real hero once in your life just may well be enough.

The Last Chance Pool Room

There were two buildings in downtown Wilkes Ferry that filled my fantasies when I was growing up. One was the huge three-story white frame Patterson's Boarding House. The other was the Last Chance Pool Room.

I was forever asking my mother to tell me about the two buildings, what went on in them, but her answers were as flavorless as Knox Gelatine. I wanted scandals, mysteries, low life. But those were things my mother, even if she knew about them, never talked about. My mother was the hardest person to get dirt out of I've ever known. She hid and protected secrets as if every one of them were her very own. It took me fifty years to ask myself why.

But when I was growing up, without my mother's information, I was left to imagine. What kind of person stayed in Patterson's Boarding House? What kind of person didn't have a home? What kind of men walked with their suitcases up from the old railroad depot, to Patterson's, stayed for one night, and then left again on the train? Where did they go next, and next, and after that?

I knew they must have been very interesting men, every one of them. They must have known about nightlife in other cities. They probably drank whiskey and put their hands on rounded, overweight women in dresses that were too tight. I imagined them, lying up there in those rooms in the morning, the shades drawn, a woman in a slip beside them, her arm hanging off the side of the bed, and an empty bottle on the floor.

I knew better than to ask if I could ever go into Patterson's Boarding House. Besides, I couldn't think up any excuse in the universe for doing so. But I would have given my left arm to have seen inside just one room.

And then there was the Last Chance Pool Room. It was down the street from the General Butler Hotel, where Mama at one time had an office. When Drew and I were staying with mother at her office, we used to sometimes walk to Wyatt's Pharmacy to get an ice cream cone and look at the comic books and magazines. When I could get away with it, I would stand across the street from the Last Chance and just watch.

The Last Chance had large glass display windows all along the front, like those at the front of a department store. But the management of the Last Chance had wisely put Venetian blinds all along those windows so that nobody could see in. The blinds were never opened so that some girlfriend or mother or wife could ride by in the car and catch a glimpse of her boyfriend or son or husband doing whatever they were doing in the Last Chance.

Nobody I knew had ever been inside the Last Chance Pool Room, or at least no one I knew would admit it. None of the fathers or older brothers of the children I knew would have been caught dead in there. It wasn't really a Wilkes Ferry hangout even though it was located on Main Street. Most of the men I saw going into or coming out of the Last Chance were from down the Valley, from the mill towns along the river. A lot of them were young.

Every once in a while, I would see one of these young men wearing tight blue jeans and a white T-shirt straining over muscles, one sleeve rolled up and a pack of Marlboros or Kools stuck in the folds. It was like watching James Dean.

I vowed that I would die if I didn't once, just once, before I left Wilkes Ferry, go out with a boy who went to the Last Chance Pool Room.

It took me years to pull it off, but I did it. His name was Maxie Earl. Not only did he play pool at the Last Chance Pool Room, he also had a beat-up old car he drove with one hand, and he knew how to smoke a cigarette without touching it, talking to you while squinting through the smoke. He was walking sex.

My parents would have had a fit and grounded me for ten years had they known I was having anything to do with this swaggering piece of trouble, but that just made him all the more delicious. I would sneak out and meet him secretly, sometimes telling my parents I was going to the weekly dance at the Teenage Club. We did go to the dance once or twice but not very often.

Once there was a party at one of the houses of the middle-class kids from Wilkes Ferry. Nobody from "down the Valley" was ever invited to one of these affairs, only the kids from town. Maxie Earl showed up with some other James Deans and crashed the party to get to me. There was a scuffle about it, and Maxie pulled a knife.

Crouched down, he held the knife out toward the circle of prep school boys as he backed up toward the door, flanked by his buddies. Just as he got to the door, he looked over at me and winked.

That was it. They got in their cars and drove away, but boy, what more could you ask for. It was like being in *West Side Story*.

But that was over forty years ago. The railroad depot stopped operating even before I found Maxie Earl, and Patterson's Boarding House was condemned when it started to display a list to the west that could no longer be ignored by the city fathers. Some years ago, they tore down the entire block where the Last Chance Pool Room stood. They replaced it with a cutesy little family park with benches and flowers. It nearly killed me.

I have no idea what happened to Maxie Earl—probably has a mortgage, a beer gut, and a house full of grandchildren.

But it seems like such a shame to me that outside the movies there'll never be another Patterson's Boarding House or Last Chance Pool Room. I would so liked to have been, just for one day, one of those buxom women in a too-tight dress being slapped on the behind while carrying beer to the pool players.

Tamyra Tanner

Tamyra says she's the only girl out of our little group who had a normal, happy, healthy childhood. She may well be right. In the 1950s when we were growing up, the Tanner family and the Tanner household was chaotic, friendly, informal, and noisy. It was as full of activity, spontaneity, and sound, as mine was of silence and tension. Tamyra's mother, Loretta, was a hair dresser, tall and black haired with the unmistakable high cheekbones of Native American ancestry. Tamyra's father, Bobby, was a big, tall, slightly overweight car salesman. He was garrulous and something like a good-natured old bull. Tamyra had two good-looking, football-playing brothers, Rod and Ricky.

There was a constant hubbub in that house, people coming and going, laughing, arguing, slamming doors in arrival or departure, calling out to be heard over the fray.

In my house a slammed door would have triggered intense anxiety and dread. In the Tanner's house, a slammed door was just part of the landscape.

The Tanners didn't have meals where family members calmly passed plates one to the other so politely you could hear the silverware clink. They had grand free-for-alls where the arms and hands of at least eight people reached over and under and around each other for dishes, salt, catsup, rolls, and turnip greens. People were likely to leave the table and be replaced by others during the same meal as neighbors and school friends slotted themselves into whatever empty chair they could find.

It was, and still remains, a close family, a happy family, an active, moving family. Believe me, there were no meals eaten in silence at the Tanners' house as there were in mine. And there were no meals where a brooding alcoholic talked nonsense or bullied his wife and children as in Margaret Ann's house.

Loretta and Bobby Tanner drank openly, liked to party, and didn't feel as if they had to apologize to anybody about it. And they were happy drinkers. Nobody chased anybody else around with a gun threatening to kill them or turn the gun on themselves. So in that sense, Tamyra did have a more healthy childhood than Margaret Ann and I. Funny we never thought about it that way at the time. I don't think Margaret Ann or I ever thought of our childhoods as unusual or particularly dreadful. Margaret Ann and I thought our families were normal. It took me over fifty years to realize they weren't.

The Tanners were not part of the Wilkes Ferry social scene. They didn't belong to the Country Club. They didn't attend afternoon cocktail parties, and Miss Loretta didn't play bridge. Miss Loretta worked full-time. The Tanners didn't even attend church every Sunday. That was probably another reason they were so happy.

The Tanners were solidly working class in culture and habit. Whereas my family and Margaret Ann's were solidly middle class in that fifties sense of the term. It's never easy to understand exactly what class distinctions are based on. In this case, it was not level of education. Daddy was the only one of the three to have a college degree, but his mother and father had been mill workers. Mr. Bobby really was a salesman, a white-collar worker just like my father. But Rebel Patterson was little more than a manual laborer even though he had the "old family" name.

Even though Mr. Rebel owned the coal yard in town, he had to do most of the work in it as well. So while my daddy and Mr. Bobby were always dressed up in a suit and tie, Mr. Rebel was always dressed in work pants and covered with coal dust. But Mr. Rebel was from old money (there were churches and roads named for the Pattersons all over the county), and so he had a name and social position that put him above the level his work would have established for him independently. None of our mothers were college educated, but Corinne Patterson and my mother were part of the hatted and gloved and high-heeled bridge set while Miss Loretta was not.

While almost every woman in the girdled and coiffed bridge and cocktail party set were having nervous breakdowns, though, Loretta Tanner was standing squarely on her rather large feet washing other women's hair, opening bobby pins with her teeth, talking and listening to gossip and women's complaints. Miss Loretta's hands were not manicured and bleached white with lemons. They were permanently stained a deep purple-black from hair dye. But Miss Loretta didn't have to be put in a mental hospital after the birth of each of her babies as did Miss Corinne. Nor did Miss Loretta have to send her two little girls to stay with their paternal grandparents for a year as did Beth Ann Jaquett's mother. Miss Paulette Jaquett had to go into the hospital for a stay when Beth Ann was born, but after Claudette came, she just found herself totally unable to cope and stayed for over a year. Now since this is just between you and me, I couldn't have coped with Beth Ann and Claudette either. I'm telling you. There were no two children that could more accurately be described holy terrors than those two in all the South. They would have had to put me into a mental hospital and kept me until the two of them were old enough to leave home, but that's another story.

Miss Loretta didn't have time for the nervous breakdowns that were all the rage for housewives in the fifties. She just carried on working, laughing, kidding, and even flirting in a feisty and straightforward way that left not a glimmer of a doubt that she either had or ever intended to have anything to feel guilty about. Neither Miss Loretta nor her children were particularly prone to existential angst, a fact that served them well later on in life.

Mr. Bobby was a big man who enjoyed his appetites. He ate well and drank copiously, hunted, fished and roared at Southern State football games up to the day he had a heart attack and died. Years later, Miss Loretta died a week after she found out she had cancer. Not a bad end, I would say. I can certainly think of worse.

Tamyra married twice. I never met the first one, but Margaret Ann told me that he pressured Tamyra into getting an abortion when she happened to get pregnant by mistake. Tamyra wisely got rid of that husband. Then it seemed as if Tamyra had hit the jackpot. She met and married a professor from Southern State University, or SSU, not thirty miles from Wilkes Ferry, where her parents and brothers lived. Robert just seemed like the nicest guy in the world. He was friendly, fun to talk to, and family oriented. He and Tamyra quickly had two children and seemed to settle in seamlessly with the Tanner extended family. I saw them some Christmases at Bobby and Loretta's big party to which my parents were always invited.

Tanner Christmases were just a more festive version of Tanner dinners when the kids were growing up. There were people everywhere, in various stages of inebriation, coming and going, laughing and shouting and slamming doors.

It seemed, during those years, as if Tamyra had it all. She had a husband from a good family. Robert wasn't from Wilkes Ferry, but his family was an established one with old money. Robert had a good job, stable and prestigious. She had her children and a large and supportive extended family close around her. Everything seemed perfect.

I was happy for her. She was one of those people you feel deserved to be happy.

Zac Fetner

For seven years, from the ages of eleven to eighteen, Margaret Ann Patterson and I were rarely apart. We went everywhere together. We moved from her house to mine and back again. When we were not together, we were talking on the phone. We were in class together. We were cheerleaders together. We attended slumber parties and dances together and would have dated together had Margaret Ann showed the slightest bit of interest in any boy who was interested in her.

But Margaret Ann's love life well illustrated the joke made by Woody Allen in Annie Hall that he would never consider belonging to a club that would have him as a member. Margaret Ann completely ignored boys who were crazy about her. She could hardly stand to be in the same room with them. But she fell head over heels in love with boys who would never have looked at her had the two of them been alone on a desert island.

There were two boys in particular she doted on for years. The first was Jobe Cobb, the son of the wealthy Cobb family branch that owned the railroad. Years later, Margaret Ann described Jobe as "Rob Lowe beautiful." I guess he was. I must admit I can't remember exactly what Jobe or Rob Lowe looked like since I don't think I ever saw either of them more than once or twice.

Jobe Cobb didn't exactly frequent the places Margaret Ann and I did. He was several years older than we were and he, like my brother, attended prep school out of town. So it wasn't like we were in school with him. Even on the rare occasions when he was at home in the lovely old brick-and-white-frame house at the top of Tenth Avenue, he was virtually inaccessible. Margaret Ann rode by his house several times a day when he was home, hoping to get a glimpse of him. When he wasn't home, she rode by every day just to check and make sure he wasn't there.

If she ever did by chance see him going out of the house to get into his convertible or getting out of his convertible to go into the house, I would have to listen to the details for months. By the time Margaret Ann was through telling and retelling the story, I would know every item of clothing Jobe Cobb had on including his socks (which he didn't wear unless he was playing tennis), his watch, and his shoes. This went on for years.

The boys who wanted to date Margaret Ann, she wouldn't give the time of day. She sometimes went out with one of them but only because I badgered her into it either out of pity for the boy or a desire to have her along on one of my dates. Afterward, she always made fun of the boy unmercifully. She had nothing but contempt for the perfectly reasonable boys who liked her and their fascination with her enormous breasts did not flatter her. It disgusted her.

Lest you think Margaret Ann was something of a gold digger because she spent several years drooling over the wealthy, old-money Jobe Cobb, I should tell you about the other boy or man who occupied her fantasies for the second half of high school. His name was Zac Fetner.

Now Zac Fetner along with his best friend, Lee Duffy, was one of the most notorious hell-raisers in the Valley. Neither Zac Fetner nor Lee Duffy had a cent to his name. Both of them were a year or two out of high school by the time Margaret Ann Patterson started writing "Margaret Ann Fetner" all over every blank surface she could get her hands on. I think there is still an old radio in my parent's house with Margaret Ann Fetner written on it.

Because Zac Fetner and Lee Duffy were out of high school, they were free to drink and party to their heart's content. It apparently took a whole lot of drink and days of partying to ever approach contentment. In fact, contentment was most probably, in the good ole' boy Southern tradition, passing out so completely they couldn't be roused.

Zac and Lee partied everywhere. They partied on the backwater in cabins like the one built by my father, walking down to a dock in the cool night air, sitting side by side with their pants' legs rolled up and their feet in the water, drinking beer.

They partied out of the back of pickup trucks at Flat Shoals Creek where some of the teenagers went to park. You could hear them hooting and singing as they wove along the moonlit sandy shoals in the creek, girls in tow.

Sometimes they partied outside the Teenage Club where weekly dances were held for the Wilkes Ferry High School students. By then, they were too old to go into the Teenage Club, but we would see them, beer cans in their hands, talking either out of or into the windows of cars.

When their friends in the most famous band around, The Bushmen, played at the Teenage Club, there was such a crowd outside they could just blend in.

When The Bushmen played, Margaret Ann was giddy with excitement at the prospect of seeing Zac and perhaps talking to him. It was hard to miss Zac. He was six feet tall and had bleached blond hair. You saw the hair before you saw the man.

It was hard to figure how he and Lee got away with drinking openly in the parking lot of the Teenage Club, as highly visible as they were. But we sometimes saw Zac and Lee standing at the open window of a police cruiser holding a beer can politely behind their backs so the officer wouldn't have to do anything about it.

Zac and Lee were just real likeable good ole' boys. They were notorious, but I never heard anybody say anything really bad about either of them. Hell, the police even liked Zac and Lee. Zac and Lee were the sort of good ole' boys the local police would arrest and then carry quite peaceably to jail. Everybody—Zac, Lee, and the police officers—would be laughing by the time they were ready to lock the cell door.

Zac and Lee were so charming they once even talked my grandmother, DeeMama, into renting them an apartment. I couldn't believe my ears when my father told me that Zac Fetner and Lee Duffy were living together in one of the small apartments in my grandmother's historic building. DeeMama was so old-fashioned she would phone my father to complain if one of her tenants hung underwear on the clothesline without putting a cloth over it. But she rented an apartment to Zac Fetner and Lee Duffy. Go figure.

Interestingly enough, DeeMama finally asked them to move, not over partying or drinking and I know it wasn't over hanging their underwear on the back line, but because she didn't like the sound of their motorcycles. She actually had no idea how loud they were since she was deaf in one ear from working in a cotton mill most of her life. If the motorcycles were loud to her, they must have been deafening to everybody else.

But, the three of them—Zac, Lee, and DeeMama—parted on good terms, which is more than I can say about most of my grandmother's tenants. DeeMama was way too nosy for most people, especially single women with fancy underwear. She and my Aunt DeWilla would carry on hissing conversations about the trashy women who lived in my grandmother's apartments or who worked in the mill with DeWilla. DeeMama was so vicious about the issue of single, loose women, she once called my cousin Biddy a whore for intending to go (not going, but even thinking about going) out of the house without a girdle on.

But back to Zac. Margaret Ann rode by Zac Fetner's house when we were in high school even though Zac and Lee lived way down the Valley. "Down the Valley" means that they lived on the Alabama side of the Catawba and south of Wilkes Ferry. It also means they were most likely mill workers, only Lee and Zac never worked a day in their lives that I could see. Margaret Ann rode by Zac's house so often Zac could not have helped recognizing her little yellow Volkswagen bug, but he never seemed to mind.

Zac Fetner was one of those unusual men who really likes women. Zac Fetner and Lee Duffy between them probably had half the women in the Valley, but again, I never heard a woman with a bad word to say about either of them, not even my grandmother (whom I am fairly certain they didn't have). One of my grandmother's sayings was "I've got no boyfriends and no gentlemen callers." I must have heard her say this a million and a half times, and always, always after she said it, she would duck her head, cover her mouth, and bounce a little in a "tee-hee look how cute I am" way. I wasn't especially fond of this little performance, especially after the thousandth time I heard it, but it drove my mother crazy. I can remember being in the car with her, driving home from DeeMama's house when she would fuss and rave the entire fifteen-mile trip about what she was going to do if DeeMama said, "I don't have boyfriends or gentleman callers" another time.

Back to Zac. Zac Fetner was the kind of man who would have carried on with an eighteen-year-old girl and a fifty-year-old woman with equal pleasure, equal enthusiasm, and equal appreciation. Zac Fetner didn't just like to have sex with women, he liked women.

This was very easy to see during the few occasions on which he actually talked to Margaret Ann. I watched them once from across the parking lot at the

Teenage Club after Margaret Ann walked over to the little knot of men, which included Zac and Lee. It was a brave thing to do for Margaret Ann, to walk up to a group of men, not school boys, with sin on her mind. Zac made it easier by breaking into a big smile when he saw her coming.

As they talked, Zac looked down at her almost tenderly like a loving older brother might, a loving older brother who thought his kid sister was just cute as hell. He never, as far as I know, made a move on her.

I don't know whether Margaret Ann would have gone to bed with Zac Fetner had he put a move on her. It may have been the sixties, but we didn't talk about such things in Wilkes Ferry. Making out, necking, was the only thing even contemplated by our little group of girls. But I find it hard to believe Zac couldn't have had her had he wanted to. Perhaps he knew that, perhaps he didn't.

Margaret Ann's sexuality was always more than a little ambivalent. It wasn't difficult to see that her romantic objects were always unobtainable. I never heard her speak as if she enjoyed making out with anybody, and her own rather impressive breasts embarrassed her. So had Zac Fetner turned around and reached for her, her fascination with him might well have disappeared.

Perhaps Zac Fetner was all too familiar with the "come, come, come-stop, stop, stop" syndrome. I wouldn't put it past him. He knew a lot about women, and as I said, he liked them. He seemed to me now, looking back on it, like the kind of man who watches and waits, not in a predatory way, but simply the way men do who are fond of women and who know the best way to please them is to let them come when and in the way they want to.

For men like Zac, watching women is as pleasurable as sex. Men like that love everything about women—the way they look and the way they smell and move, their clothes, the feel of soft fabric against skin. They like the tentative shy approach as well as the bold inviting stare. These are men who take pleasure in making a woman smile, in lighting up her eyes, in hearing her laugh. And so, they watch and wait to see what makes a woman sparkle, what she wants.

They know a woman will invite them in if they only give her time. For men like this, being invited, reached for, is the best feeling. It is the ultimate excitement of being desired. It is the difference between a gift and a stolen object.

It's all so simple, one wonders why more men don't get it, but most men, I think, really don't like women. In fact, my opinion after fifty years of dealing with them is that 99 percent of them might as well be homosexuals. They not only don't like women, they actually loathe them.

Oh sure. They have sex with women, but they don't like them. Having sex with a warm soft orifice that is socially approved of is not the same as liking the one who is in possession of that orifice. I have known many ex-cons who finally resorted to having sex with another man not because they would have ever chosen to do so ordinarily, but because they needed what they called "relief" masturbating couldn't give them.

That's what women are to most men—a warm orifice, a place to relieve themselves. They don't want to sleep with the owner, cuddle with them, talk to them. They go straight from the warm orifice back to the men's house or back to bear world as I call it. Everything they like and respect is bound up with maleness—guns, speed, hardness, lack of feeling, invulnerability, hunting, fighting, sports, competition. They hate "women things" and avoid them like the plague. They don't even really like women's bodies although they pretend to. They don't talk about women's bodies, they talk about body parts—tits, assess—as if they were doing an autopsy. They recoil in disgust from menstrual blood but regard coming in your mouth as bestowing an honor on you.

They even talk about sex as an aggressive act. You *know* women didn't start the expressions "fuck you, screw you, fucked-up, motherfucker." To be likened to a cunt is one of the worst things a man can say to another man. "Cunt. Cunt. Kill the cunts." Joe Ed Montgomery kindly left me with that quote in my head. When a man wants to insult another man, he compares him to a woman. Bitch. Cunt. As if this is the worst thing he can possibly be.

This is supposed to be love? I don't think so.

The way I see it, if men are so drawn to other men that they want to spend all their time with them doing "male things," if they hate women's sex so much that calling another man a cunt is the worst possible insult they can come up with, why don't they just go fuck men and leave us alone? Who needs a bunch of men hanging around, sniffing around, telling us they love us so they can "relieve" themselves when they hate everything about us. They relieve themselves, and once it's over, they can't wait to get away from us, criticize us, make fun of us, beat the living hell out of us, slit our throats, push us down the stairs, and vomit in the toilet over menstrual blood and afterbirth. When they marry us, they fuck around on us while we are pregnant with their children. The time that a woman is most likely to be abused by her husband is when she is pregnant.

I really think, given the amount of devastation they regularly wreak on the rest of the world, men should be confined in a big football stadium. We could fly over in helicopters and drop hamburgers and french fries and steaks to them. They could play contact sports to their heart's content. Women could check the good ones out like books from the library and then take them back where they couldn't harm anybody.

If we did this, my current husband would be one of the most dog-eared volumes in the stadium, but it took me forty years to find him. He's the kind of man who smiles with pleasure when he hears old women laughing.

I'm way off topic. What was the topic? Margaret Ann, and Zac Fetner.

Well, the other small detail that made Zac Fetner unobtainable was that he had a girlfriend. She was actually quite a nice person, but she brings to mind that song recorded by the band Alabama: "I like my women just a little on the trashy side." Cash Beasley was definitely trashy. One of those women that "war their clothes too tight and their har is dyed." Cash was a hairdresser. What else? She looked rough and acted rougher, but when half the Valley was after Zac, what could you expect? I was always afraid that one day Cash Beasley was going to come after Margaret Ann with a hot curling iron. Margaret Ann spent at least the last two years of high school in unconsummated pursuit of Zac Fetner. Thank somebody, Cash Beasley hardly even paid Margaret Ann any attention. Cash had much more serious competition to worry about.

Lint Heads

Salzburg's was the only jewelry store in Wilkes Ferry. It was where little boys went to buy silver charms for girls' bracelets. It was where high school students went to order their class rings. It was where young men going off to WWII bought wedding rings for their sweethearts.

The Hinleys, who owned Salzburg's, were German, descendants of a small group of Protestants who settled near Savannah when Georgia was first founded. A Roman Catholic archbishop named Leopold von Firmian decided in 1731 that all the Protestants in the area had to either recant their anti-Catholic beliefs or leave Austria. These Protestants followed the teachings of Martin Luther, and they refused to do what von Firmian demanded. So the Protestants were told they had only a few days to dispose of everything they owned before leaving Austria.

Twenty thousand Protestants were expelled by von Firmian, who had bought the position of archbishop from the pope. The Protestants were forced to dump their land and possessions on the market all at one time. Consequently, they got virtually nothing for them. The very religious von Firmian and his relatives confiscated or bought up most of what was left.

Not content with this little scam, von Firmian then had bonfires built and burned all the Protestant books and Bibles. Now you know, there's not much lower than burning books, but von Firmian and his cohorts didn't stop there. They even seized children so they could make sure they were raised as Roman Catholics. Organized religion has a whole lot to answer for.

But when General James Edward Oglethorpe, a wealthy British Protestant, heard about the brutal expulsion of the Protestants from Austria, he approached King George II of England, himself of German Lutheran extraction. Oglethorpe had been appointed to head the colony of Georgia, and he and George II offered aid to any of the Salzburgers who wanted to settle in the colony.

A group of around sixty exiles traveled first to London and then to Charleston where Oglethorpe himself met them. They then sailed for Savannah. The ship foundered on a sandbar off the Geogia coast, and for days, they were assumed to be dead.

Then when they finally did get to their land north of Savannah, over half of them died in the first year of disease. The location of the first town named Ebenezer proved to be so unhealthy the Salzburgers had to move the settlement. They named the new settlement Ebenezer as well so the trustees wouldn't think they had failed at the initial settlement.

Those Salzburgers who survived were some tough cookies. Later on they were joined by a second group, and by 1714 there were around 150 Salzburgers in the town of Ebenezer on the Savannah River.

The Salzburgers built the first church in Georgia, the first grist mill, the first saw mill, the first rice mill, the first silk filature, and the first orphanage. They also forged some of the first large bells in Georgia, which are still rung every Sunday morning by the Salzburger society in Ebenezer. The Hinleys who owned the jewelry store in Wilkes Ferry were descendants of those Salzburgers. They had only one daughter, Amelia. All you had to do was look at Miss Amelia's ramrod straight back, stiff neck, and clenched lips to see that she was one of the determined Salzburg Hinleys. That's part of what makes this story about her so difficult to imagine.

Miss Amelia married a man she brought home from college, Tommy Taylor. Tommy worked for the Cobb Cotton Manufacturing Company for a while, and then he joined Miss Amelia working in the jewelry store. They took over the jewelry store after Miss Amelia's parents died. It was Tommy, or at least his manner, that started all the rumors.

Tommy and Amelia Taylor never looked young. They were the sort of people who seemed to have been born looking middled aged, like Hume Cronyn, Jessica Tandy's husband who played old men in the movies from the time he was twenty.

They went to the First Baptist Church, Tommy and Amelia, so I had the opportunity to examine them weekly from the vantage point of the balcony, where all the teenagers sat. The balcony was a great place from which to observe the various members of the congregation, who tended to forget they were being observed. There was nothing even remotely entertaining about church services, so we had to entertain ourselves somehow.

I truly believe those hours spent in the First Baptist Church of Wilkes Ferry, listening to some preacher or other drone on and on were hours from the *Twilight Zone*, stretching out into infinity. They were the longest hours in my life. When I left Wilkes Ferry in 1969, I never went back into a church willingly except for funerals and weddings. The balcony was the only thing that made church even remotely bearable.

We could watch Fred Tarver, who would unfailingly fall asleep every Sunday, his head beginning to sway and bob before it finally dropped over on his chest and he settled in to snoring. His wife, at least a hundred pounds heavier than he was, would then elbow him in the side so hard Mr. Fred would jump and sometimes even let out a loud snort. When he did, new people or people who didn't attend church regularly would jump involuntarily or look over to see what was wrong. The regulars who had heard Fred snort for years wouldn't even flinch.

Other Sundays, someone from the very back of the church in the last few pews might sneak out early. A little later, someone else might join them. If the two were of the opposite sex, heaven help them. We would exchange significant glances and raised eyebrows, and you can bet your life the story would be all over town by Sunday dinner.

One Sunday, Mr. Roland Riley, a friend of my father's who rarely ever graced the First Baptist Church with his presence, came in late to morning service and sat on the first seat next to the aisle in the next-to-the-last pew. Mr. Roland captured my imagination because he looked exactly like William Bendix, the actor. Mr. Roland stretched out his legs, crossed his ankles, and propped his arm up on the side of the pew, looking like a man settling in for a miserably boring hour. Suddenly, one of the ushers appeared to his right, bending down and bowing. The usher tried to hand Mr. Roland one of the golden yellow visitor's cards that had a small red ribbon pinned on the corner with a straight pin. Now the usher knew damned well that Mr. Roland was not a visitor, but he kept offering the visitor's card, making a joke.

Mr. Roland tried to ignore him, looking straight ahead, but the usher kept bowing and reaching out offering the card. I wanted to laugh and to tell someone, but talking in the balcony was a dangerous business. The minister, the entire choir, and even the organist Miss Emily who ducked her head down and squinted into the mirror over the organ so she could get an angle to see behind her and up, monitored every move we made in the balcony and would report misbehavior to our parents the very Sunday it occurred. This made for a very unpleasant Sunday dinner, and therefore the behavior that brought it upon us was usually avoided. So there was no one I could tell. Later, though, I told my father the story about Mr. Roland and the usher. He loved it, and I loved having made him laugh. There was nothing better in the world than making my father laugh.

Unlike Mr. Roland, Amelia and Tommy Taylor were regular churchgoers. Every Sunday morning, they would walk down the left aisle—Amelia first then Tommy—to sit one pew in front of the McGregors and the McKeans, who were the first family of the church, rich and pious.

I never saw anything remarkable about Tommy and Amelia or even remotely interesting. They were pleasant enough people, but like most of the other members of the congregation, they seemed to me as a teenager to live dull, conventional lives. They weren't even on my radar screen.

Then suddenly, a rumor percolated through the town with ferocious rapidity that Amelia Taylor was somehow "involved" with another woman in the Baptist church. The next Sunday, the entire congregation watched intently out of the corners of their eyes as Amelia and Tommy walked down the aisle and took their accustomed place in front of the McGregor/McKean scions. Everybody pretended they weren't watching, but it got painfully quiet when Tommy and Amelia entered the church. No one would have done anything so impolite as to turn around and look, but the silence flowed like a wave from the back of the church to the front as Tommy and Amelia came into people's view.

Amelia sat down stiffly, her hands clasping navy blue gloves on top of her navy blue purse. There was a stain of flushed skin spreading up out of Tommy Taylor's collar and across his neck, but he held his head high. Since I was in the balcony, I didn't have to look out of the corner of my eye, but I just couldn't imagine it. Amelia Taylor, wearing those black butterfly glasses frames with the tiny rhinestones in the corners "involved" with another woman. I guess the rest of the church, especially the men, could imagine it, and I'm sure they spent the entire sermon, if not the rest of their lives, imagining it in detail. But I just couldn't wrap my mind around it.

I think the person Amelia Taylor was supposed to be involved with was Miss Antoinette Beckman, who periodically tried to kill herself by slitting her wrists. I knew Miss Antoinette used to regularly try to kill herself by slitting her wrists because every time she did it, I would have to sit in the car in her driveway, shaded by a canopy of trees, waiting for my mother to come out of her house. My mother annoyed me to no end by dragging me along on these occasions, forcing me to sit in the car in Miss Antoinette's driveway for what seemed like hours and then categorically refusing to tell me what was happening.

Miss Lotty, the church secretary, had some role in this affair, but I can't remember what. Perhaps she was the author of the smutty story. Or perhaps it was Miss Lotty that was supposed to be the object of Amelia's wild lust, but I don't think so. As hard as it was to see Amelia Taylor having a lesbian affair wearing those sparkling glasses, I just could not see Miss Lotty, with a built up shoe, a rocking walk, and a hump on her back, having anything so freewheeling and luxuriant as an affair. But you never know. Christ, when you think about it, the whole town should have been glad if Miss Lotty found somebody to have an affair with. But I have never lived in a small town where anybody cared about outcasts and strange people being sexually gratified.

The funny thing about this story was that it had less to do with Miss Lotty or Miss Amelia and their behavior than it did with Tommy Taylor and his. Tommy was, and still is to this day, well, effeminate. Tommy is very effeminate. In fact, if you put Tommy Taylor in a wig and a cocktail dress and didn't change another thing about his behavior, you would have the campiest queen east of the Castro.

Now the word "queen" and the words "effeminate" and "camp" were not even part of my vocabulary when I was in my early teens, nor do I think they were part of the vocabularies of any person in the First Baptist Church of Wilkes Ferry. I also don't think I had ever heard the word lesbian, nor knew what it meant.

How this story was passed around without even the essential vocabulary to convey its meaning, I don't know. I suppose people politely said that Miss Amelia was having an "affair," pronounced with three syllables, with another woman. This was also probably followed, at least when it was spread by women, with the sentence "Bless her heart." This "bless her heart" was supposed to make the spreading of vicious gossip a ladylike activity and absolve the teller from any mean-spirited intent. It was like saying, "Did you know Amelia Taylor is a pathological liar, a slut, and a dope fiend? Bless her heart."

I saw Jimmy Carter's sister once talking on television about a girl's home she had been working with. She said that one of the girls was there because her "daddy had had sex with her." Carter's sister smiled shyly into the camera and then added, "Bless his heart." Now I don't know whether she meant to say "Bless *her* heart." And just messed up. Or if she had gotten so used to adding "bless whoever's heart" at the end of unpleasant sentences she just automatically inserted this, but it left me sitting in front of the television staring with my mouth hanging open. It was one of those things that happen, and you want to phone everybody you know and say, "Did you see that?"

But another thing I never understood about this Amelia Taylor affair was why, given the effeminate behavior of Tommy Taylor, people chose to make up a story about a lesbian affair of Amelia. Could they just not stand the idea of an effeminate man in this football-crazy culture? I never, never heard anybody say that Tommy Taylor was "effeminate" or any other less civil word for "effeminate." And, Tommy Taylor was one of the nicest people in town.

My theory, understanding what I do now about small towns and the nature of rumor, is that some bright spark was making fun of Tommy's mannerisms. This led to speculation about the marriage. Someone then probably joked that Amelia must be a lesbian (or perhaps "that way"). Before the next morning, the story had passed from mouth to ear a dozen times, and somewhere in the mix, "Amelia must be a lesbian" transformed itself into "Amelia is a lesbian" then into "Amelia is having a lesbian affair." From there, it is just a small step to "Amelia Taylor is having a lesbian affair with Antoinette Beckman" since Miss Antoinette was always trying to kill herself.

You know, I can't even remember whether Miss Antoinette started trying to kill herself before the rumors of her affair with Miss Amelia started circulating or after. But then, I have never in my life seen fact get in the way of a good rumor. And Miss Antoinette's repeated attempts at suicide, even if they were a continuation of prior behavior, fueled the rumors.

The story, of course, was that Miss Antoinette was trying to kill herself because she and Miss Amelia had been found out, and she was outed in front of the entire community, not to mention in front of her husband and possibly her children.

For all I know, the story could have been true, but since Miss Amelia and Tommy Taylor have been together with no visible signs of strain for at least the fifty years I've known them, I can't see how she could have been having a rip roaring lesbian affair with Miss Antionette Beckman thirty years before.

But anything is possible. Wilkes Ferry might be a small town, but it had no shortage of depravity, depravity much worse than a supposedly lesbian affair.

Besides, Daddy told me that Antoinette Beckman's problems started long before the rumors of lesbianism.

Withholding

When I was a Brownie, the Scout mothers—Miss Peggy, Miss Ophelia and my mother—took us on a field trip to the Confederate Memorial Cemetery. I had never been to the cemetery before, and I don't think any of us learned a whole hell of a lot that day of the field trip. Like most little girls, the minute we were let out of the cars, we started running around. I can only marvel now at the amount of energy we had. At least three of us—Frankie Callaway, Georgia Whitney, and I—were always pretending to be the thing we admired most in the world: a horse. We galloped around, neighing and whinnying and generally acting like crazy children all the time. I can remember being in our back yard pretending I was the horse that led all the other horses down into the mouth of an extinct volcano to get away from the men chasing us.

But the really striking memory photograph I have of that day at the cemetery is a cement slab with hard-to-read names and dates on it. This cement slab rested uneasily on top of an old brick base. The grave actually was a mass grave for some of the soldiers that died in the Battle of Wilkes Ferry and didn't have identifying objects still on them. I think most of the ones in that grave were Yankees since the people around Wilkes Ferry would have known the Confederates who were fighting that day to save the city.

The cement slab, since it was out of kilter, looked very much like some grave robber had come into the cemetery at night, slid over the cement slab, and taken out all the bones. I'm sure that's not what happened. If it had, it would have been all over town. It was probably that way because grave was just so old the ground around it had settled and left the one-hundred-year-old slab catawampus and scary looking. You could tell the bricks that formed the base of the grave were old ones because they were irregular and much smaller than bricks that were used to build houses.

The same old bricks were used to build a foot-tall wall around the graves in that little Confederate Cemetery. Sometime later, somebody had come along and put cement on top of the wall just to keep the old bricks from falling down.

As with all these memory photographs, there is the question of what made an impression on me that was so powerful that it left a vivid image in my mind. I think this particular image was constructed later on in the day, after I had been taken home by my mother. It was part of trying to remember what I had done.

As soon as the little girls riding in Mother's car piled inside to be driven home, I knew there was something wrong. I had antennae that were so finely tuned even by that age, I could tell from just looking at my mother whether or not she was mad. And on that day, she was mad, really mad.

There were three or four little girls in the backseat of my mother's car. I was sitting in the front seat with another little girl between me and my mother. I was leaning on the door, my right hand on the dashboard and my left on the seat, facing my mother. I was exploring her face, trying to figure out what I had done and how bad the punishment would be. I grew more and more tense as each little girl got out of the car and walked to her house. When the last one left, the little girl in the front seat with Mother and I, I desperately wanted to leave with her.

My heart was pounding, and after that final stop to let the last little girl out, my mother turned the car toward home. I would have gladly jumped off the face of the earth if I only could, but there was nothing I could do. Mother never looked at me when she got mad. That afternoon, all she said during the drive was "Stop leaning on the door."

That was all she said until we got home, and she put the car into "Park." There was no point fantasizing that there wasn't more to come, but I did fantasize, trying to calm myself. I was probably blabbering at the same time, trying to make it seem like everything was all right, but it was no use, and I knew it. I looked out the passenger-side window and rubbed my right finger over the place where I had had a wart before DeeMama's friend charmed it off. That was one of the ways I tried to avoid what I knew was coming. I had an entire repertoire of rituals that I performed when I could feel the walls of my mother's anger closing in on me. It is a testament to faith that I kept on performing them long into my teens. None of them ever worked.

Suddenly, my mother looked over at me, and I became the most horrible, mean, wicked child in the world. In an instant, I was transformed into an irreverent, spoiled, ungrateful child who had stomped on a grave. I can remember her saying something like what I had done was just the same as if I had spit on my grandmother's grave or desecrated my grandmother and grandfather's graves. I don't really get this now, and I am sure I didn't at the time. I hadn't spit on anybody's grave, and both my grandmothers were still alive at that time, so how could I have spit on either of their graves? Besides, how did jumping off a foot-tall brick fence onto an old grave of people we didn't even know get to be spitting on my grandmother and grandfather's grave?

But I knew well enough not to argue when Mama started one of these tirades. I could beg. I could plead, but it wouldn't do any good. In fact, it would make the situation worse because in my whining, I would introduce new topics for her to get madder at me about. Anything I could or did say would certainly be used against me. So I tried at least to remain silent. I think the only word I got out of my mouth was, "Mama . . . Mama . . ." She just kept on hissing at me.

Usually, after such episodes, I wound up in my room alone and miserable. I could not rest. I could not relax. If there was something wrong with Mother, I could not do anything until I made it right. Also, there was a fear that she would yank open the door to my room, demand to know why the door was closed in the first place, and she would find me doing something that would make her even madder because she would think I hadn't taken the scolding seriously. She might, for example, find me reading and then start all over again.

"Oh, I can see just how sorry you are for spitting on your grandfather and grandmother's graves. You come right in here and start reading like nothing happened." Then she might try with all her might to slam my bedroom door. It wasn't the best door to try to slam since it ran on a track and had louvers in it. What usually happened when she tried to slam it was that it just went partially down the track and vibrated. She would almost always have to have two tries at it before she could manage to get the force she wanted to express into the gesture.

I don't remember how long she was mad over this "spitting on your grandmother and grandfather's grave" bit. But however long it was, it was torture.

When she got like this, I would usually sit in my room alone for a few hours and then creep back to where she was sitting reading a book and try to engage her in conversation. She would invariably refuse to respond the first couple of times I did this. I would say something or ask a question, and she would just continue reading, silent. I hated the withholding worse than I would have hated a beating. Sometimes she would refuse to speak to me for days.

Boss's Row

Daddy told me that before she married Bill Beckman, Antoinette Wickman was the daughter of one of the big mill managers. Mr. Wickman was not a mill owner. He was certainly not a Cobb, but he was the manager of one of the largest mills and paid well above the standard worker. That essentially made the Wickmans rich in the eyes of the rest of the workers in the Valley who did shift work in the cotton mills.

The Wickmans had a big frame house on "Boss's Row" the street of houses near the Lafayette Mill. The Wickmans's large two-story Victorian house had white gingerbread all over the wraparound porch and was at the very end of the dead-end street. The Wickman house sat by itself, facing the line of houses of the assistant managers which went up and down both sides of the street. This is where the name "Boss's Row" came from. It was an odd set up, but at the time those houses were built, few people had cars and the Cobb Manufacturing Company not only supervised the work lives of their employees, they also supervised virtually every activity of daily life.

The mill workers' houses were right next to the mills so everyone could walk to work in five minutes. If you were sick, everybody knew it. And if you were laid up with a hangover, everybody knew it as well. If you beat the living hell out of your wife or fought with your brother-in-law, every last person in that mill village knew about it. If you had bad business, you tried to keep it to yourself or you would be out of a job.

There was a big social distinction between the mill workers—the weavers and spinners and sweepers—and the bosses. Miss Antoinette, so my father told me, was not allowed to play with other children. Her mother didn't want her associating with the common riffraff children of mill hands, like my father. She wasn't even allowed to play with the other children on Boss's Row. Antoinette's mother thought these children were low class and beneath the Wickmans. So Miss Antoinette sat in the house, reading, playing the piano, and looking out the window at the other children romping and shouting on the street. When she married, she had never even been around people her own age except for a few hours every day at school.

Antoinette's mother also had a phobia about cotton lint. She went almost into a fit, Daddy said, if she saw a piece of cotton lint in her house or on her family. When Mr. Wickman came home from the mill every day, the first thing he did, at his wife's direction, was to go straight upstairs and take off all his clothes. The lint-contaminated clothes were collected by a black servant, who promptly brushed and washed them before Mr. Wickman could wear them again.

Mr. Wickman got in the tub and washed not only his body, but also his mustache and his hair to get every speck of cotton lint off him before coming back downstairs. If he missed a piece, Mrs. Wickman became hysterical.

Cotton lint, in a mill town, was like having coal dust on your face in a mining community. It telegraphed your social position. There were no safety or environmental standards in the mills until the seventies. Working in the mills meant that you came out and often went in with cotton lint all over you.

Inside the mill, it was like walking around in a snowstorm. You couldn't help getting it all over you, and you couldn't help breathing it in. Later on, after OSHA standards were implemented, the amount of lint in the air was severely cut down, and people were required to wear face masks that kept the cotton lint out of their lungs. But before that, even the mill bosses came out at the end of the day covered with lint.

As an indication of just how salient this cotton lint was, mill workers were commonly referred to as "lint heads." I heard this term frequently since I lived in the "office town" of Wilkes Ferry rather than the "mill towns" of Lafayette, River Falls, Sweet Water, Riverview and Young Harris. Some boy, for example, might refer to some other boy. "Is he going to be there?" a third boy might pipe up. "Naw," would be the response. "He's a lint-head." I remember boys using this term. I don't remember any of the girls using it. Even we knew that it was rude, if not cruel. I don't think my parents would have allowed "lint head" to be used in our house any more than they would have allowed "nigger."

Wilkes Ferry was the town where most of the white-collar workers lived. There was no mill in Wilkes Ferry, only the offices of the "Cumpny." Strung out down the river, though, were five mills and the little mill villages that surrounded each of them. Almost everybody in those towns did shift work in the mills.

Each mill was located beside the Catawba River, initially used as the power to run the looms. Each mill was surrounded by small shotgun white frame houses built by the Company for their workers. In every little town, there was a grammar school and a high school, a community center, and an auditorium—all built by the Company

Only the churches were not provided by the Company, and even they relied on the private contributions of the Cobbs and the Hopewells and the Wickmans and other owners and managers. It was the classic "company town." The Company was a fundamental part of every life in the Catawba River Valley. Everybody either worked for the Company or supplied services to those who did.

George's Record Store

George's Record Store was where my brother, Drew, spent the first twelve years of his life. Drew would stand in the store for hours, reading album covers and looking at sheet music while I cooled my heels on the curb outside watching the people come and go on the streets of downtown Wilkes Ferry.

If I got too bored or too hot, I would wander into Woolsworths and stroll the aisles. I loved Woolsworths. I wish there were still Woolsworths in every little town in America. Woolsworths had everything—needles, buttons, thread, needle threaders, stockings, sewing scissors, candy corn, red hots, sour apples, socks, head bands and hair ribbons, little bracelets and birth stone rings. It also had two water fountains along the back wall with signs up above them: "White" and "Colored." I used to wonder as a child if the water tasted different at the colored fountain.

After fingering everything in Woolsworths, I would go out the back door and check to see if my brother was through at George's. He never was. My brother could take longer to do anything than any other person I have ever known. He could go into the post office to get the mail and stay for an hour.

The George brothers, who owned the record store, loved music themselves, and they were always to be found in the shop listening to music. They would lean over the counter side-by-side, arms touching and listen to music or talk about music, or talk about the day or talk about just anything at all that pleased them. Sometimes, they sat together in the two stuffed chairs at the back of the store surrounded by account books and receipts and order forms, telling each other jokes and funny stories. When they were putting records into the bins or rearranging them, they called out to each other across the store laughing and joking. It seemed as if the George brothers found each other's company the most entertaining diversion in the world, and they were always together. They remind me of the Lebanese version of the *Car Talk* guys on radio.

The store was like a teenaged boy's attic room—records everywhere, smoke in the air, overflowing ashtrays, record players, and music magazines strewn across the counters. High along the walls near the ceiling were rows of guitars and banjos, a few violins, trumpets, saxophones, ukeleles. There was a drum set on a platform in the corner and bongo drums on the counter.

There was something dark and intense about the large-eyed, long-lashed brothers. But they were just as full of fun and full of life as they could be. I can't remember anybody in town seeming happier than the George brothers. They lived in a large frame house on Fifth Street with their mother, who wore long house dresses and had a heavy accent. I found out later that the accent was Lebanese. All of the Georges had darker skin than most people, but there was never any discussion of this that I heard.

In the South, in the fifties, people were either black or white. Nothing in between mattered very much. I was vaguely aware that Mrs. George was different, but that had more to do with her clothes and her accent than her skin tone. It took a decade of working in historically black universities for me to start to regularly notice and identify people by skin tone.

When the Georges came to the Valley, they took up residence in the large, rambling, white frame house two of the brothers still occupy on Fifth Street. They opened a tiny restaurant right next door to where the record store now stands. I don't remember the little café ever having been open, but people say the Georges sold sandwiches and hamburgers. Seems a shame, but I guess Lebanese food was just way too foreign (ferrun) for the fifties.

Papa Mansour George, the boys' father, must have expended his reservoir of life energy to get the whole family to the United States and set them up with the restaurant and the record store. He died early. He must have been dead before the fifties because I don't remember ever having seen him.

People said that Papa George was a good deal older than Mrs. George and that the two of them married late in life. People also said Papa George hadn't wanted to marry Mrs. George at all, which always seemed very sad to me. Couldn't have been a very happy marriage.

I heard about the *Titanic* for the first time listening to some adults talk about the George family. They were saying Mrs. George, her name was Fatima, was only fourteen when she came over on the *Titanic* with her young husband from Lebanon. There was a kind of American fever in Lebanon at the time. Everyone wanted to come. They were lured to America by posters and newspapers ads promising a new life to be had for only the modest price of a third-class passage to New York.

Almost all marriages in Lebanon were arranged at the time, and Miss Fatima's family had arranged for her to marry the bright-eyed Hamid George, youngest son of the George family. Most of the Georges had already established themselves in America. Mansour, the eldest son, went first, and the others followed on the money he sent home.

Hamid was a handsome and a happy boy, who liked to laugh and enjoy life. He seemed delighted with even the very simplest things around him. He was delighted with Fatima from the moment he first saw her, and Fatima was intrigued by Hamid's freedom from the formality and the dour seriousness which seemed so much a part of her own family of brothers and uncles.

Her marriage to Hamid was the most liberating experience of her life. When she and Hamid were alone together at night in their room, Fatima felt as if she were a child again, cuddling and laughing and playing with her cousins, free to be as silly and spontaneous as she pleased.

Fatima joyously bore Hamid a son not more than a few weeks before they left Beirut on a French liner for Cherbourg, the embarkation port for the *Titanic*. There were over one hundred other Lebanese passengers on the voyage. Forty-three of them would survive. Four of the Lebanese couples had planned to be married on the voyage, and they had brought along drums and musical instruments. The lutes and drums ended up on the bottom of the ocean with only the starfish and octopus and occasional current to make their sounds.

Fatima had barely had the time to get used to being married to her fine young Hamid George, when he died on the night of April 15, 1912. Fatima was frantic amid the panicking people and the listing of the boat. Uniformed men kept shouting urgent directions at her in English, which she didn't understand. Finally, Hamid took her and a group of other women, many of whom were also holding babies or trailing children behind them, up to the first-class deck and pushed through the dinner-jacketed men, demanding they be loaded onto lifeboats.

Hamid then lifted twenty children over the rail of the big boat into the arms of their mothers already seated in the lifeboats. But when he lifted his own son over the side and down toward the outstretched arms of Fatima, a rope holding the lifeboat snapped and the baby plummeted alone, helpless, screaming into the icy darkness. Fatima and Hamid's eyes met for just a second, the last time their eyes would ever meet, and Hamid went over the side after the child, diving between the ship and the lifeboats into the black water. Fatima never saw either of them again.

The other women had to hold Fatima by the waist to keep her from leaping out of the lifeboat and into the water after them. They were still holding her when the lifeboat was rowed away from the sucking of the sinking ship.

The George family was waiting for Fatima when she reached New York. But Fatima was like a shell of a human being. She remained that way for years. She never recovered from the loss of her smiling young husband, her precious little boy, and the promise of a life in America free from constant surveillance, judgement, and disapproval.

Back under the watchful eyes of her mother-in-law, Hamid's father, and all the uncles and cousins and brothers, Fatima felt as if she had been returned to prison, and the marriage to Hamid had been nothing but a dream.

For a while, the George family thought her an exemplary widow, mourning her husband and her child, but after a while, when she refused to be cooperative with their efforts to find her another husband, nothing she did seemed to please them. So she tried as best she could to do nothing.

For years, she wouldn't even listen when they talked about marrying her off to someone else. The family put more and more pressure on her to marry Hamid's older brother Mansour. But Mansour was as dour and disapproving as all the men in Fatima's family had been, and it made Fatima almost physically ill to contemplate sharing a bed with the man. She would rather die a widow without ever feeling milk in her breasts again than accept Mansour as her fate.

She scanned the faces of the men her family brought around to consider her, but she could find nothing of the open, enveloping, good-natured friendliness of Hamid. When the men left, she could hear the aunts wailing and crying upstairs in shame because another suitor had turned her down. When Fatima was around Mansour, it was painful. It was torment to see a tiny glimpse of Hamid in Mansour's mannerisms and some of his facial expressions. How could she ever live with a man who reminded her so much of her husband but who was so completely different? It would be like starving and living with fresh bread on the table you could see and even smell but never touch.

But the years went by, and it became evident to Fatima that no other man remotely like Hamid was going to come along and rescue her. If she wanted a family of her own and, even more importantly, a house of her own, she had to do something. Otherwise, she would play the role of the old-maid aunt for the rest of her life with no privacy and less respect. She would eventually be one of the old women upstairs wailing in shame every time a suitor rejected a different young relative. So finally, Fatima let the family convince her to accept Mansour. She set as her only condition for the marriage that Mansour get a house for her that was hers alone and that was in a town separate from the rest of the George family. The family thought Fatima was mad to make such a demand, especially since she was hardly in the position to demand anything, but Mansour, surprising everyone, including Fatima, agreed. She wasn't at all sure, but she thought she noticed something playful in Mansour's expression when he assented to her request. She wasn't sure where it came from, but it pleased her immensely, and it suddenly struck her that it reminded her of Hamid.

So Mansour and Fatima moved into Wilkes Ferry, bought the house on Fifth Street, and set up their restaurant. Even so, it was years before she conceived. Maybe she couldn't bear to have another man's hands on her. Maybe Mansour didn't ask her to. Maybe people were right, and Mansour didn't really want her after all. Maybe he gave into the family pressure just like she had. Maybe after all those years, it took their bodies a long time to open themselves up in that way. Whatever the reason and whatever changed, when Fatima did finally conceive, all the love she had tried so hard to keep inside her burst forth, and she not only had Harris, the first son, but then two more sons right after each other in the next two years. And whatever had been his original feeling about Fatima, Mansour was overjoyed with his sons.

Fatima could hardly take her eyes off them. She had waited so long, and when she looked into their youthful joyous eyes, she saw Hamid's eyes and Hamid's spirit, and she knew she had done the right thing. She had brought Hamid back into life.

Mama George loved her sons fiercely and evidently they her. The boys lived in the same house with her their entire lives, and not one of them married, even after her death.

The only other story I know about Mama George has to do with a tree, one of the enormous oak trees that line both sides of Fifth Street going from the General Office Building of the Company up the hill to Fort Butler and the Griggs Mansion.

The neighbors along Fifth Street woke up one morning to the sound of sawing. They were aghast when they went outside and found workmen sawing down a mammoth oak tree in front of the Georges' house. These were hundred-year-old oak trees planted at regular intervals all the way up Fifth Avenue, and Mrs. George was having one of them removed, like a bad tooth, leaving a gap in the run of trees. Everyone was shocked but afraid to confront Mrs. George. Finally someone did.

"Why?" he asked. "Why are you doing this?"

Mrs. George glared at him. Finally, she opened her mouth and said, "De trees belongs in de forest." That was it. She turned and went back in the house.

Whatever the story was with Mrs. George and her three boys, they seemed happy enough. They smiled and laughed all the time, and their faces lit up when you walked in the record shop door. Billy Cooper, the boy I danced my first fast dance with in Wyatt's Pharmacy, told me he saved up for over a year to buy his first record player at George's. He visited the record player often, and he and Mr. Harris talked about its qualities. When Billy finally had enough money, he and his mother went to George's and counted out the dollar bills for Mr. Harris. When they got home with the brand-new, red-and-white record player, one of the sacks was filled with the most popular 45 RPM records of the day. Miss Ellen, Billy's mother, phoned Harris and said they must have picked up somebody else's bag by mistake. "No," Mr. Harris told her. He had put the records in the bag. He said he thought it was a shame to have a brand-new record player and no records to play on it.

The George brothers were nice men. They loved my brother Drew, and my brother Drew loved records and classical music. So they spent a lot of time together.

My brother was a child prodigy of a sort. He took piano lessons from Miss Mary Francis Cobb from the time he emerged from the womb. Drew's life was music, and he was good at it. In fact, Drew was so good at everything, he was the perfect child. He was, and to some extent is, the hardest act I have ever had to follow.

Drew was serious, studious, quiet, respectful, and sweet. He never got in the way, never got in trouble, never demanded attention. He never cursed, yelled, talked back, thieved, drank, smoked, partied, or engaged in underage sex. So it goes without saying, I did all of them with relish. I knew I could never ever be as good as Drew was, so I decided to be as bad as possible. I did not like classical music, and my piano lessons proceeded not far beyond the *Hoe Cake Shuffle*. It was right around the time of the *Hoe Cake Shuffle* that Miss Mary Francis Cobb, in a moment of frustration, said to me, or perhaps to herself, "You will never (nevah) be as good as your brother." That was the end of me and the piano and the end of me and classical music until I was much older and read about the affair between George Sand and Chopin. Then listening to Chopin would bring tears to my eyes.

Since my brother was four years older than I was, he was always smarter, more articulate, more accomplished, and generally better than I was in every way. To my mother, he was, and would always be, the golden boy. The chosen child. Drew could do no wrong. When my brother came to Wilkes Ferry, you would think Jesus Christ and the Pope had rolled into town.

I once took care of my mother, twenty-four hours a day, seven days a week, through over nine months of serious illness, hospital stays, and emergency room visits. I had to fight nurses, hospital administrators, nursing home personnel, and she would have died had I not been there to demand somebody find out what was wrong with her. My brother came to Wilkes Ferry for three days, and the entire town genuflected.

"Not many men would love their mothers so much they would take time off work to come and take care of them."

My mother actually said that to me from her bed at the hospital after my brother had breezed back to New York and left me again quite literally with all the shit.

I just sat there staring at my mother's face. *Three days*, I thought to myself. *It's just classic. Drew was here for three days. I have been here for every illness, every emergency, every holiday, every threatened divorce for fifteen years, and nobody thinks I've done anything special at all, least of all you.*

If I get off on Mama, we'll never finish this story. The two surviving George brothers still live in Wilkes Ferry. They are now old men. But they still faithfully come to the store every weekday. Their mother, with whom they all lived, is dead. Inside the store, it is still the same—dark, musty, cluttered, like a boy's attic room. There are items on the wall of that store that I can remember being there forty years ago. And the George brothers are still there talking and laughing, still each other's very best friend.

Morphine Soaked

Mama played the part of the 1950s housewife, but she also had a job and an office. Her job as the chapter chairman of the local Red Cross was perfect in many ways. She was her own boss, worked from nine to twelve, and had no employees to get along with. But there was one big downside. She was on call most of the time.

At any moment, the telephone could ring, and all family plans were put on hold. We waited while Mama worked with families trying to get their fathers, brothers, or husbands home from the service for one emergency or another.

So growing up, I was used to phone calls in the middle of the night.

I don't know what was different about this one phone call, but something about Mama's tone made me creep from my bed and sneak quietly downstairs to lift up the other phone in the hallway.

The voice at the other end was a woman's voice, a frightened woman's voice, but this was nothing unusual. A lot of people who phoned the Red Cross were frightened or traumatized.

"I's callin' for Miss Frances Ward McPherson."

"Yes," Mama had said. "This is she."

"Miss McPherson, this Lottie." There was a pause. "I's a friend of Mattie Mae, work for you."

"Oh yes." Mama said. "What is it?"

"Miss McPherson, I hates to bother you, and I ain't never phoned nobody in the middle of the night in my whole life, but Mattie Mae, she say you gots to come down here."

"What's the matter?" Mama asked.

"Is the baby, Miss McPherson, something wrong with the baby."

"What's wrong with the baby?"

"I don't know Miss McPherson, but Mattie Mae been screamin' all afternoon and all night, and that baby won't come. Somethin's wrong, bad wrong."

"I'm coming, Lottie, but you need to phone a doctor right now."

"We don' phoned a doctor, Miss McPherson. Old Doc Fallon."

"And is he coming?"

"He here."

"Well, what did he say, Lottie? Does he think she needs to go to the hospital?"

"He don't say nothing, Miss McPherson. He won't come in the house."

"What?"

"He says he gots to have twenty dollars 'fore he step one step inside this house, and Mattie Mae upstairs hollerin' like she dying. She gon' die, and he standin' on that front porch like God hisself put him down there and turned him into stone."

Mother hissed, "You put him on the phone."

"Miss McPherson . . ."

"Put him on the telephone, Lottie."

Lottie left and came back. "Miss McPherson, he say he ain't comin' in the house without twenty dollars in cash."

"Did you tell him who it was. Lottie?" Mama asked.

"Yes 'em, I tol' hm."

Mama's voice was low and controlled, but it was the voice that sent everybody in my family, including my father, scurrying. It meant a damn was about to break, and you did not want to be standing in the way.

"Lottie, I'm on my way with the money. But you go outside and tell that morphine-soaked son of a bitch that if anything happens to Mattie Mae or that baby before I get there, I will scratch his eyeballs out and put them in his hands, and then so help me God, I'll kill him right there on that porch."

"Miss McPherson, I can't tell him that."

"You tell him, Lottie. You tell him he won't be able to come into the house because he won't ever leave the porch if anything happens to them."

Mattie Mae and the baby were fine in the end, but when mother arrived, Dr. Fallon, truly morphine soaked to the gills, was still sitting outside on the porch as big as you please. Mama would never tell me what happened on that porch, but I bet Dr. Fallon was sorry he'd ever seen Mattie Mae.

A few months later, ole' Dr. Fallon had his license taken away. Somebody reported him for getting the wrong rich lady hooked on morphine. He never spent a day in jail. He used to drive around town in a big car, and he was such a bad driver, everybody just pulled over to the side of the road when they saw him coming.

I always wondered if Mama had anything to do with him getting reported, but if she did, she never admitted it.

Class Warfare

Wilkes Ferry became part of the rail system crisscrossing the country, when in 1851, the tracks coming from the south and west reached the center of town. Three years later, the trestle bridge was completed, spanning the Catawba and thus allowing train tracks to connect Wilkes Ferry with the north and east.

The tracks ran from the south into town, parallel to the river until they reached the train depot, two blocks from the center of town. Going out of town, the tracks ran parallel to the river for another half mile and then turning east, crossed the river, ran just north of the Confederate Memorial Cemetery and then broke free through cotton fields and timberland.

Passengers could get off at the Wilkes Ferry depot and walk a block to check in or have a meal at one of the two hotels. The hotel right on the Main Street, later named the General Butler Hotel, was the same hotel where I ate with Joe Ed Montgomery and his mother. The other hotel was on the opposite side of the railroad tracks, closer to the river, a large Victorian-style structure that was never rebuilt after the war. I have only seen photographs of it.

A little up the hill from the depot, a block from the loading docks, was the mammoth boarding house. It was still there when I was growing up. The paint was peeling, and the entire structure listed a bit to the right, but it was still standing.

In the 1850s, the nexus of river and rail gave the town a boost that other towns didn't have. The railroad got Wilkes Ferry off to a fast start. Cotton from the rural interior of two states made its way by wagon to be loaded onto barges and boats and carried down river to the coast. The rest of the cotton was loaded

on railroad cars and sent north to mills in New England. As early as 1860, almost
a quarter of a million bales of cotton came out of the region annually.

At the beginning of the Civil War, the union blockade put an end to most
of the cotton export. But even during the war, if plantation owners could just get
their cotton to Wilkes Ferry, there was a chance of getting it to the coast where
blockade runners, like Rhett Butler, might just get it through to Liverpool, which
supplied the textile mills in Manchester.

Wilkes Ferry was so far inland from the coast and so far south of most of the
fighting, it was insulated from the very harshest of privations until the last year of
the war. Contrary to the picture painted by *Gone with the Wind*, a good many of
the wealthy planters in the region maintained their standard of living throughout
the war. These planters and wealthy merchants continued to have lavish dinner
parties all through the war while the rest of the Valley was starving. Some of them
hoarded cotton they couldn't get out of the region, and when the war was over,
they took full advantage of the rise in cotton prices. They dumped the cotton
on the market. They came out of the war having made a fortune. People didn't
forget which planter families shared their food and which ones threw poor whites
off their land while brothers and husbands and children and fathers were away
fighting a war, which was started to defend their economic privileges. Revisionist
popular history, started almost as soon as the war was over, glossed over the fact
that one half of all white southerners had opposed secession.

The Catawba River Valley started the war as one of the most prosperous regions
of the South. Though primarily an agricultural region, the area around Wilkes
Ferry was also the largest manufacturing center in the South outside of Richmond.
Only the most deluded would have believed that the South could secede and be
drawn into a war and come out of it having maintained that prosperity.

Even though most of the free inhabitants were pursuing some form of
agriculture, only half of those making a living from farming owned more than
three acres of land. The rest were tenant farmers, share croppers, or day laborers
working somebody else's land, usually that of the large planters. Those who
owned a few slaves worked beside them in the fields. Only about 4 percent of the
Valley's population benefitted directly from an economic system based on cotton
and slavery.

The brutal expulsion of the Creek between 1814 and 1836 had made land cheap for a few years. It was easy for the large planters to gobble up. By the 1850s, both land and slaves were beyond the reach of most small farmers. The vast majority of them had no hope of ever becoming part of the planter class.

So at the beginning of the Civil War, small farmers, share croppers, and tenant farmers had to be convinced of a lie. The lie was that their interests were the same as the big planters and slave holders of the Confederacy. The planter class represented only around 3 percent of the South's population. And even among the planter class itself, wealth was concentrated in only a few hands. Sixty percent of the slaves were owned by only 17 percent of the slave owners. So as usual, the majority had to be convinced to fight for the wealthy minority.

While the small farmers, tenants, and sharecroppers were fighting the war on the front lines, slaves continued to do the work to generate income for the planters. There were no slaves to work the poor man's fields. Officers came and went still able to supervise their interests during the war, but even the starvation of a poor man's family didn't warrant granting him a pass which he needed to even leave the field.

The class nature of this war, like all wars, was blatant, easy to see for those who cared to look. The wealthy could simply buy themselves out of military service. Some large planters escaped military service by agreeing to provide food for the troops. Most of them reneged on the offer.

Growing cotton was simply more profitable than growing crops. The result was that hunger was a problem from shortly after the beginning of the war until after the end. During most of the war, the Confederate government and the newspapers begged, threatened, and tried to shame planters into devoting less land to cotton and more to food. But the planters largely ignored both popular opinion and the pleas of their own government, desperate as that government was in the middle of a war being fought on behalf of their interests.

As one noted author has written, the Confederacy was not beaten by industrial production or the North. The Confederacy was defeated by "selfish planters, greedy speculators, corrupt officials, unscrupulous whites, and desperate slaves."

In short, the Civil War was just like every other war I know anything about. It was started by the ambitious, benefitted the unscrupulous, and killed the honorable. And just like every other war I know anything about, the class in whose interests the war was being fought squealed like little girls when class disparity was brought up. The Civil War had an impact far more devastating on the poor than on the rich. Officers could come and go as they pleased, and those with expensive rifles could join up for a year instead of three. Officers were paid thirty times more than the common soldier. Often, common soldiers were not paid at all. But when the common soldiers or their families started to complain about inequitable conditions, even the newspapers lectured vociferously about the dangers of "class warfare."

The powerful set up conditions to benefit themselves, set up conditions where they prospered off the exploitation of the less powerful. But when the common people objected, it was called "class warfare."

The result of the blatant class nature of the Civil War in the South was that desertion was a serious problem even as early as a year after Fort Sumter. Margaret Mitchell's husband was said to have remarked on seeing the scene in *Gone with the Wind*, where all the wounded and dying men were laying around the Atlanta rail depot, that if the Confederacy had had that many men, they would have won the war. The truth is that the evacuation of Atlanta was ordered not because there were not enough men to fight, but because there were not enough men *willing* to fight. By 1864, the time of the Battle of Atlanta, the common Confederate soldier had had a belly full of fighting for the planters and simply refused to stand and defend the city. That's something else the "grand lost cause" writers conveniently fail to mention.

The Civil War was the first war in which railroads were a crucial part of military strategy. When the war started, the state was already full of rail track. The Central Railway Company was set up to haul cotton in 1833. It was one of the first chartered railway companies in the country. By the 1860s, half of the quarter of a million bales of cotton that left the region annually were transported by rail. The area around Wilkes Ferry was an important part of the manufacturing capacity of the Confederacy and part of the strategy to keep the South supplied with guns, uniforms, and food by rail.

But even though the railroads were crucial to Confederate strategy, officers did not devote adequate resources to their maintenance. Southern officers, mostly trained at West Point, came out of a military tradition steeped in the movement on the ground of troops, guns, and horses. They failed to fully appreciate and therefore exploit the benefits of rail.

During the war, railroad cars often sat idle simply because of repairs that were never made. There were over three hundred railroad cars sitting on the tracks at the depot in Wilkes Ferry, when the Yankees finally got there. Mismanagement was not the only reason why so many railcars sat on the tracks at Wilkes Ferry. The gage of the railroad tracks that came into Wilkes Ferry from the west and south were one size. The gage of the railroad tracks that ran out of Wilkes Ferry to the north and east were another. This meant that every item on those cars, every bale of cotton, every stick of cut pine, had to be unloaded at Wilkes Ferry and then reloaded onto a different box car for the continuation of its journey. Because of this, Wilkes Ferry was always a bottleneck.

And even though the state was full of railroad track, most of it had been laid hastily by private companies more interested in profit than the quality of the job. Funny how things don't change. The increased traffic on those hastily laid tracks brought on by the war only contributed to their destruction.

Because Wilkes Ferry was such an important hub, it was guarded by an earthen fort. Fort Butler sat high on a hill on the west side of the Catawba overlooking the town and the river. This fort and the rail lines at Wilkes Ferry were the site of a bitter battle, which claimed the lives of Union and Confederate alike. It was fought a week after Lee surrendered at Appomattox.

By the time the actual fighting got to Wilkes Ferry on Easter Sunday of 1865, most of the city's men had already died either in battle or more commonly from wounds and diseases. Almost every available building in Wilkes Ferry had been transformed into a hospital as wounded, dying, and dead Confederate soldiers arrived in railcars. The Confederacy, adding insult to injury, commandeered the churches of the poor and turned them into hospitals. People who lived near the railroad tracks often took in soldiers who couldn't make it as far as a hospital or who couldn't find a bed when they did.

The very old, the very young, and some hospital workers were the only ones left to trek up the hill to Fort Butler to defend Wilkes Ferry when the Yankees came. There was no hope of winning the battle, and every boy and old man who walked up that hill to Fort Butler must have known it. They went anyway, along with the one-legged General Butler, who was wounded at Missionary Ridge in the beginning of the war and gave his life that day in Wilkes Ferry for a Confederacy already defeated.

There are perhaps a hundred sad little graves in the cemetery where my daddy's buried, graves of soldiers, confederate and union, buried together, who died a week after the war was over. One telegram would have made the difference. One telegram would have meant that dozens of young men and old men would have lived lives, told stories, loved, eaten, dreamed. Instead, they became dust in a cemetery thought about, if at all, only by groups of school children and an over-the-hill criminologist—me. When we lived in Wilkes Ferry, I used to go there often to sit among them and keep them company.

The Yankees fired mercilessly on Fort Butler that day, and you can still see the damage from cannonball on the outside walls of the Griggs Mansion at the top of Tenth Street, near the Fort. Dr. Asa Griggs, a surgeon and owner of the house, tended to the dead and dying while his two-story white mansion was taking cannonball fire. When I was growing up, another surgeon, Dr. Booker, lived in the Griggs Mansion. Dr. Booker, who cut off his own finger with a power saw, was a descendent of Dr. Griggs. Another doctor lives in the lovely old restored mansion now, but he is definitely not from Wilkes Ferry. He's a Yankee, and somebody told me he was a psychopath. Bless his heart.

By dusk on that Easter Sunday in 1865, Fort Butler had been taken, and the Yankees moved back to town to burn the depot. They also burned eighteen locomotive engines and 340 freight cars. It was a heartbreaking waste, especially when you consider the fact that the war was already over. But at the time, nobody knew and the North was pursuing a low-tech version of the strategy used by the U.S. to end the Pacific War eighty years later.

Sherman convinced Lincoln that the rebels would continue to fight as long as there was a one-legged man with breath in his body, an apt comment when one considers General Butler in Wilkes Ferry. The war, Sherman argued, had to be taken to the enemy, and it had to be total war. Every farm and plantation, every house, every chicken coop, had to feel the price of the war directly. The only thing that would stop the fighting and prevent thousands of additional deaths was total devastation of the South. It was a kind of atom bomb strategy, designed to bring not only the Confederate army to its knees but the civilian population as well.

What seemed like wanton destruction at Wilkes Ferry was actually part of a well-considered strategy. It was part of the same philosophy that underlay Sherman's devastating march to the sea.

At the beginning of the war, everybody along the Catawba from Wilkes Ferry south feared that the Yankees would come up the river to destroy the manufacturing capability of that part of the South. At the lower end of the river, they laid heavy chains from bank to bank and sank barges to block Yankee gunboats. But the Catawba River was so shallow and unpredictable, Yankee gun boats couldn't even get up it. Even though Lincoln decreed the blockade in 1861, the Yankees never even occupied the port city at the mouth of the river. The Union army sometimes sent small boats north on the river from the port but more for the purpose of harassment than anything else. When the destruction of the South's industrial capacity came, it came not from the river, but overland.

After the Yankees finished burning everything at the Wilkes Ferry depot, they did as everybody else had who ever occupied the region. The Yankees went to the river, this time to seize the bridge.

The Catawba river, always the river, ever-present and running through the lives of generation after generation. I don't need to imagine the muddy deep red color of it. When we lived in Wilkes Ferry, I used to see it every day running through my land. I can still feel its bottom between my toes.

The Poor Folks

All of us in the Catawba River Valley grew up swimming in and boating on the water backed up from the Catawba River. The lake south of Wilkes Ferry formed by the water damned just below the Valley was, and still is, called the "backwater." My family spent most of every summer there, first camping out and then in a small cabin built by my father. All the plumbing in this cabin was reversed, and you had to be careful not to scald yourself to death in the shower. My father was left-handed, as am I, and every time he got his mitts on plumbing, he would do it backward. It was a running joke. "Did Will Lee do the plumbing," someone might ask, "or did you hire somebody?" People would ask to get some indication of how much danger they were in.

It was a lovely little cabin at the end of a slue. The water there was smooth as silk. Few motor boats came up the slue, so it was the perfect place for children to swim and play. I virtually lived in the water every summer for nineteen years. I still feel as at home in the river as I do walking.

My father loved his cabin and the lake. I think he was happiest there, fixing and puttering, building a dock or a boathouse or a bird house, driving his boat while my brother and I skied, clearing land of underbrush, mowing. He rarely stopped when we were there except to sit down for supper.

Usually, we had grilled hamburgers and hot dogs for supper, served with sweet Vidalia onions, dill pickles, catsup, and yellow mustard. Makes my mouth water just thinking about it. Sometimes when we had visitors, we would have steaks from Byron's Market grilled over open flames and potatoes baked in the hot fire ashes. My mother would make one of her green salads with lettuce and green spring onions and luscious, wondrous tomatoes. That was back when you could still get good tomatoes or real tomatoes as I have now come to think of them.

This was before corporate farming took over, drove all the small farmers out of business, and started to breed tomatoes with hide rather than skin so they would ship well. Evidently, part of this selective breeding for a tomato that would resist bruising was a mealy tasteless inside. The tomatoes you can buy today are the kind we would have thrown out years ago.

When we were eating at the backwater, you could buy tomatoes in any grocery store that really were "homegrown." They were not the uniform size and shape of the eunuch tomatoes that now pass for real. Some were enormous, bursting with juice, having interesting sometimes grotesque shapes. Some were tiny and sweet. They each had their own individual character. They were more of a deep orange color than that puny pretend red of today's tomatoes. And they had a yellow tinge around an irregular scar, where the stem had been not that neat symmetrical stem scar of the corporate farm tomato.

Once in the eighties, after real tomatoes had disappeared even in the South, I found myself in Mexico City. I made my then husband stop on the street when I saw some sliced tomatoes being displayed by a street vendor. I could tell just by looking at their insides they were real tomatoes.

"Are you crazy?" Jack asked when I said I wanted to buy some of the tomatoes. "They'll make you sick. They're fertilized with manure from God knows what kind of animals. They may even have human manure on them."

"We'll wash them," I said, dispensing with that problem quickly. "With bottled water."

"You can't wash it off. It seeps through the skin," he said as I eyed the tomatoes covetously.

"I have to have them."

Jack shrugged. "You're going to get sick."

Later, when I put a slice of tomato in my mouth, the taste was so deep and rich I almost cried. I closed my eyes and just sat there, allowing my taste buds to go wild without being distracted by sight or hearing.

'Don't tell me," Jack said caustically. "You're having a religious experience."

"Something very like that," I replied.

I didn't get sick, and writing about the tomatoes makes me want to go to Mexico. I bet they still have good tomatoes. The U.S. is the only country in the world where people would tolerate the cardboard produce we now consume. Other countries have way too much respect for food.

When we were eating at the backwater, you could still buy ten ears of corn for thirty cents and real tomatoes from a black man in a mule drawn wagon who circulated through our neighborhood calling, "Vegetables, fresh vegebles."

After we finished eating at the backwater, we would roast marshmallows over the coals, trying for a browned and crisp but not burned outside and an almost melted inside. We also churned ice cream, cherry, vanilla, and at the first part of the summer, fresh peach.

The children would churn first, and then as the ice cream began to freeze and get hard, we would call the daddies.

"Dad-dee," we would whine as we started to labor with the churn handle.

"What-ee?" my daddy would often answer, imitating the rhythm of our lament, which invariably made us giggle.

After we were full to bursting with good food, we would sit sated and quiet around the glowing embers of the dying fire. Orange sparks would fly up in the air as a log wasted and fell. Lightning bugs made the night twinkle like a sky full of stars, and frogs big enough to have voices that could be mistaken for cows called in chorus.

My father would take a drag from his cigarettes and say, "I wonder what the poor folks are doing tonight?"

We would smile and feel contented.

That was back when my father was still allowed to say things like that. Later on, my mother would have gotten up and stalked off.

"He makes us sound like hicks," my mother once explained after one such walking-off incident.

But when I was still growing up, at the backwater, she would just smile and appear content, a seething caldron of rage bubbling evidently just beneath the surface.

Restoring Tara

I have no idea what happened to Zac Fetner. I would imagine he eventually married Cash Beasley, and they are still partying as well as old fogeys can party. You know after a while, I think you get too old to party and drink. But as Mark Twain said, you have to cultivate your vices when you are young or else you won't have anything to give up when you're old.

Margaret Ann and I graduated from high school in 1969. She went to X-ray technician school and I flitted back and forth between marriages, political activism, psychedelic drugs, and college. We came to live in very separate worlds.

Some years later, after Margaret Ann graduated, she moved back to Wilkes Ferry and got a job at the Cobb Memorial Hospital, a hot bed of melodrama if ever there was one. She lived in one of the small frame houses over near the grammar school for a while. She was not happy.

There was some man or other in there. I don't remember who he was nor how she met him. She was crazy in love with him, but he evidently was not crazy in love with her. She told me, on one of my visits, that she had gone over to the guy's trailer and tried to kill herself.

She didn't go into details. I don't know whether she took a gun to the trailer or downed some pills before she went. Maybe she did both. But somehow, I just couldn't imagine Margaret Ann with a gun. She grew up in a house where her father periodically chased different members of the family around with a loaded gun so I would bet money it was pills. In the end, it doesn't really matter.

I didn't ask too many questions when she told me the story. Maybe I didn't want to know. Probably I was just way too caught up in my own life. But that doesn't make much sense. I have always wanted to know everything, I mean everything when it came to the details of life. I can't imagine myself leaving that story alone.

But perhaps I didn't ask more because Margaret Ann had a way of signaling when she had said all she intended to say on a subject. I knew her so well, I would have recognized the signs. Her thin lips would have clamped down tight, and her down turned little mouth would have hardened, and after that, you would have had to use torture to get anything more out of her. I think that's what she did about the suicide.

A year or so after the story of the attempted suicide, I came back to Wilkes Ferry to find Margaret Ann somewhat happier and still working at the hospital. She was taking care of the two children of a new doctor who had moved to town, Wilkie Dunn.

When we were growing up in Wilkes Ferry, there just weren't that many doctors in town. There was Dr. McFadden, the Santa Clause-looking pediatrician who made house calls and did tricks with half dollars like pulling them out of your ears. He was the one who came and watched over me as I lay unconscious on a small bed in the back room of our house for several days after I was thrown from my horse. There was also the grouchy, crusty old Dr. Griggs, the town surgeon. And there was Dr. Wainwright, Lauren's father, the one doctor in town who saw black patients as well as white and about whom dark rumors circulated about a medical school scandal and a revoked license. Dr. Wainwright also shared office space with a chiropractor, which was considered at the time, little better than sharing office space with a witch doctor. Enough has already been said about Dr. Fallon.

All these doctors were well established men. They had families, they went to church, and most of them had a family history in the area if not actually in Wilkes Ferry. It was only after the Cobb Manufacturing Company merged with a Yankee company that new doctors started coming into the area. This was also around the time doctors started to change from being general practitioners to specialists. Now you have to go to a different doctor for each toenail you have a problem with. "Oh no, I'm not a little toe doctor. I'm a big toe doctor. Let me refer you. Money, please."

There are now twenty doctors in the Wilkes Ferry for every one doctor we had in the fifties. And I am not at all convinced the medical care is one whit better.

Along with the massive increase in the number of doctors was another change. The doctors who came into Wilkes Ferry after the merger were not always stable family men. The hospital recruited doctors, and at one time, they would have shot themselves before they asked into the Valley a man whose family relations were even questionable. Something changed that though, and doctors with loose morals suddenly took up residence in Wilkes Ferry and the Valley. They became one of the primary avenues of social mobility for women. I started to say single women, but even married women like Margaret Ann's older sister, Frankie, were not immune to the doctor attraction. These women were all over the doctors no matter what they looked or acted like.

There were really no other readily available ways to get rich in the Valley, especially ones that didn't require brains or chipping your nails. But if you could nab a doctor, you had your meal ticket and a whole lot more.

The local demand for doctors, of course, did not escape the attention of the doctors themselves. The single ones had the pick of the female crop, and as long as they remained single, women would even double team as did Frankie, providing sexual favors, casseroles, house cleaning, and God only knows what else.

The married doctors had to be a little more discreet if they cared at all about their reputations or their future divorce settlements, which some did not. But they could easily exchange a shop-worn, child-bearing wife model for a new sleek, tanned, fresh-from-the-gym sex goddess. She might be a little rednecky around the edges and have a vocabulary full of double negatives, but not many of them seemed to care. They came into Wilkes Ferry and just wallowed in sexual license like pigs in shit. I have no idea whether Wilkie Dunn, whose children Margaret Ann took under her wing, was one of these pigs, but I have no reason to suspect he was not.

One year, when I got in touch with Margaret Ann, she told me she was at the Dunn's house and was tied down with two young children. I agreed to visit her there. Wilkie Dunn had bought an enormous house on the west side of Wilkes Ferry a little upriver from downtown. I had never been inside the house. I had only seen it a few times from the outside when I was a child. The house was originally built by Mr. Freeman Hopewell's father when the Cobb Mills were just beginning to make real money.

The house was larger than any house I had ever seen at the time. But by the fifties, it was so run-down it looked like a haunted house, and you couldn't even see it from the street. I don't know how many acres surrounded Hopewell House, but it was set back from the river road on one of the hills near Fort Butler. The house overlooked both the river and the town. When Mr. Hopewell, Sr., first built the house, there were formal gardens all around it. But by the fifties, it was so overgrown with bushes and threes and kudzu, you couldn't even see the massive roof.

Mr. Freeman Hopewell left the house to his son, Mr. Smith Hopewell, and when Mr. Smith's daughter Jewel married, Mr. Smith and his wife built a brand-new rectangular fifties modern home right on the river, down the hill from Hopewell House. Jewel and her husband moved into the big house but didn't do a thing to it or the grounds. I don't know why. We used to play with her children in the wild brush surrounding the house during the summer. But as I said, I never went inside the house nor even very near it on more than one or two occasions. There was something scary and foreboding and unfriendly about the house.

Hopewell House was only a half mile from the Patterson's house, Margaret Ann's parent's little brick house. The Hopewells didn't live in the house year-round. Margaret Ann and I played with Robbie, Miss Jewel's son, when he visited during the summer.

By the time Wilkie Dunn bought the old Hopewell mansion, it was falling down. It was said that he spent over two hundred thousand dollars renovating it, and this was in the late seventies.

I was staggered that day when I drove up the winding driveway to see Margaret Ann and made the turn that brought the house into view. It looked like a building site with scaffolding on the front and lumber piled everywhere in the red dirt, but the house was breathtaking, much more grand than I remembered. They had cut back the bushes and undergrowth around the house, but the hill itself was thick with forty years of brush; it hid completely the transformation going on at the house. It was as if Dr. Dunn were keeping the renovation a secret.

The front of the house was completely closed off, so I walked around to the back. Margaret Ann was cloistered in a den just inside the back door with two children, a window air conditioner, and a television set. She let me in with a white-haired, wide-eyed toddler balanced carelessly on her hip. A little girl was on a quilt on the floor, the pieces of a puzzle spread out all around her.

Margaret Ann let me in and sank gratefully back onto a worn brown sofa, obviously exhausted. I moved some magazines—*Field and Stream*, *Fox and Hounds*, and *Architectural Digest*—off an old brown leather stuffed chair and sat down. The proud house had been gutted on the inside by somebody, somebody without a shred of taste. The room where we were sitting, although large, had only three, south-facing windows on one wall. Some fool had put dark fake wood paneling on the other walls covering up the windows of the west side. They had also installed cheap laminate cabinets and bookshelves. The sofa and chair were worn and brown as was the carpet. The whole room felt brown, brown, brown, dark, and depressing. The television sat on a metal rolling stand that looked like something retrieved from a trash heap.

"This is all Wilkie's old med school and internship stuff," Margaret Ann said tiredly, following my eyes around the room. "He's going to buy all new furniture when the house is finished."

I wondered why Margaret Ann was explaining this as if what Wilkie Dunn did about his furniture was any of my concern or hers for that matter.

But it didn't take more than a few minutes to see that there was something odd about the way she was situated in that house, something that let me know this was more than a babysitting job. First, there was the way she was holding the little boy. Babysitters didn't hold kids with that kind of slovenly disregard or with that particular kind of exhaustion. Only mothers looked like that, mothers who had been left alone with small children so long they are virtually mindless with the numbing routine of cereal and baths and baby talk.

"Are you taking care of them full time?" I asked, looking over at the little girl who was contentedly making herself busy with her puzzle. She glanced at me and then back down.

Margaret Ann shifted Beau, short for Beauregard, the little boy, to her knees, bouncing him. "Pretty much. But you know, Wilkie's so busy at the hospital and he's always on call. Poor thing."

Margaret Ann's accent seemed to have changed. It sounded as if it had a little more drawl, but perhaps I was imagining it. And there was something a tad proprietary in the way she was talking about "Wilkie." Her response left more than a few questions unanswered. Always on call? How did she know? Did that mean she slept at the house? Did it mean she was living at the house?

"Are you still working?" I asked, thinking that the little girl was abnormally quiet and well behaved for an American child.

"Um hum," Margaret Ann said looking into Beau's darting eyes. "But Wilkie's gotten them to cut way back on my hours."

So you can take care of his kids, I thought but didn't say.

"He's paying my rent for the house," Margaret Ann continued referring to the little frame house over near the elementary school. "And I eat over here all the time. I do the cooking. So I have virtually no expenses."

And no life, I thought. "And that's working out all right?" I said carefully.

"Seems to be," she said nonchalantly.

I wasn't at all sure where to go with this conversation. Margaret Ann wasn't offering coffee or ice water, a drink or (something I have never seen in Wilkes Ferry) a glass of wine. I sensed that I was only there for a short stay. I was having to pull information out of her. She seemed as if she had nothing to say. I felt as if even though she had invited me, I was intruding. We were not going to lapse into girlhood confidences. That was obvious.

"So where's this doctor, Wilkie, from?" I asked.

"He grew up in Heard," Margaret Ann said, laughing slightly and looking over at me. "Isn't that funny? If there's anywhere in the state that's more in the middle of nowhere than Wilkes Ferry, it's Heard. Grew up on a farm."

"So how did he get to medical school?"

Beau was flailing with his arms and legs, throwing himself tiredly but determinedly from side to side in Margaret Ann's hands. There was a long string of spit drooling from his mouth. It crossed my mind for the thousandth time how glad I was I didn't have children.

"Said he always wanted to go. Got scholarships and worked his way through."

"That's admirable," I said. I disliked doctors in general. Most of them were spoiled brats from families wealthy enough to put them through all the years of schooling a medical degree took. They never grew up.

"He had such a bad time," Margaret Ann was saying. "He's never had a life. All he's ever done is work."

I wasn't sure I was prepared to feel all that sorry for someone who was probably making $400,000 annually a few years out of school.

"This is the first house he's ever had," Margaret Ann added, looking around absently.

Suddenly, the pieces started falling together in my mind, like the puzzle the little girl was playing with on the floor.

Little Southern backwoods farm boy gets through medical school, waiting tables and working as a janitor. The minute he gets his first appointment, he buys the largest old Southern mansion he can find and sets about restoring Tara. I looked over at the *Hunt and Hound* magazine, the *Field and Stream*, the *Architectural Digest*. Wilkie Dunn was getting ready to play the planter gentleman. How predictable. He probably had foxhounds in the backyard. I wondered just where Margaret Ann fit into the picture. She certainly was not ever going to be the elegant Southern lady. Maybe she was destined to become the governess? But she didn't even speak Spanish, much less French. Maybe she was going to be a white Aunt Jemima, cooking for the family. Who knew what was going on in the probably perverted mind of Wilkie Dunn. Who in God's name was named Wilkie anyway? Maybe he had changed it, dismissing Ashley as too obvious and Rhett as inviting an unfavorable comparison.

"So where did the children come from?" I asked.

"Stacey," Margaret Ann said addressing the little girl, "why don't you go up to your room and read for a little while?"

Stacey looked up at Margaret Ann and then over at me. I got the impression she knew exactly why this suggestion was being made. But she left her puzzle without a word, docile as ever. This kid was way too obedient.

"Wilkie got married in medical school to one of the nurses in the hospital," Margaret Ann said quietly, watching the door where the little girl had disappeared. "She couldn't have children. She finally talked him into adopting when they moved here."

"Oh, so these children are adopted?" I said.

"Yes," she answered.

"Do they know?"

"Stacey does."

"The little girl?" I asked.

Margaret Ann nodded.

"So where's the wife?" I said, looking around for evidence of a wifely influence.

"She died," Margaret Ann said.

"Died?" I said, surprised.

Margaret Ann nodded her head. "Not long after they moved here."

"How awful," I said, looking around me and thinking about the two children coming to this construction site with one strange mother then losing her and having to adjust to Margaret Ann. "How long has she been dead?" I asked.

"Two months," Margaret Ann said, bouncing Beau.

Two months? The man's wife had been dead for two months, and he already had Margaret Ann installed in his house full time, taking care of his children, virtually living in his house. He'd already had her hours cut back at the hospital so she could do it. Pretty convenient little setup.

"What did she die of?" I asked idly, trying to think of something to say to hide my astonishment.

"The flu," Margaret Ann answered without missing a beat, as if she had been waiting for the question.

"The flu," I said. "How can somebody die of the fucking flu? This isn't the 1800s."

Margaret Ann cast a wide-eyed look my way that said, "Don't cuss in front of the children."

Americans have the worst behaved children in the world (rivaling only the children of the Mexican upper class). And it's because Americans (and the Mexican upper class, now that I think of it) operate under the assumption that the entire world is supposed to revolve around their children. You are expected to watch every word that comes out of your mouth just because there are children present. This is especially ridiculous in this day and age when most four year olds have heard not only curse words but seen the worst violence imaginable on the television. I turned back to Margaret Ann.

"I'm sorry," I said, "but how can you die of the flu when your husband's a doctor?" As soon as the question was out of my mouth, I knew I shouldn't have said it. It was a feeling I was well accustomed to.

Margaret Ann didn't respond at first, and then she just shrugged her shoulders. "She got really sick," she said simply. "And died of complications." There was a pause. "She was here, in this house," Margaret Ann added unnecessarily. Margaret Ann was the one with a morbid side.

"Here?" I wanted to clamp my hand over my mouth. "She wasn't even in the hospital?"

"No," Margaret Ann said. "She was here." Margaret Ann picked up Beau and started for the door. "I'm going to try to put him down," she said.

I was left sitting in the brown leather chair, thinking that it all was just too much. A wife who could never bear the offspring of what appeared to be a wildly egotistical man conveniently out of the way because of the flu. She dies of the flu in the house of a doctor who didn't even see that her condition was serious enough to take her to the hospital.

I shook my head. *Wilkes Ferry was a great place to get rid of your wife*, I thought. I had never heard of a murder investigation in Wilkes Ferry. The town should use this fact on their advertising for tourists: "Come to Wilkes Ferry, the best place in Georgia to kill your wife. In and out in six weeks. No questions asked." But maybe I was just jaded and prone to see stories where no stories existed.

Tellin' on Miss Mary Francis

Miss Mary Francis Cobb had alabaster white skin so thin and delicate you could see the veins in her temples. She had long elegant fingers. And she had the palest blue eyes, robin's egg blue eyes. She dressed like she'd just walked off a magazine cover. In all the years we were growing up, I never saw her with a hair out of place.

But she never married. That was strange in a small Georgia town in the fifties. The women who didn't get married were women like Miss Lottie, the church secretary, born with a hump and a withered leg. They were women who had something wrong with them. But there didn't seem to be anything wrong with Miss Mary Francis, at least nothing we could see.

Miss Mary Francis lived in a huge old Southern mansion, complete with immense white columns all along the front porch. As far as I was concerned, every detail of her life and that house was perfect.

And it wasn't as if she was an outcast or a hermit. She had friends and family. In fact, she lived in a town virtually controlled by her family.

So even though we sometimes wondered, we never knew why Miss Mary Francis didn't get married until we asked Pearl.

After that, everything that had seemed so perfect started to look just a little skewed. I started remembering things that had happened in that house, things I hadn't thought much about before.

I could identify something hushed and whispering about the house. As if amid all the perfection, old souls and unhappy stories remained there. Slowly, it dawned on me that the house was something like a very formal and expensive funeral home, as if the quiet was desperately necessary to keep from disturbing the demons.

I remembered how the little "gurls" who took piano lessons at Miss Mary Francis's house were met at the glass-windowed front doors at exactly the appointed time and ushered directly into what I suppose had been, at one time, a ballroom. It had become the home of two baby grand pianos, which fit without any discomfort along with the rest of the furniture.

At the end of this room was a glassed-in sun porch into which light filtered onto old, fine white wicker furniture and palms.

French doors opened off the ballroom to a dining room, but we weren't allowed to go in there, except when we were giving formal recitals and our parents were seated there in rows of folded chairs. The sunroom, was likewise off-limits except during recitals when we were seated there in rows of chairs, trying to be still until our turn to play.

In fact, after Pearl told us, it occurred to me that the little "gurls" were escorted very carefully every time we were in Miss Mary Francis's house, and we were never allowed to stray one footstep away from the path that led directly from the door to the pianos. I don't even remember ever going to the bathroom in that house.

As I was scooted through the main foyer and to the right, through the French doors to the piano room, I would sometimes glance to the left, on the other side of the hallway, and try to see through the French doors that led to all the rooms on the left side of the house. But that side of the house was shrouded with dark opaque curtains.

The right side of the house had only filmy sheers on all the doors and windows but not on the left. I don't know why I didn't figure it out, but it was like there was something hidden there. We found out there was.

I would also, when Miss Mary Francis was distracted, take a peep up the massive wooden staircase at the back of the central hall, which seemed to grow darker and darker and cooler and cooler as it ascended, sweeping up in a curve to the second floor.

I never knew what was up there. I never even knew where Miss Mary Francis's room was or where she slept. Those were the sorts of questions you just didn't ask, not Miss Mary Francis.

But you could ask Pearl.

I don't remember that Margaret Ann and I ever asked Pearl directly why Miss Mary Francis never got married. I think it just came up in the idle conversation of two twelve year olds, wiling away a sultry summer afternoon drinking lemonade at the kitchen table.

Pearl was standing at the sink cutting the kernels off corncobs.

"Miss Mary Francis got her reasons for not marrin'," Pearl said suddenly.

My eyes and Margaret Ann's locked across the table.

"What reasons?" Margaret Ann said quickly like a cat stuffing a bird into its mouth.

But Pearl just stood there, scraping the juice off the naked cobs with the back of a knife.

Margaret Ann and I scrambled up from the table and ran to the sink. Each of us grabbed an arm, and we dragged Pearl back to the table.

When Pearl sat down and started drying her hands on her apron, we knew she was going to give. Margaret Ann and I stared hungrily. We had been wanting to know this for years.

Pearl looked us straight in the eye. First Margaret Ann then me.

"Now," she said seriously. "I don' want you to be tellin' you mammas I tol' you 'bout Miss Mary Francis," she said, pointing her finger at each of us.

"We won't," we promised eagerly.

Pearl turned her head toward me. "Specially not Miss Sarah Ward. Ummmmmmmmmmmmmmmmmm, she'd cut my lips off if she knowed I's tellin' this on Miss Mary Francis."

"Telling what on Miss Mary Francis?" Margaret Ann whined impatiently.

Pearl turned her head in Margaret Ann's direction. "I'm gettin' to that. You jes be patient, child. Y'all wanna hear this story or not?"

Margaret Ann and I fell silent. We were, as usual, entirely in Pearl's hands. We held our breath, hoping she wouldn't change her mind.

Pearl leaned back in her chair and folded her arms, resting them on her rather ample belly.

"Well . . . ," she began. "Ole Mz. Cobb, Miss Mary Francis and Miss Sister mother, died when they was just little gurls. You know Miss Sister, don't you, child?" she asked Margaret Ann.

Margaret Ann nodded. "She was our Sunday-school teacher."

Miss Sister was Miss Mary Francis's younger sister and just as beautiful as Miss Mary Francis, only instead of being tall, willowy, and elegant, she was short and petite, with red hair and the figure of an eighteen year old. Jeeze and the clothes she wore were out of this world.

"Well," Pearl continued, "after Mz. Cobb died, ole Mr. Cobb decided Miss Mary Francis was gonna take her place."

"Take her place?" I said. "What do you mean?"

Pearl looked at me carefully. She puckered up her lips up as if she was trying to calculate something. "He put Miss Mary Francis in charge of everything. And her jes a little gurl, younger than y'all. From the day her mamma died, she was put to keeping all the household accounts, planning all the meals, planning the shopping, and managing all them servants."

"Miss Mary Francis had servants?" I asked, surprised.

"Oh Lord, honey, yes," Pearl said. "You don' think she ran that big old house all by herself, do you?"

I had never really thought about it. I couldn't even imagine anybody else being in that house.

"Why Miss Mary Francis?" Margaret Ann asked. "Why not Miss Sister?"

"Because she was the oldest, nitwit," I said. Margaret Ann flashed me a nasty look across the table.

"Sound to me like you two wants to fight not listen to a story tellin'."

"No, no," we protested, grabbing at Pearl's arms, petting and cooing at her. "Please tell us, Pearl. We'll be quiet." And she did.

Pearl tilted her head back and sized up our seriousness. When she seemed satisfied at our commitment, she started again.

"The Cobbs had servants, and from what I hear tell, Miss Mary Francis was fair to 'em and paid 'em a decent wage even though she weren't nothing but a little gurl when she took to running that house for her father.

"But for all them years when they was growing up, her and Miss Sister, Miss Mary Francis managed that whole big old house and took care of Mr. Cobb. And he waren't no easy man to take care of."

"Why?" I asked.

"Cause he was a mean man, a unhappy man, didn't have no consideration for nobody."

"Not even Miss Mary Francis?" Margaret Ann asked.

"Specially not for Miss Mary Francis. He order Miss Mary Francis around and talk ugly to her all the time. And he was always telling her how homely and plain she was."

"Miss Mary Francis?" I asked in amazement.

Pearl nodded her head. "See ole Mr. Cobb, he had made his mind up that Miss Mary Francis was gonna take care of him for the rest of his life and run his house and take his wife's place. He didn't want Miss Mary Francis goin' nowhere."

"So he told her she was ugly?" Margaret Ann said, staring off, letting the full seriousness of this sink in.

"That's right. Long as she thought she was ugly, she wasn't goin' nowhere. Miss Sister, now, she was the bell of the ball. There was all the time young men over there, suitors. She went to dances and out on dates but not Miss Mary Francis. She stayed right here with her daddy."

"Why did she believe him when he told her she was ugly?" I asked. "Miss Mary Francis is beautiful."

Pearl shook her head. "I knows that, and you knows that, and Miss Margaret Ann here knows that, the whole town knows that, but not Miss Mary Francis."

"How could she not know?" I continued.

"Chile', the mind a strange thing. The mind can make you see a devil in the mirror if it want to. The mind can make you do all kind of things, specially if somebody else got a hole't of it."

"And Daddy Cobb had hold of hers."

"Yes, ma'am. That old man made sure he had his fingers wrapped tight around Miss Mary Francis's mind. Squeezing all the time. He was a tellin' her no man would ever want her, she so plain an' tall an' washed out. Then he squeeze some more, tightenin' them crooked fingers round her mind. He'd tell her any man act like he wanted her was jes after her money, and he'as a lying to her. And then, he take them crippled hands with them yellow nails and be a squeezing tighter. He'd tell her if she went out with one of 'em, it'd be like making a fool out of herself, for all the town to see, an' makin' a fool out a him."

"That wasn't nice at all," Lauren said. I looked over at her and rolled my eyes.

"You right chile'." Pearl continued, "It was a evil, selfish thing to do to a young gurl, but he done it. And he done it for hisself, his own selfish, sorry self." Pearl fell silent, and Margaret Ann and I sat imagining.

Suddenly, Margaret Ann looked at Pearl. "Well?"

Pearl started laughing. "I thought you two done fell into a spell."

"No, no." We laughed. "What happened?"

"Well, Miss Mary Francis took care of her daddy for years and years, and then Miss Sister finally got herself married to one of the finest, best lookin' men in Wilkes Ferry, one of the furst families in Wilkes Ferry, Mr. Jim, and she and Mr. Jim built a big, fine, spankin' brand-new house just behind the old house where Miss Mary Francis was taking care of the ole' man." Pearl paused. "Then something happened that change Miss Mary Francis entire life."

"What was that?" We both asked, chomping at the bit.

"The ole' man got sick, got real sick, and Miss Mary Francis had to take care of him. And then weren't too long before he had a bad stroke, and Miss Mary Francis had to do everything for him. Everything." Pearl turned her eyes on us. "You knows what I mean?"

"Ugggggggggggghhhhhhhhhhhh," Margaret Ann and I groaned. "Gross."

"And after a while, Miss Mary Francis wouldn't let nobody else take care of him. And one by one, over time of about a year, Miss Mary Francis let the servants go. She paid 'em enough money to get 'em through so's they could get another job, and Miss Sister and Mr. Jim took some of 'em in, but Miss Mary Francis got shed of 'em all."

"God, that's really weird," I said.

Pearl pressed her lips together. "Don't you be taking the Lord's name," she said.

Margaret Ann flashed an impish smile at me across the table.

"I'm sorry," I said.

Pearl nodded. "But it was strange," she added. Then she leaned forward a little. "And . . . it got stranger."

"How?" Margaret Ann almost whispered.

"Well, time pass and time pass, and Miss Mary Francis was a doin' everything for the ole man. Then she wouldn't let Mr. Jim and Miss Sister see him, said he were too sick. And then time pass and time pass, and Mr. Jim and Miss Sister got worried and they called the doctor. Called old Doctor Fallon."

"And?" Margaret Ann prompted.

"And Miss Mary Francis wouldn't let him in the door."

"What happened then?" I asked.

"Everybody was worried, but Miss Mary Francis'd taken care of the old goat for so long, they just figured she was tired and overwrought. Thought it was her nerves. So they jes let it go. Well, then time pass, and Miss Sister and Mr. Jim start to think they was a'smelling somethin' powerful around that house. And people walking by on the street started a talkin' about the smell.

"And you know it embarrass Mr. Jim and Miss Sister bad, so one day, when they couldn't tolerate the talkin' no more, Mr. Jim went over there and he tried to get in the house. Miss Mary Francis wouldn't even come to the door, so Mr. Jim, he called the sheriff and they broked the front door down."

"How do you know all this?" Margaret Ann exclaimed suddenly breaking herself free of the spell Pearl was so easily casting over us.

Pearl leaned forward again, her eyes getting big and round. "'Cause I was there, Miss Priss. I happen to be walkin' by just at the minute when they broke that door down. Jes about everybody in town was there by then."

"And what did Miss Mary Francis do?" Margaret Ann asked.

Pearl shook her head in an ominous way. "Oh, chile', it weren't a pretty picture. Miss Mary Francis was a'howling and a'screaming at Mr. Jim and wouldn't let him go up the stairs to the second floor. I could see her inside holding on to the stair railing while Mr. Jim tried to push her out of the way and her just a screaming like she was fixin' to die . . . Well, finally, Mr. Jim and the sheriff pushed by her and went on up the stairs."

"And the old goat was dead," I said, anticipating the end of the story.

Pearl looked at me and narrowed her eyes. "Honey, he weren't dead. He'd done been dead. That ole man had been dead for two weeks and this was summertime."

Margaret Ann and I sat at her kitchen table, two twelve year olds mesmerized by a story Pearl was telling us.

"Well, after Mr. Jim and the sheriff broke the door down and fought off Miss Mary Francis to get upstairs, they found him. Mr. Jim and the sheriff come runnin' out, and Mr. Jim, he threw up on the grass right outside the house in front of all them people. I never thought I'd see nothing like it in my life. Specially not involvin' no Cobbs or no Hughleys."

"Then what happened?" Margaret Ann asked.

"They call the mortical, and he come with the black hearst, and they back it up to the front door, and then they all went inside the house. They wrapped that smelly ole' man up in a sheet and started a'bringin' him down the stairs, but Miss Mary Francis was a'holding onto him and trying to keep 'em from taking him out of the house. Oh, and chile' you could smell that smell of death. Ain't nothing like it in this world. And Miss Mary Francis was a'wailing and crying and tryin' to hole on to that body like she was a mad woman at a colored funeral. And . . ." A look of horror came over Pearl's face, and she put her hand over her mouth. Margaret Ann and I hardly breathed.

"What?" Margaret Ann asked. "What is it?"

"Lord, chile', they was a carrying that rotted old man out, wrapped in a sheet, and Miss Mary Francis was grabbing at him, and Mr. Jim was stickin' his arm out, trying to hold on to the stretcher and a fighting her off . . ." Pearl stopped.

"What? What?" Margaret Ann gasped.

"Honey, Miss Mary Francis grabbed at that stretcher and made Mr. Jim drop one of the handles, an' that old mad come a'rolling off that stretcher an out a that sheet and lay there in the middle of the front yard, nekked as a jailbird. He was a'laying there with everything God give him, shriveled up and facing the sun."

"Ohhhhhhhhhhhhh, barf . . . ," Margaret Ann wailed.

"He had sores all over his body, bed sores that had gone to poison and was filled with pus."

"Oh my God," I said, but Pearl ignored the blasphemy. She was there, in that front yard, staring down at those bed sores.

"And the Lord God Almighty is my witness, the mortical stepped up to the body and leaned down to roll him over and, Jesus help me, if a maggot didn't crawled out of his eye."

"Aghhhhhhhhhhhhhhhhhhhhhhhhhhhhhhhhhhhhhhhhhhhhh," Margaret Ann and I screamed, covering our eyes and mouths. "Oh, Pearl, no more, no more."

But Pearl wasn't through.

"I didn't 'spect to see no white folks act like that, and I sure didn't 'spect no Cobb in it. And my God, I ain't never smelled nothing like that in my life. Mus' be what hell smell like."

Margaret Ann shivered. "Ohhhhhhhh, Pearl."

"What about Miss Mary Francis?" I asked softly.

Pearl looked down like she might cry.

"Miss Mary Francis just stood there and stared at him. Well, everybody just stared at him. What else could you do? But didn't nobody move, 'cept Miss Sister. She went into a faint. Jes' fainted dead away. I got to tell you, I felt like having a fainting spell myself. I ain't never seen nothin' like that before or since.

"Finally, the mortical, he threw a sheet back over the ole man, and it were like everbody started to move again. Miss Mary Francis gave her daddy one last look and, chil', it were such a mean look I thought she might just spit on him. But she turned and went back in the house. She went upstairs and she didn't come out."

"That day?" I asked.

Pearl shook her head.

"She didn't go to the funeral?" Margaret Ann asked.

"Honey," Pearl replied. "She didn't go to the funeral, and she didn't come out of that house for over a year. She didn't have noting to do with nobody. Folks said she sat up there in his room, rockin' and a'starin and didn't hardly do nothing but feed herself some of the time.

"Miss Sister and Mr. Jim took food over there every night and left it outside the door. Sometimes she'd eat it, but most times, when they sent the girl back for it in the morning, it'd all be there, nothin' gone."

"How long did Miss Mary Francis stay in the house after her father died?" I asked.

"Long time, honey," Pearl replied. "Not for years after Mr. Jim and the sheriff broke down the front door and fought Miss Mary Francis to take that stinking old man out of the house. But little bit at the time, she started to eat and dress herself and bathe . . ."

"You mean Miss Mary Francis didn't bathe all that time?" I said astounded at the very thought of it.

"Not for a long time after her daddy died. Folks said she look terrible bad, hair all stringy and fingernails long and dirty."

"I cannot imagine it," Margaret Ann said.

"I can't either," I joined in.

"Did you see her?" Margaret Ann asked.

"No, chile', but they tole' me."

"Who told you?" Margaret Ann asked suspicious again.

"People that went inside the house to clean up and bathe Miss Mary Francis, when she'd let 'em."

"So," Margaret Ann continued, "how did it end? How did she get out of it and start teaching us piano lessons?"

"Why did she start teaching us piano lessons?" I suddenly thought to ask. "Why didn't she just take all that money and go away, have a life finally after taking care of her daddy for all those years."

"It's that mind, chile', that mind. A body get a hold a your mind, that grip don't let go, even when nothin' but skeleton fingers still a'holding it."

"Uhhhhhhh, Pearl, you're so creepy," Margaret Ann said. "This is making me scared."

"Makes you scared," Pearl said. "That's why I'm a telling you. That's what stories is for. To make you sit up and pay attention. You got to be careful all your life. You got to watch and ask God to watch with you, to keep them fingers from around your soul. See folks think that they only got to be afraid of the devil. That it's only the devil can get a hold of you and squeeze you and make you mind like one of them crazy mirrors in the county fair, but sometimes people, they might as well be the devil, they so mean."

Margaret Ann looked at Pearl wide-eyed. "But how do you know? I mean, which people?"

Pearl gazed at her steadily. "You just got to watch honey, like a fox watch, like a cat watch, wid your ears shunt forward and your whiskers a' tremblin' with every whisper of the wind."

Margaret Ann and I both sighed deeply. I was thinking about the enormity of this task and the unimaginable evil that must be at work in the world.

I wondered if there was anybody trying to curl their fingers around my soul, and I wasn't at all sure that I would know it if there were. I wished I had Pearl around all the time.

"Besides," Pearl was saying, "there weren't no money."

I sat up straight and looked at Pearl in surprise. "No money?"

Pearl shook her head. "Nothin' 'cept the house."

"Where did it all go?" Margaret Ann asked.

Pearl looked at us in satisfaction. "Now that's another story entirely."

Get Rid of the Baby

Carolee Linley was beautiful. My mother said so often. Carolee's dark eyes gave her an Asian, slightly exotic look that was added to by her long straight black hair, curled gently under at the ends, and her bangs. Mothers in the fifties didn't wear bangs, or long straight hair.

My parents and the Linleys sometimes went out together, but more often, they took all the children and carried us to the backwater. The Linleys had a cabin on the water near ours and two children the same ages as Drew and I. We would all spend weekends together, going back and forth by boat and car from one cabin to the other for meals and afternoons.

It always seemed to me at the time that the two couples enjoyed each other, but Mother, in the last few years of her life, talked about how she hated spending every weekend at the backwater with the Linleys. That she spent weekends at the backwater with the Linleys was, of course, Daddy's fault, as was almost every other thing in her life including her weight. The rest was my fault.

She told me once, in the year before she died, that she had never wanted children. "It was your father that wanted children," she said, and I remembered what was, and I guess still is, a funny photograph taken of her and my Aunt Karen. The two women are sitting together in rocking chairs, each of them holding their babies. The year was 1951. Karen, my uncle's German bride, looked so happy. She was smiling at the camera, proud of her son. Mother, however, looked miserable, like she was standing before a firing line waiting to be shot. You could tell she just wanted whoever it was, probably my father, to get finished with the photograph so she could get rid of the baby (me) and do something else. I think it was a sentiment she maintained most of her life.

After I moved back to Wilkes Ferry, mother talked about those weekends with the Linleys at the backwater in much the same way she talked about going to my grandmother DeeMama's house every Sunday for lunch. Mother had a little story she used to tell about this. She told the story in much the same way every time, as if she had rehearsed it in her head, which she probably had.

"We used to go down to Mrs. McPherson's every Sunday," she would say petulantly and with distaste. "Then I just put my foot down and said I was not going to do it anymore. I was just not going to do it." These lines were always delivered in a smug, self-congratulatory tone of voice, as if Mother was announcing a blow struck in behalf of justice and righteousness. She obviously expected some adulation for the action of having stopped the weekly Sunday dinners. I am sure for years I dutifully provided that adulation. After all, I was well trained to tap dance to my mother's tune.

When I was around forty-five, however, I began to see my mother a little more clearly. My husband at the time told me once he read a study that indicated that when a person was around sixty-five, they stopped caring what their parents thought of them.

"They stop caring because their parents are dead," I remarked.

Anyway, Mother, with her exquisitely tuned antennae, sensed that I was beginning to catch on to her. She stopped telling all of the "Sunday dinner at DeeMama's" story. She started to realize that I considered the story to be yet another implicit criticism of my father, which it was.

The general meaning of the story was that my overbearing and thoughtless father dragged the entire family to his horrible, trashy mother's house for dinner every Sunday until Mother courageously stood up and saved us all from the oppressive obligation.

Mother started to realize, when she started to tell this tawdry little story, that I simply was not going to respond. But she could not seem to stop herself from trying it on every now and then anyway, just to see if I had weakened.

These little vignettes about Sunday dinner at DeeMama's and weekends with the Linleys and a million other similar stories were part of the half-century campaign my mother conducted against my father. I found out, purely by accident, that this has a name—Parental Alienation Syndrome. The syndrome, however, is usually used to describe the actions of one parent who is already divorced from but who works tirelessly to turn the children against the other parent. Mother, however, did not even have the decency to divorce Daddy; she just inserted herself probably from the day Drew was born, between Daddy and his children, and tried to make them hate him. The campaign succeeded surprisingly well. To this day, my brother still hates my father although he would never admit it. He has probably constructed some story that pleases him and allows him to think well of himself, about how Daddy mistreated him. Since I have spent very little time around my brother, I don't know the details of this story. I'm sure it's interesting. I only heard snippets of it when he once visited me. It was the only time in his life he did visit me, and I suggested that visit. For work reasons, Drew was coming to Atlanta. I suggested that he fly to Florida and drive up to Wilkes Ferry with my husband and I. To my surprise, he did.

When we were in the car driving up to Wilkes Ferry, Drew trotted out the little resentment stories he had been harboring for fifty years. One of Drew's complaints involved some incident that had happened when he was a boy scout. Some boy lost his swimming trunks in the water and got out naked, and my father and the other fathers around laughed at this. The obvious intent of harboring this story was to illustrate my father's coarse and crude sense of humor and low-class behavior.

Another story involved a jacket that my brother had wanted when he was a teenager. I remember that jacket. They were all the fashion at the time. They were made out of some insulated material like foam rubber, but they were jackets with ribbed material at the cuffs and the waist and the collar. Anyway, my brother wanted one so badly, and my parents took him to Atlanta to Rich's and had him close his eyes to try on the jacket. His version of this story was that having him close his eyes and trying it on ruined the entire thing. According to him, they ruined the surprise and pleasure he might have had at getting this jacket for Christmas because they tried it on him.

Hello? They didn't have any money. They didn't have any money partly because they had borrowed so heavily to send him to prep school that there wasn't anything left over. My mother probably found the jacket on sale, and they couldn't afford to buy the jacket and surprise him at Christmas and take the risk that it didn't fit. I can easily understand him being disappointed at the time and thinking that they had spoiled his Christmas present, but for Christ's sake, still to be going on about this when he was almost fifty. Give me a break.

It was in especially bad taste to be still pumping this organ when he was an adult and knew or should have known that we all—Mother, Daddy, and I—did without things to pay for his private schooling and then his university degree.

When I got accepted to a private school in Atlanta, Mother told me that she was not going to "lose another child." Even though this was the reason she gave, I think they just didn't have the money to send me because they were already deeply in debt for Drew's education.

In the years before Daddy suddenly died, I came to know him well enough to partially understand the outlines of the narcissistic mind control wielded by my mother all those years. My father and I became close friends. Our friendship enraged my mother and continued to enrage her even after Daddy's death, over which my mother cried not one single tear. She waited a moderately decent interval and then renewed her attempts to discredit my father at every opportunity. She couldn't even leave a dead man alone. If anyone had ever asked her, though, she would have told them she loved my father "better than anything on earth." I heard that so many times it made me want to vomit.

When we were going to the backwater with the Linleys, it seemed as if Mother got along well enough with them and was enjoying herself. But now that I look back on it, there were telltale giveaways indicating the contrary. I suspect, for example, that her frequent comments about Miss Carolee's beauty were an attempt to ward off a murderous jealousy. My mother was a violently jealous person. And she was capable of being jealous of anything and anybody. She sublimated this jealousy only by convincing everyone, not least of all herself, that she was immensely kind and generous and religious. By repeatedly talking about how beautiful Miss Carolee was, she prevented herself and everybody else from realizing that she wanted to slash Carolee's face with a razor blade. It took me years of close contact with my mother before I figured this out.

Another of the little tales Drew told on the one occasion in fifty years he visited me had to do with pocketbooks. My age group was one that, later on in high school, donned Midi skirts bought from flea markets. We were never snobbish brand-label buyers as were the children a few years older. At least, that's how I remember it. Drew remembers it differently. I think I had two brand-name John Romaine handbags in my life. I bought both of them partly with my own money from working in the hospital. But Drew, who got educated in a swanky prep school and then an ivy league college, evidently deeply resented my having them. He harbored his resentment over the John Romaine handbags for forty years and brought it up on the drive from Florida to Wilkes Ferry. It just made me want to spit. He also ate peanuts in my brand-new van all the way to Wilkes Ferry and flicked the greasy skins on the floor. When I finally asked him to stop, he closed down emotionally and refused to continue conversation with Lee Ray and I for the rest of the trip. Just like Mama, the Queen of Passive Aggression. If he had to, Drew would say yes or no, but nothing else. I tried hard to resist the temptation (ingrained over fifty years) to tap dance for him and thereby try to get him back into a good mood.

The Position that Befitted Him

When Tamyra Tanner's son, Luke, was eight years old, Tamyra started to notice something strange about the way he walked and carried his head. Robert poo-pooed her concerns, but Tamyra headed to the doctor. A few weeks later, she got the diagnosis. She was told that Luke had a degenerative muscle and bone disease. Luke, they told her, would gradually lose control of his muscles, his bones would slowly deteriorate, and his internal organs would then begin to fail. He would never live past the age of twelve. Tamyra just kept getting up every morning, her jaw set.

Luke, in his mid-twenties, finally finished college. He was confined to a wheel chair and went through countless excruciatingly painful operations, the last of which was to put a steel rod in the place of his spine which had all but disintegrated. He depended on Tamyra for everything. For some of the time after he graduated from college, he could operate a wheelchair with his finger. But then, he could no longer even do that. Tamyra faced every day with a kind of determination I can only admire.

She talked in a matter-of-fact way about the machine she used to hoist Luke, who weighed over three hundred pounds, up out of his wheelchair and swing him over the bathtub before letting him down. She had to pump the handle of this machine with her arm every time Luke bathed. This was only one among a thousand things she did every day out of love for that child.

An interviewer once asked Marlene Dietrich if she didn't miss the war. "No," she answered. "I don't miss the war. I miss what people are like when they are trying to be brave."

Tamyra is one of the bravest people I know. The courage with which she faced every day astounds me and humbles me. I have never once heard her complain or feel sorry for herself. While being the primary care giver for Luke, she worked full time and maintained an active social life. She went to church, played bells, played tennis, and had season football tickets. But she was never ever free from that cell phone. She was a second away from an emergency or a disaster all the time.

So what about the great guy she married? What happened to the wonderful college professor?

Robert Forrester, it turned out, wasn't anywhere near as nice a we all thought he was. And he was also a deeply ambitious man. None of us had any idea just how ambitious he was. He turned himself into an alcoholic working fifteen hours a day writing articles for the very "best" academic journals. He sucked cock at every conference to get his research published in the very "best" academic journals.

After ten years of this, when he finally landed a job at a prestigious Old-South private college, Duke, he felt he had arrived.

Robert's father had taught at Duke, and Robert was always headed in that direction. Southern State University, where he was when he met Tamyra, was just a way station, a temporary but necessary bit of slumming Robert had to put up with on the way to the position that befitted him.

There was a wee problem, though, as the Scottish would say, a wee fly in the ointment, or as Southerners would say, a mosquito in the batter, a testicle in the frogs' legs. The problem was a little matter of his wife and children. You see, they were also evidently a part of the slumming he did at Southern State, a temporary but necessary way station on Robert's rise to take his place among the academic elite. Robert Forrester was as disgusted by his family and as ready to put them behind him as he was to put behind him the partitioned cubicle of an office he had at Southern State University.

She Was from Atlanta

I never told my mother what Pearl told Margaret Ann and I about Miss Mary Francis. But after that, every time I went to Miss Mary Francis's house to take a piano lesson, I was filled with images. Miss Mary Francis's daddy telling her she was ugly and plain. Miss Sister, the bell of the ball. Miss Mary Francis sitting in that upstairs bedroom by her daddy's bedside for all that time. The old man, lying naked on the front lawn. The maggot.

No, I never told my mother about all that, but I did ask her about something else that happened in that house.

"Mama?" I said one evening sitting at our kitchen table while my mother cut up salad vegetables into unrecognizable pieces.

"What?'" she answered.

"I saw somebody at Miss Mary Francis's house today."

My mother's eyebrows raised, but she said only "Oh."

"I saw a woman."

My mother didn't reply. She just kept cutting tomatoes, spring onions, and radishes up into itsy-bitsy pieces. I guess it was a fifties things.

"Mama?" I whined.

"What?" she answered, a bit cross.

"I never saw her before."

"Well, she must have been visiting Miss Mary Francis."

"She wasn't visiting," I said with finality.

"Oh, and how do you know that?" she asked.

"I don't know," I admitted.

My mother ran her forearm over her brow to wipe away some perspiration. She puffed out a stream of air. "Did this woman bother you?" she said.

"No, it was just strange, that's all. Miss Mary Francis opened the front door to let me in, and this woman opened the french doors on the left side of the house, and it was like Miss Mary Francis and this woman scared each other, like they didn't think they'd meet."

My mother put her hands down on the counter and leaned on them. She looked over at me. "People do that. Sometimes we scare each other in the house when we don't expect to come up on somebody."

I looked over at my mother and narrowed my eyes. I knew she was trying to slip something by me, as usual. "But we live in the same house."

She was cutting radishes. "Well, that's true."

"Well, that's what I'm talking about. It was like two people who lived in the same house, coming up on each other when they didn't expect it. If it was a visitor, Miss Mary Francis would have known exactly where she was in her house and wouldn't have been surprised when she opened the door. And she would have introduced me. You and Miss Mary Francis are always the ones talking about manners. She didn't even introduce me."

"What did she do?" my mother asked.

"Nothing, that's just it. She stared at the woman and the woman stared at her, and the woman just closed the door on the left side of the house."

"The left side of the house?"

"Mama"—I knew she knew what I was talking about—"the left side of that house has dark curtains over it. You can't see in. This woman came out of there."

My mother put down the knife and washed her hands at the sink. I watched closely as she walked to the table and sat down. I wasn't sure whether she was mad at me or not.

"I'm going to tell you this once," she said. "Once. And I'm never going to talk about it again. Do you understand?"

I nodded.

"The woman you saw lives in Miss Mary Francis's house. She has lived there for years. She is a friend of Miss Mary Francis. Do you understand?"

I knew I was supposed to say yes. "No," I said. "Not really."

"Miss Mary Francis would be lonely without her," my mother said carefully.

"But why haven't we ever seen her?" I asked. "Where does she come from? Who are her people?"

"It doesn't matter," my mother said.

"Why doesn't she go to church?" I asked.

"This woman you saw keeps Miss Mary Francis from being lonely. She makes Miss Mary Francis a little happier. And if you tell anybody anybody, it will hurt Miss Mary Francis, and I don't think you want to do that, do you?"

"No," I said.

"Then you'll drop it, and you'll never never breathe a word of this to anyone, not to Margaret Ann, not to Pearl, not to anybody. You promise me?"

I just nodded my head.

I never knew any more about the woman who shared Miss Mary Francis's life, her private life that is. I think someone told me once she was from Atlanta, but that was all. But like I had promised Mama, I never said another word about it.

Good Enough for Duke

When Robert Forrester imagined running his hand over the oak bookshelves lining the brick walls of his office suite at Duke, when he thought of the building where the English Department was, with its white columns, old brick and ivy, he could not stand the thought of Tamyra in her purple-and-white track suit with her loud voice and slang-filled Southern accent joining him. He cringed when he thought of her at the welcoming reception given for new faculty by the president of Duke at his home.

Robert thought of his white-haired mother in an elegant black or beige silk suit standing at the cocktail party, a glass of good French white wine in her hand, looking at him disapprovingly from across the room as Tamyra slapped her thigh and brayed in laughter at one of her own jokes.

"Unsuitable," his mother had pronounced after the first time she met Tamyra. Ten years later, her opinion hadn't changed although she was unfailingly polite. Her opinion and her behavior would be exactly like that of everybody at Duke. They would be cordial and gracious to Tamyra, but Robert could already hear their tongues clucking. "What a dreadful shame," they would say. No. He just couldn't let it happen. He could not take Tamyra to Duke.

Finally, finally, he had what he always wanted, what he was entitled to. Duke was where he belonged, had always belonged. That office had his name written all over it. But Tamyra didn't fit. There was no place for her there.

Tamyra had been fine at Southern State. She fit in well enough there. She was at least part of the surrounding culture, and she and her family had made him feel less depressed and lonely. He had been lonely, very lonely at SSU, stranded there as he was in that southern backwater of an agricultural college. He had been the fish out of water when he first got there. He had been the person whose accent caused raised eyebrows.

Robert Forrester had always been the fair-haired boy, the center of attention, the up-and-coming student and then graduate student. But in the middle of what he considered to be the red-neck, bum-fuck capital of the South, people treated him like he was a curiosity. The rest of the people in the English Department were all right. But they were there for life. They would die at SSU. None of them were real academics, and they were certainly not intellectuals.

The other faculty members were not movers and shakers and they never would be. They didn't even have enough sense to appreciate the fact that he was a mover and shaker. Oh, they were civil enough, but they knew he wasn't like them. They didn't exactly take him to their bosoms.

Outside the university, in town, people were often downright hostile to him. He had eliminated so much of his Southern accent they thought he was a Yankee. He didn't hunt or fish or like football or water ski, and he didn't have a gun rack in the cab of his pickup truck. He didn't even have a pickup truck. The students thought he talked funny, and even his virility was questioned behind his back because he didn't fit the Southern male hunt-'em-down and shoot-'em, macho stereotype. He felt when he first arrived like he had been stranded on Mars. That is, before Tamyra and her family came into the picture.

But how could he have been so stupid as to marry her? And then to have children with her? What was he thinking? Did he forget about Duke? Wasn't that always in the forefront of his plans? Did he begin to doubt he'd ever get back to Duke? He couldn't have been so crazy as to think he could take her with him, could he? The odd thing was that he didn't remember ever even thinking about it.

He had married Tamyra Tanner shortly after he met her and then turned every bit of his energy toward research and publication that would get him back to Duke. He had not ever even consciously considered the incongruity of the two separate parts of his plans.

He felt, on the brink of achieving what he had spent his life working for, that he had been living in some kind of dream. This woman and these children didn't even seem like his. They had nothing to do with him. When he stood back and looked at them like the people at Duke would, he could see that they were coarse and unrefined. They were like somebody else's wife and children, certainly not the wife and children of a Duke University professor of English.

He couldn't let this happen. He couldn't. He had to get rid of her. But how? How could he get rid of her now, dump her right before he left for Duke? It would look terrible. And there was Andrea Drafer on the English faculty at Duke, a feminist postmodernist. She loathed men. She had made a career out of loathing men. She would ruin him if he dumped his wife of ten years and two small children, one of them handicapped, right before he accepted this plum of a job.

Robert Forrester might just have heard Tamyra then, in the background, shouting to the children, trying to get them in bed. She did it every night, every goddamn night. She never did anything in less than a shout. She was never going to do anything in less than a shout.

Robert might well have tightened his jaw at the sound of her. Sitting in his study, he might well have felt the muscles in his upper back and neck, pulling his shoulders up toward his ears. He might have massaged his neck with his hand, squeezing hard to try to get what felt like gristle to relax.

He had to get rid of Tamyra. His eyes darted to the credenza, where he kept the liquor. He then looked reflexively at his watch. Before he knew what was happening, his fist came down on the top of his desk hard, hard enough to hurt his hand.

"You're in a damn good mood tonight," Tamyra said, flouncing into his study, chewing gum, a dish towel thrown over her shoulder. The children had stopped spitting up on her at least eight years ago, but she still went around with a towel over her shoulder most of the time. He had no idea why.

Tamyra collapsed into the large leather chair beside his desk and threw one leg over the arm. In the ten years they had been married, Robert had never seen Tamyra sit down in a chair like a lady. She threw herself at a chair or a sofa and, like now, sat there with her crotch in everybody's face

"Lemme guess," Tamyra said, leaning her head on the back of the enormous chair and looking over at him. "We're not going out."

"No," Robert said, getting up and moving toward the credenza.

"Buddy Roe, why don't you try something different tonight and not start that until the children are in bed?" Tamyra lowered her head in the direction of the credenza.

Robert ignored her.

Tamyra shrugged her shoulders, took her leg down from the arm of the chair, and changed position to look at a printed invitation from the Duke University faculty laying on the ottoman.

Robert poured his whiskey and turned around, leaning against the credenza, circling the ice in his glass. He looked at Tamyra. She was sitting on the edge of the chair, hunched over, reading. Her legs were spread wide apart, and her elbows were propped on her knees. Both her large, stubby hands hung limply from the wrist between her thighs.

It occurred to him for the thousandth time that she looked like a man. Her knees were enormous, and her thighs threatened to burst out of the pair of stretch shorts she had worn for at least seven of the past ten years. She had on a pair of dirty blue flip-flops he had asked her to get rid of for what seemed like years.

She had worn the flip-flops for so long they had the permanent grimy print of her foot ground into them. The prominent balls of her feet had made a depression in the rubber that remained even when she took them off. She had not only failed to throw the flip-flops away, she had actually packed and taken them along on their vacation.

Robert had allowed himself to be badgered into taking the family on an expensive Caribbean cruise to celebrate the new job. Every woman on that boat looked fabulous, and there was Tamyra in her shorts and flip-flops. Robert was grimly embarrassed, but when he asked Tamyra to wear something else to the dining room, she had brushed him off.

"I ain't walking all over this damn boat in high-heeled sandals like all those twenty-year-olds," she said. "So just get that out of your head. You like the damn high heels so much, you wear 'em. These flip-flops I broke in just right. They fit my feet perfect."

Robert took a gulp from his drink and tried to sigh quietly, his eyes lingering on the disgusting flip-flops. He noticed that not only were the flip-flops dirty, but Tamyra's feet were also dirty as well. And she had painted her hideous toenails a bright tomato red and then allowed it to chip off for weeks. Robert looked back down into his drink and then walked back over and sank into his desk chair.

"Whores de overs," Tamyra said, looking up and over at him, smiling, adopting an even more redneck, low-class accent than normal. "Hot damn, we gon' have 'whores de overs' with the English faculty."

Robert didn't even smile. He had heard this joke so many times it made him want to scream . . . or . . . perhaps . . . clamp his fingers solidly around her sweaty, fat, football player's neck.

"Robert," she said, putting the invitation down on the leather ottoman to the chair, "you been wantin' this job your whole life. I been listening to how you can't do this and can't do that, don't have the time for me or the children, for ten years 'cause you got to write some article or read some book. All so we can get to a better school. And now, you got it, not just a better school but Duke, your dream, where your daddy taught, where you always wanted to be, so why don't you just relax and enjoy it?"

Robert nodded his head as if considering this seriously as an alternative.

"Yeah," he said. "Relax." He then let out a small snort, got up, and walked to the window. "Don't you have enough sense to realize that's absolutely the last thing I can do right now?"

"Why the hell not?" Tamyra asked, flopping against the back of the chair.

"Tamyra, think, think for once. I just got this job. I'm the new kid on the block in that faculty at Duke. I have to prove I deserve it, to be there."

"I thought that's what you been doing for ten years here, proving you deserved it. That's what you been telling us."

"I have to prove I belong at Duke. That's not the same as proving I belong at . . ."

"A fifth-rate cow college."

"I didn't say that."

"You didn't have to. You've said it enough times in the past."

"That is not true and you know it."

"What I know is that for ten years I been listening to you whine around, telling me you didn't have the time to go anywhere with me, do anything with the children. You didn't have enough time to help me out, even with your own son, who needs you."

Robert tried to interrupt, "don't let's start this . . ."

"That little boy up there needs you . . ." She spat out the words one at the time.

"Stop it," Robert shouted louder than he intended.

"No, I won't stop it," Tamyra said, trying to keep her voice down. She walked over to the study door and slammed it shut. Her voice lowered to a fierce whisper. "Your son may not live more than a few years. Do you hear me? Have you heard anything I've told you in the past two years about that child?"

"Of course, I have. Who do you think I've been working all these years for? I have been working my ass off so I can pay his medical bills and still keep the rest of us in food."

There was a silence.

"There are so many things wrong with that statement, I don't even know where to begin," Tamyra said finally

"I'm sure you'll find a place," Robert retorted.

"That is my child up there," Tamyra said, poking the air with her finger. "That fine, sweet little boy is my child, and I intend to fight with every inch of my being for him to have the best possible life for just as long as he draws breath."

"And don't you think I'm dong the same thing?"

"No, I don't."

Robert threw up his hands then picked up and gulped down the rest of his drink. He started for the credenza and another one.

"You do not spend a minute with him, with us. You are gone all the damn time, and when you're here, you don't show the least little bit of interest in what goes on in this house," she said to Robert's back. "Do you know," she continued, "that he is going to have to go into the hospital again soon?"

"Of course, I know," Robert said sourly, pouring his drink.

Tamyra came up out of the chair, strode across the room, and slapped Robert's hand away from the drink. "Stop it," she said angrily. "Stop trying to drink us away."

The glass with the ice and whiskey flew out of Robert's hand and landed in the center of the room on the oriental carpet given to them by Robert's mother.

"Please," Robert said, walking over and bending down to pick up the glass from the floor. "Can't you control yourself? Look what you did to the rug." He straightened up holding the glass but made no move to clean up the mess himself. He stood there looking down at the stain on the carpet.

Tamyra stared at the rug and then at him, wanting very much to hit him again in sheer frustration.

The words came out between her teeth, low, in an almost growling sound. "I control myself every minute of every day. I have to control myself to keep from collapsing in tears and grief over what has happened to my baby. I have to control myself to keep from screaming while I'm doing things for him I had to do when he was two years old. I have to control myself just to go on talking and watching and explaining and cheering him up, hour after hour after hour after day after week. I control myself when I watch my daughter watching me. Robin is like a neglected child, an orphan. Do you realize she's just been pushed to the side since Luke's been sick? She doesn't get half the attention she needs."

"Robin doesn't need that much attention," Robert said, standing next to the credenza, trying not to pour himself another drink.

"She does," Tamyra said, her voice faltering. "She needs as much attention as Luke. She just doesn't get it. She's started to mess up at school, to fall behind. She's going to fail a grade if we don't do something."

"Robin's never going to be smart, Tamyra . . ."

"Don't you ever let me hear you say that again," Tamyra said balling up her fist and shaking it at him. She would dearly liked to have hit him about the face at that moment.

Images came into her mind, images of Paul Newman beating his opponent in the ring in *Somebody Up There Likes Me*. She and Luke had watched the black-and-white movie the afternoon before. Newman was playing Gratziano, hitting an opponent in the face twice with one fist. He would swing in one direction and strike the man across the face, and then swing back in the other direction, getting the man with a backhand. You could see sweat and blood flying off the man's head with every hit. Tamyra, standing there in Robert's study, wished she could hit like that.

"You stop saying my children aren't smart or can't be whatever they want to be," she said shaking off the boxing images.

"Tamyra, at some point in your life, you're just going to have to start being realistic. Luke is . . ."

"Luke is fine. He's just fine. He's going to be just fine. He's not . . ."— and here she lowered her voice to a rough whisper—"going to die. He's not. He's going to live, and I'm going to help him live just as good a life as anybody else in this world."

Robert shook his head. He could feel his hands fidgeting, moving over the buttons on his shirt, slipping inside his pockets, and then out. There were some pills in his desk somewhere. *Some Vicodin*, he thought. That would be great. Vicodin would smooth him out, allow him to regain control over this discussion. He had to have something, and he was not going to give Tamyra the opportunity to slap another drink out of his hand.

"And don't you tell me he's not," Tamyra was saying furiously.

"Okay, fine," he said, moving behind the desk and opening drawers. "And Robin's going to be a genius."

"She may not be a genius," Tamyra responded as she watched him thrashing through his desk drawers, "but she isn't dumb like you keep saying."

"I never in my life said she was dumb. You said she was dumb."

Tamyra stood there, staring at Robert as he opened and closed drawers. "I did not," she said, unable to think of anything else to say.

"You did," Robert retorted, taking something from the bottom corner of his desk drawer and concealing it in his fist. "You just stood there and said your daughter was dumb. Not thirty seconds ago."

"You . . ." Tamyra smacked her forehead in exasperation.

Robert walked to the credenza and poured himself half a glass of water. "I don't think you even know what you mean."

He was using that professorial tone Tamyra detested. For her, it was like fingernails dragging across a chalkboard.

"And besides," Robert was saying, "why do you keep saying they're *your* children?"

He walked to the window again and stood with his back to her. He popped the pill into his mouth from out of his fist and drank the water. If Tamyra noticed, she didn't say anything.

"Because you don't have anything to do with them," Tamyra said, feeling back at least on some ground she could understand.

"That's not true, and you know it's not true. Didn't I just take you all on a cruise?" Robert turned around and walked over to his desk.

"And spent the whole time in the cabin writing or sitting on the deck talking to somebody else. You didn't spend five minutes with your own children."

"Tamyra," he said, scoffing at her ignorance the way he might at the failure of a bubble-brained freshman coed to appreciate the deeper significance of George Elliot. "I'm a professor of English. I have to talk with other people, different people, people who talk differently and think differently. It's part of my work."

"Well, why do all the people who talk different and think different always turn out to be women between the ages of twenty and thirty-five?"

Robert cast a long-suffering, disappointed look in Tamyra's direction as he sat down behind his desk. "You can't even have an adult discussion without resorting to cheap accusations and innuendos."

"I don't even know what innuendos are." Tamyra shouted.

Robert sighed.

"And don't sigh at me." she screamed. "I hate the way you sigh at me."

"You hate the way I sigh at you?" Robert said, a tight smile curling up the ends of his lips.

"And I hate the way you smile at me," she added.

"And the way I smile at you," he repeated. "Well, is there anything about me you do not hate?" he asked, glancing at the credenza again.

"The way you used to be," she said after a pause. "I don't hate the way you used to be."

Robert nodded his head and ran his eyes up and down Tamyra's body. "You're not exactly the way you used to be either," he said cruelly.

Tamyra lowered her eyes. It was her turn to sigh. She sank down in the leather chair and massaged her forehead with her hands. A stony silence filled the room.

"Tamyra, I can't take this anymore," Robert said, putting his palms flat on the top of his desk and pushing himself up.

Tamyra looked at him as he crossed the floor headed like a moth to the flame for the whiskey. "You can't take it anymore?" she said. "You? What exactly is it you're having to take?"

"The constant fighting, arguing, the wild accusations."

"Accusations? It seems to me that you've done your share of accusing. You even—"

"Don't, Tamyra. Don't start that again." He was warming to the debate, starting to feel the first telltale rushes of opiate-induced power tickling his being.

"Why not?" Tamyra was asking. "Are you ashamed of hearing your words back?"

"I was drunk, Tamyra," he said turning around to face her, fresh drink in hand, posing as if he were on the inside jacket cover of a book. "I keep telling you I was drunk." He should use that credenza with the cut glass decanter as a background on his next book cover, well, his first book cover, leaning back just like this, casual in a sweater and tie. *The new literary sensation out of Duke* . . . He could already see the typeface.

"You can't use that as an excuse anymore, Robert," Tamyra was saying.

"I didn't mean it," he said, trying to remember what he was talking about.

"People don't say things they don't mean when they're drunk. They say things they do mean but just don't have the goddamn courage to say when they're sober."

"That's not actually true," Robert said, latching on to the ill-conceived theory Tamyra had just advanced. "The research . . ."

"Don't you fucking dare . . . ," she said.

"There's no need for that kind of language. I was just going to tell you that . . ."

"If you start telling me about some research paper, I will tear this study down. Do you hear me?"

"I hear you," Robert said after a pause.

"You don't believe I'll do it, do you?" Tamyra asked staring at him.

"Unfortunately, my dear, I do believe you'd do it."

"We are not talking about some research project. We're talking about our lives."

"Tamyra, only the ignorant dismiss scientific—"

"Stop it, Robert. Just stop it," Tamyra said tiredly but firmly.

"You were the one who was making broad generalizations about the affects of alcohol on the brain."

"I was not making broad anythings, I was talking about *you* and your brain and you when you're drunk. And you meant every word of it when you blamed Luke's disease on me."

"I did not."

"Robert, you said it. You said that there had never been anything like this in the history of your family."

"That's quite different from blaming you."

"Well, what else is it? You were saying it couldn't have come from your side of the family, and so it must have come from mine."

"It's just that we know our family. We can trace the Forresters back to the Revolutionary War."

"Oh my God, not this again. Don't you dare tell me about the fucking Daughters of the American Revolution."

"I know you don't like it, but the Forresters are a well-known American family."

"That doesn't make you perfect."

"I never said anything like that, never. That conclusion does not follow logically on from the previous assertion. It's just that you don't know anything about your family history. You can't go back more than three generations and even then . . ."

"Even then what?"

"Well, look at your skin and that of your brothers. And look at your mother's cheek bones. It's obvious."

"What's obvious?"

"That there's been some race mixing, combining of gene pools that should have never been combined."

"My great-great-grandmother was a Cherokee. You call that race mixing?"

"Tamyra, you're overreacting to this. You overreact to everything."

Tamyra was exhausted. "Robert, nobody's to blame for this. It just happened. Even if we knew which side of the family it came from, what's the difference? Luke is here. He's our son, and we have to try to make him as happy as we can."

"I'm goddamn doing the best I can."

"Well, your best is just not good enough."

"How much more do you think I can work? I've worked like a slave for the past ten years, trying to keep up with the operations and consultations, paying for you to drag Luke to every rip-off specialist in the country chasing after a cure that's not out there. I finally got one of the best jobs in my field in the country. I will make more money, live in a better place, be able to pay the medical bills. What more do you want?"

"Robert Forrester, you didn't work for or get this job for us, for Luke, you got it for yourself. We're paying the medical bills now. We have insurance. What your son needs is for you to be part of his life. He needs you to be a father." Tamyra paused. "Robert, he thinks you are ashamed of him."

Robert turned around and stared at Tamyra. "That is not true."

"Isn't it?" she said. "You never go anywhere with him"

"Do you have any idea how much work it takes just to get Luke into the car?"

"Do I have any idea? Do I know what it takes to get him into the car? Who do you think you're talking to? I get him in the car every day. I get him out of the car every day. In fact, I get him up, bathe him, dress him, and fix his breakfast, and I get him off to school. I pick him up, and I bathe him again, and I help him with his homework, and I feed him, and I put him to bed. Do I have any idea? Who the hell do you think knows better than I do?"

"You have time for that sort of thing. I don't."

"That's right. You don't have time, for any of us."

"How do you know he thinks I'm ashamed of him?"

"I know because he told me."

"He didn't."

"He did."

"You've probably just planted that in his mind for your own reasons."

Tamyra stared at Robert in disbelief. "Do you think I would ever suggest to my own child that his father was ashamed of him even if I knew it was true? What kind of person are you?"

"Okay, Tamyra. Have it your way. I'm ashamed of Luke. I'm ashamed of all of you. Is that what you want me to say? Does that make you feel better?"

"It makes me feel terrible."

"You asked for it."

"No," Tamyra stated flatly. "I didn't ask for it. I didn't ask for any of this. But I don't think of Luke as some kind of mistake that we have to find somebody to blame for."

"I think you blame me."

"I don't blame anybody," Tamyra said softly. "This just happened, and you know, Robert, it happened mainly to Luke, not to you. You act like you are the one who's been left in a wheelchair without a backbone, rotting every day from the inside out, stinking your pants, and having to be cleaned up by your mother, knowing that everybody thinks you're going to be dead before you can get to high school. It's Luke that's diseased, not you."

"I'm warning you, Tamyra, I just can't take this kind of constant upheaval in my life in this new position."

"What does that mean?"

"It means that this job is a big step up for me, for all of us, and I can't perform in the way I'm expected to with all this turmoil always swirling around me."

"What turmoil? Luke being sick? Luke having to go to the hospital? And just what do you propose we do about it?"

"All of it. Luke's emergencies, your demands, this constant nagging for me to spend every minute I'm not in class with you. I've got to be able to concentrate up there, concentrate on my work."

"Well, maybe you just shouldn't have gotten married and had a family. Then you could have . . . concentrated on your work. But Robert, you did get married, and you did have children, and you have a son with a terminal rotting disease, and you have responsibilities. That's just a fact, Robert. A damn fact."

"You think you're telling me something I don't know? I live with that fact every day of my life."

"The difference between us is that I'm not sorry about that fact."

"You're not sorry? How could you not be sorry? You're actually standing there trying to tell me you're not sorry you have a ruined, defective child?"

"Luke is not . . . ruined. And he's not defective."

"I thought you were the one talking about facts. That, Tamyra, is a fact. You have a son who will never get into college, who will never amount to anything. Who will spend his life vegetating in a wheelchair, stinking in his pants. And you're not sorry about that."

"I'm sorry for Luke. I'm so sorry for Luke I could tear the world apart. Sometimes I wake up in the middle of the night, and I just want to go outside and howl at the moon, howl my lungs out. I hurt so bad for him and what he's got to face. But I'm sorry for Luke, Robert, Luke, not myself."

"And I'm sorry for myself."

"Yes. You are. Ever since we got the diagnosis, you have climbed more and more into that bottle you're guzzling down over there and more and more into your work. You have buried yourself but not because you hurt for Luke. You hurt for yourself and your disappointment because your son won't teach at Duke after you, because you won't be able to go to the award dinners when he's declared a Road Scholar."

Robert closed his eyes. "A Rhodes Scholar, Tamyra, a goddamn Rhodes Scholar."

"Whatever."

"Okay. So I see it now. You hurt for Luke, but I only hurt for myself. You're the heroic mother, and I"m just the selfish bastard of a father."

"If the shoe fits . . ."

"Highly original. Just like everything else you say."

"If you wanted to marry another English professor, you should have damn well done it, but you happen to be married to me."

"Yes, I do know that. Boy, do I know that."

"You know, Robert. You can say anything you want to about me. You can even say you're sorry we ever got married, if that's what you want to say, but don't you ever say you're sorry to have those children."

"How can I say anything else?" said Robert. "Robin's just as lazy as she possibly can be. She's never been anything but a B student at best. And you never pushed her. And Luke? You've allowed Luke to get so fat and gross, he's disgusting. He talks like your brothers . . ."

"Which is how?"

Robert looked at her. "Truthfully?"

"Why not?"

"Like a backwoods redneck who's never seen a book, much less read one. Are you telling me you're glad you brought something like that into the world?"

"Something?"

"He eats with his mouth open, shoveling food in while he's talking at the same time. Globs just drop out all over the table. He doesn't even try to have manners. Sometimes I think he revels in his sloppiness and crudeness. And you do nothing."

"Luke has a hard time controlling his muscles, Robert. If you ever stayed home or out of this study long enough to find out what's going on in your own house, you would know all that. Luke does the best he can, and he tries to cover up by making jokes. He doesn't revel in it."

"You let him . . . encouraged him to get this way."

"What way?"

"Obese and crude."

"And you think I planted in his mind that you were ashamed of him? You are ashamed of him, Robert, and he is smart enough to pick up on it."

"I'm ashamed of how he looks and how he acts. There's no excuse for letting him become revolting and act like a cretin. Tamyra, at some point, you are going to have to be realistic about this. If you were honest, you would admit that you are ashamed of him too."

"No, I wouldn't because I'm not ashamed of him."

"Come on. Can't you just face the truth once? Don't you ever get tired of playing the martyr? Just this once?"

"Robert, it's not the truth. I have never been ashamed of Luke, not for one minute."

Robert threw up his hands in frustration.

"You just don't get it, do you, Robert?"

"No, Tamyra, I don't get it."

Tamyra sat down in the leather chair, thinking. She tried to start off softly, in a conciliatory tone. "Robert, you know this move to Durham is not going to be easy for Luke. He has friends here who have known him for years. They're used to him. He feels comfortable around them. You know how difficult it is for him to meet new people, to have to go through them staring and laughing at him. It's just going to be heartbreaking. And he's getting older now. He's almost a teenager, and you know how difficult that's going to be for him, watching all the other boys start dating and having girlfriends. You must remember what a cruel time that is to be different."

"He'll be in a better school in Durham. The schools are excellent. He'll get a better education. If they stare at him, it'll probably be because he talks like a mill hand."

Tamyra sighed, trying to maintain her self-control. "It's not a better school he needs. He needs to be around people that are used to him and who accept him as he is. That's what he's got here. He's also got Ricky and Rod here," she said referring to her two brothers. "They pal around with him and do men things and take him to the lake so he can get away from me once in a while. He's not going to have anybody to do that for him when we move."

"Well, why don't you leave him here if all that's so important for him."

Tamyra stared at the man who had been her husband for over ten years. "Leave him? What are you talking about?"

"Leave him here. Make some kind of arrangement so he can stay here."

"And just what sort of arrangement did you have in mind?"

"I don't know."

"Just what sort of arrangement do you think it's possible to make for a severely handicapped child to live and be taken care of and educated and fed and entertained?"

"I don't know, Tamyra. I was just suggesting you explore the alternatives. You were the one saying that staying here was so important to him."

"Important but not more important than being with his own family. Who would do such a thing? Move away and leave a child behind."

"We wouldn't be leaving him behind, just making an arrangement for him to stay here. It's done all the time."

"Well, it's not being done this time. Luke goes wherever I go."

"Do you think Luke can't live without you?"

"No. I think I can't live, don't want to live, without him."

"Well, stay here with him."

Tamyra was stunned. She sat looking at Robert, feeling as if she was married to a stranger. "You're planning to leave us all behind," she said slowly. "Is that it, Robert? You've got this job you always wanted, and you are planning to leave us all behind like so much beaten-up luggage."

Robert turned around and looked at her. "No, Tamyra, of course not. That's not what I'm talking about."

"What are you talking about? You've just said to leave Luke here and then for me to stay here with him. What is that other than leaving us behind?"

"I just meant temporarily, Tamyra, until Luke has time to make the adjustment, the change."

"Robert, if you . . ." Tamyra drew herself up. "If you want to divorce me—"

"No, Tamyra." Robert interrupted her, his hands out, coming toward her. She put one hand up, palm toward Robert to stop his approach.

"If you don't want me anymore, you are going to have to say so. You are going to have to look me in the face and tell me you don't love me anymore and you want a divorce. But you are not going to tuck Luke away somewhere out of sight and act like he doesn't exist. You're not going to do that to him."

"No, Tamyra," Robert said, coming closer and squatting down to take her hands in his. "I didn't mean that," he said and slid his hand down her arm. "Nobody's going to tuck anybody away. You're my family," he said, trying to be convincing. When Tamyra didn't move or look at him, he added, "I'm so sorry, Tamyra. I'm just so scared. I can't do this new job without you."

Tamyra didn't melt in his arms like she used to, but she thawed a little. He felt it. He took both her hands in his and looked up into her face. "You see, the problem is that we all need you so much. We're all afraid of not having all of you."

She met his gaze, and a smile softened her face. He put his arms around her and drew her to him. He patted her back tenderly. Finally, her arms relaxed and encircled his shoulders.

Robert sat back on his heels and patted her thigh with his hand. "Everything's going to be all right," he said, groaning a little. His knees cracked when he got up.

Tamyra wiped away the few tears she had allowed to stream down her face after he took her in his arms.

Maybe, she thought, *maybe now that he finally has this job he wanted for so long, he'll be happy. Maybe finally he'll back off and not be so hard on Luke and Robin.* She knew how much the job at Duke meant to him. He had been working for this for the entire time she had known him, dreaming about getting a job in a school like Duke, hoping against hope that a position would become available at Duke before he got too old to accept it. Maybe, just maybe, their lives would be better now that he had what he wanted. Maybe the disappointment about Luke wouldn't eat him alive now that he had fulfilled his lifelong dream.

"I have to go finish up upstairs and get them into bed," Tamyra said and paused, hoping Robert would offer to help. Robert didn't offer to help.

It was exhausting, just getting Luke into bed for the night. But Robert Forrester was already back behind his desk, standing and looking down at some papers.

"Yes," he said without looking up. "And I have to work through these financial papers transferring our investments and setting up our medical coverage." He sat down, avoiding her gaze. "It's very complicated with Luke's condition," he said.

Robert picked up some of the sheets of paper and leaned back with his drink. He took a long sip.

Tamyra watched him. "Don't you ever think," she said, "that I would like to climb inside that bottle with you and just forget about everything?"

Robert didn't look up and didn't answer.

"But," she said softly, "everybody needs me."

She didn't even expect Robert to answer her. She pushed herself up with her hands on her thighs and walked out of the room leaving the door open behind her.

As soon as her back was to him, Robert looked up over the top of his papers and watched her go. Her fat ass rolled from side to side as she walked. God, she had gotten big. She hadn't just gotten fat. It wasn't like she was a petite little thing who had softened around the edges and become a little comfortably plump. She looked like a football player. She looked like her bones had gotten bigger. She and her brothers were looking more and more alike every year. And she wasn't shy about it. She didn't even try to hide what had happened to her body.

The image of her taking off her clothes in the bedroom came to him—her puffy skin, the red marks that the elastic in her underwear made on her fat. Robert closed his eyes.

He couldn't remember ever even seeing her with a book in her hand. She didn't read books, didn't read the newspaper, and her knowledge of current events, politics, or social conditions amounted to her oft-repeated stories of where she was when she learned John Kennedy had been assassinated or Elvis had died.

When she was around people who talked about politics and social conditions, she spouted the most simplistic Republican cliches, and she got nervous. When she got nervous, she got louder, more aggressively trite, and obnoxious than usual. Whenever they were at some university function, it was usually a disaster. She hated the people on the faculty and their wives and husbands, and they regarded her as a horror.

Robert wanted to cry, thinking of her at the welcome reception at Duke announced in the invitation she had been holding. She would probably repeat the same tired old "whores-de-overs" joke at the party itself, and he would be ruined, utterly ruined. None of them would ever think of him the same way afterward.

He had to do something. He just had to keep her from ruining him at Duke before he even got started. He imagined her walking up the stairs and going into their bedroom. He wished she would lay down on the bed and die before he went upstairs. That would solve everything, if she would just die. Then he could go to Duke a widower. She didn't look so bad in the photographs they had of her. He glanced at some of the photos on the walls. She could pass for acceptable in those pictures. He could put their wedding photo on his desk at Duke, and everybody would ask about her, and he could tell them she died tragically just the spring before he came to Duke. They would feel sorry for him then. And an added bonus would be that if he didn't do as well at Duke as everyone expected, as he expected, he could fall back on her death. "He never recovered from his wife's death," people would say. And it would be all right.

He could put Luke in some home or institution. He certainly couldn't take care of him. He wasn't going to spend fifteen hours a day cleaning up somebody else's shit. Robin. He'd send Robin to a boarding school. That would solve that problem.

Yes, he needed Tamyra to die. That was all there was to it. When he thought about her telling that "whores-de-overs" joke at the welcome reception at Duke, he felt as if he could have killed her himself. He could have strangled her. No blood, no poison, no mess. Then he could say that somebody broke into the house after they went to bed and overpowered him. He could hit himself over the head with something and say that they must have strangled Tamyra while he was out. Hadn't he heard that story before? Damn, wasn't that some variation of *The Fugitive*?

He scanned the titles of the books on the bookshelf. What was he looking for? A manual on how to strangle your wife? That would be handy. Agatha Christie? No, that was way too old and out of date. There must be some novel about a man who killed his wife successfully. O.J. Simpson, but he wasn't a celebrity football player.

Luke in an institution. That wouldn't look good at Duke. His wife dies, and he puts his only son in an institution. And then, he sends his only daughter off to boarding school. No, it wouldn't look good. Especially not to Andrea Dyer. She would crucify him. It would definitely dilute the sympathy factor of Tamyra's untimely death. Besides, God only knew how much money it would cost to keep Luke in a home with twenty-four-hour-a-day care and send Robin to a boarding school.

Robin had already started to be a problem, making bad grades and getting into trouble at school just to get attention. He could just see himself in the middle of an important faculty meeting or an international conference being called to deal with his daughter's emotional problems.

Besides, what was he thinking about? He couldn't kill Tamyra. She'd gotten so big, and he was so out of shape she'd probably just kick him in the balls, toss him off her, and go right on ahead with whatever she was doing.

No, if he was going to kill anybody, he would have to kill all three of them. Something could go wrong with the car. He could do something to the car when all three of them were going somewhere, and they could all die together. That would get him sympathy for sure.

But he knew absolutely nothing about cars, never had. How was he going to fix a car so that they would all die. Besides, they all might not die. Maybe everybody but Luke would die; that would be just his luck. And then he'd really be stuck. He certainly couldn't put him in an institution after that.

No. It was possible, just possible that he might be able to bring off killing Tamyra, but he knew it was not reasonable to think that somebody who had never done that sort of thing in his life could bring off killing three people without getting caught. If he got caught, he'd spend the rest of his life in a cell instead of in his nice, tasteful office suite at Duke.

No. Tamyra was definitely the least expensive way to keep the children out of his hair. He couldn't kill her. It didn't make sense. Even paying child support was less expensive than a home and boarding school. She'd have to stay, but there must be a way to keep from taking them all to Duke.

As Long as Everything Is Us

The Civil War gutted the South. But fortunately, a few men escaped who had foresight and courage. They looked around them at burned out houses and blackened, abandoned factories and warehouses, but what they saw was an opportunity to transform the South into an industrial powerhouse. While others were pulling out of the South what investment there was left, Lafayette Cobb decided to put money in.

Lafayette Langdale Cobb was not from one of the big planter families in the region. He wasn't even from Wilkes Ferry. He had come to the Valley before the war as a cotton buyer for the Lowell Mills. He traveled back and forth between the Lowell warehouses near Columbus and those near Wilkes Ferry, where much of the cotton came in from the interior. He much preferred Wilkes Ferry. Columbus was a rough, crude town filled with drunken mill workers, gamblers, prostitutes, and thugs. Wilkes Ferry was a quiet, sleepy little town filled with lovely old homes lining wide streets. Commercial activity was confined to the small business district on the west side of the river. On the east side, there was peace and order. Houses with wide verandas still lined the streets, and ladies strolled with parasols. To Lafayette, Wilkes Ferry still looked like a painting. It looked like what life could be, a thing of harmony, filled with beauty and comfort and contentment. Harmony, beauty, comfort, contentment all supported by, but separated from, money and industry.

Lafayette Cobb might just have stood on the high bluff overlooking the Catawba River near the loading docks one afternoon in the summer after the war's end, looking at the white water rapids that became apparent only when the river was at its lowest.

The Catawba dropped nearly three hundred feet in the twelve miles of river that ran south of Wilkes Ferry. If it could even be partially damned, the force of the water could be increased much more. There would be no need for the South to continue to function as a colony of the North—exporting precious raw materials and importing expensive manufactured goods. That was what big cotton and slavery had done for the South, turned it into a colony. They were better off without it. Besides, Lafayette Cobb had never liked the taste it left in his mouth when he saw human beings kept in conditions little different from those of domestic animals.

He had seen officers during the war, from some of the big planter families, treating their men in the way Lafayette supposed they treated their slaves. The common soldiers, the backbone of the Confederacy, hated officers like that, and they wouldn't fight for them. Lafayette had been at Selma when Major General Wren replaced a trusted and loved officer, General Drew Beau, with the arrogant and pudgy Gen. Pickford Kyle. The soldiers would have walked the last mile into hell to fight a battle behind Gen. Beau. But when Kyle replaced him, the men became surly, short-tempered, and unwilling. They grumbled and complained. Every order was regarded with suspicion and chewed over like an old bone. Some of the men just spit the bone out and disappeared, put down their rifles, and walked home, unwilling to fight anymore.

"He'd sit on that damn horse and order a thousand of us to our deaths without so much as turning a hair," one of the soldiers said one night over Lafayette's shoulder, up close to his ear. Lafayette was standing around a campfire, studying Pickford Kyle, who was sitting alone at his own campfire. "Oh, he's willen' to sacrifice everything for the cause," the man said, breathing whiskey into Lafayette's face. "As long as everything is us."

Men like that weren't going to like coming back home and having to be beholden to officers like that, having to work for them like slaves themselves since many of their families had been pushed off their own land for failure to pay taxes. Those men who fought for the rights of the planters to own slaves were now faced with the prospect of sharecropping and tenant farming for those same planters. They started the war thinking they were fighting for their way of life. They wound up, at the end of it, on the bottom of the social heap, virtually slaves themselves.

To add to the humiliation, free blacks were now going to compete with them for the opportunity to sharecrop, shoe horses, and butcher hogs. The common soldiers weren't going to like that either.

Lafayette Cobb had watched and listened during the years building up to the war, how the planter class had used propaganda and fear to enlist poor whites to its cause. Common white men, they argued publicly, would suffer even more than the planters if Lincoln freed the slaves. The first time Lafayette heard this preposterous argument, he let out a guffaw of involuntary laughter. The men standing around him in the crowd listening to the speaker, a well-known Columbus preacher, stared at him. But then, some of them, a few, had smiles of amusement playing at their lips, indicating that they understood why he was laughing.

Six months later, Lafayette was hearing this ludicrous argument come off the tongues not only of planters and their buddy preachers, but also out of the mouths of small farmers and blacksmiths, people who should have known better.

It amazed Lafayette, watching the common people pick up and repeat like parrots the words and ideas of the planter class, the preachers, and the politicians. The sentiments seemed to spread like the ubiquitous kudzu plant, and just like that plant, the ideas would cover and kill off the independent life of everything they touched.

Lafayette sat in church and listened to the preachers argue for a literal interpretation of the Bible, which became intertwined with biblical support and legitimation for slavery. Blacks were what they called "natural slaves," and the white man was intended to be the steward of the black man, taking care of these inferior creatures. "Taking care of them" was what they called keeping them in bondage, working them to near death, and beating the living hell out of them from time to time, for their own good.

Lafayette watched men who had never owned a slave in their lives nod in agreement with the pastor, say amen, and grow flushed with emotion. What could make them so vehement about this issue of slavery? Did they really harbor deep in their imaginations the belief that they were going to come out of a war with hundreds of acres of cotton land and a thousand slaves? How could they be so deluded?

Lafayette had no doubt that some of them were just this deluded, but others were consumed with fear. Public meetings sprang up everywhere with speakers who were talented fear mongers. Blacks were carefully kept away from such meetings, even moved blocks away to keep them from overhearing. Men with voices sounding the death knell of doom predicted that if Lincoln had his way, "niggers" would be sitting in judgement of them on juries, asking for their daughter's hands in marriage, or just taking by force the honor and purity of white women they wanted. Nothing would be enough for these newly freed "niggers."

Lafayette Cobb wasn't sure anything would be enough himself. That part of the hooey might well be right. It would have been one thing if they'd never been slaves. But once slaves, would there ever be enough to make up for that? He didn't think so. They might be saying now that they just wanted their freedom from slavery, but once free, they would want more. They would want revenge. He wasn't sure they didn't deserve it, but it would be a fool's search. No amount of payback would ever be enough. How could it?

No, some men had made fortunes off the cheap labor of slaves, but their decedents were going to pay for it for generations and generations. *And the rest of us as well,* Lafayette Cobb thought. That was the real tragedy. Hundreds of thousands of people never even involved would suffer for the greed of a few. Mankind never seemed to progress far away from greed. The form of it just changed over the centuries.

The planters and the politicians filled the heads of the common people with bluster and banter. The North, they bragged, couldn't get by without cotton for a week. Their mills would shut down, and they would be back in a month begging for Southern cotton. The English and the French were in the same position. Even if the North held out, the English and the French would fund the Southern war effort to keep their supply of cotton coming.

"When they're ready to quit wearin' clothes," one speaker blustered, "we're ready to quit usin' slavery."

In addition to the prospect of black men having white women, a thing that seemed to linger in the minds of white Southern men much more than Lafayette Cobb thought normal, was the fear of everyone being turned into what they called "factory slaves." Whites in the South, they said, had to stick together to preserve an agrarian, farm-based, family-oriented independent way of life. The

Northern industrialists wanted to break up the family and turn people into individual cogs, each working only for wages for himself. They wanted to turn people into machines, lock them up inside a windowless factory doing the same thing all day long.

This wasn't how men were meant to live. At least the slave was outside in the fresh air, working alongside his family. And the master had a personal relationship with the slave and an investment in him. The factory owner didn't care anything about his workers. Lose one, he'd just get another.

Before long, it became dangerous to show even neutrality on the slavery issue.

Poor farmers and yeoman bought the ballyhoo. They marched off to war believing they'd be back in a month, covered with honors and telling high tales of adventure. None of them had any idea what a battlefield was going to look like or sound like or smell like. They had no idea that they were going to be hungry and sick and wet, with rot setting up in their boots when they were lucky enough to have them. They could not have imagined that they would find the bodies of men dead and, worse, men still alive on a battlefield days after the battle was over, screaming, crying, begging—men laying beside corpses in Confederate uniforms being feasted on by pigs working their way around the battlefield.

There wasn't much cheering and clapping and throwing hats up in the air after the war started and certainly not by the end. There had to be something for these men after all the misery, something other than poverty and more hunger and a backbreaking lifetime trying to squeeze a living out of worn-out land.

Lafayette Cobb squatted down at the crest of the bluff looking out over the Catawba River. He picked up a hand full of red clay. After squeezing it into a clump, he threw it out into the water. He stood watching the swift current as it took the water of the Catawba to the sea.

Lafayette Cobb then walked along the old Creek Indian path, still there beside the river, running over the bluff and down until the land ran low, close to the level of the river, onto the fertile flood plains. Lafayette squatted down again and gazed out at the river. He reached out and put his walking stick into the water. He watched as the water swirled around it, climbing up on the side against the current.

The power of that river. What enormous power there was in that river. Lafayette thought of all the spindles he had seen working off one water wheel at the exposition in Boston. How many hundreds of spindles could you turn with the force of this river. He leaned down even further and put his hand into the water. He flattened his palm against the current and watched the water flow around the tips of his fingers. A dam that extended even halfway across the water would speed up the flow around it enough to turn a shaft in the driest season.

He stood up and gazed south, down the river. With a mill, they could spin the cotton themselves. Instead of shipping all that beautiful raw cotton to the mills in New England or Manchester and letting them make all the profits turning it into cloth, they could do it themselves. They could do it even more cheaply than the New Englanders or the British. There would be no expensive transport hundreds or thousands of miles to the mills, and labor had always been cheaper in the South.

Most of the men in the Valley were now out of work and without land. They needed jobs. Even women and children had worked textile mills around Columbus before the war. There was no reason why they couldn't do so again. Lafayette looked across the river at the fine old houses still remaining, the magnificent Crawford house atop Booker hill. It was a beautiful, majestic old home in the best Southern Greek revival tradition. Five immense fluted columns lined the width of the wide front porch, all the way to the roof two stories up. There was a gracious balcony outside the landing of the second floor. Even though Lafayette couldn't see the balcony from where he stood at the river, he could remember before the war arriving there in a carriage and seeing the daughters of the house in their wide-skirted dresses standing together on that balcony, kited out in a rainbow of colors. Hats and streamers, long lustrous hair, dainty lace gloves over their white hands.

Would that ever come back? What would happen to all that if Wilkes Ferry turned into Columbus, grimy mill hands and their women taking over the quiet streets? What good would he have done if he had helped to bring that about?

At least in Columbus, the city fathers had finally moved the mill workers across the river to the Alabama side, to get them and their ways apart from decent folks. But after that, they had pretty much wiped their hands of what happened in the mill tenements. The squalor bred more squalor and crime. It wasn't safe for even a grown white man to venture over to Phenix City after dark.

And in the mornings, most of the low-class workers crossed the Fourteenth Street Bridge and came over to the good part of town to work in the mills, which were still close to where their owners lived.

Lafayette Cobb thought there had to be a better way. Mills didn't have to mean squalor and tenements. He was well acquainted with the mill villages around Lowell, Massachusetts. They weren't crime-ridden nor were they filled with temporary lean-to housing. To be fair, New England was too cold for temporary tar-paper shacks, but in many of those mills near Lowell, only young women worked, young women from surrounding farms, decent girls, saving money to send to their parents on the farm or for anticipated betrothals. Those mill communities were fine places to live.

There was one thing Lafayette Langdale Cobb knew for sure. That was that there was nothing that could be done up North that couldn't be done better here.

Lafayette envisioned a mill, no mills, textile mills lining the twelve-mile stretch of the Catawba all down the Valley. Textile mill villages with decent housing to attract hard working farm people. There were enough of those sorts of people around, and most of them didn't have farms left. The ones that did could barely support one person, let alone a whole family.

So Lafayette Cobb stayed put, set down roots, and found the money locally to build the first textile mill in the Valley, a mile south of Wilkes Ferry. They built a stone wall out into the river when the river was at its driest, and then they extended water shafts out into the riverbed. The flow of the Catawba turned the shafts, which turned all the pulleys and spindles in the Lafayette Mill.

There were jobs enough for everyone, decent jobs. Lafayette Cobb made sure there were enough profits to make everyone's life bearable. The company built neat little four-room white frame houses all around the mill close enough for the workers to walk the few blocks to work. The Company built and maintained the houses for a reasonable amount of rent deducted from each wage packet. Lafayette Cobb paid out of his own pocket the wages of the first school teacher hired to set up classes in the little school house. He made it his business to see to it that families came to and stayed as workers in the mill. Troublemakers and thugs were sent packing. Lafayette was a mill community setup for decent folk, not the kind of mill trash that had worked in Columbus.

With the building of the first mill, the Lafayette Mill, Wilkes Ferry was transformed from simply a little town where the rail lines didn't match up and the river met the rails, to a magnet for cotton and for decent farm folk in need of jobs.

Shipping out cotton at ten cents a pound hadn't been nearly as lucrative as separating, combing, and turning that cotton into cloth. Lafayette Cobb got the pick of the finest cotton coming through Wilkes Ferry to the railroad. He hired workers to grade that cotton, and he outbid the Northern and English cotton factors. Lafayette Cobb could offer the planters a higher price because he didn't have to ship the cotton to mills far away to pick, comb, separate, spin, and draw the cotton. He made a fortune.

Lafayette and his sons and cousins, who came later to help out, didn't stop with one mill. The Cobb family built mills all down the Catawba River Valley. First there was Lafayette Mill and then River Falls Mill and then Sweet Water Mill, and on and on.

They built not only mills, but also community centers for each mill village. Then they provided something like a system of socialized medicine. The Company hired doctors who stayed on call. Each worker paid a certain amount out of his weekly paycheck, and when he needed a doctor and medicine for himself or his family, one came for free.

It was way better than anything most workers had ever had. And even people who had managed to hold onto some of their land through the war, left it for the more predictable work in the mills.

As long as Lafayette Cobb and his sons and grandsons owned the Cobb Manufacturing Company, textile workers in the Valley had better conditions than any other textile workers in the country. Don't get me wrong, the Cobbs made money, lots of it, and conditions were good in part because the Cobbs were afraid of the unions, but they could also hold their heads up in front of any man who worked for them, from mill managers to janitors. They had nothing to be ashamed of, and they opened their house twice a year to the workers for a giant

Christmas party, where every child got a gift, and on the fourth of July when they shot off fireworks from on top of the hill where they lived.

Lafayette and Miss Mary Fanny built an enormous house with extensive grounds way down in the Valley not in Wilkes Ferry where the rest of the Company management lived. The symbolic act was not lost on the workers in the five Cobb mills.

Whores de Overs

Robert Forrester did not, in the end, figure out a way to keep from taking Tamyra and the children to Duke. The family went, and Tamyra told the "whores-de-overs" joke at the welcoming reception just as Robert had feared.

He watched from across the room as tight smiles spread over the faces of the people around Tamyra at the buffet table when she told the joke. And he watched as looks passed from one to the other. Tamyra saw him watching, and she threw up her hand and shouted to him. "Hey baby," she drawled. "Just entertainin' ya' friends with a little South Alabama humor. They didn't know when they hired you they'd be getting a redneck country girl too."

Robert clamped down his jaw and wanted to throw something at her, but he tried to smile. She was nervous, loud, and a little drunk. This was going to be a disaster just as it had been every time she came to a faculty gathering.

But to Robert's surprise, most of the faculty members were kind the next morning. They treated Robert with sympathy just like they did when they found out about Luke and his disease. Robert thought that perhaps they thought there was something noble in the situation, like Robert had chosen to marry this horrible woman with a handicapped child because he was just such a great guy.

Over the next few years, Robert settled in at Duke, and Luke just kept getting worse. They lived perpetually on a roller coaster of emergencies and operations.

Luke lived past the predicted twelve years and just kept going. He didn't die; he just became more and more obese and, in Robert's mind, disgusting. And like his mother, the more obese and disgusting Luke got, the more he tried to compensate for it by being loud and obnoxious and crude. Three years after Tamyra went to the first welcoming reception at Duke, she attended another welcoming reception, this time for a new faculty member that Robert, she learned at the reception, had been instrumental in recruiting. The new faculty member was a young assistant professor named Barbie Tombs. She had been Robert's graduate student at Cummings University, where he had had his first job before going to Southern State.

A year after that, Tamyra and Luke learned that Robert and Barbie were virtually living together in her small apartment in a fashionable part of Durham. Tamyra took Robert straight to court, and Luke went with her. Luke sat in court in his wheelchair right beside Tamyra and the attorney. Tamyra took Robert Forrester to the cleaners. Then she packed up her things, sold the house they built, put Luke in her van, and drove home. She enrolled Luke as a freshman at Southern State and got a job in the provost's office. With some of the settlement money from Robert, she built a small brick handicap-friendly house for herself and Luke, and they began life again. They were near enough to Tamyra's two brothers for Luke to have male companionship, and for his twenty-first birthday, they took him to a whorehouse.

Robert had almost no contact with them, and when he and Barbie married two years later, he didn't even want his family at the wedding. Tamyra threatened to tear the wedding party apart if he didn't invite his own son, and Robert reluctantly relented. He sent money for Robin and Luke to fly in. Robin declined the invitation, and so Tamyra carried Luke to Durham to Robert's house and went home. Robert and the Barbie doll, as Tamyra and Luke referred to her, were supposed to drive Luke home after the wedding on their way to Miami.

After virtually ignoring Luke during the wedding and the reception, Robert got into a quarrel with him when he took him back to the motel where he had arranged for Luke to stay. The quarrel ended with Robert screaming at Luke that he (Luke) had ruined his (Robert's) life. Robert then threw a fist full of money at Luke and told him to get a taxi to the airport and go home. Robert and Barbie then left on their honeymoon, a walking tour of Wales.

Luke phoned Tamyra to tell her what had happened. Tamyra got in her car and drove all night to Durham so she could bring Luke home. After that, neither Luke nor Tamyra had anything to do with Robert.

Luke not only started at Southern State, he finished there three years later with a degree in French, having outlived his doctors' predictions by over fifteen years. Robert visited periodically, infrequently and fought a constant battle with Tamyra over money. He resented every penny he had to spend on Luke's and Robin's upkeep, and on more than one occasion, Tamyra could hear the Barbie doll in the background while Robert was on the phone, yelling ugly things for him to say to Tamyra.

The last visit Robert made to see Luke was when Luke was twenty-four. Robert came into town calling Tamyra only after he had left Durham and was on his way. Tamyra reluctantly agreed to allow him to see Luke, and Luke agreed to see Robert. Tamyra made an appointment at the local spa and planned on spending the day, one of the first she had had to herself for years. When Robert arrived at her house, she left.

A few hours later, Tamyra received an emergency phone call at the spa. Wrapped in hot towels with cucumbers on her eyes and green mint mask all over her body, she raised up as the attendant held her cell phone for her.

"Mama." It was Luke's panicked voice. "I've had an accident. You've got to come home."

Tamyra was used to emergency phone calls, and she sprang into action without a word. Ripping off towels and scattering cucumbers on the floor, she called for water to wash off her body. She was terrified that she was going to arrive home and find Luke covered in blood.

What she did find was Luke and Robert calmly watching television, eating out of the same bowl of Tostidos. The house smelled like shit.

"What are the two of you doing?" she asked, trying to catch her breath from rushing home, fearing the worst.

Robert got up and went into the kitchen while Luke explained that he had had an accident in his pants and in the bathroom and needed cleaning up. Tamyra cleaned him up, cleaned the bathroom, and sprayed air disinfectant all over the house before walking into the kitchen where Robert had planted himself.

"Hey." Robert looked up at her as if nothing had happened.

"Let me just get this straight," Tamyra said. "You had Luke phone me and make me come home from a prepaid day at the spa because he had an accident in his pants?"

"Yeah?" Robert answered like he didn't understand what she was on about.

"The one day I have to myself in years. I pay the fee for the whole day at the spa, and you phone me to come home and clean up shit?"

Robert threw up his hands. "I knew he'd be humiliated if I did it."

Tamyra stood frozen in the middle of the kitchen floor blinking. "Humiliated," she said. "You knew he would be humiliated. Why, Robert, would he be humiliated? You are his father. I clean him up all the time. He has these accidents almost daily, and I get down on my hands and knees and clean him up. But you have him phone me because you are too good to touch your own son's shit. Is that right? Have I got it?"

Robert only shrugged.

"You get out and don't ever come back. Ever. Do you understand?"

Robert got up and left.

A week later, Luke received a giant flat-screen television set sent by Robert and delivered by UPS. Tamyra and Luke called it the television that shit bought.

The Depression and Ruby Gem

Workers who got jobs in the Cobb mills were proud to have them and proud for the Cobbs to make money off their backs, their lungs, their eyesight, and their hearing. They were proud when the Company got them through the Depression. That's how they thought of it, the Company getting them through the Depression.

It wasn't as if they didn't feel the effects of the Depression; they did. But they were luckier than most people. They didn't go hungry or at least not often. As conditions got more and more desperate, workers had their hours cut back and then cut back more, but nobody was let go and everybody shared the cutbacks, even the managers.

Still, my grandparents had a difficult time supporting the two children they had, my father Will Lee and his sister DeWilla. They were probably lucky that a third daughter, Ruby Gem, died shortly after she was born. She would have only been another mouth to feed. But my grandmother, DeeMama, mourned this little girl for the rest of her life. Whenever DeeMama got really upset and emotional, she would start to rock slightly and repeat Ruby Gem's name. DeeMama was eventually buried between my grandfather, Will Henry McPherson, and Ruby Gem in the Valley Cemetery.

It was around the time of the Depression, or so I am told, that my Grandfather McPherson started to drink seriously. He had always been a drinker, but as my grandmother proudly said, he never missed a day of work in his life because of drinking.

I suspect this wasn't true, primarily because she said it so often. Nobody denies something over and over without being guilty. I suspect that with the Depression and idle time on his hands, Will Henry MacPherson spent entirely too much time sitting in the woods, telling stories with his blue tick hound Jake, his buddies, and a bottle. I suspect that the "never missed a day of work because of drink" line was just another of the convenient fictions that seemed to be manufactured by our family like Ford motor cars off the assembly line. Massive denial appears to be one of the few things the two sides of my family had in common.

No one talked about my grandfathers, either of them. One of the reasons DeeMama came to like me so much and leave me her lovely Hoosier cabinet was that I once asked her when we were alone whether my grandfather had been alive when I was born. Now DeeMama was a strange woman. I don't think anybody ever saw her real self, if indeed there was even a real self left inside her to see.

She kept up an act all the time—cute, sweet little DeeMama—but I never got the sense that behind the facade there was a person in there. Her conversation was a collection of cliches. I cannot remember her ever saying or thinking anything original.

Maybe DeeMama just pretended so much for so long to be brave, to be cheerful, to be happy, she just somewhere in it all forgot how to do anything else. When I asked her whether Granddaddy was alive when I was born, I was sitting on my mother's sofa. DeeMama looked up at me, and it was as if she seemed to see me for the first time, and I her.

I realized later that everybody else in the family avoided talking about Will Henry McPherson. I had never heard my father or Aunt DeWilla or one of the grandchildren so much as ask a question about him. They either knew or had been told or somehow just realized that this was a forbidden topic. Of course, forbidden topics were, and have always been, my specialty.

DeeMama was touched that one of us was not ashamed to ask about my grandfather. Will Henry McPherson was, incidently, alive when I was born, and it meant a great deal to me to know that. I have no idea why it meant so much to me, but it did. DeeMama saw that it meant something to me, and she was grateful—not that she ever said anything about it, but I could tell from her expression that day in my mother's living room. And there was the Hoosier cabinet. DeWilla would have spit nails to get that Hoosier cabinet, but in the one time Daddy stood up to DeWilla, he was adamant that DeeMama had wanted it to go to me. It now lives in my kitchen.

Anyway, the Depression was hard for my grandparents—two adults living in rented mill housing with two small children and only working a few hours a week. They did what everybody else in the Depression did, they improvised and they shared. DeeMama told me once that every night, the people on Tallasee Street where they lived, got together for a meal. Each family brought what they had. One might have a little flour, another a little cornmeal, another a slice of fat back to season the vegetables. The men and boys brought catfish from the river and whatever vegetables and roots they could gather from the gardens everybody kept on the bottomland down near the riverbanks. My father gardened on an island in the middle of the Catawba, where the soil was especially fertile since it was flooded regularly every year.

The women combined all the resources and fed everyone. From each according to his resources to each according to his need. But all of them hated and feared Communists. None of them had ever even read Karl Marx. I suspect that most of them hadn't even heard his name.

Daddy said that when the union organizers came around, the men from the mill villages would get up on top of the mills, some with shotguns and other with shotguns made out of wood (Quaker guns they had come to be called in the Civil War), and call themselves protecting their jobs. Daddy also told me that "fightin' the strikers" always turned into one big drinking party, an excuse for all the men to get away from their wives and families and drink to their heart's content.

My grandparents survived the Depression, but my grandfather didn't survive the drinking. His blue tick hound met my father at the mill gate one afternoon and led my father back to his master's body. The dog, Jake, lay down on the front porch, put his head down, and never got up again. He died of a broken heart a week later. It's a good story. I have no idea whether or not it's true. My father swore up and down it was, but swearing up and down that a story is true is just a part of good Southern story telling. Besides, after a while, all really good stories become true, for the teller if not the listener, and often for both.

My father always said that my grandfather's death was an accident. There were a lot of "accidents" in the family. This accident was that my grandfather burned to death in a brush fire while he was sleeping. Now this little piece of fiction never struck me as strange until I happened to contemplate how unlikely it was that someone would sleep through their own death, especially death by being burned alive.

It did not escape my powers of imagination, especially since I had found myself in such a state on more than a few occasions in my life, that my grandfather was passed out, dead drunk, stinko, instead of merely asleep. Still, even though I am acquainted intimately with the effects of overindulgence of every sort, I found it difficult to contemplate being in such a profound state of drunken unconsciousness I allowed myself to burn alive. I also, years later, found it difficult to accept that an inmate could hang himself with a metal telephone cable even though the warden and the guards assured me it was true. There is a strange kind of determination that pervades those desperate for oblivion.

My cousin Biddy once suggested that my grandfather and hers had been murdered, and then the brush fire started. This seems to me a much more likely possibility, but Biddy offered nothing more than this vague speculation. She mentioned no motive, and I didn't know enough about Will Henry McPherson to even guess at one. And that's certainly not something I could have asked DeeMama or Daddy. Daddy choked up every time he talked about my grandfather. Mother, of course, hated Granddaddy MacPherson's guts.

Like most people who lived through the Depression, my grandmother saved everything—newspapers, my father's letters, my mother's letters to my father (my mother never found out about this, I had them hidden), sticks which could be used for toothbrushes, soap ends, string, rubber bands. When I was really young, she cooked huge vats of soap made with chinaberries in her backyard in a big round black pot. She used the same pot for washing clothes. I can remember seeing her sitting in her backyard, stirring the steaming clothes in the pot with a stick.

DeeMama told me that this tendency to save everything, use everything, didn't just come from the Depression. She said her grandmother taught her how to save and use everything from her experiences during the Civil War. Not too long after the war started, so many things became scarce or so expensive regular people couldn't even hope to buy them. So just like during the Depression, everybody improvised. DeeMama said her grandmother used chinaberries to make soap and old newspapers as envelopes. She turned used bottles into glasses. Walnut hulls were ground down and used as dye or ink. Gourd shells made excellent buttons;

corncob ashes were used to make bread when there wasn't any flour. They started growing peanuts seriously during the Civil War and used them to make candy and burn in lamps. It was also during the war that sugarcane started to be commonly grown in the South to replace refined sugar, which they couldn't get at all.

When DeeMama died, my father found hundreds of old newspapers underneath her apartment building, where she had hidden them from his periodic attempts to purge her apartment of items that were certain to cause her death by internal combustion.

DeeMama adored my father. Several years before she died, I went to her apartment with my father to check on her. We were sitting in her little den, and my father was talking about something. My grandmother and I were listening. At least I was listening. Then as my father paused, my grandmother said to no one in particular, "Isn't he precious?"

My father looked over at me and rolled his eyes and we both laughed.

From then to his death, I would refer to him as "Precious" when my mother wasn't around to overhear.

This was exactly the sort of comment that would have sent my mother into fits. Mama hated the relationship between my grandmother and my father and was insanely jealous of every minute he spent with DeeMama. My mother actually hated DeeMama although she would never have admitted this. It wasn't, after all, Christian to do so.

There seemed to be two lifetimes of accumulated slights between Mama and DeeMama. Of course, I only heard them from Mama's side. Mama, of course, used these stories to legitimate her constant dogging-out of DeeMama. I heard all of them many times. One slight occurred during WWII. For some reason, when Daddy first went into the army, Mother stayed with DeeMama for a while. I am sure it was the last time the two of them ever shared the same roof. Mama was working, and she ordered a lipstick through a salesman who came round knocking on the doors. When the salesman came back to leave the lipstick and get his money, Mama wasn't there and DeeMama (according to Mama) had a hissy fit.

When Mama came home, DeeMama lit into her yelling at her about wasting money on face paint and running up bills. Further, DeeMama accused Mama of getting them into debt and prompting bill collectors (the guy collecting for the lipstick) to come around demanding money. To DeeMama, this was the worst thing that had ever happened to her. Mama had shamed the McPherson family name. I don't know if it happened that way or not, but that was Mama's story and, by God, she was sticking to it. She stuck to it and told it over and over again until shortly before she died, about sixty years later.

My mother would go through phases with my grandmother. There were periods when she would refuse to have anything to do with DeeMama. She wouldn't even talk to her on the telephone. DeeMama would call. If mother answered the phone, which she avoided doing since she might have to talk with my grandmother, and my grandmother started talking, my mother would interrupt her with a flat statement like, "I'll get Will" or "Will isn't here. I'll tell him you phoned." After that, she would abruptly put down the phone. She was civil but barely, and she made plain by her tone that she did not intend to exchange pleasantries.

During other periods, my mother would, for some reason or other, decide she was going to be magnanimous and make a stab at loving DeeMama. That's right, the effort wasn't just to like DeeMama or be decent to her. Mother was going to love DeeMama. When these magnanimous turns came on her, the most surprising things would come out of her mouth, things I never thought I'd ever hear, about what a hard life DeeMama really had, or that my mother thought (on the basis of no empirical evidence that I could see) my grandmother had finally started to realize how much she (my mother) loved my father. Aunt DeWilla usually got dragged into and out of favor with DeeMama. When Mother decided that DeeMama could be treated decently because she (DeeMama) finally realized how much Mother really loved Daddy, DeWilla somehow miraculously seemed to make the same discovery at the same time.

Mother would then proceed to drive Daddy crazy, asking him why he didn't do this or that for DeeMama or DeWilla, why he didn't invite them for dinner or to the backwater or out to eat. She would proceed to drive me crazy by making these discomforting statements in supercilious tones. "DeWilla's always been so good to Will, and she's worked so hard taking care of Mrs. McPherson," she would say, referring to DeeMama.

I never once heard my mother call my grandmother anything but Mrs. McPherson, not DeeMama or Delia, which was her name. It was unmistakable that this bit of formality was obviously intended to maintain a distance between Mother and DeeMama like a stiff arm.

Back to the business about DeWilla being so nice to Daddy or her working so hard to take care of DeeMama. Let me tell you, DeWilla was never ever good to anybody, least of all to my father, who she drove crazy with her incessant demands all his life. DeWilla and Mother were the two people in all the world who could reduce my dear father to tears of frustration and sheer exhaustion later on in his life. To say that DeWilla had worked hard at anything in her life except being mean and manipulative and mercenary would have been to fly in the face of God.

DeWilla was, in fact, so hateful Mattie Mae was afraid to stay in the same house with her. There was almost nothing Mattie Mae wouldn't do for us. But she drew the line at spending time around DeWilla. Mattie Mae never said so directly, but I do believe she truly thought DeWilla to be an instrument of the devil. I truly believe Mattie Mae was right.

You can see why these magnanimous phases were so disquieting. Daddy and I had to tiptoe around listening to the most outrageous nonsense coming out of my mother's mouth without ever revealing so much as a hair's breath of an eyebrow twitch of disbelief or, God forbid, amusement. When mother was being loving to DeeMama and DeWilla, it was damn near suicidal to do anything to remind her that only a few weeks (or days) before, she would have gladly wiped her feet on their faces.

Given all the time my father and I spent walking around on our toes, it was fortunate I took up ballet. It was unfortunate, however, that I became so accustomed to dancing I could not stop or feel comfortable without my toe shoes. By the time I was fifty, I was so exhausted I could barely breathe.

These magnanimous loving phases never lasted long. Something would happen, some small offhand comment would be made, some look exchanged, and mother would fly into another "refusing to speak to DeeMama and Dewilla" phase. The refusing-to-speak phases were actually much less stressful for Daddy and I than the loving phases. The not-speaking phases were more stable, long lasting, and not as likely to blow up in our faces.

The final phase lasted fifteen years, during which my mother spoke not one word to DeeMama. I actually saw my mother turn her back on my grandmother and walk away when DeeMama, then over eighty, approached Mother at a family gathering. This gathering was at DeWilla's house, and Mother only came along because she couldn't stand the thought of being left alone while we all went without her. It was one of those rare times when we just all decided to do what was reasonable instead of what Mother wanted us to do, which was to stay at home. The final fifteen-year chill started over one silly little story my grandmother told.

Now DeeMama was not an educated woman. A lot of her conversation—well, all of their conversation consisted of cliches and repeating the same cliches over and over again, if they remotely fit into what was being said. I cannot count the number of times I heard her say, "You have to go where the work is." Every time something was said abut jobs or work, she would come out with, "You have to go where the work is."

It is interesting, now that I think about the era in which my grandmother lived, that she repeated this sentence so often. There is a picture of her and Will Henry when they were first married, only kids, neither of them very good-looking, neither of them very happy standing in a meadow looking up at the camera like they were about to step off the end of the earth. They looked like immigrants getting off the boat at Ellis Island. Neither of them were very tall. Both of them had dark circles around their eyes. My grandmother had on dark stockings and dark chunky shoes, a dark skirt and sweater and a white blouse. Will Henry had on checkered knickers, ribbed knee socks, a pullover sweater that showed off his slight frame and a cap.

They were, I imagine, leaving the farm, the two of them, and going to the Valley to find work in the mills. They had just been married. It was 1916. What an amazing step this must have been for them. It must have seemed like stepping off the end of the earth. To leave the family and the farm must have been exhilarating and terrifying at the same time. Somebody, perhaps my grandfather, must have said to her, "You have to go where the work is" and she must have repeated it to herself a thousand times. "You have to go where the work is." All these years later, she was still saying it.

My grandmother and grandfather walked from the farm to the mills, and for the next fifty years, my grandmother stood in the spinning room of one of Lafayette Cobb's mills. I never saw her pick up a book and read anything but the Bible. She raised two children, saw one through a world war, and buried her childhood sweetheart before she was fifty.

She got two children through the Depression. My father got up at four every morning and went down to the river. There he got in a little John boat and rowed across part of the river to an island where he had their garden. After tending to the garden, he rowed back, walked home, and cleaned out the grate in the fireplace for DeeMama. She would have biscuits waiting for him and clean clothes for him to wear to school. She might have been up all night washing those clothes and drying them and ironing them. They might have been the same clothes he wore to school the day before, but they were clean and pressed and ready for him to wear to school again. Daddy was proud of that story, and he told it many times, outside of the hearing of my mother. The story made my mother furious.

Some mornings, if he hadn't had time to finish studying the night before, DeeMama would get him up at four to study instead of having him go to tend the garden. He was proud of that as well and choked up when he told it.

He told it once when Mama came into the room. She picked up the thread immediately.

"Can you imagine?" she said to me. "Can you imagine a mother sending her child to the river to row across all that current in a tiny boat? I think it is horrible, irresponsible."

Daddy and I, of course, didn't say a word. Daddy didn't even protest the implied insult. Mother had worn him to a nub.

So DeeMama wasn't a sophisticated woman, but she liked to tease and to be funny. She liked to make people laugh, who doesn't? Unfortunately, though, she was not good at it. That day, the day of the beginning of the fifteen-year chill, my grandmother was giddy with excitement because my father, my mother, and I had come to see her. It was a rare event when my mother agreed to go to DeeMama's house, and DeeMama couldn't be faulted for being somewhat anxious and nervous.

She was kidding around and telling fragments of stories about when my father and mother got married. She was trying to be the Miss Delia she liked so well to play, cute little four foot seven Miss Delia, the spry little old lady. She stupidly blundered into some statement about having to talk my father into going to the church the morning of their wedding, implying that he had second thoughts about marrying my mother. Well, no. She didn't imply it. She said it. When she came out with the offending sentences, she leaned over toward me, put her hand up over her mouth, and winked.

Now I know this was an insulting thing to say, and even though she was kidding, it wasn't really funny, and I wouldn't have especially liked it had someone been teasing me in that way. But the woman was almost eighty years old at the time, and to turn this clumsy attempt at teasing into a fifteen-year-long vendetta was ridiculous, but it was just like what always happened to end the loving phases my mother orchestrated with DeeMama and DeWilla. It hurt my father more than I can say, but my mother found so many ways to hurt my father, it's hard to keep track of them all.

Stomping Her Foot

The damn funeral wasn't even about Beth Ann.

If I hadn't recognized her mama and daddy—still good-looking in their seventies—sitting less than a foot away from the sleek gray coffin, I would have thought I was at the wrong ceremony.

The family had, for reasons I could not fathom then and still cannot fathom today, asked a fifth cousin, half-removed, that nobody had ever set eyes on before to give the eulogy at the grave site.

The man droned on and on for a tortuous half hour without even mentioning Beth Ann. I felt my soul flittering around the edges of ill temper and mean-spiritedness.

Then mercifully, half-removed, or half-wit as I was beginning to think of him, informed us that he was finishing up—with a short amusing anecdote.

I do not think amusing anecdotes (short or otherwise) have any place at funerals, especially not funerals where the deceased has had a stroke forty years before her time. And the anecdote turned out not to even be amusing.

The half-wit told us with great delight that once while Beth Ann was in college, he had been traveling through the town in which her college was located. He had arranged to meet Beth Ann for lunch. Beth Ann showed up in a dress.

That was it. That was the "amusing anecdote."

Half-wit stared out at the assembled crowd with that Richard Nixon used-car-salesman smile, waiting. For what? A roar of laughter, a titter of appreciation, a smile of recognition? I have no idea.

I didn't understand the joke, and nobody else did. Half-wit stood there with that look dogs get when they're caught in the chicken coop—part smile, part embarrassment, part supplication.

Finally, the preacher rescued the half-wit by gently taking his arm and pulling him backward. "Shall we pray?" the preacher asked.

Pray for him. I wanted to but did not say.

I folded my arms across my chest and while everybody else was praying, I stood wondering what in the world I was doing there on the hillside of the Confederate Memorial Cemetery, watching the body of a forty-year-old woman I had known since I was five be lowered into the ground.

I knew everybody there—parents of children who grew up with Beth Ann and I, some decrepit former school teachers like Mrs. Hawkins, preachers and their wives. But there was no one who belonged to the second twenty years of Beth Ann's life—no husband, no children, no coworkers, not even a dog. And there was no mention of that part of her life, as if it had been buried long before the body.

I felt more than a little bit insulted, partly because I could see my own funeral turning out just like this if (God forbid) I should die suddenly between husbands.

I could just hear some idiot reducing my entire life to a joke about wearing a dress. Beth Ann and I were clearly something more than what we had been during the twenty years we occupied that tiny, sweltering, incestuous little town, but nobody there seemed to know it.

If we'd had children and husbands, I guess it would have been different; we would have been eulogized as loving mothers (even if we hadn't been), faithful wives (which would have only been true if Beth Ann had a major personality change since high school), and dutiful daughters (which I knew damn well didn't fit either one of us).

As it was, we were single and without children and therefore invisible as functioning adults. Nobody would be able to think of one single thing to say about us at our funerals except stories that were twenty or twenty-five years in the past and that said nothing about the struggles and triumphs, the tears and loneliness, the sleepless nights, the exhilarating days or the sheer stubborn independence of the other twenty years.

They would understand nothing about the value of our accomplishments, our reckless gambles, lost causes, hard-won battles, or desperate losses.

And it's really funny, but the most vivid memory I have of Beth Ann is her, beet red with frustration and rage, stomping her foot. I can just see her, and I know if it was at all possible, she was either looking down or up at that funeral, stomping her foot.

Sweet Honey Terrace

Mother always maintained that Sweet McKean was her best friend. I have no idea why she felt Sweet McKean was her best friend. As far as I could see, Sweet and her disreputable husband, Reese Tate, did little, if anything, for mother except phone me to ask how she was doing between their cruises. Every once in a while, the two of them showed up when Mother was in the hospital. They never stayed over ten minutes and then took off for dinner and a movie. This is not a best friend in my way of thinking.

Sweet McKean and Reese Tate were never involved in the dirty work of life. They never seem to put themselves out in the slightest. That's what I think a best friend is, a person who is there to do the dirty work when dirty work is needed, a person who doesn't even mind doing the dirty work when needed. But there was no dirty work for Sweet McKean. And as far as I could see, there never had been. Reese Tate made sure he would never have to do any more dirty work by marrying Sweet McKean.

Sweet's parents, the McGregors, were the scions of the First Baptist Church when I was growing up. They sat in the same place on the same pew every Sunday, third pew from the front on the left-hand side near the center aisle, as you would see it from the balcony.

The McGregor/McKean clan sat together every Sunday—Miss Fiona, old Mr. McGregor, Sweet and her husband Ben McKean and their three boys. I liked Miss Fiona. I had her once as a Sunday school teacher. I didn't know the rest of the McGregor/McKean clan very well then. I had no bad feelings about them, didn't think much about them at all, except to watch the scene as they paraded into church every Sunday and took their places, watched by the rest of the congregation.

The McGregors and the McKeans were rulers of the roost, and they knew it. They weren't obnoxious about it or not that I remember. But then, they didn't have to be. They were just the richest, most deferred to members of the church. They were like a lot of rich families in Wilkes Ferry. They weren't snooty. They didn't have to be. They always got their way. If you couldn't be nice when you got everything you fucking wanted, you were just plain ill-mannered.

Old Mr. McGregor owned a chain of furniture stores. So the McGregors were not "old money," part of the planter class with generations of inherited wealth. Maybe that's why they were nicer than the old-money planter families. Or perhaps it was because they were truly religious and among the ten people on the face of the earth who took seriously the dictum that it was easier for a camel to pass through the eye of a needle than for a rich family from Wilkes Ferry to go to heaven. Anyway, they were nice enough, virtually supported the church single-handedly, and were there every time the doors opened. None of this saved them, though, in the end.

Sweet McKean was one of the McGregors' two daughters. She and Ben McKean had three boys. The boys were a handful and the delight of their grandparents. They were all three as cute as buttons and had the diminutive stature determined by their double dose of Scottish genes—one set from the McGregors and the other from the McKeans. Sweet and her sister Honey were tiny, perfect, rich and, thoroughly spoiled.

Daddy told me that old Mr. McGregor made his money selling and reselling furniture to every poor person in the Valley. If you invested in the furniture and then sold it to poor people, you could be sure to repossess it before very long and then sell it again, and again, and again. I have no idea of the truth of this story, but Daddy seldom told outright lies, at least not about other people. He embellished as all Southerners do but just to make a story better. He was not above stretching the truth, but he was above breaking it altogether. Daddy might outright lie about something that had happened to him, but he wouldn't have lied about somebody else.

Anyway, old Mr. McGregor made a fortune. He and Miss Fiona built an enormous house on some land they bought along the east side of the Catawba

River, downstream about two miles from the bridge. From that day to this, the house has been referred to as the "McGregor Mansion." When we moved back to Wilkes Ferry and I needed to give directions to someone who didn't know which house was ours, I used the name. "We're just two houses down from the McGregor Mansion," I would say. It worked every time because everybody who ever lived in the Valley knew where the McGregor Mansion was. The neighborhood around the McGregors' mansion was sometimes, not very kindly, referred to as "McGregorville."

The reason the neighborhood came to be known as McGregorville was that the enormous house and lot of the McGregors was flanked by two others. On the right was the sprawling brick ranch house belonging to Sweet McKean. To the left was the summery, informal white brick house of Sweet's sister, Honey, and Honey's husband, Ed Fist. Old Mr. McGregor named the semicircle road that passed through the neighborhood, arching toward the river, Sweet Honey Terrace. He divided up the rest of the land into lots and sold them off. He made even more money.

Somewhere along the way, the McGregors started a bank and added even more to the fortune. For a while there, it seemed like everything the McGregors touched turned to gold.

And whatever truth there was about repossessing furniture from poor people, there seemed to be no shame in it. As I said, they were the first family of the church. This was possibly because they were selling furniture mostly to black people. But you could argue that if the McGregors hadn't sold them furniture, who else would?

Sweet McKean was one of the mothers in the small group of mothers having children my age, the mothers of the children I started kindergarten with. She did not, however, seem to be part of the bridge circuit. My mother, like the mothers of most of the children I knew, was involved in Scouts, cocktail parties, and bridge parties. You would not believe, had you not seen them, how elaborate the bridge parties were and how dressed up the women got.

They just sat for an afternoon playing cards, smoking cigarettes, and drinking coffee, but every woman had a hat on and heels and gloves. The hostess set out card tables with elaborate settings of napkins, cards, plates, place cards, score books, little picks for the food, and gifts for the guests. Everything matched from the tablecloths to the score pads to the matchbooks. The tablecloths had little pockets in the sides like fitted sheets and were quilted with intricate lines of stitching. To a little girl, it was just magic that everything matched. I, of course, wasn't allowed to touch any of the tantalizing favors until after the party. It took all my self-discipline to leave them alone.

The women talked, laughed and, smoked and sometimes drank but only coffee since these bridge parties were in the afternoons. Sweet was not part of the bridge circuit. She had three young boys, and I guess that took up a lot of time, but still, I don't remember seeing Sweet McKean anywhere but church.

The McGregors, Sweet's parents, followed a pretty traditional religious path. The McKeans started a more modern, jet-set type of religious activity. They started traveling to revival meetings but more often to what were called "retreats." The "retreats" were overnight gatherings of religious people in rustic, camplike settings. The places were like summer camps for adults. Everyone stayed in cabins and walked to daily religious services and Christian recreational activities and pep rallies.

The McKeans started going away for long weekends with other couples chosen to be among the select who were invited to ride in the McGregor bus. It was a matter of intense competition among the young couples in the church to be among the chosen who rode free on the bus to and from "retreat." It was like a rolling Christian party, and Sweet McKean was the gracious, pert, petite, master of ceremonies—the select of the select. Ben McKean went along.

Mr. Ben was a pleasant man. Well, they were both pleasant, but Mr. Ben's pleasant behavior seemed to be genuine. He was just a nice, kind man. He was very handsome, but the most appealing thing about him was his eyes. He looked at you like he really liked you, like he saw something in you that nobody else had seen. I can still see his face in my memory with the crinkled skin around his eyes and the tenderness in his smile.

He always seemed to be kind and gentle and quiet. Having married into the wealthy McGregor clan, he just seemed to good-naturedly go along with the plan, whatever the plan was. Don't get me wrong, he was a principled and perhaps even a religious man. But Mr. Ben was the type who, left alone, would have attended church every Sunday morning, tried to lead a decent life, and left it at that. Miss Sweet was the driving force behind the social whirl of the retreats. Or at least that was my impression.

After a while, weekend retreats didn't seem enough anymore. So Miss Sweet talked the McGregors into building what was called a "playhouse" back in the wooded area toward the river between their two houses. Let me tell you, the "playhouse" was like nothing anybody in the Valley had ever heard of. It was one enormous room with a small kitchen and bathrooms and some storage rooms. And it wasn't a playhouse for children. It was a playhouse for adults.

The adults started having mini-retreats during the week at the playhouse. It was said that sometimes talking in tongues occurred. Now even though we were all members of a First Baptist Church, nobody ever did anything at church as tasteless as talk in tongues. This was something new, sort of like a New Age talking in tongues, not the trashy talking in tongues that went on in country churches.

The "talking in tongues" thing was certainly inconsistent to me with the modern, hip Christian image of Sweet McKean and her crowd of hangers-on. So I don't know whether this detail of the story is true. My guess, however, given what happened later, would be that one night somebody was confronted with a reality they found unacceptable and just couldn't think of anything else to do so they suddenly fell to tongue talking.

Anyway, the shifting set of Christian couples became a little bit less shifting when Reese and Millie Tate wormed their way in near the center of the vortex. Before long, the Tates and the McKeans were an item. They were always together. They didn't change pews at church. That would have been too much. But the minute that last prayer was over every Sunday morning, the Tates were over at pew three, left side, smiling and shaking hands like they were part of the receiving line at Buckingham Palace.

It was a strange pairing from the outset, the McKeans and the Tates. They were so different. Sweet McKean was outgoing, pert, a middle-aged belle. Millie Tate hardly ever opened her mouth. She was as sweet and pleasant as she could be but someone who would shy away from any spotlight for miles around. It didn't make sense, her in the middle of the Christian social swirl.

That Sort 'A Behavior

Less than a year after I sat in the dark back room of Hopewell House with Margaret Ann and the two Dunn children, she phoned and asked me to come home for her wedding. I was not surprised, but I was skeptical. After all, nobody knew anything about this Wilkie Dunn, and the story about his wife's death seemed more than a little strange to me. But when I got to Wilkes Ferry, nobody but Daddy and I seemed to have any reservations about Wilkie Dunn or the coming nuptials. Nobody mentioned the dead wife.

The Pattersons, Margaret Ann's parents, and their entire extended family of Hendersons and Woodruffs and Luces and a few Cobbs sprinkled in, had come out in full force. Preparations were proceeding hot and heavy for the wedding of another Patterson to a prominent doctor. Two of the sisters of Mr. Rebel Patterson, Margaret Ann's father, had married doctors in keeping with the elevated social position of the Patterson family. The remaining sister, Miss Dee, had formed a somewhat disappointing alliance with a man who opened a tacky business on Highway 29 called The Tic Tack Shack. This marriage was definitely a step down for Miss Dee and so for the family. It was an embarrassment. With such a marriage, Miss Dee could not be received in the socially superior homes of her sisters, or at least not at anytime other than at family gatherings.

Miss Dee must have known she was marrying beneath her when she chose Mr. Tic Tack Shack. So it's a puzzle to me that she seemed to resent her consequent exclusion from the charmed circle. But people have a strange ability to blind themselves from consequences. They will freely take an action sure to bring about a particular result and then spend the rest of their lives embroiled in resentment over the outcome. Mr. Tic Tack Shack seemed as well to be bitter over their social position. Perhaps he expected to be elevated into the social circle of the Pattersons, benefitting from their wealth and connections. But this social elevation seems only to work when the woman is elevated into the social sphere of the man's family, not the other way around.

It probably never occurred to Miss Dee's husband that he would ever actually be called upon to make a living. After all, he was married to a Patterson. But the days when a family would financially support a brother-in-law just to keep up appearances were over.

All this must have come as a rude awakening to Miss Dee and her husband, making them seethe with envy over the lifestyles of the other two Patterson sisters and of Miss Sudie herself, who lived well until her death on the investments her husband had made when coal meant profits. She didn't share, and when she died, Miss Dee and her husband considered themselves entitled to more of the estate than Miss Dee's already wealthy sisters.

So Miss Dee and her husband were like wild shoppers at a fire sale in the bargain basement of a department store when Miss Sudie finally died. Miss Dee and her husband argued over every table, every chair, every cup, and every saucer. It was ugly and the family never really resumed friendly relations after the fighting over the spoils. Death, I find, brings out the very best and the very worst in people.

Miss Dee and Mr. Rebel represented the disappointed, bitter side of the Patterson family. When they were growing up, the Pattersons had as much money as any family in town. The Patterson family owned one of the enormous white-columned frame houses near the Baptist Church. Mr. Rebel, being the only son, was spoiled and babied by his mother and given the lucrative family coal business by his father. The daughters were given the consolation prize of a college education.

Who knew that the bottom would fall out of the coal market, leaving Mr. Rebel so broke he wound up shoveling coal himself with his one black employee. I think the black employee was kept on mainly so Mr. Rebel could feel superior to someone and order someone around as he was intended to from birth. The spoiled, rich Rebel Patterson, who was to be the central and most important member of the family, who thought he was going to spend his life after the war in decorous, indolent luxury supported by the profits of coal, became peripheral to the family at best, marginalized by his embarrassingly diminished social position, his lack of money, his bad manners, and then his alcoholism.

Margaret Ann was, through the one act of marrying Wilkie Dunn, pulling the family up out of the social hole Mr. Rebel had dug for them. Margaret Ann was about to be welcomed into the socially prominent fold.

Daddy was the only person other than myself who expressed any unease about or dislike of Wilkie Dunn. When my mother proposed asking Margaret Ann and Wilkie over for dinner right before they were married, my father overheard the plans and said, "Do we have to invite Wilkie?"

But invite Wilkie we did. Anything else would have been rude. Unfortunately, Wilkie accepted the invitation. He was just as obnoxious as Daddy had warned. Wilkie dominated the conversation throughout dinner, conducting a monologue on the general theme of what a hard life doctors had.

He loved talking about the sacrifices doctors made going to medical school, the long hours of hospital work they did as interns, the lack of sleep, constantly being on call. He also found it necessary to pontificate on how doctors deserved every penney they made. It was really hard for me to keep my mouth shut when he started this line of argument. Nobody deserves the amount of money doctors make, and the least they can do about the obscenity of their profits is to keep their fucking mouths shut about it. But Wilkie Dunn's mouth was almost never shut. I am sure that I am far from the only person who fantasized about shutting it for him.

The night Wilkie and Margaret Ann came to my parents' house for dinner, Wilkie's beeper went off. He promptly phoned his service and, in a very loud and overbearing tone, proceeded to harangue the poor girl on the other end of the line for phoning him. This little performance seemed to please him immensely. He was the center of attention just like he wanted to be, always. He was unutterably irritating. I kept catching Daddy rolling his eyes.

At one point during the evening, Wilkie launched into a diatribe about some kind of rude behavior perpetrated by a member of the Country Club. Some man had (surprise, surprise) gotten drunk and started cursing (or cussin' as Southerners say) in the dining room of the Country Club. Wilke was incensed.

"I'm not havin' my (mah) wife (wiiiiif) exposed to that sort 'a behavior (behavya)," he announced, his chin jutting out in righteous indignation.

My eyes went to Daddy's before I could control them, but it didn't matter. We both had to stifle conspiratorial smiles, but Wilkie wouldn't have gotten it if we had laughed out loud. He wouldn't have noticed the rest of us if we had set our hair on fire. Wilkie Dunn was so obsessed with himself, he was oblivious to the feelings of anyone else, even those of us sitting at the same table.

In addition, the offended Southern gentleman act, protecting the flower of Southern womanhood, was ridiculous. It was way too late to begin protecting Margaret Ann from either cursing or anything else. Margaret Ann had worked in the emergency room of Grady Hospital in Atlanta during the entire time she was going to X-ray-technician school. She spent every Friday and Saturday night dealing with gunshot and knife-stabbing victims—fighting, cursing, dying, screaming, and doing whatever else the poor souls who ended up in the emergency room every weekend did. She told me stories about having to break dead people's arms just to get them into overcrowded freezers. But Wilkie was going to duel at dawn over her being exposed some cursing. It was preposterous.

But that was Dr. Wilkie Dunn. Preposterous. His pretensions and his ego were preposterous. His opinions were even more preposterous. He was one of those poor-boy successes who firmly believe that anybody could make $500,000 a year if they just wanted to. He bitterly resented every jar of baby orange juice given to a welfare mother and thought the poor were poor because they were too lazy to be anything else. Good Lord. I don't see now how Daddy and I resisted jumping him at the table and shoving a napkin down his throat. As I look back on it, everybody would have been a whole lot better off if we had.

Fortunately, I was not around enough to really get to know Wilkie Dunn. I think had I been, I would have had to kill him. When I asked him about his parents' farm that night at dinner, he spun a tale, which he had obviously told before, about his family's "plantation." I could feel my mouth twitching to keep from smiling while Wilkie was telling this obvious falsehood. Margaret Ann wouldn't even raise her eyes to meet mine.

The long and the short of it was that we didn't like Wilkie, but what could we do? Were we going to tell Margaret Ann she shouldn't marry the son of a bitch? No. And her family certainly wasn't going to tell her. They were perhaps the only people in town who actually did like Wilkie, and they liked him mostly because he was a doctor and marrying their daughter. Also I suspect, they were almost grateful because they thought nobody would ever marry Margaret Ann or perhaps that Margaret Ann would never accept a proposal.

And you couldn't do much better in the Valley than to marry a doctor, except to marry a Cobb. Margaret Ann's parents, especially her mother, were virtually crowing with pride over the prospect. Years later, they would even ignore Dr. Dunn's abuse of their own daughter because he was a doctor and rich. They told Margaret Ann to go back to him. But that's another story.

It was obvious that Wilkie Dunn was a man who you would not wish on your worst enemy, but Margaret Ann didn't exactly have a good track record with men. The only person I knew who had a worse record was me. So given the facts, who was going to object to her marrying a doctor, even if the doctor's former wife had died in suspicious circumstances? Having wives that died in suspicious circumstances wasn't exactly unique in Wilkes Ferry. The Pattersons would later on add one more to the list themselves.

Besides, who was going to tell Margaret Ann not to marry Wilkie Dunn just because he was an insufferable asshole, an egomaniac, and one of the most arrogant people on the face of the earth? That made him not too much different from most of the doctors in town, hell, most of the doctor in the country. The outrageous hubris of doctors is matched only by the near insane hubris of lawyers.

I just spent only one week listening to Wilkie Dunn. I also spent much longer than that just being glad I hadn't married him.

But Margaret Ann did marry Wilkie Dunn in an elaborate wedding that put her mother into a nervous fit. Corinne, Margaret Ann's mother, had always been the nervous type. She was one of the '50s housewives who went off to a sanitarium for a brief time after both her daughters were born. My mother, by the way, was an exception to this pattern. My mother wouldn't have dared get close to a sanitarium. She was way too smart for that. They might have kept her for life. We would have all been a lot better off had they done so, but she wasn't about to chance it. No, my mother was the queen of control, of her emotions and feelings, and that was just fine with me. I didn't want her to get more in touch with her feelings. I used to think about writing a book entitled *When Mama Got in Touch with Her Feelings and Other Horror Stories.*

But Miss Corinne was just beside herself with excitement over the marriage and the wedding. Corinne was like a second mother to me, but I had never seen this side of her, the social-climbing side. I would never have imagined Miss Corinne lording over other people the fact that her daughter was marrying a doctor. But when Margaret Ann decided to marry Wilkie, Miss Corinne turned into somebody I barely knew.

I guess that had the bottom not fallen out of the coal business and the Pattersons had had all the money they were supposed to have, Miss Corinne would have been like this all the time. I don't know. She surely married Rebel Patterson for something other than his good looks or his personality. She paid an awfully big price for that decision.

But at the wedding, it was obvious that Miss Corinne had just been wanting all those years to be taken in as a part of the wealthy social set belonged to by Rebel's mother and his two sisters. Finally, she was going to have what she wanted. And with their money, she was going to put on a wedding that would be the pride of the Patterson family.

Skinny-Dipping

While presentable enough physically, Reese Tate was just . . . smarmy. There was something ugly about him, something that left you feeling oily after being around him. He was, in this, the opposite of Ben McKean, who was quiet, upright, self-contained, and clean as a scrubbed show horse.

Reese Tate was too loud, told jokes and laughed at them, and thought much too well of himself. Reese Tate thought . . . well, Reese Tate still thought, at the age of eighty-five, he was the cutest little thing in shoe leather. And Reese Tate was always a man on the make.

But how could anybody fault the two couples—the Tates and the McLeans. They were always in church, at prayer meetings, at retreats. They were together because they were the most dedicated Christians in town. Weren't they? But one day, some kid around my age told me a story about somebody coming up on the Tates and the McKeans at the backwater — skinny-dipping.

I thought it was just one of those ridiculous stories that people tell solely because the idea is so preposterous. I thought it was a joke. The idea of the two most Christian couples in the community skinny-dipping at the backwater was just crazy. But the kid maintained it was the truth.

Of course, this kid had gotten the story from somebody else who had gotten it from somebody else. It was rumor on top of rumor on top of rumor. It was in that spirit that I repeated the story to my parents. I was standing in my mother's mauve living room facing the sofa. Mother was sitting in her usual position on the right side of the sofa and Daddy, on the left. Mother was settled in, as she often was, with the newspaper folded to some crossword puzzle, a pen in her hand

(Mother didn't make mistakes). Daddy, as he often did, perched on the other side of the sofa tentatively, as if he were ready at any moment to take flight.

I still remember the look of fury on my mother's face as soon as the story was out of my mouth. Now I must admit I got some little devilish pleasure out of telling the damn story. My mother thought Sweet McKean was destined to sit on the right hand of God. Mama was always preaching at my father and I, who took a relaxed attitude toward spiritual matters, that everyone should be a lot more like Sweet McKean.

So I suppose there was something of the smart ass in my telling the story. No, I know there was something of the smart ass in my repeating the story. I can't imagine what made me do it. I should have known better. I regretted it immediately and for a long time as Humphrey Bogart said to Ingrid Berman in *Casablanca*. I watched as my mother settled into an icy rage even as I spoke the offending words.

"How dare you repeat such a thing?" she hissed venomously. "How dare you go around spreading that kind of malicious gossip?" Now you have to understand that I didn't tell the story as truth. I just said that somebody had told me that somebody else said that this happened.

But of course, after I had opened my mouth, nothing I could say afterward would appease her. I tried to explain that I had told no one but the two of them, and I reminded her that I had prefaced the story by saying it probably wasn't true. But, it didn't matter. It was another in a long list of incidents in which I was magically transformed into the embodiment of everything my mother hated.

In that one minute, I became all the people who had talked about my Grandfather Ward and his less-than-illustrious history. I became all the people that hurt my mother's feelings when she was growing up. The scandal of my grandfather, her poverty, her shame, came back with a vengeance, and I became, in an instant, all her tormentors rolled into one.

She hated me in that instant. I see it now, even though at the time I didn't. I became the spoiled, privileged child that had taunted her with words and tortured her by just being comfortable and self-assured.

I could not apologize enough to my mother for repeating this story, and I was made to swear on punishment of death that I would never repeat it again. I did not repeat it, that I can remember, not even to Margaret Ann, my best friend. But I didn't have to. The boys who saw the couples skinny-dipping in the backwater did their own repeating everywhere, and soon, the story was all over town.

A Nobody from Eufala

Reese Tate, somebody years later told me, was just a "nobody from Eufawla." Reese Tate didn't even have the damn sense to use the GI Bill to go to college like the other young men who returned from WWII. Reese Tate did some kind of business certificate and went to work for the Company.

One thing you had to give Reese Tate, though, was that he was smart enough to realize he was never going to make anything out of himself on his own. He was smart enough to realize he was a lazy, limited man who was going to need some help to get on in life. Reese Tate knew he had to be nice, and he knew exactly who he needed to be nice to.

Now my father was a nice man, an intelligent man, but he firmly believed he didn't *have* to be nice to anybody. He carried his own weight in the world. He got a college degree and he did a good job. And he would have eaten his left arm off before he would ask for anything from anybody. He had worked himself out of poverty, away from the mill villages, but he was never ashamed of having a mother who worked in the mills and having grown up with an alcoholic father on Tallasee Street. He was, in that way, a typical Southern man who would have helped anybody on earth but made damn sure he never had to ask for help himself. Beholden was something Will Lee McPherson was never going to be.

After Daddy died, I found a pencil-written sheet where he and the yard man, Looney, had made careful and dated entries tracking Loony's dollar and five-dollar payments on a loan of five hundred dollars from my father. There was no interest, and sometimes there were months between payments.

It was so like Daddy. That one page was just Daddy summed up to a tee. He believed any man (for in his world, there weren't women coming around asking for money) deserved a chance if he was willing to work.

The sheet made me cry as I ran my eyes down the entries, following my father's increasingly erratic handwriting. I knew Mother would just throw it away. I was lucky the sheet had been inside a book and had escaped the clean out and delousing conducted by my brother and his wretched family. So I took it back to Florida and framed it along with a flower from Daddy's coffin. It hangs on the wall of my study, and every time I look up at it, I long for him—for his goodness, his basic decency, and most of all, for his laughter. They don't make men like my daddy anymore. I can't even count the times people came up to me after his funeral and said exactly that.

My daddy had a set of core principles he believed in and lived. He didn't wear them on his sleeve. He didn't take them out and dust them off on Sunday morning for church. He just lived like he thought people ought to live—decent people, that is. And he expected nothing more of other people than he expected of himself.

I don't know what Reese Tate believed, if anything. But I knew his eyes. When my daddy talked to someone or listened to them, he looked them right in the eye. Reese Tate didn't look you in the eye. He grinned a lot, but his eyes slid off you like they were greased. Reese Tate was always thinking something he knew deep inside him he should be ashamed of. It was as if he felt that if he looked at you for too long, you might guess what was really going on inside his mind.

But after he and Millie started skinny-dipping with the McKeans, he was given a whopping promotion in the Company and put to dealing with the cotton buyers who came to town. This was a good job. It meant more money, travel, and an expense account he could spend on fine dining, golf tournaments, and booze. My father was dumbfounded.

"If you were going to hire somebody to meet cotton buyers," he said to me not long after Reese Tate was promoted, "and represent your company, would you want Reese Tate?"

I considered this unlikely scenario.

"No," I said. "I would want you."

My father looked over at me and smiled. He didn't say a word. He just smiled. There was nothing in the world I loved more than making my daddy smile.

But my poor father never got it. Even after he had been retired for years and gotten away from the Company, he never got it. I don't think he wanted to get it. It was just more than he could take.

By the mid-sixties, the days of honesty, integrity, and grit were over. Everything my father believed in was a thing of the past or holding on by its fucking fingernails for dear life. Men like my father were obsolete. Independent men—men who stood their ground and rolled over for no one—were dinosaurs. They had been replaced by boastful, back-slapping sycophants who ran around on their wives and told dirty jokes about women.

The beauty and the con of WWII was that it was a time when talent and brains were important. The country was fighting for its life and that of western Europe. It wasn't a time to be putting your bets on the weak or the unprincipled. If you were good and smart, you were valued and promoted.

Men like my father thought when they came home from the war, it would be the same. They were proud of themselves and, with the GI Bill, pulled themselves up into a middle-class life better than anything they ever thought possible before the war. And they had done it on their own. They didn't need to doff their hats to anybody. They had stood up, been men. They had fought and come home. They'd given a square deal to their country and they'd gotten one in return.

What few, if any of them, foresaw was that twenty years later, the rot would have set in. By then, what it took to get ahead was completely different from what they believed in. What was needed was a flexible moral code and an eye for the main chance. Right and wrong were things you left for the preacher to talk about on Sunday morning. And if the preacher talked about what happened at work, he was *meddlin'* and not *preachin'*. Men like my father found themselves living in a world of sleazy deals at cocktail parties, kickbacks arranged on the golf course, and cruelty in the form of jokes told behind people's backs. My father, instead of bending to the new wind, straightened. He refused to allow himself to be sullied by the unscrupulous and the tawdry. He didn't go to the cocktail parties or the golf games, where deals were struck with nods and winks. My daddy felt like these things were beneath him. He also thought the men engaged in them would get their comeuppance. He died before they did. We will all die before they do.

While he was alive, they snickered behind his back, made jokes about the "saint," and passed over him when raises and promotions were given out. My father was a team player, but only on a team for which he could have respect.

The Sputnik Family

Years ago, I started calling the family I grew up in, the Sputnik family. One incident in 1957 involving the Soviet Sputnik, summed us up completely.

My family was always . . . on a different note, off-kilter, a little odd. It's not as if we were all noticeably crazy; there was just a basic disjuncture between the way we thought and commonly held reality. I guess you could say we passed for normal the way some black people used to pass for white.

It took most people a while to realize how out of it my family truly was. Some people, however, noticed right away. Real crazy people, for example.

I was on a subway car in London once when one of these completely nutty street people got on the car dressed in nothing but a rather elaborate diaper. He scanned the assembled passengers and within seconds, his eyes were riveted on mine.

"You." he thundered, pointing a long finger at me and causing every head in the car to turn and look.

Yeah, it's me. I felt like saying. One of the Sputnik family, but you don't have to tell everybody.

But the Sputnik family name came about like this.

In Wilkes Ferry, people would compete every year to win a prize for best outside Christmas decoration. We had tried to win for as many years as I could remember but had never succeeded. One year, we built a train out of painted paper boxes and put it in the front yard. A waving Santa Claus sat in the engine of the train, holding the reigns of reindeer who were tethered out in front of the train engine. I know, it doesn't make any sense, but remember who you're dealing with here. Each car, or painted paper box, was filled to overflowing with elaborately wrapped Christmas presents.

We thought we were sure to win. We didn't.

After we got over the initial defeat, we drove by the houses that won. Daddy pulled over and we sat in the car, eyes narrowed, studying the technique. The most significant thing about the winning house decorations was that they were all on the roof. Next year, we decided, we would perch our decoration, whatever it was, on the roof.

Then one day the telephone rang. I remember distinctly, standing beside my mother and father's bed, the telephone in my hand, listening to someone explain to my father that the Russians had successfully launched the Sputnik into outer space.

This person made it sound terribly serious, but Daddy was elated. When he hung up the telephone, he began shouting and dancing about the living room, his arms raised over his head.

"That's it. That's it." he exclaimed. "The winning Christmas decoration . . . the Sputnik . . . Just imagine it."

Daddy put his hands out in front of him and spread them as if he were showing us a marquee. "Santa Claus riding the Sputnik, lit up on top of the house." He was so excited he was vibrating. "This is a marvelous scientific achievement," Daddy went on. "Just marvelous."

Daddy was filled with admiration for the Soviets. During the next year, he brought home articles about and pictures of the Sputnik. We would all pour over them at night, reading everything we could get our hands on.

And come Christmas, there it was—the same waving Santa that had been in the train the year before was now riding the Sputnik off our roof. Daddy had spotlights all over the front yard and up on the roof. It could have been mistaken for a landing strip.

Then the real excitement began. We started counting the cars that came by. There were hundreds, literally hundreds of cars, not just from Wilkes Ferry, but from down the Valley. We were sure to win. When we weren't counting the cars coming by our decoration, we were riding around looking at the competition. None of the other displays had cars stopped in the middle of the street like ours.

When the day of the announcement of the winner arrived, my brother tore out the front door, grabbed the paper from the startled paperboy, opened it and stood frozen—staring. My mother, Daddy, and I crowded around.

But it wasn't a waving Santa and the Sputnik on the front page. It was a creche—a stable, mules, a manger, Mary, Joseph, and the frigging wise men.

We had lost, and we couldn't figure out why.

"But all those people," my brother protested, "came by and stopped their cars to look at our display."

"It's a testimony to the damn power of mediocrity," was Daddy's one and only comment.

It took me over forty years to understand what had happened.

People were building bomb shelters in their backyards in 1957. During the height of the cold war, the McPhersons put up an elaborate Christmas display celebrating the scientific accomplishments of the Soviet Union. And, to illustrate even more clearly just how out of it we were, we didn't even have enough sense to make the connection between our display, the anti-Soviet mood and the stopping cars.

See what I mean? The Sputnik family.

The Servant Problem

The Patterson aunts and cousins indulged in a series of elaborate parties and showers to celebrate Margaret Ann's upcoming marriage to the horrible Wilkie Dunn. Before the engagement, Miss Corinne and Mr. Rebel were never invited to the parties the cousins gave. The rich relatives wouldn't even have stepped inside Miss Corinne's house unless it was on family business.

Miss Corinne was not considered high class enough to attend their bridge parties or their parties at the Country Club. And they certainly didn't want Mr. Rebel there in his dirty, coal-stained clothes and displaying his coarse manners. The Pattersons, Miss Corinne and Mr. Rebel, didn't even belong to the Country Club.

But now, Miss Corinne was going to have the social recognition she had evidently wanted since her marriage to Rebel Patterson thirty years before. She was enjoying it. She was nice to me at the wedding and at the showers. She always was. But she was distracted almost to the point of madness with the Fergusons and the Cobbs and the Woodruffs, the extended Patterson family. She barely had time to hug me or talk to her own daughter, Margaret Ann, who was the one getting married. We were definitely secondary.

The Episcopal minister who presided over the wedding was a study in narcissism. He was good-looking, with large, black-lashed blue eyes and dark hair. He looked stunning in his vestments (I think that's what you call them), and you got the idea that he had perhaps known he would look good in the costume before he went into the ministry. He was the type to have gone into the ministry just so he could stand up there in the center of everything officiating, all eyes glued on him. I was surprised Wilkie Dunn was able to get through the wedding ceremony without getting into a fistfight with the minister over who was going to be center stage. It must not have been easy for Wilkie to see somebody else hog the attention for ten minutes.

The wedding and the series of showers given before it were eye-openers for me. I associated social climbing and snooty behavior with an older generation. I certainly never expected to see people I had grown up with acting like their mothers, in some cases, worse then their mothers.

I was, for example, utterly floored to see Rachel Burke (now Rachael Henderson) in a navy sheath and pearls complaining about the servant problem without the slightest bit of irony. She actually meant it.

I sat in the Henderson' s living room, watching Rachel and feeling like I was an anthropologist observing a rare tribe. This was the same wise-cracking, irreverent, don't-give-a-damn girl who had stuffed bottles of illegal vodka up the pants of her cheerleader's uniform when the police stopped off at Flat Shoals Creek one night and caught us. Smart-talking, quick-witted, rebellious Rachel Burke with her nails polished sitting on her mother-in-law's sofa talking about the servant problem with a dainty plate of cheese grits and shrimp casserole in her hand.

How had she become this imitation, this parody of the very people who had driven her mother to the grave? She had joined the very people that had caused her family so much pain. She had not only joined them, she had become them.

Most probably, mother said, Rachael Burke had gone away to college for a few years and seen what the rest of the world was like, outside of Wilkes Ferry. She'd then beaten a path back to where everybody knew just who the Burkes and the Hendersons and the Pattersons were. Rachael wasted no time marrying a Henderson, even though he was much older than she. She then donned the pearls.

The strangest part of the whole story was that the Hendersons and the Pattersons and the Cobbs had made Rachael's mother's life a living hell.

The Burkes were cousins in some way to the Hendersons and the Zacherys and the Cobbs. Rachael's father, Henderson Burke, had displeased the family by marrying a Jewish woman—Rachael's mother. I suppose as long as the Burkes lived in New York and stayed the hell out of Wilkes Ferry, Miss Sarah had a life. But when they moved to Wilkes Ferry, the Hendersons and the Zacheries and the

Cobbs just refused to accept her. I don't know the details, I just know that Miss Sarah drank. It was said in hushed tones, just like that.

Someone would say, "You know . . ."—and the teller would glance around to make sure no one was listening—"she drinks." Pause. "Bless her heart."

The blinds were always drawn in Miss Sarah's house, and I don't remember ever having seen her. I just heard about her. Finally, she drank herself to death. It was a very sad affair.

Years later, Rachael, for whatever reason, joined the ranks of the family, donned the pearls, and became interested in the servant problem. And, she was always such a plucky, mischievous person. What a waste.

In Their Element

Men like Big Ed Montgomery, who also worked for the Company (didn't everybody), and Reese Tate were in their element in the changed world of the 1960s and 1970s. They were crafty, and they were on the lookout for the fast buck, the quick lay, and the main chance. They were into that new sleazy business world game like rats up a drain pipe. Finally, it was their world, a world they were as comfortable in as pigs in shit.

It must have been heartbreaking for my father to watch them. He was a young man in 1951, Young Man of the Year, in fact. By 1965, he was a joke, at least to the Reese Tates and Big Ed Montgomerys of the world. Big Ed Montgomery was a talker, a drunk, and a loud, boastful, clumsy womanizer. Reese Tate was a butt licker, a backslapper, a yes-man, a skinny-dipper, and an adulterer. He wasn't many years away from being worse. They both got promotion after promotion.

When I was visiting Mama and Daddy once during that time, I fell asleep on the sofa in the back bedroom. The next morning, after I awoke, I could hear Daddy in the kitchen, making his coffee. I knew every sound, having slept in that little back bedroom often when I was a teenager. Sleeping downstairs was a way of coming in later than I was supposed to and not waking anybody up.

I knew the sound of the spoon hitting the inside of the coffee cup—one clank for the coffee, two for the sugar. I knew the sound of the boiling water being poured into his cup. I knew the sound of the chair being pulled out from the table, the straining sound of the wicker seat as Daddy sat down in it, the slow deliberate sound of his coffee cup being placed back on the table after each sip. He was alone in there, early in the morning, drinking coffee and thinking before he left for work.

When I was laying there listening to him as an adult, it struck me that it was the saddest thing I had ever heard in my life. I couldn't see him, but I somehow knew that he was dreading that drive to work, dreading having to spend all day there dealing with people he no longer had any respect for. I felt unutterably sorry for him, and there was not one thing I could do about it.

My daddy was a man who hadn't asked much out of life. When he came back after the war, he thought he was the luckiest son of a bitch in the world. He was alive; he was going to get a college education, something that would under ordinary circumstances have been unattainable for him. Not only was he going to get to go to college, but it was paid for by the government. He had a job in the Company virtually assured to him. He had a beautiful little wife who had followed him from town to town when he was stationed all over the United States before he went overseas. She went everywhere he did until he went to Scotland, then France.

Not too many years later, he had not only completed his college education, he had an invitation to go to graduate school. He had bought a brick house in Wilkes Ferry away from the mill villages and had a white-collar job. His mother and his father had come off the farm with nothing but their willingness to work. His father had died an alcoholic, and his mother had struggled through the Depression with two young children. She had worked in the mill her whole life and then stayed up sometimes all night to make food and wash his clothes for the next day of school. And there he was, Will Lee McPherson, putting on a tie and a coat to go to work. He must have been proud of himself and for himself. He was the young man in the Norman Rockwell *Four Freedoms*.

It was a bright world in the 1950s, full of promise. There is a photograph of my brother, my mother, and I at Christmas before I could even walk. I was being held up for the camera by my mother who was seated on the floor. I was wearing one of those little pajama suits with feet in them and gathered material at the wrists. My brother is sitting cross-legged beside my mother. In the background, you could see a Christmas tree with lights and presents piled all around it. It is a happy picture, a picture of a young family just starting out in life, posing for a proud father who was taking the picture. That was the 1950s, my father's time.

Daddy didn't change. The world changed around him and became cheap and tawdry, slick and underhanded. It was a world that regarded men like my daddy as losers.

Granny Pearl

When I was a child and my parents started talking about going out of town, or even away for the day, I would beg to go to Granny Pearl's.

Granny Pearl was my grandmother's sister. She was short, soft, funny, and comforting. But most importantly, for a mischievous child, she never got mad at me, no matter what outrage I perpetrated. I think Granny Pearl must have been a mischievous child too, and she still had a good healthy store of mischief inside her in her sixties.

At whatever time of day or night I was dropped off at Granny Pearl's; she was making pulled taffy. I can still see her in my mind's eye standing in her dining room talking to me while pulling out and smacking together the shiny strands of taffy. When the taffy was setting, we would make tea cakes in all kinds of shapes. There were star-shaped tea cakes, circle tea cakes, triangles, and hearts. Then Granny Pearl would make tiny finger sandwiches with three or four layers of white bread without the ends. We put chicken salad, cream cheese and olive, cucumber, or pimento cheese between each layer.

While Granny Pearl was finishing up the meal, she would send me outside to pick figs off the tree in her backyard. Nothing in this whole world tasted better than those figs off Granny Pearl's tree.

I wasn't supposed to do it, but every time I was sent to get the figs, I would crawl up under the shrubbery at the far end of the yard and look down at the back of the funeral home. If I waited long enough, I might get lucky and see a hearse drive slowly up to the back door and a white shrouded body taken inside. I have no earthly idea why this was so fascinating to me or why it was forbidden. But it was.

I knew if I stayed too long, Granny Pearl would start calling from the back door; worse still, she might come looking for me, and she knew exactly where to look. She never got mad at me for sneaking a look at the back of the funeral home, but she knew my mother wouldn't like it, so she got me back inside.

After I went into the kitchen with the figs, Granny Pearl would pick out two perfect specimens and stand them on end in two sparkling sherbet glasses. Then she would pour some kind of sweet, clear liquid over the figs and put the glasses on a silver tray.

After the figs went on the tray, it was time to dress.

I can't remember Granny Pearl wearing anything but flowered house dresses. They were nice house dresses—thin cotton shirtwaists—but they were house dresses just the same, and every one of them had a belt made out of exactly the same material as the dress.

But on the days I stayed with her, Granny Pearl and I would open up her enormous cedar chest and take out her treasures. Where Granny Pearl got these things, I don't know, and where she could ever have worn them, I don't know either. But there they were, always waiting on us for their day out.

Sitting on the floor, we would go through gloves, shoes, handkerchiefs, jewelry, stoles, scarves, and hats. There were several dozen pairs of gloves—long gloves, short gloves, gloves that flared at the wrist, gloves with beading on them, with embroidery on them, with piping on them. White gloves, ivory gloves, pale blue gloves, pink gloves, and gloves in yellow, lilac, black, and navy blue.

We would match the gloves with shoes—open-toed slippers, sling backs with spiked heels, shoes with ankle straps, bedroom slippers with pink puff balls on the toes. She had little delicate shawls and even a mink wrap. She had earrings and pearls and rhinestone tiaras. But the crucial decision, and the one that was fussed over and discussed for the longest time, was the hat. The hat had to be just right. She had dozens of hats too—a black hat with one long thin red feather sweeping back from the crown, a little mink hat that was almost like a headband, a large sun hat with tiny flowers and flowing ribbons on it, and a dainty little pink Sunday school hat with one tiny flower on the top.

When we had made our selections, Granny Pearl would then set up the card table in the backyard and cover it with a white starched tablecloth. There were ironed cotton napkins and napkin rings, flowered plates, cups and saucers, a vase of freshly cut flowers, and our figs in crystal sherbet glasses.

When we were properly attired, Granny Pearl and I would float grandly down the back steps and out into the yard for afternoon tea. We had a plate of taffy, tea cakes, finger sandwiches, a sterling silver teapot, creamer and sugar dish, and a glass pitcher of milk dyed whatever color I fancied that day—green, yellow, blue, or crimson.

We drank milk and tea and ate tea cakes and figs and watercress sandwiches, while we discussed the world of ladies. I loved every minute of that ritual, and part of what was so much fun about it was that Granny Pearl enjoyed it every bit as much as I did. She never seemed fussed or hurried or distracted, and she never got mad at me for deciding not to wear a particular hat or bracelet. Whatever I did was just fine with her. When I was with Granny Pearl, I didn't have to worry about anything.

Granny Pearl, I am sure, would be pleased to know that I now possess probably a hundred pairs of gloves—pink gloves, lilac gloves, mustard-colored gloves, gloves that flare at the wrist, lace gloves with no fingers, gloves with piping, and I almost never go out of the house without a hat.

Showing Up Dead

The religious retreat circle continued merrily along despite the rumors about the Tates and the McKeans and their skinny-dipping. My mother steadfastly defended Sweet McKean and the Tates over and over to the family and outside it. My father and I, of course, never spoke so much as a word on the subject again for fear of enraging my mother. We just listened when she went into yet another tirade about yet another person who was spreading ugly gossip about Sweet. Whenever she did this, I could feel the words jabbing into me like little needles she was propelling across the room in my direction. Whenever she talked about the subject, it was always, somehow, my fault that it had all happened since I was the first one to mention the story to her. I felt miserably guilty about it.

Then all of a sudden, in the middle of daily life, Millie Tate turned up dead. That's right—dead. People's mothers just didn't turn up dead in Wilkes Ferry. I couldn't remember anyone ever turning up dead in Wilkes Ferry. It just wasn't done. Daddy's friend, Mr. Riley, turned up dead, but he had a legitimate excuse, a heart attack. That was different.

It's probably hard to imagine how shocking it was for the mother of one of the children I grew up with to turn up dead. People now show up dead every day, and the nightly news is filled with drive-by shootings and pop stars masturbating children. But you have to remember, that didn't go on in the 1950s, and if it did, nobody talked about it. There were no sex scandals on the nightly news, and people died unexpectedly only from heart attacks and in the movies.

When I was growing up in Wilkes Ferry, life on the surface was the closest thing to *Leave It to Beaver* or *Father Knows Best* you can imagine. It was a small Southern town made up of a few hundred people. As a child, my world consisted of a handful of other children my age and their families; our extended family and cousins. I not only knew everybody in town, I also knew their dogs. It used to amuse my father no end that when we were driving together, he could spot a dog and I could invariably tell him whose dog it was. Maybe below the surface there were scandals galore, but in my life outside the house, life was pretty much like it seems on *Leave it to Beaver*. I can remember being absolutely astounded when a girl started school in my class and I found out that her family lived in an apartment.

Nobody's parents lived in an apartment. It was just such a novel concept to me, like someone's parents living on the moon. I must have seemed a truly demented child the first time I was allowed to go over to Ginger's house—apartment—to spend the night. I couldn't have done much more than stand around and stare.

Not only did Ginger's parents live in an apartment, but Ginger's mother walked around in that apartment wearing nothing but a slip. And it was not only a slip. It was a black slip. And that black slip had black lace on the top and the bottom. Underneath it was a black bra and black panties. Now let me tell you something; there is no doubt in my mind that my mother in her entire life never owned, much less wore, a black bra and panties. She never even thought of such a thing. Ten minutes in a black bra and panties, even in the privacy of your own bedroom, would have condemned women like my mother to perpetual damnation in the next life and the inner conviction that they were certainly whores in this one.

My mother, and Margaret Ann's mother, who I knew almost as well, steadfastly wore the most hideous undergarments imaginable. They did so not out of any lack of personal pride. They did so because the type of underwear you wore made a statement about your character. It said it all about the type of woman you were. Good women, wives, and mothers, didn't wear sleazy underwear. I am sure that had any of the mothers of my little group of friends considered wearing sexy underwear they would have immediately thought, *What if I get in an accident and taken to the hospital? Everybody in town will find out.*

In the fifties, wives and mothers did not don floozy underwear. They wore standard, respectable white cotton or nylon panties with elastic (tight elastic) waists and legs. Over this, they wore girdles that you couldn't get a squirrel's fingernail underneath and that froze any whisper of a possibility of a jiggle of fanny flesh. Going out without a girdle was akin to walking naked and wet down Main Street. My grandmother DeeMama once called my cousin Biddy a whore because she said she *intended* to go out of the house without a girdle on.

The night I stayed over at Ginger's apartment, her mother and father were going out dancing. Now where on earth they were going dancing within a hundred miles of Wilkes Ferry, I don't know. But they were going and going dressed up, not like you'd dress up for church or even dressed up like you were going out for dinner which my parents sometimes did. Ginger's parents, or at least her mother, was dressing up like someone in a movie getting ready to go to a night club.

I cannot imagine what this woman must have thought of me. She probably thought I lived on the moon, but she didn't let on. Ginger and I hung around her dressing table for what seemed like hours, watching her put on makeup, paint her lips, do her nails, and fuss with her glistening short curly black hair. All the time she was wearing the black slip and black bra that showed alluring cleavage and black panties. The door to her bedroom was wide open even though Ginger's little brother and the maid were there.

When Ginger's father came home, I immediately started to become anxious, waiting for Ginger's mother to jump up and cover herself. But into the bedroom he walked, big as life, throwing his coat on the bed. Coming up behind her, he bent over, wrapped his arms around her half-naked shoulders, and kissed her . . . on the neck. It wasn't just a peck either.

I had never seen anything like it.

Anyway, the point, least you had forgotten it, or thought I had, was that if Ginger's mother in her black slip, and the fact that they lived in an apartment made that much of an impression on me, you can imagine what Millie Tate showing up dead did to me.

The Bottom Fell Out

Miss Corinne Bell grew up in the Valley, the daughter of a mother whose husband died young. Miss Corinne and her sister, Miss Opel, were the only two children. Needless to say, the Bells had no money with no man in the family to work. Miss Corinne's mother provided for them by sewing for other people which she did with proficiency.

Very early on, it was obvious that Miss Corinne was going to turn out to be a beauty. I know this because Mama knew Miss Corinne when they were both teenagers. Mama sang, and Miss Corinne was part of a singing group that performed at churches, parties, and old people's homes. Mother said that Miss Corinne played the piano and sang like an angel. She had a tall, thin body, which was important to my mother who was five feet tall and always on a diet. Miss Corinne, Mama said, could wear anything. Miss Corinne just had that model's type of body that made anything look good on her. And she had a sense of style. She could take a simple dress and make it look like something that came out of a fashion magazine, and her mother taught her how to sew.

So Miss Corinne Bell, the beauty of the Valley, went around playing the piano and singing. Everybody loved her. She was funny and fun, and she had long wavy black hair. She was sweet to everybody and liked to laugh and have a good time, a very clean and modest good time, but a good time. I am sure that's one of the things that made her so attractive, her humor and lightheartedness. When Margaret Ann and I were growing up, she was still funny. She was sort of ditsy and scatterbrained and made jokes her own expense.

"Why, Margaret Ann, ya mama has gone completely insane," she might say when we were growing up, making fun of one of her mistakes or explaining when she forgot to pick us up from the movies or somewhere else. Miss Corinne forgetting was a regular event, so regular that we always knew what had happened when she wasn't there waiting for us when we came out of the theater or a party.

"I'll go call Mama," Margaret Ann would say and disappear. She knew the location of every phone in town.

At some point, Miss Corinne might have sung for a group that Rebel Patterson was a part of. He laid eyes on her and fell in love, or as much in love as somebody as self-centered as Rebel Patterson could ever be. Miss Corinne was swept off her feet. In retrospect, it seems that she was as much swept off her feet by the Patterson's money and social standing as she was by Rebel himself, who was much shorter than she, stocky, and well, earthy. I can't imagine Rebel Patterson was much nicer or much more well behaved when he was younger, perhaps just better dressed. He was a spoiled only son of a wealthy family and remained so his entire life.

But Miss Corinne learned to overlook Mr. Rebel's faults, or the most glaring of them, and she fell into her own large wedding to Rebel Patterson attended by the very cousins and aunts who later on put on Margaret Ann's wedding to Wilkie. The Pattersons paid for the entire wedding, even down to Miss Corinne's wedding dress. Miss Corinne's mother certainly couldn't have afforded a large elaborate wedding.

The wedding, though, turned out to be the high point of the marriage. After that, nothing seemed to work out the way it was planned.

When Miss Corinne and Mr. Rebel married before the war, the coal business was thriving and making oodles of money. Rebel did his service in WWII and came back from England to a lovely, talented wife, a new brick house across the river, a wealthy family, a good name, and an established and lucrative business.

But, even though the economy was booming, coal was starting to have trouble even then. Coal was a pain in the ass, having it delivered and poured down a shoot in your house, and coal was dirty. It was much more convenient to use heating oil, and before long, coal became nothing but a relic in home heating. By the time Mr. Patterson, Sr., and Miss Sudie were dead and the girls married, the bottom had fallen out of the coal business. Mr. Rebel was left with not the prize but the booby prize. Coal never paid again, and Rebel Patterson, who thought he was going to be pampered and idle his whole life, had to work for a living. He never got used to it, and it turned him into an even more bitter and often violent man than he would have been had he wound up with all the money.

I remember him coming home at lunch when I was a child staying at the Patterson's for the day. He was dirty, with coal dust all over him. He rarely talked. He just sat and ate and drank his glass of water and went back to the coal yard. In the afternoons, he would sometimes show up unexpectedly in the house and scare us. When we were teenagers, Margaret Ann and her sister, Frankie, warned me about leaving the bathroom door unlocked when we were there in the house alone. Mr. Rebel, they said, had a habit of walking in while one of them was on the toilet or in the bath tub. It was a little creepy. I never knew Mr. Rebel to do anything like that, and I always thought they were exaggerating about him coming into the bathroom, but who knew?

What I do know is that Mr. Rebel would show up in the afternoon, go into the bathroom off his bedroom, and stay a long time. Margaret Ann and Frankie used to laugh about this. I have no idea what he did in there, and I don't want to know even now.

Putting Everything in Order

I guess it was a normal day in Wilkes Ferry the day Millie Tate died, at least for everybody except Millie, but no one knew that. People were going about their business, getting children off to school, instructing maids on how not to break off the legs of silver coffee pots while polishing them, going to the beauty shop, talking about a neighbor who was in the hospital.

Someone, I don't remember who now, dropped by the Tate's small neat brick house. Who knows what this woman was doing—dropping off some little something, the program of Bible verses for Wednesday night prayer meeting, a borrowed cake plate, a cupcake tin. The woman parked her car in the Tate's driveway and rang the bell at the kitchen door off the carport.

Up until that moment, everything was just humming along in Wilkes Ferry. Everything was taking its daily course. After that moment, there was an awareness that something was not right. Something was off-kilter, off center.

Something was wrong in Wilkes Ferry. The sunlight looked a little different. The leaves in the trees and the blades of grass paused a millisecond in their movement, swaying in the gentle morning breeze. The cardinals and mockingbirds hesitated just a fraction of a God's breath in their songs. A woodpecker stopped pecking on a rotten tree down near the river, distracted by nothing. In an alley behind the Piggly Wiggly, a stray kitten crawled into the cool darkness of the interior of a spare tire. A beaver's head disappeared under the surface of the water of the Catawba River.

At Millie Tate's house, no one came to the door.

The woman was almost sure Millie was there. At least that's what they said, but she didn't know why she was sure. The woman started knocking louder.

When she thought she saw a curtain move in the kitchen window, she began calling out.

"Millie. Millie. Are you there?"

From behind the door, the woman heard what sounded like a mew, a cat's mew.

"Millie," she called again, knocking. "Are you all right?"

"I'm all right," Millie answered in a thin, frail voice, startling the woman because the voice was just the other side of the closed door. The door didn't open.

"Is something wrong?" the woman asked, feeling a chill. She looked toward the street, at the houses across the way as if someone might come out and tell her what to do.

She waited. She heard the mewing sound again.

"I'm all right," Millie said softly.

The woman stared at the door. She'd never known Millie to act like this, but she certainly wasn't going to make a scene. If Millie didn't feel like coming to the door, what could she do but go back home. The woman backed away from the door and walked to her car.

Nobody ever talked to or saw Millie Tate alive again. At least nobody who would admit it.

God only knows what was happening in that house behind that door. I am sure of one thing, though, Millie Tate wasn't standing there in a black bra and slip. In fact, Millie Tate was completely dressed, not in a fancy dress, as if she were going to a night club, but in a good respectable house dress, the sort of thing you might wear out to the grocery in a town where everybody knew everybody else and watched everything that moved.

Millie Tate was dressed that morning, had her shoes on, and her stockings. She had on her glasses. And her hair, that mousey, thin, dirty blonde hair of hers that she curled with bobby pins, was fixed just like it was every day. She had done everything—gotten up, dressed, put on her makeup, fixed her hair, chosen which shoes to put on, straightened her house. Put everything in order.

I wonder sometimes if she knew when she got up that morning what was going to happen. I wonder if beforehand, she took one last walk around her house to make sure everything was just right, make sure she had done everything she was supposed to do. She had made up the beds—hers and Reese's and the beds of her three children. I wonder if she lingered in her daughter's room, picking up a doll or folding a sweater discarded at the last minute before Patty left for school. I wonder if perhaps Millie Tate loved every little girly things she'd been able to buy for Patty after six years of nothing but boys.

What depths of despair were driving Millie Tate to leave that house with every item lovingly put in its place. Every stick of furniture was polished. Every dish washed, dried, and stacked neatly in the cabinets. Every cabinet door was shut, and every dishcloth was folded. They said she had even washed all the clothes, folded them, and put them away. So did she walk from room to room saying good-bye to an especially loved bedspread, a porcelain figurine, a set of wedding china?

You see, it had all been enough for Millie Tate—the small, neat brick house with a car in the carport, three healthy children, a husband who wore a white shirt and worked in an office. It was more than enough. It was so much more than she had ever dreamed possible growing up in the country with a family trying to feed itself off a few chickens and a garden.

For Millie Tate, all of it was like a dream come true. Standing in church wearing a hat and gloves, matching shoes, and handbag—it was so much more than she had dared to hope for. Standing beside a husband who wore a coat and tie, sharing a hymnal with her eldest son, her youngest son and her precious daughter dressed in their Sunday best lined up down the aisle. After church, they went home to have Sunday dinner, the five of them sitting around a table. There was no war, no Depression, no red dirt in the yard and in the back of her throat, no chickens. There were clean beds, a steady income, church, meals, nice neighbors, white gloves.

So where, she must have wondered that morning as a cat standing in tall grass flicked its tail, did it go so wrong? She must have failed in some crucial way. But how?

She might have looked around her. What else should she, could she, have done. Maybe she shouldn't have had that last baby. She ran her hands absently over her belly. It was soft but not that bad. Certainly, it wasn't any worse than any of the other young mothers in their set.

Maybe at that moment, Millie Tate walked to the mirror in her bedroom and gazed at her small frame. She had always been petite, and she didn't look that much different in a dress than she had when Reese married her. In fact, she remembered having a shirtwaist dress very like the one she had on, with small flowers in the print and a gently gathered skirt, years ago, before Reese had asked her to marry him. Only then, the material for the dress had come from flour sacks.

Maybe then she turned to the side to examine her shape. A little thicker in the waist certainly, she might have thought, but not overweight.

Then an image of Sweet McKean came into her head. Sweet McKean with her even more petite, hard little body, dressed to the nines. Sweet McKean, with all that money, looked very much like Debbie Reynolds.

Millie smoothed her skirt with her open hands, suddenly feeling a wave of shame creep over her. A housedress with little flowers in the print just like she had worn years before. Her hands went to her wispy hair—thin, washed-out, and permed. She had never had thick lustrous hair. Reese knew that when he married her. But it was . . . decent, respectable, perfectly presentable hair.

Sweet McKean came back into her head, and Millie's hands closed into fists. Sweet McKean's hair was shiny and teased, not in a cheap way, no never that, teased just the right amount. Sweet McKean looked like she just walked out of a fashion magazine for the perfect wife. Sweet McKean and her money, her clothes, her hair, her carelessness.

Millie looked down at her clasped hands. She was ashamed of herself. She dropped her head in her hands. What was the matter with her? How could she be so mean and envious. A Christian, a real Christian, didn't covet what other people had. They didn't envy their best friends, and that was what Sweet McKean was, wasn't it? Her best friend?

Sweet, she had to admit, had been wonderful to them. Millie reminded herself for the thousandth time. It wasn't right to resent her because of her money. If she hadn't had money, she wouldn't have been able to help Reese with his promotions. Sweet had helped because she was kind and good, not for herself. She got nothing out of it. If she hadn't had money, she would not have been able to help Reese or to take them on trips in the bus.

Millie closed her eyes. "Help me," she murmured. "Please help me to see thy purpose." Despite herself, she started to cry softly, unobtrusively, even though there was not a soul there to hear her.

She thought of Reese, of how he had looked years ago in his uniform, of how proud he had been when he had finally gotten it. Like a little boy, smiling and pulling on the bottom of his coat, glancing at himself in every mirror and window. Where had she failed Reese? Hadn't he been in love with her then? He seemed in love. He said he was in love. It felt like he was in love. But how would she know? She had never had another boyfriend, certainly never been in love before. What did she know about love?

She had done everything she was supposed to do. She had remained chaste until her marriage night even during a war. She had borne him children, cleaned his house, fed him, taken his clothes to the cleaners, shined his shoes herself. She had stood beside him in church and at cocktail parties. She had even . . .

No. She wasn't going to think about that. She hadn't wanted to do it. She hadn't wanted to at all. But he was her husband. She had been told her whole life by her family and by her church that her husband's needs were hers to fill. Even if . . . even if she didn't agree with those needs. But was that right? Was it right for her to . . . even though every fiber of her being told her she was doing wrong.

But he was her husband. The father of her children. Wouldn't it be wrong if she refused him and lost him. Wouldn't she have sinned against God if she had allowed her home to be broken up? Millie began to cry. But that happened anyway. She had done what her husband asked her to do, pressured her to do, to keep him, and she had lost him anyway.

She had always kept herself clean, never talked about female troubles, never let Reese see her when she was pregnant or nursing. She always closed the bathroom door and even tried to wait until he left for work in the morning.

She never wanted the light on, but she had let him finally. She hadn't refused like most wives would have. Maybe she made him feel guilty about it even though she really tried not to let him know how humiliated she felt.

And then when he . . . when they . . .

It was all too much. She couldn't think about it anymore. She'd gone over it, over and over it, until she wanted to scream. She had tried. She had tried to do what was right, to save her marriage. Wasn't that what she was supposed to do?

Judy, Judy, Judy

The most important thing about Judy Tatum was the way she looked. If I could just take the photograph I have of her from my mind and show it to you, you would understand.

When I think of Judy, I see her leaning with her back up against the door frame of the door that divided Jewel's apartment from Granny Pearl's. They built a lot of the houses that way in the mill villages. I remember the first house my parents lived in after they had children was just like the one that Granny Pearl and Jewel lived in.

The houses were white frame, with a large front porch, one central staircase leading up onto the porch and two wide front doors—wide so they could get a casket through. Inside was one door that connected the two sides of the house. When we shared the house with the Vinsons, that door remained locked. And it was never opened. Granny Pearl and Jewel, however, were both already widows when we were growing up. Their husbands had already succumbed to a life of hard work, cotton lint, and hard drink. So their door stayed open all the time.

It was standing in that connecting doorway that I saw Judy for the first time. Jewel and her daughter Judy it seemed, walked freely into and out of Granny Pearl's side of the house all the time. For them, it was like one big house. In fact, I seldom remember being in that back den without Jewel being there. At night, Jewel and Granny Pearl and I would sit in the dark and watch television together. Jewel could see better in the dark.

We would have to carry on a running narration for Jewel though, since she was almost blind. Jewel was one of the plethora of elderly people around in the Valley who had diabetes and who periodically lost parts of their bodies to the disease. Toes were usually the first things to go and then feet and then legs. Blindness was also common.

Jewel, fortunately, hadn't lost more than a few toes, but the toes she had left, she joked, were the very ones that had corns on them. She was not totally blind; she could still see a little but she wore sinister-looking glasses, thick and dark. They were the kind of glasses that children regularly referred to as "coke bottle" glasses, and they made her look like a mad scientist in a horror movie. Because of the thick glasses that she wore all the time, her eyes were sunken back into the head the way that eyes always do when the person can't see very well and the glasses are necessary all the time. When her eyes moved, they seemed to take on a new life seen through the distorting waves in the lenses. Jewel took some getting used to, but she was sweet and a funny. She and my Granny Pearl were good company for each other. They liked the same things and laughed at the same things. They both teased and made jokes at each other's expense all the time. They were both always just on the verge of a laugh or a smile at whatever happened in life.

In the dark, watching television in the back room, I didn't have to look at Kate's eyes, and the running commentary on the television was always funny. Granny Pearl was always objecting to and adding to my narration of the events on the television. She would say, for example, that I hadn't told Jewel all the essential details or that I had added something that wasn't in there. Sometimes, she would sit down with the popcorn and elbow me in the ribs for falling down on my job of narrating for Jewel. We laughed and joked the whole time we were watching our programs. I loved being at Granny Pearl's house and I loved Jewel.

But even though Jewel and, to some extent, Judy had the run of Granny Pearl's side of the house, I don't remember ever watching television in the dark with Judy. The thought of it makes me shudder even now. I don't think I ever saw Judy without Kate. I was not permitted the same freedom of movement as were Jewel and Judy. I can't, in fact, remember ever being in Jewel's and Judy's side of the house. I don't think I ever saw it.

Even though I don't remember anybody ever sitting me down and telling me I was never to go into Kate's side of the house, someone must have, because I knew I was never to set one foot past that door stop, the raised piece of white wood that ran along the floor of the door separating the two sides of the house.

Because I can't remember who told me I was forbidden to enter Kate's side or how they explained it to me I am not entirely sure how I came to have the strong sense of this prohibition. But I would never ever have gone over that threshold. Wild horses couldn't have stampeded me or dragged me there. And this could not have been simply because I had been told not to. I was not that obedient. And as with the prohibition about setting up surveillance on the funeral parlor from Granny Pearl's backyard, my usual response to adult prohibition was to promptly do whatever I had been forbidden to do as quickly as possible. Somehow, this was different.

I had a profound sense of unease about Kate's side of the house. Even if the entire house had been empty, I would not have ventured even close enough to the adjoining door to peer over into the other side of the house. The reason was Judy.

There was something dangerous about Judy, about being around Judy. Don't ask me how I knew this. No one told me she was dangerous. No one told me never to be alone with her. But whenever she was around, there was something different in the air, a tenseness that was totally absent in Granny Pearl's house at other times.

That first time I saw Judy, I stood staring at her for a long time, much longer than anybody could conceivably have considered normal. But nobody said anything—not Jewel, not Granny Pearl, not Judy. Perhaps it simply seemed like an extraordinarily long time. Perhaps it was the case that I stood in the middle of the floor riveted, my eyes frozen on hers and then traveling up and down her body examining every detail. I can't imagine that Jewel or Granny Pearl would have allowed me to do something that outlandishly rude. But perhaps they were reluctant to make an issue of the fact that I was looking like I'd just laid eyes on a Martian. Perhaps they feared calling attention to my behavior would only serve to embarrass or even hurt Judy—I just don't know.

I don't think Judy would have been looking at me in quite the same way had either Jewel or Granny Pearl been actively engaged in the interaction. They had their heads down, looking at some piece of sewing or some magazine or something. Judy was looking at me over their heads.

One of the things that was so strange about the encounter, and part of what fixed me to the spot, that immobilized me, was that Judy was saying something to me, and I didn't know how to respond.

I don't think she wanted a response. I don't know what she wanted, didn't at the time and don't now. Maybe given my experience with my mother, what disturbed me profoundly about the exchange was the feeling that Judy wanted something from me but that I had no idea what she wanted. I was probably wondering where my toe shoes were from habit, the habit of dancing for my mother.

I was trained very carefully as a child to pay attention to people, to be hyper-vigilant as they now call it. My emotional survival depended on sussing out my mother's moods and responding ahead of time by doing what she wanted. As anyone who has ever had to play this guessing game knows, it is almost impossible to win, but that doesn't keep you from trying. I never knew I had been trained to jump before being told, but I had. I can now see the effects of this training on my entire life.

But that day, standing in my Granny Pearl's den, gazing at Judy across the room, I only knew that I had never seen anything like Judy in my whole life. Judy had not always lived there, I knew that. She had been away for years. Where she had been, I don't know. The first time I remember seeing her in the doorway, she had just come back.

Judy appeared from around the door frame, out of nowhere. She put her two hands behind her back and leaned on them. She lifted one foot and put it on the door frame so that her knee poked out. After that, I don't remember her moving. After that, the only thing that moved were her eyes and the corners of her mouth.

She was wearing pedal pushers that day, pedal pushers that were old and faded. They were a light salmon color, light because they had been washed so many times. And the legs of her pedal pushers had a cuff on them at the bottom with a cloth tab that was fed through two metal loops and then drawn tightly against her legs below the knee. She had on a white cotton short-sleeved shirt with the shirt tail out, penny loafers, and white socks.

Her skin was pasty white, and her arms, neck, face, feet, legs had a puffy, unhealthy look that even to a child seemed disturbing. The tops of her arms were tight like the skin stretched over a sausage. Her neck had rings around it, lines where the skin puffed out above and below. Her eyes seemed small, peering out from between swollen lids, which came together slowly instead of quickly in a blink. The tops of her feet arched up out of the penny loafers, stretching the white threads of her socks. Even though her calves were almost nonexistent, her thighs were tightly packed inside her washed out pedal pushers.

Her hair was dark brown and short and fixed like no other woman's hair I had ever seen. It was brushed straight back, and it separated so you could see the rows made by the comb as it had been pulled through it. It was like her hair wasn't clean or she had put hair oil on it like men did. At the base of her neck, her hair flipped up in what boys used to call a ducktail.

The clothes were not much different from what a lot of women wore to the mills in those days. The hair was strange, masculine I realize now, but not so much that you'd stop and stare at her on the street. You'd just think she had an unfortunate combination of features and hairstyle.

It was the puffiness that really held my attention. That and her body language. It was that kind of puffiness that tells you, even if subliminally, that something is very wrong. I had no idea at the time what it all meant, but the strangeness of her seemed to creep into my pores from all the way across the room.

I suppose I would now describe her body language as dykey—bull dykey to be more exact. There is just no other way to describe it. There are homosexual women that are dykey and those who are not. There are gay men who queen about and those who do not. Judy was a dyke. It was just that simple although I had never heard the word at the time. I could also not have explained what was so strange about Judy to anyone else. But boy, was she strange.

There are two things I now know about Judy that made her strangeness explicable. The first is that she was a lesbian at a time when such a thing was an abomination. The second thing was that she was a morphine addict, a patient of old Dr. Fallon's. The odd, unhealthy puffiness is now familiar to anyone who has seen photographs of Judy Garland in the 60s or Elvis Presley in his cape and sequins phase or even Errol Flynn in the latter stages of his life. In the mid-1950s, though, I had never seen anybody who looked like that, and I had never heard of morphine.

But Judy was only one among a long list of Southern women addicted to morphine by doctors. These women were regularly supplied with injections because they couldn't face their lives or their husbands or their families or their children or even because they wouldn't do the housework or fuck their husbands with the lights on. Many of these women found themselves in the old state mental hospitals like Miledgeville or Catawba. Others, like Judy, spent their lives in a morphine haze. Most of them died early.

So the puffy Judy Garland look-alike in pedal pushers who leaned against the door frame and smiled at me from across the room may have been tasting me as a potential sex object. She may have been looking out from an opiate haze, smiling simply at the glow within her own body. Or she may not have even known that the heel of her loafer was on planet earth. I have no idea.

I have stared at the photograph of her in my mind off and on for over forty years, but I still cannot figure out what she was thinking. I can see the expression in her eye, but I cannot, for the life of me, figure out what it meant. But there she is, in a mental photograph that will never leave consciousness until I do.

Come Get Me

When I was around twelve, the middle-of-the-night phone calls from Margaret Ann started. The phone would ring at our house, and it would be Margaret Ann. "Come get me," she would say. That was all.

My mother would throw on some clothes, and we would drive across the river to the Patterson's house. Margaret Ann would usually be waiting out on the street, holding some clothes to wear the next day. She got in the car and rode home with us, saying not a word about what happened. My mother drove up the drive and to the back of our house. The three of us—Mother, Margaret Ann, and I, would get out of the car, file in the back door, and all go to sleep. In the morning, everybody just acted like Margaret Ann being retrieved from her house and brought to ours in the middle of the night was the most normal and natural thing in the world. After a while, it became so. Years later when I was talking about this in front of my father, he said, "Where was I?"

"I don't know," I responded.

"You mean I let you and your mother go over to Rebel Patterson's house in the middle of the night when he was threatening his family and his daughter was waiting out on the street she was so afraid?"

"I guess so," I said. In fact, I don't have any idea where Daddy was when all this was going on. He was asleep, I guess. He certainly wouldn't have thought in the morning that Margaret Ann being in his bathroom or the kitchen was odd. She was there all the time. Besides, he probably considered all this coming and going my mother's territory and knew it was safer not to ask questions.

Margaret Ann never told us at the time what had happened at her house to make her want to leave. We never asked. It would have been rude.

I only once actually saw Rebel Patterson in the act of threatening his family. This had to have been years later since by that time, I was old enough to drive. Margaret Ann phoned the house, and rather than waking up my mother, I pulled a sweatshirt top over my pajamas and drove barefoot over the river bridge and parked across the street from Margaret Ann's house. Margaret Ann came out in her nightgown and walked calmly across the front yard and got into the car. We sat there looking at the house.

"Daddy's got a gun," she said quietly. For some reason, this didn't shock me. Maybe because my father also kept guns in the house, maybe because the gun had been mentioned before. I don't know.

Margaret Ann and I sat there in my little blue Falcon car, looking across the street toward the house. Suddenly, Mr. Rebel came out the front door in nothing but his undershorts. He marched across the lawn looking for something or somebody, perhaps Margaret Ann. He was carrying a handgun. My father kept rifles in the house when he was still hunting, but since when she was young my mother had been shot in the chest by her brother, there weren't any guns laying around the house. And I had never even seen a pistol outside the movies. Mr. Rebel, though, looked more ridiculous than frightening. He was running barefoot in his white boxer shorts, around the outside of the house, swiping aside the branches of the azaleas to look under them.

"Let's go," Margaret Ann said after a few seconds.

I don't think Mr. Rebel ever even saw us drive away.

Years later, after Lee Ray and I moved back to Wilkes Ferry, Margaret Ann told me Mr. Rebel had beaten her mother repeatedly from the time Margaret Ann was a child. She told me that before she started phoning us, she would hide in the garage of a neighbor's house to get away. She never told me about this when we were growing up, and I am ashamed to say I was surprised to hear it. I thought Mr. Rebel made a fool out of himself on a regular basis, but I didn't ever think about his beating anybody. I don't remember anybody talking about it, not even the adults. People like the Pattersons, the Wyatt's, and my parents, didn't do things like that.

We're All Friends

They told her it was a new way of thinking, modern, up to date. They told her God wanted his children to worship him with their bodies. God, they told her, didn't want his children to be ashamed of their nakedness. He wanted them to rejoice in their bodies, to give freely and receive, to share God's bounty. The only rule was that it had to be shared among other Christians, caring couples. It was a celebration.

That's what they had called it. A celebration. It hadn't felt like a celebration. It felt dirty and tawdry. It felt shameful, at least to Millie Tate. But it seemed she was the only one who thought so. The rest of them hugged, exchanged pecks on the cheek, and "Praised Jesus" afterward when they had all come back together. Praise Jesus. She had felt so unclean she couldn't even permit the words on her lips.

How had she ever gotten herself into something so crazy?

But she was just a country girl, old-fashioned. She hadn't grown up in Wilkes Ferry. Reese was a country boy too, but since he had been promoted with the Company, he hobnobbed with the gentry and with out-of-town buyers. People had started moving into Wilkes Ferry from outside, people with no family history to rely on, people with new ideas. They were having an influence. People seemed now to have ideas Millie Tate had never even considered.

Even Yankees were coming now that the Company had merged with another company.

She supposed she'd just didn't know enough or understand. Reese said she was behaving like a little girl. There had been a time when that was exactly what he wanted, a little girl. No longer. Or at least, he didn't want the little country girl she was.

What he wanted, he said, was freedom. His freedom. Who ever heard of such a thing? What kind of freedom was there in being alone, leaving your family? She shouldn't have had that last baby. But after two boys, she wanted a girl to dress and buy clothes for. Maybe she had been selfish in this. Maybe she had brought this all on herself.

They had told her what she was doing was good for her marriage—good for all their marriages. But now, Reese said he wanted a divorce, said he was getting one whether she agreed or not. What had she done that was so wrong?

The image of Sweet McKean came into her mind. Sweet McKean smiling, stretching out her arms to embrace Millie afterward. "My sister in Christ," Sweet had whispered joyously in Millie's ear. But Millie didn't feel joyous. She felt shy and uncomfortable, very uncomfortable. Her hand flew to cover her mouth as she felt the hot messy gush of fluid come from between her legs and wet her underpants.

They all stared at her, and Sweet and Reese started laughing. Millie turned from one to the other in confusion. How had they known? They couldn't have. Ben McKean reached out and cupped her elbow in his hand.

"Millie, you all right?" he asked sympathetically.

She stared into his eyes. At that moment, she thought she saw pain in them, a kind of fond pain, like he knew what she was feeling, like he was complicit. Even so, she removed her elbow from his hand and couldn't believe that a few minutes before . . . She felt the blood rise to her face. Even there in her own living room, she blushed just like she had that night.

Sweet and Reese were still laughing. Sweet hugged her again and patted her on the back like she would comforting a child. "There's nothin' to blush about, Millie," Sweet said. "We're all friends."

Millie let out a loud sigh, startling herself. She got up and walked into the kitchen. She stood in the middle of the floor looking around. Nothing left to do.

Gas Pains

At Margaret Ann's wedding, Miss Corinne flitted around like a butterfly. Of course, it was as if it were her wedding, not Margaret Ann's, but the first wedding is always for the mother. All the Patterson aunts and cousins were also flitting around, making sure that every detail of the elaborate wedding, paid for by with family money, was perfect. It was the social event of the Wilkes Ferry season, and we all know just how important that was.

Margaret Ann's attitude can be summed up in one incident. Not ten minutes before the wedding, she was standing on a platform receiving last minute alterations to her wedding gown. She was completely dressed and veiled in a stunning dress with tiny pearls all over a bodice, which tastefully revealed her ample bosom. Her train was twice as long as the skirt of her dress, and her veil came down almost to her ankles. She was standing there on a pedestal, and I was watching her, thinking that I had never seen her look lovelier.

Suddenly, her face changed to a grimace, and she put her palm on her stomach. I was alarmed.

"Margaret Ann, are you all right?" I asked moving forward thinking I might just have to catch her if she fell.

She looked down at me with a pained expression on her face. "Gas." She pronounced and put her hand behind her to wave away the supposed fumes.

It was Margaret Ann all over. No pretensions, no fuss, no snobbery. She was getting married surrounded by all these flitting society women, but she was in no danger of allowing it to go to her head. To her, there was nothing really that special about marrying Wilkie Dunn although I suspect her mother's encouragement had not been a small factor in her deciding to do it. I'm not saying that Margaret

Ann wouldn't have married Wilkie without the pressure, but she was just never going to be overimpressed by Wilkie's social status. This one fact would turn out to be the pivotal issue in the eventual end of the marriage. I think Margaret Ann married because she was lonely, because she wanted children, and because Wilkie Dunn asked her, in that order. That makes her not that much different from women who get married every day.

After the wedding, Miss Corinne and Rebel Patterson went back to their small brick house on the other side of the river with the newly filled living room. Even with the addition of the new furniture from Miss Sudie's house, it was very different from the immaculate and tastefully decorated old South homes of the Fergusons, the Cobbs, the Luces, and the Woodruffs.

"I'm glad she finally got her living room before she died," Margaret Ann would comment years later referring to Miss Sudie's furniture, which finally filled the Patterson's living room and dining room. She said this when we were back at her parent's house after Miss Corinne's funeral. Rebel was upstairs eating potato chips and talking to the television.

As Close as Sisters

Millie Tate might have thought that morning about going somewhere, getting out of the house. She might have looked out the kitchen window and remembered that Reese had the car. *Phone someone. Phone somebody, anybody.* But if she did, everybody would know. Everybody in town would know.

She went to the telephone stand in the hall, picked up the receiver, and started dialing before she realized she was phoning Sweet's house. Sweet was, after all, her best friend. That's what Sweet had said. She had told Millie that night when the couples were together that they were now best friends, as close as sisters. Millie had never had a sister. Reese had looked on beaming, proud that his wife was Sweet McKean's best friend.

That was what cinched it—what Sweet had said about being friends and sisters. If it hadn't been for that, Millie would have started crying, started howling, and she would have embarrassed herself and Reese. She would have lost him then for sure.

Millie stopped dialing and put the phone down. Sweet McKean was the only person she could, and the one person she couldn't talk to.

Close as sisters. Close as sisters. Millie kept repeating the words to herself. So why couldn't she phone Sweet. Close as sisters. Millie went through the house and sat down on her bed again.

She knew why she couldn't talk to Sweet. She just had to admit it to herself. Sweet McKean was the reason Reese wanted a divorce. One time with Sweet and Reese was willing to throw away everything, or at least throw away her. One time. That was enough. One time and he wanted a divorce even though Sweet and Ben McKean were happily married. They were happily married. Weren't they? They looked happily married. They said they were happily married. They acted like they were happily married.

One time with Sweet McKean and she, Millie, had become so repugnant to Reese, he could no longer share the same house with her, no longer share the same bed. But he had been sharing that bed with her. He still was sharing that bed with her even though he said he wanted a divorce.

Millie glanced to her right and looked at herself in the mirror. She saw herself as Reese must see her. Sitting there, her hands folded primly in her lap, her legs crossed at the ankles, her sweet little housedress. Who could blame him. Who would want her—mousy, little Millie Tate—after, whatever he had done with Sweet. What had Sweet done with him, to him? Millie stood up and shook her head. She didn't want to think about it. She didn't want the image in her head. It was sinful. Thinking about it was as sinful as doing it. It was the devil who was visiting her with indecent images. It certainly wasn't God. God was the one punishing her for having done what she did.

Maybe that was it. Maybe Reese was repulsed by her because she had been with another man. She should never have let Ben McKean touch her, much less . . . Even though Reese had been with Sweet, men didn't think about it as the same. It didn't matter that he had been with another woman, with Sweet, but it might have mattered very much that his wife had been with another man.

But they said they were one in Christ, all of them, afterward. But Reese might have felt different after he got home and thought about the mother of his children in bed with another man. She should never have done it. Never. She should have walked out.

But how could she? It was what Reese wanted. What they all wanted. How could she disappoint them? They said that it wouldn't happen unless everybody agreed and she was the holdout. She just couldn't ruin everybody's good time. Reese had wanted her to do it. Reese had almost forced her to do it.

No, she couldn't blame it all on Reese. That wasn't right. It wasn't just. She was a grown woman. She could make her own decisions. She was responsible to God for her own decisions. God wouldn't have liked her to blame Reese for her behavior. She had just done the wrong thing, and now God was punishing her, or Reese was punishing her, or the devil . . .

Popcorn for Dinner

It was a real surprise to those of us who grew up in Wilkes Ferry with Jimmy Wade when he cleaned up his act, went to work at for a major corporation, and wore a suit and tie every day.

The way Jimmy was raised, it was a surprise to most of us that he grew up at all. He didn't exactly have your average 1950s Beaver Clever upbringing like the rest of us, or at least like what the rest of us thought we had.

I remember exactly where I was standing when I first heard as a child that the Wades were having popcorn for dinner. It was so unheard of it was almost scandalous. None of our mothers would have permitted such a thing. Housewives in the 1950s cooked three meals a day. My father might have hated the hotdogs my mother boiled sometimes for dinner, but he always had a meal ready when he got home. The bridge set would have been shocked to the core had they heard of anyone besides the Wades having popcorn for dinner.

The Wades lived in a house right next to ours, and their backyard was separated from ours by only a little white fence. Every morning at around 9:00 AM, June Wade, Jimmy's mother, would usher three little boys—Jimmy, who was my age; Bobby, a year younger; and Joey, year younger still; down the back steps of their house and outside into the enclosed backyard. She would bring with her a loaf of bread or some crackers and peanut butter or whatever else she had grabbed on her way through the kitchen.

After spending a few minutes issuing instructions, she'd go back inside. The door would slam, the bolt would lock, and after that, Jimmy, Bobby, and Joey were on their own, at least until lunch (that is, when she remembered to give them lunch). Sometimes they had to pound on the door at lunchtime to get her attention. My mother and I would sometimes watch this, peering over the top of the half curtains in our back room.

Now you can imagine what three little boys, unsupervised, got up to in that backyard. They were always either planning or perpetrating some outrage. They played Tarzan, army, cowboys and Indians, anything that involved dying. It seemed as if every time I looked out the sunroom windows, one of them was clutching his heart or his stomach in a simulated death agony. They also ripped shingles off my father's garage. They yelled at and generally tormented any of the neighborhood animals foolish enough to get near them.

One day, they set fire to our garage. After the fire department left, they were punished severely first by June and later by their father. The next day they set fire to their own house.

On another occasion, Jimmy tried to hang Bobby from the big oak tree in the backyard, nearly killing him. Had my mother not just happened to be passing through the sunroom and seen Bobby's little tennis-shoed feet swaying underneath the branches of the tree and then had the clearheadedness to fly out the back door through the gate and grab him in time to lift him up and relieve the pressure of the noose around his neck, Bobby Wade would have certainly passed onto the afterlife, if indeed there is such a thing.

After that, whenever there was crying or screaming from the Wade's backyard that seemed to indicate someone was being killed, June Wade` would fling that back door open so hard it's a miracle it didn't come off the hinges. She would come down those stairs like a Tasmanian devil, hair flying.

June Wade had so much long black wavy hair that it seemed to be enough for three women and it just seemed to stick out everywhere. From the look of it, I can't think that she ever brushed it. I don't see how she could have gotten a brush through it. Jimmy told me she used to pull at it all the time, sometimes so hard it would come out in her hand.

She scared the bejesus out of me when she came tearing down those stairs. And I was inside my own house just watching. I wasn't going to get a spanking.

When June Wade came out the back door, little boys scattered in all directions. But it was no use. June would eventually catch them and jerk them up by the arm or the shirt collar, if they were even wearing shirts, and beat the living daylights out of them. I don't think she really hurt them. If she had, they might not have been so devilish. She just had this sort of dramatic flair that made the whole thing look terrifying. Then just as suddenly as she had appeared, Miss June would turn on her heel, stomp back up the back stairs, go inside, and slam the door. You could hear the bolt locking from our house.

Miss June Wade was definitely not part of the hatted and gloved and pearled bridge set the rest of the mothers hung out with. She was often in her bathrobe in the middle of the afternoon—something else that would have shamed any of the other mothers. That little clique of women who had children around my age would have been dressed by nine had they been dying. You have to remember these were women who put on clean underwear before leaving the house for fear they would be stricken by some illness or injured in some accident and taken to the hospital where they would be found to have moth-eaten under panties on.

Miss June wore tortoise shell glasses with lenses that were as thick as the bottoms of coke bottles. They were not nearly as bad as the ones Jewel wore, but they were not very fashionable. But then, Miss June wasn't the least bit concerned with fashion. Miss June wore no make up, and she didn't even pluck her eyebrows. She was definitely not a June Clever mother.

Jimmy told me in high school that June locked herself in the house all day to write country and western lyrics. But nobody I knew ever saw a song sheet or even saw her go to the post office. But Miss June remained cloistered in that house for most of my childhood.

Then one day, Miss June disappeared. It was all hushed up by the adults. Nobody would talk about it. But all of us knew she was gone. The Wades had moved by that time, over near the elementary school, so I didn't get to observe the situation first hand, but I heard the adults talking about it in hushed tones.

Jimmy told me years later that Miss June had just left them and gone to Nashville for a while to try out her country music career. I guess she didn't have a lot of success since nobody's ever heard of her, and she finally wound up in a mental hospital in Mississippi where she had grown up. Miss June remained at the mental hospital until the day she died. Jimmy regularly visited her, and he told me she spent all her time writing country and western lyrics and sending them off to Nashville. He said she was never happier in her life than when she was in the mental hospital.

Some women just weren't cut out for the fifties.

Cats Don't Work for Nazis

A few years after they were married, Margaret Ann and Wilkie moved away. They couldn't sell the enormous remodeled Hopewell house, so they rented it. Margaret Ann started having children. She had three of them—girls, one after the other so that by the time she was through, she and Wilkie had four girls and a hyperactive little boy. Five children.

Margaret Ann was through having children after three girls, but Wilkie wasn't. He still kept wanting her to get pregnant again so he could try for a boy. You might think, he already had a boy, but Wilkie Dunn wanted a boy of his own, not the adopted hyperactive misfit.

I don't know how Margaret Ann managed it. Perhaps she took birth control in secret, perhaps she just refused to have sex, perhaps she just didn't get pregnant again. But after the third girl, she never had another baby. She loved her children, and she was a good if weird mother.

But after a while, it all started to get to her—alone there in the house, isolated in another state with five children. She started to take Beau's Ritalin just to be able to keep going. This went on for years until finally, she looked like a walking skeleton. She lost so much weight even her head looked like nothing but a skull, the skin sunken back around her eyeballs like a victim of a concentration camp.

Wilkie couldn't be bothered with her and her problems. When he wasn't working, he was traveling around the country showing his Dobermans in the dog shows. Anybody would have known that he would breed Dobermans. Cats would never have worked for the Nazis, Dobermans did.

In the fine old tradition of the Southern planter class, Wilkie had Margaret Ann commit herself to a mental institution. That was how much control he had over her by that time. She drove herself to a mental hospital, a private clinic run by one of Wilkie's friends near the Valley. She committed herself, but even so, the staff wouldn't allow her to make a telephone call or leave. They had orders from Dr. Dunn.

Margaret Ann did what she had done for most of her early life—she escaped and found a phone and phoned mother.

"Come get me," she said simply into the telephone. Mother knew immediately who it was. She was transported back twenty years.

"Where are you?" Mother asked.

By the time Mother got to the all-night donut shop from where Margaret Ann had phoned, the police and the staff of the clinic were already there to take her back. Mother was shocked at the way she looked.

"Does Miss Corinne know you're here?" she asked Margaret Ann as she was being led away and put into the squad car. Margaret Ann just looked over at her and nodded her head. "She told me to stay."

In less than twenty-four hours, Margaret Ann was on the telephone again asking mother to come get her. Mother got Tamyra this time, and the two of them showed up at the clinic and demanded to see Margaret Ann. The staff adamantly refused. Margaret Ann was isolated, and no one could see her—on orders from Dr. Dunn, her husband, and also the owner of the clinic. Mother and Tamyra just pushed past the staff and started going from room to room to find Margaret Ann amid threats of phoning the police.

"Call them," Tamyra said at one point. "If you don't let us see her, I'm going to phone them myself." This made them back off.

What Mother and Tamyra found in the clinic was shocking. It was like something out of Dickens. It was the middle of winter, and there were broken windows with newspaper stuffed in the holes in rooms where the patients were kept. Mama and Tamyra were appalled at the conditions and the dirtiness of the place.

When they finally found Margaret Ann, she flew into their arms and begged to be taken home, in other words, to Mother's house. They bundled her up in a coat and amid the screams and accusations and threats of the staff, they ushered her out of the clinic and took her to Mother's house where she finally rested.

As strange as it may seem and as predictable as it may seem, Margaret Ann went back to Wilkie after that. She rested and gained some weight and got better and then she got in her car and drove back to Wilkie. The marriage lasted a few more years. Then Wilkie ditched her and the children for a slim, social climbing "barracuda" as Margaret Ann termed her. She was the opposite of Margaret Ann.

The Barracuda liked designer clothes, jewelry, country clubs, going to night spots, expensive cars. She was delighted to be in the social whirl of Little Rock. I cannot imagine how glamorous that must be. She had no interest in children.

Margaret Ann, after going through a severe depression, got a settlement from Wilkie and moved into a small brick house out in the country near Wilkes Ferry.

Love on the Coffee Table

"Oh, for heaven's sake," Millie Tate said out loud standing up from where she sat on her bed. "I can't think about this anymore."

She stood looking around her for something, perhaps she was looking for something that needed to be done—a shirt that needed a button replaced, an end table that needed polishing with Johnson's Wax, a pair of socks needing to be laundered. There was nothing.

"I can't think about anything else," she finally said and sank down on the bed again.

She had been with another man, another man that Reese saw almost every day, and now he thought of her as unclean. What had she done? God help her.

But Reese hadn't stopped having sex with her. And she hadn't refused him. She had done everything in the world to avoid another rendezvous with the McKeans. She had pled headache, flu, exhaustion. She had gone to visit her mother for as long as she could stay away. She had made so many excuses she couldn't even remember them all. But she hadn't refused her husband. She would never have done that. She knew she was displeasing him by not going back for another experience of being "one with Christ." But she couldn't help it. She just couldn't do it again. She preferred, as much as humanly possible, not to think about it again, not to speak of it ever again. But she hadn't refused Reese.

In fact, she had tried, in her own pathetic way to entice him, to win him back. She had read the magazines in the doctor's office waiting room like everybody else. Those articles advised letting your husband come home and find you cleaning in an apron and nothing else. She had thought about it.

But when was she going to be standing around wearing an apron and nothing else when three children weren't running in and out? And how were they going to make passionate love on the coffee table (just the thought of it made her reach instinctively for a cleaning cloth) while three children stood around waiting for supper.

It was just something she could not imagine in her wildest dreams doing. Ever. But she had tried to make herself alluring, wearing gowns instead of pajamas, and wearing her good gowns, the ones that she saved in the cedar chest for trips. Reese couldn't help but notice. He knew those gowns and negligees were special. He had given them to her to put in the cedar chest to take along on the business jaunts that he never managed to be able to take her along for.

She had not worn cold cream to bed in months and months and had started rolling up her hair in the mornings after Reese left for work and the children left for school. She would wash and set her hair and let it dry while she did the rest of the housework. She had the bobby pins out and her hair done well before Reese came home from work just in case he came early and caught her.

She tried to remember to put perfumed cream on her body so she would smell good at night. Every night, no matter what happened, she would reach her hand out and touch him on the shoulder just to let him know that she was there, available to him in case he wanted her.

He usually didn't, but that was nothing new. He sometimes did—enough so that she couldn't believe he was completely disgusted by her. But there had been a change in his lovemaking, a slight change, a change so slight nobody else would have noticed. Well, how could they? But Millie noticed even though she tried to ignore it.

Reese, when he did want her, seemed even more excited than ever but by a different thing. He had started to say things. He never did that before. Things like "Yeah. Yeah baby. Like that. Just like that." And he had started to guide her in a way that he never had, even once pushing her head down his chest toward his stomach. She didn't have a clue what he was doing, or at least she didn't think she had. If she did, she didn't want to.

But even though she resisted the pressure of his hand on the back of her neck, he seemed even to be excited by that.

No, when he wanted to do it, he didn't seem to be repulsed. So why now did he want to leave? Where was he going to go?

Maybe it was because she wouldn't go back for another session with the McKeans. He couldn't do it without her. If he wanted to have another go at Sweet McKean, he needed Millie even to do that. What were they going to do just the three of them—Reese, Sweet, and Ben? She just couldn't see it. She didn't think Ben McKean would stand for it.

Millie clutched her throat as she thought about that afternoon with Ben McKean. She thought she sensed that he didn't want to be there with her any more than she wanted to be there with him, but she wasn't sure. He was nice enough and tried his best to make her feel like he wanted her, but his heart wasn't in it.

He made love to her but not like a man who wanted a woman, really wanted her, or at least not like Reese had done in the beginning, before all the children had come. Ben had held out his arms to her and kissed her on the cheek before he started. But it wasn't the same. There was no immediacy of desire like there had been with Reese when they were first married.

But then, and Millie might well have blushed again thinking about it, making love with Ben McKean, even though he didn't really mean it, was in many ways better than it had ever been with Reese Tate in his prime. Millie felt ashamed of herself for thinking this. Reese was her husband, and she had never wanted another man besides Reese in her life. But there was something different about it with Ben McKean.

First of all, Ben had watched her. Not like Reese watched her. When she made love with Reese, he watched her body, her breasts, her nipples. He liked to watch her nipples get hard and almost always twisted them even though she had often told him it hurt. Reese liked to look at her sex, which made Millie feel like she was going to throw up, and he even sometimes turned her around to look at her butt and smack it. That just made her feel ridiculous.

Ben McKean had hardly looked at her at all, at her body. He had looked right into her eyes. His kind, gentle blue eyes gazed into hers as if he were watching her to make sure he didn't hurt her. It was as if he were looking for her, and she didn't know how to respond.

Millie Tate liked Ben McKean. They had spent so much time together, riding in the McGregor's bus, eating, picnicking, sitting beside each other in churches, tents, auditorium, choir lofts. He was a nice, friendly man, and she was genuinely fond of him. She felt also that Ben McKean was fond of her. When he made love to her, it was like making love to an old friend. It *was* making love to an old friend, and this was a new experience for Millie.

Ben was patient and slow and gentle. He seemed in no particular hurry to get anywhere, do anything. Making love with him was something like a warm handshake or a friendly hug. It wasn't like making love at all, or at least not what she was used to as making love.

Ben McKean didn't pinch or twist or smack anything. And the parts of her body he might have pinched or twisted or smacked didn't feel like things anymore. Millie, well she shouldn't feel this way, but Millie was probably more relaxed with Ben (even though she felt she was committing a mortal sin) than she had ever been with Reese.

Ben McKean had looked fondly into Millie's eyes the entire time, almost up to the very beginning of the end. When he finally did take his eyes away from hers and start the rhythmic path to the finish, she felt, for the first time, as if it were Sweet's face he was seeing, Sweet's body he was worshiping, Sweet's sex into which he was releasing himself, and always out there, the possible gift of new life.

When it was over, really over, and Ben McKean gently pulled himself out of her, she thought she saw just a flicker of apology in his eye, an apology that had not been there before. It was then that she knew that in those last few minutes, both men had been loving Sweet McKean.

No matter how they tried to talk it away to cover it up. No matter what the physical arrangement was of the coupling of bodies, in those last few minutes, Millie was the odd man out, and she knew it. They had said that nobody would be hurt, nobody would be left out, nobody would be excluded, but Millie had been excluded as truly as if she had been forced to wait in the hall.

Ben McKean knew it as surely as did Millie, and there was just a hint of pity in his eyes as he glanced at her afterward. Millie had never felt too alone in her life, not when she had been a little girl in the big farmhouse waiting for her parents to come home, not during the war when she had prayed and waited for Reese to return, not in the labor room at the hospital.

Mama Won't Leave

Wives dropped like flies in Wilkes Ferry. There's no better locale for getting rid of a wife than the small town South. Entrenched class distinctions and privileges combined with subservient, incompetent law enforcement to make small town Southern America the playground of wife murderers. Miss Corinne's death was not even investigated even though Mr. Rebel and her doctor were clearly at fault. If Mr. Rebel didn't pull the trigger, he might as well have, and Dr. Luce, through just plain sorry negligence, let it happen.

At the time of Miss Corinne's death, I had not had a lot of contact with Margaret Ann for years. Once when I was home in Wilkes Ferry, I ran into Miss Corinne at the Kroger. She was a nervous wreck, even more of a nervous wreck than usual. She didn't bother with preliminary niceties. The minute she saw me, she started grasping at me and crying. She begged me to phone Margaret Ann. She wanted me to phone and get Margaret Ann to phone her. What could I say? That I wasn't going to phone? I had no real understanding of the situation. Miss Corinne just said that Margaret Ann wouldn't speak to her. I felt so bad for Miss Corinne I didn't see what else I could do.

So I did phone Margaret Ann, and she explained that Mr. Rebel and Miss Corinne were driving her out of her mind. She said that they would phone her while in the middle of a murderous battle. Miss Corinne would be crying and screaming in the background. Mr. Rebel would be yelling and trying to beat Miss Corinne while he was talking on the telephone.

"I just can't deal with it anymore," Margaret Ann said. "I'm three states away. I can't do anything about what's going on. It's been going on for years, decades, and Mama won't leave him." In an effort to preserve her own sanity, Margaret Ann had just finally washed her hands of them.

I tried to reason with Margaret Ann, a fact that I am now ashamed of. I argued that when Miss Corinne grew up, women just didn't leave their husbands, and besides, where would she have gone? People just didn't get divorced in their generation.

I can see now that I took a detached, academic view of the matter and completely missed the impact all this was having on Margaret Ann. I had no idea because she had not told me at the time that Mr. Rebel had been beating Miss Corinne all those years. I should have figured it out, but I didn't. I suppose I was victim of the same set of idealized notions that protected so much slime in Wilkes Ferry. Even with all the evidence, late night phone calls from Margaret Ann, Mr. Rebel parading around the yard in his underwear holding a gun, I just didn't get it.

I thought Mr. Rebel's behavior was just bravado. I never saw Miss Corinne hurt or bruised. Even if I had, I don't know that I would have put the two things together even if she had been black and blue. And I am sure Miss Corinne would have made some self-deprecating joke about her condition, blaming herself for falling, and I would have accepted it hook, line, and sinker.

Margaret Ann listened to me, as always. I could tell she wasn't convinced. But, she agreed to phone Miss Corinne. Margaret Ann and I have never talked about that phone call. We have never talked about so many things, and I doubt now that we ever will.

Miss Corinne and Mr. Rebel continued to be just as dysfunctional and miserable as they always had been. Now that I think about it, I don't remember being anywhere where they went as a couple, not at church, not anywhere. I guess Mr. Rebel just didn't go anywhere with Miss Corinne. He spent most of his time in front of the television. I am sure this was not the life a young Miss Corinne had in mind when she married into the Patterson family so many years before.

A Trunk Full of Guns

When I talked to Brennan O'Hara that summer afternoon in my parent's backyard, I had never seen him look happier or healthier. Two hours later, he put the barrel of a rifle into his mouth and splattered his brains all over the back wall of his dead mother's toolshed.

He made two phone calls between the time I saw him and when he killed himself. He called me and asked me to go to Atlanta with him for dinner, and he phoned Joe Ed Montgomery.

Afterward, I regretted not accepting his invitation to dinner, but it was already three o'clock in the afternoon when he called, and I was driving to DC to pick up some furniture I had stored. I just didn't have time to drive to Atlanta to have dinner.

Later that same afternoon, Brennan phoned Jo Ed with less ambitious plans. He wanted Joe Ed to meet him somewhere in Wilkes Ferry for coffee. But Joe Ed was fixing dinner for his two little girls. He didn't have time either.

Had Brennan ever said, "I'm depressed" or "I'm desperate" or even "I need somebody to talk to," Joe Ed and I would have set aside anything we were doing and met him. There were dozens of people in Wilkes Ferry who would have dropped everything to talk and listen and even to hold him had he only said something, people who would have stayed with him all night if that's what it took—but he never said a thing.

Those two telephone calls were the extent of his reaching out.

Brennan Quinn grew up with us. I played with Brennan, walked to school with Brennan, and later on in high school, partied with Brennan. He was the first boy who ever kissed me. And he was the first boy who ever, walking home from school, carefully steered me to the inside of the sidewalk so he would be walking on the side near the cars. Good, sound Southern gentleman manners.

Brennan Quinn grew from being a short, pudgy redheaded and freckled little boy into a young man over six feet tall, solid as a rock. He played guard on the football team, and nobody could get around him. He wasn't afraid of anything or anybody.

After high school, Brennan, like so many of us, did more than just experiment with drugs and drink. As the years progressed, he moved on to more sinister activities. Jimmy told me Brennan would show up at their annual drinking binge at the lake with guns, a trunk full of guns—automatic, semi-automatic, enough ammunition to take out a small city, even hand grenades.

"Why?" I asked Jimmy.

He shrugged his shoulders. "Beats me, but it scared me to death. Somebody would lock the guns up in the trunk and hide his keys, just in case," Jimmy continued. "But you know how Brennan was. He was always happy. He never got mean, even when he was drunk. The guns? I don't know."

After the drug and gun episodes, Jimmy told me Brennan became, of all things, a charismatic minister. I don't know how long that lasted, but later, I got word that he had settled down and married a very proper young woman from Wilkes Ferry who was a child when we were in high school. Within a short time (too short for some people's taste), they had a child. Brennan fell in love with the little boy. He stopped traveling around the country preaching, got a very good job with a large corporation, a house and a swimming pool. But unfortunately, he kept drinking.

Then after a few years, his employer told him he had two choices—quit or go into drug treatment. Brennan opted for the latter. After a year of drug treatment, it seemed like he finally had everything together. That's when the proper young woman up and left him. She said he wasn't "fun" anymore. She took the child.

Maybe losing the child was why he did it, or maybe it was because his mother had died the year before. This had been a close family—Brennan; his older sister, Mary; his younger sister, MaryAnn; and their mother, Aideen. Nobody really knew why he did it or why he did it in that particular, violent way.

His sister Mary and Mary's husband had bought Mrs. Coffee's old house next door to my parents. Miss Aideen's house, the house they all grew up in, was just behind ours facing the other way. Their back fence was the back fence to our yard when we were growing up. Later, that fence was replaced by a bank of flowers. The afternoon Brennan called Joe Ed and I, he was staying in Miss Aideen's house. He walked down to Mary's house and started a fight. Mary was so devastated by Brennan's death I never got to ask her what that fight was about.

In the middle of the fight, Brennan stormed out of Mary's house, walked up to his mother's house, and went into the toolshed. Afterward, they said he had practiced the suicide, set everything up beforehand, because it wasn't ten minutes after he left Mary's house that my parents and Mary's husband heard the shot. Brennan sat on the ground and leaned back against the inside of the shed. He took off his shoe, put the gun into his mouth, and pulled the trigger with his toes. Afterward, the usual rumors circulated around town. One person said that Brennan was about to be arrested; another said he had just found out that he was dying of incurable cancer. I don't think any of the stories were true. I think Brennan just got tired, tired of trying.

But he adored that little boy. I saw him with the child once at Mary Ann's swimming pool. He could hardly take his eyes off the boy. How, how could he leave him? How could he take his own life and leave behind a son to grow up wondering why it happened. How could he leave a child knowing that the child might well blame himself. And how, how could he leave a child to imagine what his father looked like with his brains spattered on the inside of his mother's toolshed.

Soon after the suicide, they tore down the shed, of course, but every time the child went down that street, he would remember where his father had sat and decided to blow the back of his head to smithereens.

Another thing I just didn't understand, really, was that Brennan purposefully provoked an argument with the sister who had loved him so much and supported him through so many difficulties. He provoked the argument, walked out and went straight to the toolshed to blow his brains out. Perhaps he just couldn't do it alone. Perhaps he needed Mary to give him the impetus.

Suicide is such an extraordinarily selfish thing to do. The way Brennan chose to do it was even more selfish.

In the years after Brennan killed himself, he has floated into and out of my consciousness. He'll never see another hibiscus, I'll think to myself. He'll never see another blue heron rise slowly and heavily into the air. He'll never see another horse gallop across a snow-covered field, his tail up, flying with the sheer delight of being alive. He'll never see another cat flick it's tail in anticipation as it reads something captivating on the wind. Hell, he'll never even by able to go to Wal-Mart on a spring day and buy herbs.

Mary, Brennan's sister, was never the same after that summer afternoon. She and MaryAnn wouldn't let Brennan's ex-wife and the little boy sit with the family at the funeral.

Brennan Quinn was in this world and then he wasn't. He was bone and flesh and muscle, and then he was not. He was desire and ambition, pleasure and dreams, and then he was . . . nothing. And as good as he was, as kind and loving as he was, as hard as he tried, he left behind him an avalanche of pain and bitterness.

Pulling Away from the Wall

Millie Tate might have been able to have Ben McKean make love to her again, even if his heart wasn't in it, even if he finished by pitying her. She might have been able to stand that. What she could not stand and what she was determined to avoid at all costs was that dreadful feeling of loneliness she had experienced in the room with Ben McKean after he had made love to her, had had her.

But wasn't that what she felt now? Alone?

Millie put her head in her hands and started to cry again. It was then that she heard the tapping on the kitchen door.

She sucked in her breath sharply and tried not to make a sound. Her body froze, the instinctive response of an animal seized in the sure knowledge of being observed. "Who on earth?" She wracked her brain trying to think. Who would be at her door at this time of the day. She glanced over at the clock on the dresser. 11:00 AM. Who could possibly be at her door?

Millie tried to hold down the sobs so she couldn't be heard even though overhearing her was virtually impossible. She was in the bedroom, and the tapper was outside the kitchen in the carport.

"Millie," a voice called out. "You there?"

Who was it? Millie asked herself. The tapping started again. Whoever it was, she wasn't going to go away. *The car wasn't there*, Millie thought. Their car wasn't in the driveway. Maybe she would think Millie was not there.

Millie crept, like a prisoner in her own home, to the bedroom door and peered around the door frame. She walked across the hallway and then peered to her left and tried to see the kitchen window without being seen. She closed her eyes.

Part of her wanted to run to the kitchen door, fling it open, and fall into the arms of whoever was there. "Oh, my God." She could imagine herself saying. "Thank God you've come." But a stronger part of her, the part that had for so long held everything inside her, not made a scene, not screamed out even in the hospital in labor, hushed her breathing and stood still. She knew she wouldn't fling open that door just as Reese did.

When the tapping and the calling stopped and Millie heard the car door slam and the car start and pull out of the driveway, she knew it had been her last chance. She walked back into the bedroom and patted her hair in front of the mirror. She turned around and went to the dresser she shared with Reese and pulled open the top drawer. Moving some balled-up socks aside, she curled her little fingers around the handle of the gun. She walked calmly into the bathroom, stepped into the shower, and made sure the shower curtain was pulled tightly closed after her. As she raised the gun to her temple, she noticed that the curtain hadn't completely closed and that there was a little gap just at the edge of the tub, where the curtain was pulling away from the wall. She reached down with the hand not holding the heavy gun and smoothed out the shower curtain so that it made a leak proof seam with the tile. She raised the gun to her head, and she pulled the trigger.

Afterward, there were a lot of variations of the story around town. Some people said Reese Tate had been at home when it happened. Some people said that the neighbor had indeed tapped on the door earlier in the morning but that Reese had come home from work at lunch time, and Millie had shot herself then. That made a certain amount of sense. Reese came home, and they got into a fight about the divorce and she shot herself.

Other people said that Reese shot her. Now I wouldn't put it past Reese Tate for a minute, but even if he had the motive and the intent and the desire, how the hell would he have talked her into walking into the bathroom, getting in the shower, and letting him do it there. How, if he had done this, did he avoid getting blood all over him?

I suppose he could have stood outside the bathtub, facing her, with the gun to her temple, his body shielded by the shower curtain. He could have removed his clothes and stood with her in the shower. He could have put the gun in her hand and then raised that hand to point the gun to her head. There were ways to do it.

Reese could have pulled the gun on her and forced her to march into the shower, and it would make sense then that she would have still had her clothes and shoes on and even her glasses. But I just don't think Reese Tate was smart enough to get away with murder. Maybe I'm wrong. O.J. Simpson is no genius. Maybe it takes a certain kind of crafty stupidity to get away with murder.

But I don't think Reese Tate murdered Millie, at least not directly. I think Millie murdered herself, and I think she did it in the shower so it wouldn't mess up the house. She couldn't bear to think about quarts of blood and guts all over her carpet and walls, so she did what every good housewife would do; she got in the shower, where all of it could be washed down the drain. I can see it now: Tips on Blowing Your Brains Out with Minimal Mess by the Queen of Clean. Make sure the shower curtain is completely closed . . . don't leave any telltale gaps . . .

There are parts of the story about Millie Tate that don't make sense. For example, I can't imagine Millie Tate blowing her brains out in the shower, knowing that her children would be the ones to find her when they got home from school. Reese Tate didn't come home every day for lunch, or at least my father didn't. It was irregular. And even if he had said he was coming home for lunch, there was always the chance that he wouldn't. The Millie Tate I knew would not take the chance that Reese would not be able to get home, and her children would come in from school and find their mother blown to bits in the shower. She just wasn't that kind of person.

Some people said that she phoned Reese at work and asked him to come home and then went to the shower with the gun. That's possible, but it certainly wasn't part of the original story I heard at the time. Seems like if that was part of the original story, it was an important detail that would have been included.

But if Reese wasn't there, who loaded the gun? I do not believe for one second that Millie Tate knew how to load a gun for herself. So did Reese leave a loaded gun in his dresser all the time with three children in the house? Or did he load it that morning?

Did he load it in front of her? Whose gun was it? How long had it been there? Did he sit on the bed and watch her load it that morning before he left for work and not say anything? Did he tell her to load it and then just walk out of the house?

Of course, you can't ask anybody now. Nobody will talk about it even though it happened thirty years ago. The McGregors, Sweet McKean's parents, are dead now, but Sweet McKean and her money still make her the center of the church social scene, and everybody is afraid of talking about her behind her back, having it found out, and being kicked off the McGregor bus, which still runs back and forth to activities and carries its select group of now geriatric hangers-on.

Ben McKean is in a nursing home. He developed Alzheimer's and can't even recognize his own sons, much less Sweet. Sweet, who is now Sweet Tate (what a name), and Reese lived in what is still called the McGregor Mansion even though there is now a town full of houses much larger and grander than the McGregor Mansion. Sweet and Reese, who married shortly after Millie died, moved out of the McKean house and next door into the McGregors Mansion when Miss Fiona died. Patty Tate and her husband now live in the McKean's old house.

I saw Patty one day, thirty years later, jogging in the neighborhood when I was driving to the store. When I saw her, I was so startled I hit the breaks. I thought I was seeing Miss Millie jogging toward me in a sweat suit and sneakers. It took me several minutes to realize what had happened. It was literally like seeing a ghost.

Patty, grown up, could pass for Millie's twin. It must be disconcerting to Reese and Sweet, although something tells me that nothing is disconcerting to those two. When Patty married, the write-up in the paper, or so I'm told, didn't even mention Millie. Patty was said to be the daughter of Reese and Sweet Tate, granddaughter of the McGregors, so on and so on. It was as if Millie had never existed.

Mark Tate, the Tate son who was my age, just as stupid as his father, inherited his craftiness. Mark must have gotten through school by cheating and buying papers. But no fool, he followed in his father's footsteps and married an extremely wealthy Jewish girl from Savannah. After that, he was set for life. Like father . . .

And Sweet's new husband, Reese, worked his way further up the corporate ladder. He eventually became president of the bank formerly owned by the McGregors and passed down to the McKeans and the Fists, Honey and her husband, Ed. The insertion of Reese Tate into the bank caused something close to a war among the remaining family. First, Ben resigned. He wasn't about to share his work life as well as his wife with Reese Tate. Since Ben was an attorney, he opened his own practice and did very well for himself without the McGregors' money or Sweet.

He and his new wife (some doctor or other's ex) built an extravagant new house over in the old Pine Grove behind the Peach Hills neighborhood. The house said, "I have done very well without you and your money. Thank you very much." Ben also dropped out of the church. I never saw him there again.

At the church, you would have thought nothing happened. Reese and Sweet got married in a quiet ceremony presided over by the minister, and the Tates (the new Tates) assumed their position at the center of the Baptist social scene and on the third pew from the front, left side as you see it from the prospective of God or the teenagers in the balcony.

If almost anybody else in the church had been involved in such a sorted series of events, they would have been driven out of the congregation and shunned. As it was, money, like blood and history, always wills out, and Sweet McKean and Reese Tate just continued along as they had before, only now a couple.

Reese Tate, now an extremely wealthy man driving a Volvo and sporting expensive clothes, became even more obnoxious than he had been when he had been a poor white-collar working man for the Cobb Cotton Manufacturing Company. He told even more tasteless jokes, and he became a drunk and a loud, a lecherous, dirty-minded, insulting drunk. My mother maintained until the day she died that Sweet McKean/Tate was her very best friend.

Honey and her husband tried to fight Sweet and Reese for the bank, but they finally gave up. It just wasn't worth it. Sweet and Reese were always grounded in Wilkes Ferry in a way that Honey and her husband weren't. Honey and Ed spent almost all of their time out of town and even when they went out to dinner, they went to Atlanta or Columbus. They never really either socialized or went to church in Wilkes Ferry. I have no idea why. But I could guess.

Needless to say, the bank went to shit after Reese took it over.

A Pact with the Devil

After the chance encounter at Kroger, I saw Miss Corinne one more time before she killed herself, if that's what indeed happened. Mother and I went over to the Patterson's house once when I was home visiting. We drove up and parked on the other side of the street, where we used to park when we came to pick up Margaret Ann in the middle of the night.

Mr. Rebel and Miss Corinne came out of the house at just the time we drove up, but they didn't see us. They were both walking with their heads down, looking at the ground. They were headed toward their car. I have never seen any two people who looked more miserable than they did that day, especially Miss Corinne. In those few brief moments before she knew we were there observing her, she looked like the most miserable woman on the face of the earth.

I have only ever seen one other woman look so miserable. That was my mother in the only photograph we have of her and me when I was an infant. My mother was sitting in a rocking chair holding me in her arms wrapped in a blanket. Beside her was my Aunt Karin, holding my cousin Gary who was the same age as I was. Karin was smiling into the camera. Mother looked like she would have been grateful to have a loaded gun.

I felt almost embarrassed to see the naked unhappiness on Miss Corinne's face, and I hurried to get out of the car so she would notice us. When she finally looked up and recognized me, she broke into a full smile, a weary smile, but at least a smile. We talked for a few minutes.

"How do you stay looking so young?" she asked, hugging me close to her.

"I have a pact with the devil," I quipped. It was the wrong thing to say.

She pushed me away from her and looked carefully into my face. "Don't ever say anything like that again," she said, meaning it. "Never."

"It was just a joke," I explained, confused by the severity of her response.

"Don't ever say it even in a joke." She added her face looking serious and unhappy again.

I just stood there staring at her, wondering who this woman was. We had joked about everything when Margaret Ann and I were growing up and certainly said things much more irreverent than this. But you would have thought I had sacrificed a baby in front of her in a ceremony of devil worship the way she reacted.

I found it hard to believe she was serious. We didn't stay long, and as we were leaving, Mr. Rebel and Miss Corinne got into their car, once again looking like the two most miserable people in the world.

"I can't believe she got so serious about what I said," I commented to my mother as she was turning the car around to go home.

"Corinne has become very religious lately," my mother said.

"I would call that a little more than being very religious," I said.

"She has started going to these meetings organized by Kitten Kelly's mother. They've started their own church."

"Their own church?"

"They don't go to a church anymore. They meet over at the Kelly's house every Sunday and conduct their own service.

"That's weird."

"I went once because Corinne wanted me to so badly, but I never went back."

"What was it like?"

"They were way out there, talking all this Southern Baptist stuff about the inerrancy of the Bible and the leadership role of the minister."

"While they don't have a minister?"

"Precisely."

"That doesn't make much sense."

"No, it doesn't. They went over to Susan Ivy's house when she was dying of cancer and told her that the illness was her fault."

"No," I exclaimed. "You don't mean it."

"I certainly do. They told her that she was sick because God was punishing her for something she had done."

"No."

"The God I believe in does not punish people by giving them diseases."

"I can't believe Miss Corinne would do something so unkind."

"She and Frankie just went head over heels for some evangelist in Texas, and Corinne came home and didn't even sound like the same person."

"I've never seen her look so unhappy."

"It's sad, isn't it?"

"Yes."

"And she was so beautiful and bubbly and happy when she was a girl."

"Before she married Rebel Patterson," I said.

"Before she married Rebel Patterson," my mother confirmed. "But you know, she was the one who married him, and anybody could see then that he wasn't ever going to be anything but a big spoiled child."

"Why did she marry him?"

"The Pattersons were among the wealthiest families in the Valley at that time, and Rebel Patterson was the only son. He was going to inherit everything. Miss Corinne was a sweet, kind, happy girl, but she was the one who married him."

I pondered this for a while as we were driving over the river bridge, the new river bridge that replaced the one I feared so much. When they tore down the old bridge and built a new one, they moved it a block north and thereby ruined the lovely vista you got looking east from Main Street. When I was growing up, you could stand in the middle of Main Street and look up and see the street as it swept up onto the hill where the elementary school was. At the time the school was built, it was the only school in Wilkes Ferry. Other towns put the courthouse in the most prominent place; Wilkes Ferry put the school there. It said so much about what used to be. Oh, and I later on found out that the bridge was moved a block north because the then mayor, one of the planter family descendants, was afraid that if the bridge stayed in the same place, it might decrease the value of his downtown property.

After Mother and I saw the Pattersons that day, I went back to where ever I was living at the time. It wasn't more than a few months after this that I received a call in my hotel room in Chicago. It was Mother telling me that Miss Corinne had killed herself and that Margaret Ann wanted me to come home.

I was at a criminology conference, and my then Colombian lawyer of a husband had shown up as a surprise at the conference. But there was no hesitation in my plans. If Margaret Ann wanted me to come home, I was coming home directly from Chicago. I began putting things in a suitcase while I was talking with Mother on the telephone.

I got the story for the first time as Mother and Daddy and I were driving home from the Atlanta airport to Wilkes Ferry.

That night, the night of the shooting, by the time Mother and Daddy got to the hospital in Columbus, Miss Corinne was dead. Mr. Rebel was in the hallway of the hospital wing. Miss Corinne had shot herself in the chest.

As Rebel Patterson told the story, he woke up in the middle of the night hearing Miss Corinne calling out to him. "Rebel, Rebel."

He got up out of bed and walked to the bathroom. He bent down to pick Miss Corinne up. She was on the floor. He felt something wet. He thought she had spilled water on herself. That's what he said.

Somehow, he figured out she was hurt or sick. He got her down the stairs and into their car. He then drove her to the Columbus hospital, twenty-five miles away.

Now there are a lot of things wrong with this version of events and had I been a police officer, I would have started suspecting that something was wrong when I got the call. But do you think anybody in Wilkes Ferry conducted an investigation? No. There was not an official peep about the incident. A few days later, Rebel Patterson was back in his den watching television and being cooked for and cleaned around.

I sat in that den with him before the funeral as he commented on the action on television like a child, like nothing had happened. It was as if Miss Corinne was going to walk in from the next room with her nightgown on. I had to leave. It was just the strangest thing I'd ever experienced.

The first thing that should have tipped off any investigator when they got the initial call was the fact that Rebel Patterson put his wife in the car and drove her twenty-five miles to Columbus to the hospital. Rebel Patterson was not a large man. He was short and stocky and perhaps he was strong enough to lift Miss Corinne and carry her down a flight of stairs and out to the car. But who would have done that? Who would have tried to pick up another human being

306 CHRISTINA JACQUELINE JOHNS

that badly hurt and carry them to a car. Who would have tried to stuff a limp body into the car, and who would have driven twenty-five miles with that limp body in the car?

Rebel Patterson was at least sixty at the time. I have a hard time imagining that he whisked Miss Corinne up like Rhett Butler in *Gone with the Wind* and carried her out to the car. This must have been quite a scene. It was just lucky it happened in the middle of the night, and there were no witnesses. I can imagine that Rebel carried, half dragged, Miss Corinne's body to the car. But why not just phone 911 and get an ambulance with EMT people on board who could administer medical attention immediately?

Then rather than take her to the local hospital that couldn't have been more than a few miles away, he drove a long twenty-five miles to another city. The woman had a gunshot wound in the chest, and Rebel Patterson drove twenty-five miles with her in the back of the car bleeding to death. Why would he not have gone to the closest hospital?

After all, the closer hospital, Cobb Memorial, was the hospital used by almost everybody in the Valley. It was the hospital he was most familiar with. He knew the direct route to the emergency room entrance there. Everybody in the Valley was familiar with that hospital, having been there at least once. If you had been thinking under pressure, this would have been the hospital you would have thought of, not Columbus.

There were, however, two doctors at Cobb Memorial who were relatives of Miss Corinne's. I sometimes wonder if that was the reason for heading north to Columbus rather than south to the Cobb Memorial Hospital. Also, the notion that Mr. Rebel did not hear the gun go off has always struck me as impossible. I know the Patterson's house as well as I know my own, and I could draw a detailed plan of the rooms and spacial arrangement of that house. The bathroom in which Miss Corinne was supposed to have shot herself adjoins their bedroom. Now this bedroom is not as big as a football field. It is a small bedroom with a bath which could not have been more than six feet from the bed.

Mr. Rebel's story was that he did not hear the gunshot but woke up when he heard Miss Corinne calling out his name. Now if you think I believe that for an instant, you're wrong. And why any law enforcement person believed it, I don't know. Well, that's not right, I do know. Law enforcement just didn't ask those kinds of questions. Nobody wanted them to. Nobody wanted the questions answered. Even Miss Corinne's relatives didn't want the question answered. If the question were asked, and the answer was that Mr. Rebel Patterson murdered his wife, it would have caused a scandal. My God, it was bad enough to have a suicide in the family, why court having a murder? And then, by the 1980s, there would have to be a trial. More scandal and public notoriety. Heaven forbid.

Even Miss Corinne's relatives swallowed the suicide story hook, line, and sinker. Even Margaret Ann swallowed it. She never once expressed any doubt about her father's version of what happened. It was easier for her as well to think Miss Corinne killed herself than to confront the distinct possibility that Rebel Patterson had finally, and I say finally, killed his wife. He had been murdering her for years. The gunshot wound was just the final and conclusive act of violence.

The "I thought she'd spilled water on herself" argument was preposterous. Anybody who has ever had contact with blood knows that water and blood do not even feel similar. I find it difficult to believe that you could mistake blood for water under any circumstance. And why should he? She had already shot herself. Why find it necessary to add this last, exculpatory detail? Why say that he thought it was water unless he had a guilty conscience?

I doubt that it would have taken a professional long to break Rebel Patterson down. He was not a sophisticated man, and he was a man with a temper. All you would have had to do was make him angry enough, and he would have boasted of killing Miss Corinne and then broken down and cried. But there was no interrogation. That would have been just too rude to the wrong people.

There were some other interesting details to this story. Just before Miss Corinne died, there had been a letter, a letter out of the past. The letter was from a middle-aged woman who lived in England, who said that Rebel Patterson was her father.

It seems that Mr. Rebel, while stationed in England, was not as upright as he should have been and didn't evidently use the government-issued condoms that he must have had as part of his kit. The object of his lust had recently died, and her daughter was trying to make contact with her roots.

The letter came just days before Miss Corinne's death. Did they get into some kind of argument about this? Did Miss Corinne go into a hysterical fit and Rebel just decide to silence the hysteria. Who knows. You might think that this sort of thing wouldn't matter forty years later. But it did. Think of Miss Corinne's position. She would have found out that her entire marriage had been a lie—that she had put up with Mr. Rebel's abusive, neglectful behavior for no reason, that all this suffering had been stupid. It is a tragic thing to think about. He had never loved her or never in the way she had thought. She couldn't say to herself that the economic ruin of the coal company had brought on all Rebel's bad behavior. He had been behaving badly from the beginning. Why had she suffered all these years? It must have been devastating.

Now I realize this is as much an argument for suicide as for murder, and I have no idea what happened in that house in the early hours of the morning. Added to this fact is the fact that Miss Corinne's brother-in-law doctor had abruptly taken Miss Corinne off her antidepressant the week before her death. Why would a doctor who must have been aware of the complications of suddenly taking someone off an antidepressant just taken her off cold turkey? Had he as well thought everybody was just better off without Miss Corinne? What threat did she pose to the family? Or did they just tire of her and think she was better off dead. In the past, families in this situation just sent their bothersome female members to a mental institution or addicted them to morphine. And the troublesome ones just faded away.

Margaret Ann's behavior after her mother's suicide was bizarre to say the least. Margaret Ann had never liked her father. Who could like a man who spent his time beating up on your mother and running around in his boxer shorts with guns, walking in on his teenaged daughters? Why like him? It would have made sense at that point, given the suspicious circumstances of Miss Corinne's death, for Margaret Ann to have walked out on Rebel and never looked back.

She did the opposite. Whereas she had hardly spent fifteen minutes with Mr. Rebel and Miss Corinne over the past ten years before Miss Corinne died, after Miss Corinne's death, Margaret Ann started driving over to Wilkes Ferry every few weeks to take care of Mr. Rebel. She would get somebody to cook for him and put all the food in the freezer. She would hire somebody to clean up the house, and she would herself dote on him for the time she was there. She would work in the garden and get people to come and help her.

In fact, Rebel Patterson was probably cared for to his satisfaction in this period of his life like no other. He was the sole focus of attention, the baby boy again.

For Margaret Ann, all his past bad behavior seemed to melt away, and she had justifications for everything he had ever done. There was no talking with her about any of it, not that I tried. Listening to her, you knew that there was not a hope in hell of changing her mind and that there was a risk of destroying the friendship if you said anything negative about Mr. Rebel, even reminding her of his bad behavior in the past. It was a case of revisionist history that rivaled that of Joe Ed Montgomery.

Brainwashed

I was there when Margaret Ann married Wilkie Dunn. But after that, we didn't see each other very often. She was busy having children, and I was busy with school. But even though we rarely saw each other, we had a good relationship. When we did see each other, it was as if we had never been apart. We had a special place for each other in our hearts, a special tenderness. All this changed when Mother managed to insert herself in between us. But this was Mother's specialty—inserting herself in between people.

Margaret Ann used to say I was the only person who had never criticized her, who had always supported her. That was important, important enough for her to tell me about it. It never occurred to me that she would allow Mother to make her turn on me, but it should have. Mother had been doing it all my life. But it did surprise me, and I allowed my anger and frustration at Mama to spill out on Margaret Ann.

I allowed myself to express the anger I felt, something Margaret Ann was not used to. She never forgave me. She was, in that too, like my mother. When someone crossed her, she cut them off forever and for good. Both of them were grudge holders. Even though Margaret Ann tried after I moved back to Wilkes Ferry to be civil, she never missed an opportunity to let me know I had been crossed off the list. She would clearly see me in the grocery store or the post office and studiously pretend she didn't. Once, she apologized for her snippy behavior, but then the next time I saw her, she could not contain her resentment.

This deep resentment came because I lost my temper and yelled at her over Mother. I thought at the time, and still think now, she deserved it, but it was the end of our relationship. I could and should have expressed myself differently, but she and Mother had just pushed me too far. Yelling at and hanging up on somebody is seldom the best way of dealing with a situation. But nobody has ever accused me of being a diplomat.

This all started because Mother had decided to schedule some kind of surgery and then inform me. This was a shoulder or knee replacement. I can't even remember now which. Mama, like always, had pressured me into doing what she wanted me to do. She was counting on me to take care of her. I drove to Wilkes Ferry in the middle of a school term.

Every day for over a week, I drove to Columbus to the hospital where Mother was staying. After sitting in the hospital all day, I drove back to Wilkes Ferry at night. I managed her case, talked to her doctors, shopped for her, read to her, got her whatever she wanted, sat with her. After ten days, I was exhausted, and I had to go back to work. When you teach at a university, you can't just leave for several weeks in the middle of a term.

I got Mother through the surgery, and she was recovering nicely. I even managed to convince her at one point when they gave her some codeine that there were not bugs crawling around on the walls of her hospital room. After her condition had stabilized and she was ready to leave the hospital, I arranged for a woman to come in and see about her every day. This woman was to do errands and just make sure that Mother had what she needed. And Mother also had Mattie May, who could come over and clean and stay with her anytime she wanted. Mother was to be released the next day, and I just had to go back to work. When I was talking to Margaret Ann about the situation, she offered go and pick Mother up and take her home from the hospital.

I returned to the university having missed an entire week and a half of classes. It had been a strain to say the least, but I felt as if I had done what a daughter was supposed to do. I had taken care of my mother at a time when she needed it. I should have known that this happy conclusion to the episode was more than my mother could allow.

A day after I got home, Margaret Ann phoned to tell me Mother was furious with me for messing up her house. To hear Margaret Ann talk, you'd have thought I'd trashed the place. The only thing I did was to leave without putting every single item in the house back exactly the way Mother wanted it. I was worn out when I left, and she had two women coming in who could clean up and straighten. But Mother expected her house to look as if I'd never been there.

It was Mother down to the ground. I traveled from another state to help her, spent over a week in the middle or the school term managing her affairs, driving to and from Columbus every day, sitting in a hospital for ten or twelve hours a day, going shopping for whatever little thing she happened to think she needed. I had done a good job, but my feeling of satisfaction with anything I ever did was like a red flag in front of a bull. Mother couldn't allow it. You might think she would have thanked me, but no, she was in a rage because I didn't put her house back together so it looked like an add for *Home and Garden*.

"You knew she was going to be mad," Margaret Ann reasoned with me. "You said so yourself before you left."

"Knowing she's going to be mad and having her have you call to tell me so are two entirely different things. And thinking she's going to be mad is different from thinking it's reasonable for her to be so."

A few days later, I received another phone call from Margaret Ann telling me I needed to come back to Wilkes Ferry right then.

"She's almost eighty years old," Margaret Ann kept repeating.

"I know how old she is, Margaret Ann." I could feel the anger rising in me like bile at the back of my throat.

The problem as reported by Margaret Ann was that Mother had diarrhea. I was supposed to jump in the car and drive two hundred miles, leave again in the middle of the term because my mother had diarrhea.

"Has she gone to the doctor?" I asked.

"Lydia, she can't," Margaret Ann responded. "She's too weak. She's just dragging herself to the bathroom and back."

"Has she phoned the doctor?" I asked again.

"She's got some kind of pills, but they aren't working." Margaret Ann's frustration was beginning to overflow.

"Why doesn't she phone the doctor and get something else?" I asked.

"You can't just abandon an eighty-year-old woman to fend for herself," Margaret Ann responded. "You just left her."

I could not believe my ears. Abandoned an eighty-year-old woman? Left her? It sounded like I had walked out to party and told my mother to hitchhike home from the hospital.

"You just went home and left her at the hospital," Margaret Ann was saying as if she were reading my thoughts.

I was just speechless, astounded at what was coming out of the mouth of a woman who had been my friend for half a century. The fact was that I had most certainly not left my mother at the hospital, and the woman saying I had was the very woman who had offered to pick Mother up and get her home. I knew, by that time, that Mother was crazy, but it sounded like Margaret Ann had also taken leave of her senses. Margaret Ann knew, because I had told her, that I had made arrangements for Mother to be cared for after I left. And Margaret Ann herself had offered to be part of those arrangements. I was used to Mother's utter disregard for objective reality, but for Margaret Ann to join in on it was just a stunner.

This little piece of manipulation was, now that I look back on it, one of my mother's most impressive accomplishments. She managed, at the age of eighty, to convince a grown woman, Margaret Ann, to disregard what she (Margaret Ann) knew personally to be true and join mother in a reality she had created out of whole cloth. It was like Margaret Ann had been brainwashed. Margaret Ann took Mother home, and after a few days, Margaret Ann completely divorced herself from what she knew to be true. And she was so convinced of this story line Mother had manufactured, she had the effrontery to phone me and accuse me of doing something she knew I didn't do. How many people could single-handedly brainwash another human being completely in the span of a few days. It was, and still is, breathtaking.

At almost eighty, my mother was one of the most impressive people I'd ever met. As Lee Ray once commented, how can a four-foot-seven, eighty-year-old woman manage to cause this much havoc?

That evening, when Margaret Ann phoned me to tell me black was white, I felt all the frustration and anger of fifty years welling up inside me. I had spent ten miserable, exhausting days taking care of a woman who was difficult to deal with in the best of circumstances. In the hospital, she was outrageously demanding, even more out of her mind than usual with the codeine, but I had dealt with it. I had done a good job. I had done what I was supposed to do. And I was feeling good about myself. She tried her best to make me feel guilty about leaving after ten days. She would hardly speak to me that last day when I had to leave.

That I had a husband and six cats, four classes of students who were obsessed with grades and made paranoid by the least upset in their schedules, and a chair who never wanted me on the faculty in the first place, a radio and a television show to do every week, never seemed to cross her mind. If it did, she dismissed it as secondary to her needs. I was supposed to be there when she wanted and for as long as she wanted. The fact that I went home at all enraged her. Of course, it also never occurred to her to ask Drew to do any of this. Had Drew farted in her direction, she would have considered it an immense sacrifice on his part.

But for me, there was not even a word of thanks. For me, the reward was having my childhood friend turned against me and used as an instrument of revenge for daring to thwart my mother's will. In mother's world, I hadn't stayed with her for ten days in the middle of a school term; I had abandoned her. I hadn't lived out a suitcase and spent every waking minute sitting by her bedside for ten days; I'd messed up her house. I hadn't gotten up every morning and driven forty miles to the hospital and driven forty miles home at night; I'd neglected her and failed to come to the hospital on time. A few days with Margaret Ann and she had managed to make Margaret Ann see reality in the same lunatic way.

This woman who had known me her entire life, turned on me and treated me as if I were some selfish, negligent daughter. I was tired. I was under enormous pressure at work. And after Margaret Ann's depraved accusations, I was close to tears and absolutely furious.

"I'll take care of it," I yelled and slammed the receiver of the telephone back into the carriage. After that one conversation, nothing was ever the same between Margaret Ann and I. Fifty years of friendship disappeared in ten minutes.

One telephone conversation with Margaret Ann a year after Lee Ray and I moved back to Wilkes Ferry forced me to a realization that had been staring me in the face for a half century. It may well turn out to be the last conversation Margaret Ann and I ever have.

In an effort to reestablish some kind of a friendship with Margaret Ann, I phoned to ask her a question about feeding chicken bones to a raccoon, who had set up housekeeping in our backyard. Margaret Ann wasn't there, so I left a message on her answering machine. This was on Friday. On Monday morning, I found a voicemail from Margaret Ann with the answer. The message was largely silence—long gaps between phrases. She sounded like someone ready to put a bullet through the roof of her mouth.

Fool that I was, and still am, I walked right into the trap and phoned her immediately to see what was wrong.

When Margaret Ann answered the phone, she sounded like she had a gun loaded and in her mouth when I had disturbed her.

"Margaret Ann, hey," I said, uncomfortable at hearing this flat, mildly irritated hello.

"Hey," she said.

I cannot tell you how flat her affect was when she said this. The "Hey" was the "Hey" of someone who has dreaded your phone call and is steeling herself for an extremely distasteful conversation.

My response to this implicit rejection was that I chattered. I had been raised on passive-aggression, and it always generated what I had taken to calling "tap dancing." All my mother had to do was sound the least bit annoyed, and I babbled like a child, trying to ward off her venom.

"Were you about to go for a walk? No, you couldn't be. It's . . . is it raining there? It's raining here. The cats are depressed because they can't go outside."

"Ah," Margaret Ann said.

This was the first even remotely positive response I had heard in over a year.

"It's like being cooped up . . . ," I rushed on, anxious to capitalize on the response I had gotten, "in the house with six two-year-olds fighting and competing over who's going to stretch out where." There was dead silence on the other end of phone.

Running out of chatter, I asked her about a name I had been trying to remember.

"Oh," I said, "what was Zac Fetner's girlfriend's name?" There was a long pause.

"I have no idea," she finally responded as if I had asked her something unutterably boring and stupid.

"You don't remember?" I heard myself exclaiming, unable to keep the disbelief out of my voice. Margaret Ann remembered everything that happened to us in high school. In fact, I was the one who usually was saying "I don't remember" while Margaret Ann recounted in amazing detail some incident that happened forty years before. Zac Fetner consumed years of Margaret Ann's life. I must have listened to enough discussion of him to fill three books. I could not and cannot believe she didn't remember the name of his girlfriend.

"What girlfriend?" Margaret Ann asked in an irritated voice as if she was just now learning Zac Fetner had a girlfriend.

I know damn well she remembered the girl's name and to act as if she didn't even remember Zac Fetner had a girlfriend was preposterous. Instead of saying so, I verbally tap danced away. "Well, when we were teenagers he . . . I remember . . . ," I launched into a monologue, feeling my blood pressure go up and my nerve endings beginning to fray. "I remember one time when we saw him over at the beach. He had the girlfriend with him."

There was dead silence on the other end of the phone. I was worn out.

"Well," I finally said. "I just thought I'd phone and see how you were."

" All right," Margaret Ann said as if she were talking to somebody she disliked intensely and wanted to get off the phone. "You've done that, now hang up," her tone said.

I had initially hesitated to phone her because most times when I did, she acted as if my very phone call was an insult. Afterward, I was left going over the conversation again and again trying to figure out how I had insulted her. Was it because I had said I was phoning to see how she was? Did she find that patronizing? Did she feel as if I were saying "I phoned because you needed me" instead of "I phoned because I needed you?" Was that what was bothering her? To demonstrate how perverted her thinking was, that was a likely possibility. Most people would consider it a compliment if you phoned to see about them, and most people would find it insulting if you were always phoning them because you needed something from them. Not Margaret Ann, or so I mused.

Not long after the conversation was over, I was going round and round in my mind trying to figure it all out when I stopped myself mid-thought. It suddenly struck me that what I was doing was what I did every time I talked with my mother.

First, I was verbally tap dancing. I had told Lee Ray for years that whenever I was with my parents (well, with my mother really, I never felt this way with my father), I felt as if I were always furiously tap dancing, wearing myself out trying to keep her entertained, trying to make her happy, throwing out sentence after sentence, thought after thought to her. At the same time, I was trying to dodge anything that might cause her to be offended. I never knew what would offend her. One careless sentence or phrase could trigger an outburst. After all, one of DeeMama's stupid jokes provoked a fifteen-year silence.

I had that same uncomfortable feeling talking with Margaret Ann. That feeling of something being wrong. There was a conversation in which I was giving, but the other person, Margaret Ann or Mother, was withholding. "You've done something wrong. I am displeased with you," the tone and the silences said. I am not going to tell you what I'm displeased about. I'm just going to communicate displeasure in every inflection and gesture. You have to guess why I am withholding. Because I know you are sensitive to such subtleties, I know you will get the message. Dance. Dance faster. Maybe if you dance well enough, fast enough, long enough, or just the right combination of steps, I'll stop withholding. I'll respond. I'll give. But right now, dance a little more. A little more. A little more.

The demonic beauty of this strategy is that if the target—me—turns around and confronts the aggression openly, says, for example, "What's the matter with you?" the other person simply denies the withholding.

"I don't know what you're talking about," they can say. "There's nothing wrong with me."

My mother would take the game one step further. If I ever made the mistake of asking "What's the matter?" she would answer "Nothing. There must be something the matter with you. There must be something you feel guilty about or you wouldn't be asking what the matter is with me."

Then she would have me (or Daddy). Caught. The focus of suspicion was then on me, not her.

Over time, I learned not to confront her aggression. It was always a losing game. I am sure my father learned the same thing. So Mother could get away with the most outrageously aggressive behavior and never be called on it. She could do the most vicious and aggressive things, and my father and I would just ignore it. So she could express all this aggression and never have to take responsibility for it because my father and I knew that confronting the aggression was more dangerous than just letting it go.

This was my mother's game. My mother's MO. And suddenly, Margaret Ann was playing by my mother's script. Margaret Ann was somebody I thought I could trust with my life, but how long, I asked myself, had she been playing this passive-aggressive game?

I had told Lee Ray a number of times after we moved to Wilkes Ferry that Margaret Ann hadn't always been like this, handing out passive-aggressive signals right and left. But I wasn't so sure of that anymore. Margaret Ann was always called "moody," but that was almost the same thing. She would clam up and refuse to respond to you, and she never told you why. I had developed a close lifelong friendship with someone who treated me very much like my mother did.

Giving, withholding, rejection, tap dancing, and then a slap across the face. Giving, withholding, rejection, tap dancing, and then a slap across the face. Just what I had always needed.

I thought about the message Margaret Ann had left on my cell phone. She must have known how odd it sounded, how depressive. She must have known that in response to such a disturbing message, I would phone to see what was wrong. It was like putting out bait. It was so like something my mother would do it terrified me. Put out the bait, bait that would make me feel like a callous, heartless bitch if I didn't respond. Then when I did respond—withhold, reject, and slap me in the face.

Come here, come closer. Let me make you feel bad, like you've done something wrong, without ever saying a word of accusation. Let me punish you and make you feel it's your own fault you're being punished. Let me have you wondering and wondering, trying to figure out what you've done wrong to deserve this punishment. And while you're pondering, you'll be focusing on me, thinking about me, coming back to figure out whether I'll forgive you, tell you what you've done, let you back into the fold. I know you. Every time I slap you, you will just crawl back with your ears flat on your head, your tail between your legs, wagging just the tip of it, hoping to please me and to be petted rather than slapped. God, what a pathetic statement about Margaret Ann, about my mother and about me.

It's horrifying to think of how much of my life has been controlled by these patterns my mother set up for me fifty years ago.

The State Championship

"There are a lot of people in Wilkes Ferry who are still loyal to him."

This statement was made by William Wyatt, Elizabeth Ann's older brother, about Heston Dwyer, the high school football coach who dominated the lives of most of the students of Wilkes Ferry High School when I was there, especially the males. I hadn't even so much as thought about Heston Dwyer for decades, and I can't remember exactly how his name came up in a casual conversation at Elizabeth Ann's house.

We were all talking in the small den at the back of the house, which used to be Elizabeth Ann's bedroom when we were growing up. I spent so many hours in that bedroom it felt strange to be sitting there forty years later. I couldn't shake the uncomfortable feeling that I was doing something wrong, sitting in Elizabeth Ann's bedroom with her brother.

William and his wife, Anne, were visiting Elizabeth Ann and Miss Fern. Elizabeth Ann moved back to Wilkes Ferry at about the same time as we did. She and Miss Fern bickered like an old married couple. I had stopped by to leave them some whole wheat rolls and was ushered back to the den to say hello to William even though I didn't particularly want to. I had not seen William Wyatt since he was in college, perhaps graduate school. I remember exactly when I saw him because he left another of those photographs in my mind.

William Wyatt was sitting at one end of Miss Fern's dining room table, probably where Mr. James William, Elizabeth Ann's father, sat before he died suddenly of a heart attack. I was sitting at the other end. There was no one else at the table. It was another one of those long, dim, green unsupervised afternoons at the Wyatts.

William was doing an experiment, and Elizabeth Ann and I had been recruited as subjects. Elizabeth Ann had already been in the diningroom with William at the table, and it was my turn. William was asking questions, and I was responding. The questions must have been designed to elicit one of two responses or types of responses. I can't remember exactly.

Every time I gave one type of response, William would make an affirming *um-hum* noise. If I answered the other way, he said nothing. I now know he was doing a study of "experimenter effect." At the time, I had never heard of an experimenter effect. After a list of questions, he asked if I knew what he was doing. I explained it to him. He didn't seem surprised I figured it out. He just said thank you.

It's impossible to know why a particular image sticks in your mind, why some experiences leave detailed photographs and others do not. I still have no idea why that afternoon scene in the dining room was significant enough to leave a snapshot that remains mentally visible and retrievable forty-five years later.

I did eventually wind up doing my own *effect of experimenter* studies years later. It was fascinating to me that you could get an experimenter effect for almost any reaction or activity. *Sex of experimenter* was usually the strongest experimenter effect. What this means is that for almost any activity or task you can think of, people will perform it differently depending on whether the experimenter is a man or a woman.

I wound up as a criminologist. William and his wife were both psychologists with their own practice. But when I was led back to Elizabeth Ann's bedroom and sat down, the conversation was not professional. The talk centered around Wilkes Ferry and the people who lived there.

How exactly we wound up on the subject of Heston Dwyer, I don't remember, but I think it had something to do with "suicides" or the history of wife "suicides" in Wilkes Ferry. It may even have been Miss Corinne Patterson's "suicide" that was the lead in.

"There was also Coach Dwyer's wife," William remarked casually.

"That was a suicide?" I asked, genuinely surprised.

"Of course," William said smiling over at me, clearly pleased he had been able to tell me something I did not know. William's obvious satisfaction at telling me something I didn't know reminded me not only of Drew, but also of academics in general who are notorious for intellectual one-upsmanship. And here in Elizabeth Ann's bedroom, William Wyatt was not only an academic, he was an older brother.

"How did she die?" Elizabeth Ann asked. "I don't remember that one."

I was still staring at William, processing information. "She went between the guard rails just before the interstate bridge," I answered Elizabeth Ann, immediately understanding the unlikely nature of this "accident." I was staring at William, but I was seeing the two double-lane highway bridges that spanned the Catawba about two miles down from the Wilkes Ferry bridge.

It was highly unlikely that a car would go neatly between the two bridges, down the bank, and into the river by chance. The space is not much wider than a medium-sized car. But then, what was the probability that a drunk and distraught woman could navigate a car neatly between the bridges and be assured of plummeting down to the water? It would be more likely that she swerved off the road and hit something that stopped the car than that she threaded this needle and went careening down the embankment and into the river. It took days to discover the car and the body. So she was going fast enough to submerge her car.

"Wasn't she an alcoholic?" Elizabeth Ann suddenly asked, breaking into my musings.

"Who in this town wasn't?" Ann, William's wife, quipped. "There seems to be an extremely high rate of alcoholism in this little town."

"It was probably the only way she could have survived all those years with Heston Dwyer," I commented.

"That's for sure," Elizabeth Ann added.

"And I always thought she just got drunk and drove into the river," I said.

"She did," William said, and we all laughed.

"Incredible," I said. I had never heard any speculation about Rose Dwyer's "accident." I do remember driving past their house after the accident. It always looked closed up, vacant, sad. Miss Rose and Heston Dwyer had a daughter, a sweet little girl. I don't think she was ever the same after losing her mother.

"But, back to the original thought," I said. "Why would people remain loyal to a dead man?"

"He took them to the state championship," William said without missing a beat.

"Took them to the state championship," I repeated. "Let's see. He either drove his wife to a drunken accident or a drunken suicide . . . but . . ."

"He took them to the state championship," William and I said together. I rolled my eyes. "I guess I missed that fundamental point."

"I hated the man," William added. "I left here because of him."

"Left because of him?" I asked.

"He told Mama and Daddy I wasn't smart enough to even get into college."

"What?" I said. "Heston Dwyer? How would he know anything about getting into college?"

William just shook his head.

After Lee Ray and I moved back to Wilkes Ferry, I had to go to the county courthouse over in Alabama for some document or other. While I was there, I ran into Dr. Ray, an old high school teacher of ours, a rather eccentric math teacher. I especially liked Dr. Ray because he could never hide his contempt for the intellectual capabilities of the goody-two-shoes, memorizing-instead-of-learning, captain of the cheerleaders.

Also, I think he was important to me because he was the first authority figure who ever genuinely liked me. He would ask a question from the chalkboard and then turn around and flash me that look of inquiry, knowing I was going to give him the right answer. I was great at math. He not only didn't mind that I was a wiseacre and a troublemaker. He actually seemed to enjoy it.

At some point when we were in high school, Dr. Ray said something complimentary to my mother about me. Mother passed this compliment along to me while I was standing in the kitchen ironing a blouse. It made me feel great. "I didn't know he liked me that much," I said.

"Well," my mother huffed, "he's not in love with you, if that's what you think."

It was another of her stunners. I stood there, the iron in my hand, reeling, embarrassed at my reaction, betrayed by my own feelings. I had never ever meant to imply that he was "in love" with me. What had I done to make her think I thought he was in love with me. It hurt, and it made me ashamed.

Dr. Ray was a real find for that high school full of teachers who were (with a few exceptions like Mr. Strother) mediocre, to put it kindly. I can remember feeling like I would surely die in Georgia history class or Spanish class. By the time I graduated from high school, I never wanted to see the inside of a classroom again. Most of those teachers could have easily made sex a boring topic.

Heston Dwyer, the foul-mouthed, shambling, abusive football coach, was principal of the school. That one fact tells you a lot about the priorities of the school board. They put far more care in choosing assistant coaches (who all taught academic courses) than regular teachers. The assistant coaches were probably paid more as well.

I never liked Heston Dwyer, but I especially didn't like him in high school. Heston Dwyer had me expelled once for distributing a questionnaire about the quality of education in the school. Well, I had also said "hell" within his hearing and refused to apologize while telling him that I didn't see why I had to apologize for something he did (cussin'). I guess that didn't help. Joe Ed piped up and said that the class accepted my apology for saying "hell," hoping that would get me out of trouble, but Heston Dwyer demanded that I apologize to him. I wouldn't do it.

Dr. Ray hated Heston Dwyer. Dr. Ray was the first adult I had ever met who was as disrespectful of authority as we were and who not only questioned, but also openly ridiculed the established order of things at that school. Dr. Ray was his own man. He was brilliant, funny, cynical, and totally unwilling to pretend respect for those he didn't have any regard for. I remember once while we were talking a test in his classroom, he walked over and stretched out full length on the lab cabinet and announced that he was taking a nap. Then he did it. I had never seen an adult do anything like that.

Years later, when I ran into Dr. Ray at the county courthouse, he was watching over an antique store on the square owned by one of his daughters. He told me that he had threatened to leave his job at the high school several times during those years he taught. At one point, he told the school board that he would stay if and only if Heston Dwyer signed an agreement never again to teach another math course. For whatever reason, Dwyer signed.

But, back to William. William Wyatt not only got into college, he graduated with a PhD. Heston Dwyer had predicted he would never get into college.

William said that the comment was made because first, William and his father, James William, objected to Heston Dwyer's decision to start William in a big game when he had a shoulder injury. Dwyer was enraged that somebody had dared to question his authority. Mr. James William said something like, "You hurt him here and he might not be able to play in college."

"College," Dwyer scoffed. "That boy's so goddamn dumb he'll never get into college."

James William not only took his boy off the field, but he also took him out of the school.

"Do you remember Neal Spraggins?" William was asking me. "He was around yours and Elizabeth's age."

"Yes," I said. "I remember him. He died shortly after we graduated from high school of some kind of brain disease."

"He didn't die of a brain disease," William said.

"What did he die of?" I asked, wondering if I had missed another choice story.

"He had some kind of neurological problem," William explained. "When he was in high school, playing for Heston Dwyer, he was already starting to develop problems."

"Oh," I said. "He may have had problems, but I remember him catching a lot of touchdown passes thrown by Joe Ed Montgomery."

"He did, but he would also have these clumsy spells. Don't you remember?" William asked.

"No," I said. These men amazed me with their ability to remember the details of thousands of football games. But then, I suppose they would find it amazing that I could remember the buttons on a dress Margaret Ann wore forty years ago.

"In the state semifinal game, when Neal was a junior, he lost the game for Wilkes Ferry by fumbling two passes."

"Oh," I said. I must have missed that.

"Not long after that, some of the football players walked off the field when Neal was missing passes and Heston Dwyer started kicking him."

"Started kicking him?" I almost gasped. I knew Heston was bad but not that bad.

"Neal missed a couple of passes right in front of Heston. With the last one, Neal divided for it, juggled it in midair, and then fell on the field, fumbling right in front of Dwyer without anybody ever even hitting him. Dwyer just started kicking him."

"My God," I said. I wouldn't have guessed that anything Heston Dwyer could have done would have surprised me, but this, this was way beyond anything I had ever imagined possible. "Kicking him," I repeated, finding it surprisingly easy to create the scene in my mind. It had been difficult to imagine Miss Amelia sucking on part of Miss Antionette's body, but Heston Dwyer kicking a player was right in character.

"And he died?" I said, suddenly looking up at William.

"Well," William admitted, "nobody knows that Neal died from the kicking. I don't actually think so. It's just the fact that he kicked a boy who was developing a neurological disease."

"Well, even if he didn't die from it, it couldn't have bloody helped," I said. "Did he kick him in the head?"

William paused. He was looking at me, but I could tell he was replaying the scene in his head. "He kicked him everywhere. His head, his stomach, his back, his butt."

"Oh my God." I found myself squirming in my seat. "How did you know about it?" I asked. "You couldn't have been there?"

"No. I was away at school by then, but it was all over town. You know how things travel here."

"Boy, do I," I said.

"People who hated Heston tended to phone other people who hated him with the horror stories. Hating Heston Dwyer was like being a member of a club," William said. "A couple of the football players, good ones, walked off the field because of it."

It suddenly hit me. "Joe Ed Montgomery?" I asked.

William thought a second. "I think so, and that kid whose father, a little wiry Irish guy, an alcoholic, was so tight with Heston."

"See, I told you," Ann interjected from beside me on the sofa. "Every story about this town has an alcoholic in it."

"Brennan Quinn," I supplied William the name.

"That's it," William said.

"Brennan Quinn's father was that tight with Heston Dwyer?" I asked.

"Oh yeah," William answered. "He was always hanging around the football field. Came over straight from work during the football season."

"Even before Brennan played?"

"Oh yeah," William answered.

"Where did he work?" Elizabeth Ann asked.

"The telephone company," I said, answering Elizabeth Ann and then turning back to William. "You know that Brennan Sr. and Big Ed Montgomery stopped talking to Joe Ed and Brennan over that, don't you?"

"Stopped talking to them," Elizabeth Ann exclaimed.

"I remember something about that," William said.

"Why would they stop talking to their own sons?" Elizabeth Ann asked.

"Because they walked off the football team," I answered.

"It was Heston Dwyer that was kicking players with brain diseases."

"He didn't know that at the time," William corrected Elizabeth Ann. I hated this big-brother correcting game. "And it was a neurological problem, not a brain disease."

William, I was starting to notice, very much liked correcting people. I could also tell he was very well accustomed to correcting Elizabeth Ann. This was not because she was always wrong, but because she was the younger sibling, and William considered her beneath him. I noticed this especially because I found myself frequently in the same position whenever I was around Drew.

With Drew, I could say, "The sun is shining," and he would respond with, "Well, not exactly shining . . . it's . . ." Drew and his dreadful wife had fine-tuned this verbal pattern into a conversational style. Whatever I said, either Drew or his dreadful wife would find it necessary to correct me. Sometimes, they would say it in a laughing way, just to underline the point that they were the smartest people in the room. This, of course, is an extremely self-aggrandizing way of interacting with people. William or Drew or his dreadful wife, thereby, placed themselves in the superior position, always talking down to me or to Elizabeth Ann. It was unutterably tiresome. Elizabeth Ann was talking. "Neurological problem, brain disease, whatever," she said.

"I know, I know," William responded, dismissing Elizabeth Ann.

"It would have been horrible no matter who he was kicking," I interjected so I wouldn't have to smack William in the head.

"I can't believe they wouldn't even support their own sons," Elizabeth Ann continued.

"I know," I said, pondering a betrayal that was even more hurtful and significant than I had thought.

"As I remember it, they had to apologize to Heston Dwyer to get back on the team," William said looking at me.

I nodded in agreement. "That's what Joe Ed told me," I responded. "But Joe Ed never told me what Heston Dwyer had done to make them walk out."

"Probably he was too embarrassed," Anne said.

I nodded.

"What did he have to be embarrassed about?" Elizabeth Ann asked.

"His father taking sides against him and with a man like Heston Dwyer, I guess, a man who could do something like kick a boy laying on the ground," I said.

"That's just unbelievable," Elizabeth Ann said.

"You know," I continued, "the last time I talked to Joe Ed, really talked to him, I asked him how it felt when Big Ed would scream abuse at him from the sidelines in front of all those people. You know what he said?" I looked up and scanned the faces.

"What?" Elizabeth Ann asked.

"That his father never did that. That I must be confusing his father with Heston."

William snorted a laugh.

"He denied his father was ever anything but supportive of him," I said.

Ann shook her head. "He just rewrote the past to make it more palatable."

"Yep," I said. "Amazing isn't it?"

"Do you think Miss Rose killed herself because of it?" Elizabeth Ann asked William.

"Because of what? The walk off? The apology?" William asked impatiently, annoyed.

"No," she said. "Because of the kicking."

"No," William said simply. "I don't think so."

"I doubt if she even knew about it," I said. "I think she probably stayed in a alcoholic haze just to be able to share the same house with him." I grimaced at the thought. "To share the same bed with him."

"I doubt if she shared the same bed with him very many times," William said.

My ears perked up.

"I'm gong to bed," Anne announced getting up off the sofa and stretching. "I don't even want to hear the rest of this."

"What?" I said, genuinely shocked.

"Well, now," William held up his hand. "I don't actually know this for a fact."

"Know what?" Elizabeth Asked.

William hesitated as if he were trying to decide whether to go on.

"William Wyatt," I said narrowing my eyes at him in mock seriousness, "you cannot simply drop a comment like that into a conversation and not explain it. You can't."

William shrugged. "Heston Dwyer was a homosexual, and none of the parents would believe it."

I sat there blinking. "You know, I have heard people say that," I said. "But I never took it seriously."

"Neither did anybody else outside the locker room," William added.

"You never observed him in the act did you?" I said.

"No," he responded. "But I saw more than enough touching in the locker room."

"What? You mean more than the usual male macho fanny patting that goes on all the time?" I asked.

"Well, you have a point, but they usually wait until everybody has on padding to do that," he said.

I must say this point never occurred to me. "You're not talking about nude fanny patting, are you?" I asked. The fanny-filled locker room in *Steel Magnolias* came immediately in mind. It would have been hard for me to resist patting some fanny in that locker room.

"On occasion," William answered.

"How did he get away with that?" I exclaimed sickened by the addition of Heston Dwyer's enormous overweight frame into my fantasy. He was reaching out for a butt with one hand and rearranging his hemorrhoids with the other. I tried to shake off the image.

"He got away with it," William said. "The same way he got away with everything else. He'd do things like that and then laugh at anybody who acted like they felt uncomfortable with it."

"You were a sissy or a wimp if you didn't want you naked fanny patted?" I said.

"Exactly," William agreed. "Real men weren't sensitive about things like that. Real men walked around naked. You were a sissy if you wore a towel."

"Well, that was convenient as all hell for him."

"Wasn't it? You can imagine what men like Big Ed Montgomery would have said if Joe Ed came home and told him there was something funny about the way Heston Dwyer stared at his butt in the locker room."

"He would have made Joe Ed feel like he was the one something was wrong with."

"These guys would have accused their own sons of being homosexuals before they would have thought such a thing about the great Heston Dwyer."

"What a perverted mess," I said. "And this man had so much power and influence over so many lives."

"If Heston liked you and your family, it was one thing," William said. "But if he ever got it in for you, he could make your life a living hell, and he didn't hesitate to do it."

I remembered for the first time in decades that there was a problem with Heston Dwyer and my father. My mother was, at that time, the secretary for the grammar school. I have no idea exactly how this worked, but Heston Dwyer was able to make all the teachers in the high school and the elementary school take up tickets and stand at the concession booth during the high school football games.

My mother had more than a few words to say about this. After working all week and all day on Friday, the teachers and my mother had to go home to prepare a meal and then go to the football field and put in more hours for free, for Heston Dwyer. My mother, quite rightly, thought this was insane.

My father finally got so tired of hearing about it, he told Heston Dwyer my mother would not be doing any after-hours work. He also told Heston Dwyer if he (Heston) had any problems with it, Daddy wouldn't mind beating the living hell out of him since he richly deserved it for much more than just making my mother work for free.

That was the end of Mother working at the football games. I guess to save face, Heston Dwyer told all the elementary school teachers they didn't have to work at the football games anymore. But the high school teachers still sat there every weekend taking up tickets and making Coca-Colas.

Now I must explain that my daddy was not a large man. He was maybe five foot nine and slim, but when he said he just might beat the living hell out of somebody, that somebody tended to believe him. They either knew my father or they knew stories about him or they could just look in his eyes and know he wasn't bluffing. Daddy was never big, but he wasn't afraid to take on anybody. A friend of Daddy's who had grown up with him on Tallasee Street told me that Daddy, from the time he was a kid, would fight anybody, anywhere, any time.

So I knew that Heston Dwyer could make life difficult. He had done so for my own family. It was probably one of the other reasons why Drew was sent away to school, to keep him out of the tender mitts of Heston Dwyer.

"It is just astounding," I said, coming back to the discussion with William, "that an entire town full of people allowed this man to abuse their children and even paid him to do it. But I guess . . ."

William and I said together, "He took them to the state championship."

"Do you remember where Byron's market was?" William asked. "Not where it was downtown, but where it moved?" William asked.

"No," I said, trying to remember.

"Over on this side of the river near the baseball field."

I tried to remember which one of those fields was the baseball field and what buildings were close.

"Lambe's. Do you remember where Lambe's meat market moved? Over near the Boy Scout Hut."

"Oh, yes," I said. "I do remember." It was a small cinder block structure across the street from the old baseball field.

"Not that building, but in a building behind that there was a garage apartment, and this man lived there who was supposed to be a homosexual." I looked at Elizabeth Ann. "Where was I while all this was going on? A homosexual man living in a garage apartment next to the baseball field, and I didn't know it."

"Nobody talked about homosexuality then," Elizabeth Ann said.

"They talked about it," Walter corrected her. "They just didn't use the words. Heston would go over to this man's apartment and watch . . ."—Here William raised his hands to indicate quotation marks—"'pornographic' movies."

"Oh, barf," I said, unwillingly imagining the scene. "How do you know this?"

" He used to take some of the football players with him."

"Heston Dwyer used to take teenaged boys to the apartment of a homosexual man and show them pornographic movies? Why did they go?"

"They didn't have much choice. You didn't want to get on Heston's bad side," William said.

"Or he might kick you," I said.

"Or worse," William added.

"Two closet homosexuals and a bunch of teenaged boys watching 1950s porn. What a scene." I hated even picturing it in my mind.

The whole thing fit perfectly with my theory that most men are closet homosexuals. When they're with women, they're just performing for the other men that run around in their heads.

"Did any of the parents know about this?" I asked William.

"I'm sure none of the mothers did. But a lot of the fathers did. They just considered it part of male initiation."

"Male initiation. What a nightmare. To have your son initiated into manhood by Heston Dwyer and porn movies. And he was coach and principal of that school for decades. It's a wonder any of you came out normal."

"Who said we did?" William quipped.

Mattie Mae's Comforting Arms

Mattie Mae Hollis became part of our family in 1947, when my brother was born. My father had only been back from the war two years, but he was already working a full-time white-collar job and going to college at night. That left all the responsibility of running the household to my mother.

Now my mother hated housework, and her one source of independence from the 1950s family pattern of stay-at-home, martini-drinking, pill-popping wife was her part-time job at the Red Cross. She was not going to give it up. So the family got Mattie Mae.

Four years later, I got Mattie Mae as well. She was there at the hospital when I was born. They wouldn't let her into the waiting room with my father, of course. Things were still segregated then. There were "white only" signs all over Wilkes Ferry. But when my daddy rolled Mother out the front door of the hospital in a wheelchair, cradling me in her arms, the first thing Mother did was deposit me in Mattie Mae's huge and capable hands.

I stayed in those hands until I was about twelve and felt myself much too grown up and sophisticated to be rocked in Mattie Mae's comforting arms. But Lord, there were great many times later on in my life when I would have given anything to have those arms around me again.

Mattie Mae didn't talk much during all those years when we were growing up. She was a pretty closemouthed individual unless she had something important to say. She didn't tell stories like Pearl or hypnotize chickens like Mary or gossip like some of the other women who worked for the families of my friends. It would have never crossed Mattie Mae's mind to gossip. I don't even really remember Mattie Mae playing with us. While she was there in the house, she worked.

Oh, she took care of us; she knew where we were every minute, and I know that she was always listening out for us. I know this because she had the uncanny ability to appear out of nowhere just before we were about to wreak serious damage on the house or when we were about to kill ourselves.

I remember one afternoon, especially, when Mattie Mae appeared in the doorway of my brother's room just in time to find my brother and I peering down the barrel of a lighted Roman candle.

"Git back," she ordered just in time to save the eyesight of two children. Five fireballs hit the ceiling in rapid succession while my brother sat too dumbfounded to do anything but hold the candle upright. We were fortunate he did. Had he not, we might all three have died by Roman candle that fateful afternoon. It would have not been a romantic way to go.

"Lord, have mercy on my soul," was all Mattie Mae said as she walked back to the kitchen to get something to clean up the smut all over the ceiling. But that's all she said. She didn't scold us or even tell on us. She left that for us to do.

When my mother came home, she would have to have been struck blind during the day not to have noticed the scarred ceiling in my brother's room, but even then, Mattie Mae stood silent when my mother asked what happened.

We had to confess.

But curiously enough, my mother didn't scold us this time. She just listened, her face growing ashen. She closed her eyes and shook her head. She then turned and went to her room.

So for twelve years of my life, Mattie Mae Hollis was the one who was there to tend skinned knees, bandage scraped arms from bicycle accidents, put tobacco on bee stings, and phone my mother at work when I stuck an ice pick through my hand. But she didn't talk. That's probably why she and my mother got along so well all those years.

My mother was an intensely private person, a person who liked being alone. Having someone in her house six days a week was not something she became accustomed to easily. But over the years, Mother and Mattie Mae came to understand each other about as well as two people can separated as they were by race, social position, and class.

During over fifty years of shared experience, sympathy, and mutual help, the bond between my mother and Mattie Mae became solid as a rock.

Mattie Mae Hollis was there when I was born, and she was there when my father died. She stood uncomfortably in the receiving line at the funeral home, and when we both became too heartsick to go on standing, we shared a huge overstuffed chair, and I rested in those arms once again.

Dancing for Mama

Lee Ray and I moved back to Wilkes Ferry for a number of reasons. After struggling with fibromyalgia for seven years, I could no longer handle the stress of university teaching. Since we didn't have to live in a university town anymore, I thought moving back to Wilkes Ferry made sense. The cost of living would be low, we could buy a nice house there, and we would be among friends. We would also be around to take care of Mother and make sure she could stay in her own house for just as long as possible, something I knew was important to her. We didn't have to move back to Wilkes Ferry. We could have moved anywhere, something Mother's own doctor at the time, Dr. Markov, pointed out to her when she was once complaining about me to him.

Very soon after we moved back to Wilkes Ferry, Mother started to resent our presence there. We would run into her at the gas station or at the grocery store, and she would say things like, "I just can't go anywhere without running into y'all" or "Every time I go somewhere, y'all are there." She wasn't joking. It was one of those statements she specialized in, statements that she could claim were jokes but weren't at all. It took somebody as familiar with her as I was to really know this.

We did everything we could for her. I cannot even remember all the things that Lee Ray did—mowing grass, climbing up into the attic, changing light bulbs, fixing the garbage disposal, putting up a mailbox for her when the post office demanded she do so, on and on and on. And even though she asked, she resented us every time she had to.

Looking back on it all now, I think that for Mother, I was always the wild card, the one she couldn't control. She told me once that even when I was a baby,

I wouldn't allow myself to be held. But I love to be held. One of the photographs I have in my mind is being held by my much older cousin, Casey, at DeeMama's house. It must have been one of those dinners at DeeMama's house that Mother hated so much. All the adults were talking, and I was sitting in Casey's lap. He rocked gently in DeeMama's rocking chair and held me. It was a lovely experience.

But I think that the first time I struggled out of Mama's arms, she interpreted it as rejection, and forever afterward, I was the embodiment of everything that had ever hurt her, embarrassed her, or shamed her or rejected her. Even though she needed Lee Ray and I around, she didn't want us there, and the more she needed us, the more she hated us, or me really. I don't think she ever hated Lee Ray; he was far too useful and unlikely to say what he thought. He was, and still is, a lot like Daddy.

But things were livable when we first went back. I could ignore her for the most part, and I didn't have to be with her all the time. A few months after we moved back, though, things changed completely.

Mother got sick and was rushed to the emergency room at Cobb Memorial Hospital. This started a nine-month run of hospital stays and emergency room crises. She would go to the emergency room with a sky-high temperature, get antibiotics, and then come home. A few days later, we would go through the same thing. It happened so often, I got to where I could just talk to her on the telephone and tell whether or not she had a fever.

They couldn't figure out what was wrong with her. They would keep her on antibiotics for longer periods of time and then let her go home. A few days later, we were back in the emergency room. They would try different antibiotics. As soon as she got settled at home, her fever would sky rocket again. Then they took to giving her intravenous antibiotics and keeping her in the hospital for longer and longer stays. That didn't help either. It was like living on a roller coaster, and I was with her all day, almost every day. During this time, nothing I could do would please her. There had never been much I could do to please her anyway, but during this hospital fever run, it was especially so.

She would complain about how badly she was being treated in the hospital or the nursing home. I would try to sort it out and make sure she got better treatment. I must have sat in the hospital administrator's office more than he did. But when I would try to intervene, she would rip into me for making her life more miserable than before. This was a version of the "I have to live in this town even if you don't" line, only it was "I have to stay here, you don't."

So she would complain that she was being mistreated, and I wasn't doing anything about it. Then when I tried to do something, she complained that I was alienating the hospital staff and making sure that she would be even more mistreated after I left. She would do this and then turn around, sometimes in the same day, and brag on some friend of hers who had come and given the hospital staff "a dressing down" and stood up for her.

Every day or so, there was a withholding episode where she would refuse to do more than say hello to me when I got to the hospital. I would have to try to figure out whether I was too early or too late, had forgotten to buy her something, had bought the wrong thing, had spent too much money, was ignoring her. There were so many options it made my head spin. She would see me wearing something and ask me to go out and buy her the same thing—a blouse, some shoes, some pants. When I did, she would accuse me of buying it for myself or say that she didn't like it. Then I would have to try to find time to take whatever it was back to the store in between taking care of her and my own family.

The upshot of all this was that I found myself back in the same situation I had fled when I was nineteen. When I wasn't with Mother, I was at home, crying and telling Lee Ray that I couldn't stand it and that she was driving me crazy.

Dr. Markov was telling me the same thing.

Mother had gone through every doctor in town, first loving them and idealizing them beyond all recognition and then turning on them and dogging them out as the worst doctor in the state. It was very much like the cycle she went through with DeeMama and DeWilla. At some point in this nine-month episode, she accused her then doctor, Dr. Ben Markoff, and I of trying to kill her because she had a bad reaction to a medication. This may sound like a joke, but it wasn't. Ben Markov was a friend of mine, and we talked and joked together all the time. When she had this reaction to the pain medication, he stabilized her, and we were outside her room talking. She must have heard one of us laugh at something. She decided we were laughing at her. She was furious, and after I came back inside her room, she started the accusations. She never wanted to see Ben again because we were trying to kill her and laughing about it. She promptly stopped going to Ben, told everybody who would listen that she never wanted to see Ben Markov again, and got another doctor.

After a few months, her new doctor (someone who was widely referred to as Dr. Death for obvious reasons) decided he couldn't do anything else about the fever cycles. He wanted to send Mama to Birmingham to let them try. This was announced late one afternoon when I had just come back to the hospital after running home. When I walked in, I found out that Dr. Death had arranged to get an ambulance to take Mama to Birmingham.

Mother, of course, just assumed that I was going to follow the ambulance to Birmingham in my car and be there for her when she got there. That I didn't have any clothes, had doctor's appointments myself, and had a husband and five cats at home, was insignificant to her. She was furious at the suggestion that I couldn't go. I tried to explain that I had a doctor's appointment in Auburn. Her response was that I could to go the doctor's appointment and then drive straight to Birmingham.

I was so exhausted and so fed up with her, I just said no. That's something you didn't do with my mother. Saying no was a major crime. But this time, I said no. I told her I was going to Auburn and then home and pack some clothes, make arrangements for the cats and Lee Ray, and that I would drive to Birmingham the next morning. She would barely speak to me when I left her room. I could see the rage welling up in her, but I just walked out the door.

By the time I got to Birmingham the next afternoon, she was, strangely enough, subdued. I thought she must be drugged, but I found out that when she had been delivered by ambulance to the hospital the night before, she was in a rage and evidently behaved with the hospital staff the way she regularly behaved with me. Their response was to put her in a straight jacket.

My initial reaction was shock, sympathy, outrage, and guilt. After all, had I come with her, followed the ambulance like she wanted me to do, this wouldn't have happened. But the more I thought about it, the funnier it seemed. I finally had to leave her hospital room for a few minutes to keep from breaking into laughter. That one episode just said it all.

Mother was in the hospital in Birmingham for six weeks. They found out she had an infected lead to her pacemaker, and they had to remove it and start another round of antibiotics. I was there every morning and stayed until almost night. She got her pluck back from the straight-jacket incident and started the complaints again pretty soon. I would walk into her room in the morning, and she would light into me for being late and ignoring her. She especially didn't like it that I got so exhausted that I just went home to Wilkes Ferry for a couple of days just to rest. She acted like I was abandoning her again.

When she was recovering, they had to start the intravenous antibiotics again. She could stay in the hospital and get them or go to a nursing home. The administration of these antibiotics required specially trained personnel, and she had to be supervised carefully. It was not like taking a bottle of pills. But Mama wanted to go home, and wild horses were not going to prevent her from doing what she wanted to do. We all, the doctors and nurses and even her lawyer's assistant, a wonderful person named Meg, tried to reason with her.

If she stayed in the hospital or a nursing home, she could get the antibiotics free with Medicare. If she went home and somebody had to supervise the administration of the antibiotics eight hours a day, it would cost something like $35,000. But mother wanted to go home. No amount of reasoning was going to change her mind. Now I knew as did everybody concerned that if she chose to go home and have someone come in and administer the antibiotics every day, I was going to have to stay there with her all the time. She couldn't be left alone in her own house with this going on. When we tried to get her to see reason by bringing that up, she said that she "had friends" who would take care of her.

I stood there staring at her, wondering just who these friends she had were who were going to stay at her house and take care of her every need while she was hooked up to an intravenous feed. Sweet McKean? Even Meg finally commented that Mama was delusional.

But home she went, just like she wanted, and after nine months of this medical roller coaster, we added two additional weeks of constant care. And I was the constant care. It was the most amazingly irresponsible thing I'd ever seen her do.

By the time all this was over, I was a basket case. I went back to Ben's office trying to get some more fibromyalgia medication. Mother called four times on my cell phone while I was trying to talk to Ben. Finally, Ben got up, took the cell phone out of my hand, and threw it on a couch in his office. He went and sat back down behind his desk.

"Don't answer that again," he said, pointing to the cell phone. "You are the person least able to deal with this situation in your family." He sat there looking at me and then leaned back in his chair. "Go home, get on the computer, and look up Narcissistic Personality Disorder." He ordered. "Spend some time reading, or you are going to wind up in the hospital yourself."

I spent the next couple of days on the computer, in my pajamas, reading. I could hardly take my eyes off the screen.

A couple of weeks later, Mama had to go to Atlanta to the hospital to have the pacemaker reinserted. I just couldn't do it. I phoned Drew and told him he would have to deal with it; I couldn't.

Drew came to Wilkes Ferry, took Mama to Atlanta, and brought her back in a day. He never phoned me. He never asked me how I was doing. He had to deal with Mama for three days, not nine months, not fifteen years, which was how long I had been close enough to drive to Wilkes Ferry. But Drew never even drove the half mile to my house. What he did do, along with Mother, before he left was to have Mama's attorney draw up a letter accusing me of misusing her credit card and demanding that I bring it back immediately or face "further legal action." That was Drew's reaction to being asked to help out for three days.

I was floored, absolutely floored. If I hadn't spent a week reading about the children of narcissists, I think I might well have killed myself. And in Wilkes Ferry, a letter like that would be all over town in hours. Mama, and now Drew, had tried to publicly humiliate and shame me rather than phoning and asking me or driving a half mile to pick up the American Express card themselves.

I drove to Mother's house, put the credit card in the mailbox, and returned home. I never talked to either one of them again. Lee Ray and I moved from Wilkes Ferry, and Drew e-mailed me when Mother died. I did not go back to Wilkes Ferry for the funeral.

I wish I could tell you in these last few pages that I had settled my score in Wilkes Ferry, confronted the demons that had been driving me for over half a century, but it wouldn't be true. I could easily write that, a nice story to make an end of all this. It would just be a matter of typing out the words. But what would be the use?

Until I settle the score for myself, find the story that I have been trying to tell for fifty years, I will have to keep going back in my mind—to Daddy and Mama, to Drew, to Margaret Ann and DeeMama, to my grandfathers and their stories, to Wilkes Ferry. I have looked for so long into these memories, I don't know anymore which are true and which are fictions created to weave together the unquestioned myths that make up the family lore. But I know that somewhere in the mix, somewhere in these stories and histories lies the truth. I just have to find it.

Reference

Most historical information adapted from *Rich Man's War: Class, Caste, and Confederate Defeat in the Lower Chattahoochee Valley.* Historic Chattahoochee Commission: University of Georgia Press, 1998.

LaVergne, TN USA
30 January 2011
214586LV00002B/29/P